Book One of the World of Hetar

LARA

BERTRICE SMALL

Book One of the World of Hetar

LARA

HQN™

ISBN 0-373-77026-X

LARA: BOOK ONE OF THE WORLD OF HETAR

www.HQNBooks.com

Printed in U.S.A.

For Ethan Ellenberg with thanks.

Prologue

SHE WAS NAKED. The girl reached up to touch the thin gold chain that she had always worn about her slender neck. It was still there. Her fingers gently wrapped about the delicate crystal star that hung from the necklace. It also remained, and relief flooded through her. She lifted the star to her sight, and whispered silently, "Are you there?"

A tiny golden flame flickered within the star. "Of course I am here," the familiar voice murmured as silently back to her. "Where else would I be?"

"I am afraid," the girl said.

"The unknown can frequently be frightening, but you need not be fearful," the voice reassured her. "All will be well. This is but the beginning."

"The beginning of what?" the girl wanted to know. She simply could not keep her eyes open a moment longer. They were closing in spite of her efforts to stay awake.

"Your journey," came the reply as the flame within the star flickered again and died, dropping from the girl's fingers as she fell into a deep and dreamless sleep.

 Chapter 1

"WE MUST SELL Lara, husband. There is simply no other choice if you are to have your chance," Susanna, wife of John Swiftsword, said quietly. She was uncomfortable with this matter, but sometimes her husband would not face simple facts. And the simple fact was that John had a beautiful daughter for whom he could no longer provide. But that same daughter could provide for them all, given the opportunity.

"I cannot," her husband replied, but his voice was filled with the desperation that came from knowing she was right. Lara was all he had left of his brief union with the faerie woman, Ilona. The faerie had loved him for a brief time, given him their daughter whom she had named Lara—shining one, in her tongue—and then disappeared from his life as easily as she had entered into it that midsummer's night so long ago. He had not married until two years ago, and while he loved his Susanna, the memory of Ilona would remain with him forever.

"Listen to me, husband," Susanna's voice penetrated his thoughts. "Have you considered what is to become of Lara? We are poor people. There is no dowry for her. How can there be, given your situation? Many fear her faerie beauty and her faerie blood. Who will wed a dowerless girl like that? And if she is not married, what will happen to her? All your life you have wanted but one thing—to become a member of the Order of Crusader Knights. You have served as a mercenary soldier since you were fifteen, and your reputation as a great swordsman is known throughout the land. But you know as well as I do that your poverty prevents you from attaining your greatest desire. The tournament for entry into the ranks of the Order of Crusader Knights is to be held in just a few months, husband. It will not be held again for another three years." Could he not see, or understand? Why did she have to be the one to point out these things? She very much liked her stepdaughter, but John needed to advance, and she wanted a better life for their son. There was but one way to achieve their goals.

"But to sell my daughter into slavery," John Swiftsword protested weakly.

Susanna sighed. "I know, husband, how much you love this child, but she is all we have that is of any value. She is so beautiful that it almost hurts the eyes to look upon her. I have grown to love her, too. Still, think of what little we have, and consider the son I gave you but six months ago. What will happen to Mikhail? The hovel we live in is yours only by virtue of your service to the Guild of Mercenaries. Your sword gives us food and small necessities, but nothing else. What clothing we possess is ours, but when your sword is no longer useful, where will we go? How many of your kind have deliberately allowed themselves to be killed in battle rather than face a homeless old age? And how many of their women roam as beggars without sons to provide for them?"

"But if Lara is sold into slavery what will happen to her?" John Swiftsword asked his wife. His gray eyes were troubled, and he ran a nervous hand through his brown hair.

"She will most likely be bought and trained to be a Pleasure Woman for one of the great Pleasure Houses here in the City," Susanna said. "It will be a good life for her, and in all likelihood some magnate will eventually purchase her from the Pleasure House to be his own personal Pleasure Woman. She will enjoy a life of lux-

ury, husband, which is a far better future than we can offer her."
Susanna put a comforting hand on her husband's sinewy arm. He
was a good man, but like many men he needed to be led in the right
direction. Such was a wife's duty.

"How can you be certain that she will be so fortunate in her
fate?" he demanded.

"I have already gone to Gaius Prospero, husband," Susanna answered honestly.

"You went to the Master of the Merchants of the Midlands, and
he saw you?" John Swiftsword was astounded by her admission.

"The Master of the Merchants holds an open audience once
each month for any who would come to proffer him something of
value. I took Lara with me several days ago that he might see what
we had to offer him. Gaius Prospero is who he is because he is a
clever man, and always eager for profit. He has told me what he
will pay for Lara. It is a more than generous sum. With it I can purchase the finest materials to make your application garments. With
it you can order up the best suit of armor, new weapons, and the
best warhorse bred, for whom I will sew the most beautiful capar-
isons that you may be proud of yourself, your talent with the sword
and your perfect appearance. I have already alerted the armorer
and the swordsmith. They are eager to service you, husband, because they know that if you enter this tournament you will win
your place among the Crusader Knights, thus burnishing their own
reputations. Gaius Prospero was particularly pleased when I told
him why we were selling Lara. Your skill as a great swordsman precedes you, husband." She spoke strongly. He must be convinced that
this was the right thing for all.

"Susanna…"

"Think, husband!" She interrupted him. "When you gain your
rightful place we will be given a house in the Garden District
where all the Crusader Knights and their families reside. Oh, it will
be small at first, I know, for until you have made your mark among
the knights in battle you will not merit a large home, but one day

we shall have one, I know. And even the lowest of the Crusader Knights is given a servant. I will have someone to help me. Our son, Mikhail, will be raised as a knight's son with an automatic place within their ranks should he merit it, but if he is not the warrior his father is, he will receive an education that will keep him in the upper strata of our society. Selling Lara to Gaius Prospero will benefit us all. She will live a life of luxury, and we will climb into the ranks of the elite. You will have your dream. Our son will have more opportunities than even we can imagine. There is no honor or advancement in poverty, husband. There is only the certainty of death." Her eyes suddenly filled with tears.

John Swiftsword nodded. Susanna was absolutely right in this matter. This was an opportunity that would not come again for him. His daughter was exquisitely beautiful even as her faerie mother had been. But he could not provide Lara the kind of life to which she was entitled. And of late, the Mercenary Guild had not been as active as they had always been. Those needing their services were seeking men-at-arms not allied with his guild to whom they might pay a lower wage. It mattered not that these outsiders had no real training, or skills. They were cheaper to employ, which meant more profit, and if they died, they died. It was no great loss. Most of the assignments that did come into his guild these days were going to those men willing to share a percentage of their wage with the guild sergeants.

"I will need to speak with Lara," he said. His eyes mirrored his anguish.

Susanna looked up into her husband's face. "Yes," she agreed. Reaching up she touched his rough cheek with her fingertips. "I would wish it otherwise, husband," she said. "If Lara were plain of face and meek of spirit we might have put her as a maidservant into the house of a magnate's family. She would have earned her keep, and even been able to put a bit aside for a dowry portion. But she is beautiful, and high-spirited."

"Like her mother," he half whispered. "Ilona was glorious to look upon, and fiery of temperament. I can understand why she left me. But at least when she did, she left Lara so I should never forget the faerie who once loved me." He sighed sadly.

Susanna felt a stab of jealousy, but she hid it from him, saying instead, "Your faerie woman was a fool, John Swiftsword, for you are as good a man as ever was born!"

He looked down at her, and marveled that after all those lonely years he had found Susanna of the Lea. He had been heartbroken when Ilona had departed despite his pleas. He was a man with an infant daughter, and an old mother. It was his mother who had taken charge of his child, finding a wet nurse, and raising Lara while he was off in service to whoever was willing to pay for his skillful sword and his temporary loyalty. And then his mother had died when Lara was ten years of age. To his great surprise, his daughter took over the household chores. Whenever he returned home she would be waiting for him with a hot meal, lively chatter and a clean bed for him. He was grateful that his mother had trained his daughter so well, but he found himself growing lonely for the companionship of a good woman. Pleasure Women he had aplenty, but John Swiftsword wanted more now. At Lara's suggestion he went to the matchmaker.

Susanna of the Lea was the daughter of a farmer from the Midlands. She was the youngest of eight daughters and a son. Her family was delighted to find a husband for her who was willing to accept her miniscule dower portion, consisting of the clothing on her back, her shoes, a second skirt and bodice, a woolen cloak, a feather bed, two down pillows and a single silver coin of a small denomination. And she was willing to leave the country for the City.

"You'll not find a better wife," the matchmaker had told him. "She is pretty enough, but most important, sweet-natured. She is not fearful of that faerie child of yours, either. She will be a good mother to your daughter."

"If she is such a good catch then why is she still unwed?" he asked the matchmaker.

The matchmaker sighed. "It's the dowry, John Swiftsword. She's the last of her parents' children, and there is practically nothing left for her. Usually these girls remain at home to care for their eld-erly parents, but her mother died last year, and the old farmer, her father, took himself another wife, a widow. The girl is not needed any longer, and the new wife wants her gone. She has an ugly daughter who will be the one to stay home and look after the farmer and his new wife. Only when I told the farmer there was no way I could get a decent husband for her without silver was the coin offered, and grudgingly at that. The new wife is not happy about it, but the girl's brother spoke up for her, and as he is the one who will inherit the farm one day, his voice carried weight."

John Swiftsword nodded. He understood what it was like not to be wanted. He had been born on a Midland farm himself, but being one of his parents' younger children, he was encouraged al-most from birth to find his own way. He had been fortunate in that his eldest brother's wife was the daughter of a mercenary, who had come to live with them in his old age. It was the old soldier who had taught John how to use a sword, and encouraged him to join the mercenaries that he might have a life of his own.

"I'll take Susanna of the Lea for my wife," he had told the match-maker, and it had been done. He had gone to her father's farm, found that the matchmaker had not lied, and they had been united on the next Marrying Day, along with twenty-two other couples, by the Squire who ruled the Midlands region. The Squire per-formed this service one day each month.

And Susanna had come back to the City with him immediately afterwards, spending their wedding night in their hovel. She had shrieked satisfactorily when he broke through her maidenhead, so he knew with certainty that any children he got on her would be his. She was a good bedmate, and he quickly realized he had found a treasure of a wife in her. His hovel was kept clean. His daughter was cared for and his meals were excellent. When he got a child on her he knew his life was a good one. Good except for the fact he could not think of a way to make his dream of joining the Order of the Crusader Knights come true.

When he had first come to the City and joined the Mercenaries, he quickly learned that mercenaries were not a particularly respected group. They were needed, yes, but not well-regarded. Mercenaries were the cannon fodder used by the Crusader Knights in the wars they had once conducted. Nowadays mercenaries were hired to protect the caravans that traversed the four kingdoms. They were the men-at-arms used when one traveled the streets at night or carried valuables. They had no stature at all. The district in which they lived was a poor one, and their hovels were not their own. They were at the mercy of their guild, and the only escapes available to them were death, or entry into the Order of the Crusader Knights. Having earned the appellation Swiftsword for his skill with a blade, John wanted more than anything to be a Crusader Knight.

Entry into this high order was not an easy task. Every three years the Crusader Knights held a great tourney in the City to replenish their ranks, due more to old age and death than battle these days. But the Crusader Knights would not take just any man. Men who applied to enter the tourney had to appear before the entrance board properly garbed in fine garments. If they gained a place in the tourney they had to arrive that first day well-equipped with a warhorse, a good suit of armor and an array of fine weapons. Any man not appearing as required was immediately disqualified, and sent away.

For the next five days the applicants would battle with each other. At the end of each day the winners would be separated from the other aspirants. And on the sixth day all the previous winners would battle. At day's end, the last few men remaining were paired to fight Crusader Knight opponents. One run only with horse and lance. If the applicant was not unhorsed he would be accepted into the order. Those men who tumbled from their mounts were sent away. It was a grueling tourney, but John Swiftsword knew in his heart that he could prevail if he could only enter.

But it was such an expensive undertaking, and he had never made enough coin to be able to put some aside. He barely managed to support his family. It was very rare for a mercenary to be able to enter the tourney. Most applicants came from families of some means with second and third sons who had been trained to fight in hopes of joining this vaunted order. But now his wife had offered him a solution to gain his dream. He could still not bring himself to sell his beautiful daughter, but at Susanna's suggestion he invited both the armorer and the swordsmith to a local inn so that they might speak together. Both were enthusiastic at the possibility of his entering the tournament.

"You're a warrior born, John Swiftsword," Rafe the armorer said enthusiastically. "I would be proud to make your armor. You'll win, too, you know." He grinned. "I've seen you in the practice yard wielding your blade. There isn't a man who can stand against you."

"I'm not as good a horseman as I would want to be," John replied slowly.

Rafe leaned forward, and lowering his voice said, "I've three Crusader Knights among my patrons. I have told them you may enter this tourney, and they all evinced enthusiasm at the prospect, for your reputation precedes you, though you are too modest a man to realize it. If I ask, and you have but to give me the word, they will tell me the trainer you will need to polish your other battle skills, John Swiftsword." He picked up his tankard and drank deeply from it.

Now Bevin the swordsmith leaned forward to speak. "I made the sword with which you have always fought. My own skills have improved over the years, and I will make you the finest sword ever created. It will sing a song of death as you wield it, John. You will be envied by all, for this sword's beauty will almost equal your prowess with it."

The mercenary sighed deeply. "To realize all of this I must sell my daughter," he told them. "You know I am a poor man."

"As you have said, you are a poor man," Bevin said quietly. "But the faerie you mated with left you a most valuable gift in the person of the lass."

"And what is to happen to the girl, John Swiftsword, if you do not sell her?" Rafe asked. His direct gaze pierced the mercenary's own.

John Swiftsword nodded. "I know I have no choice in this matter," he replied to them. "I will go tomorrow and speak with Gaius Prospero myself."

"Come just after sunrise to be measured so I may begin working on your armor," Rafe told him. "We want time to make any adjustments needed." He downed the remaining ale in his tankard and, standing, bid the other two men farewell.

"You are doing the right thing," the swordsmith told John. "What good is the girl to you now that she is grown? You have a good wife, and a little son to consider now. Your daughter's beauty will give her the future that you surely cannot."

John Swiftsword nodded slowly in reluctant agreement, and then he ordered them each another tankard of ale. He said nothing to Susanna when he returned home late, and the next morning he left their hovel to go into the Golden District, where the magnates had their City homes. He had dressed carefully in his best tunic—he had but two. He had polished his worn boots. His sword hung from a wide leather belt.

Reaching the tall gates of the Golden District, he said to the two guardsmen who guarded those gates, "I am John Swiftsword of the Guild of Mercenaries. I have come to speak with Gaius Prospero."

"Are you expected?" one of the guardsmen asked.

"I do not know if I am or not," John answered.

"Wait while we check," the guardsman replied. Then turning he went back into the little guardhouse, and leaning out a window that opened beyond the gates he called out for a messenger to come.

John waited. Riders and travel wagons carrying the women who lived in the Golden District came in and out of the great gates. He could glimpse what appeared to be a parkland beyond those portals as they opened and closed. Finally after some time had passed the first guardsman motioned him forward.

"You must leave your sword with me, and then you may be admitted," he said.

"You know who I am," the mercenary replied, "and I will find my sword here when I return?"

"Do I look like a common thief?" the guardsman responded indignantly.

"Nay, not at all, but so many pass by here, and you could be distracted," John quickly said. "The sword is my livelihood."

"I understand," the guardsman replied. "I am a member of the guild, too, John Swiftsword. I was injured several years ago, but was fortunate to obtain this post. Your sword will be safe in my care. Now go! Gaius Prospero doesn't like to be kept waiting. You will find a conveyance directly inside the gate that will transport you to his house." He then took John's sword from his hands, and ushered him through the gates where the cart was awaiting the visitor. John climbed aboard, and the vehicle moved quickly away from the entrance to the Golden District.

All around him was an incredibly beautiful green parkland. There seemed to be huge trees everywhere, and the grass was neatly manicured. They trotted down a well-paved road. Here and there through the greensward and trees he could see great houses of shining white marble. He had never imagined a place such as this within the City, and Susanna had said nothing about it. How like her, he smiled to himself, to want him to be surprised, and see for himself. And it was quiet. Several feet past the entrance the cacophony of the City had disappeared entirely. He wondered if the Garden District, where the Crusader Knights lived, was quiet like this, too. A man could actually think in such quiet.

John grew alert once more as the cart in which he traveled turned down a narrow road of white gravel. As his transport passed by, liveried servants stepped from behind the flowering bushes to rake the path smooth again. Such a thing would have never occurred to him had he not seen it for himself, he thought, amazed. The cart drew up before the house now. He had no time to observe but that it had a rotunda over the main entrance, before a servant stepped forward to help him from his transport and usher him into the building. He was taken to a wide marble bench in the rotunda, and told to sit. Before him was a rectangular pool at one end of which was a bronze boy on a dolphin. Water spouted gently from the fish's mouth. There were green water hyacinths floating in the pool.

"Someone will come for you when the master can see you," the servant said, and then he was gone.

John Swiftsword sat. The day was warm. He was thirsty, and had had nothing to eat as he had departed early from his hovel. First he had gone to the armorer to be measured for the suit of armor he would need, and then he had walked across the City to the Golden District. A cup of water would have been nice, he considered, but John Swiftsword knew he was of little importance, and would be offered no refreshment. He waited. He was startled when a small goldfish leaped up from the pool, splashing back down into the water. The sun reached its zenith, and poured into the rotunda. The air was still, and it grew hot. He struggled not to doze in the still heat. It had not seemed so warm in the City outside of the Golden District this morning. And then finally a man came forward, and spoke to John.

"I am one of Gaius Prospero's secretaries. You will come with me." He turned without waiting for any reply. John stood and quickly followed the man into a side hallway, down its length and into a large room. "Wait here," the secretary said, and disappeared through a door at the end of the room.

John Swiftsword stood quietly. In the center of the room was a great round black-and-gold-flecked marble table with solid gold legs that had gold balls and claw feet. Upon the table was a great round polished stone vase from which a colorful arrangement of exotic blooms spilled. One side of the room was an open colonnade, and beyond it a small garden. He would have liked to have looked into that garden, but he dared not move. His manners, for he did have them, overcame his curiosity.

"Come this way," the secretary's voice snapped, breaking his reverie.

He was ushered into another large room where sitting at a long marble table was the man he had come to see, for it could only be Gaius Prospero in that thronelike chair.

"You may go, Jonah," Gaius Prospero told the secretary. Then he looked at John Swiftsword.

The mercenary bowed politely, and waited for the Master of the Merchants to speak. You did not speak unless spoken to by a great man, he knew.

"So you are to become a Crusader Knight," Gaius Prospero began.

"I should like to, but nothing is certain, my lord, as you surely know," the mercenary replied.

"It should please me if you did," came the surprising reply. "And there are others who agree with me. Your battle skills are legend, John Swiftsword. The Order of Crusader Knights is where you rightfully belong."

"Thank you, my lord," John said.

"This will be, of course, about your decision to sell me your beautiful daughter," Gaius Prospero began the negotiation.

"Yes, my lord," John replied.

"I had your wife remove her garment. She is exquisitely made. Every Pleasure House in the City will want her. The bidding will be unprecedented. And I had my physician validate her virginity. I am pleased that she is fully intact. Her first-night rights will bring her owner a fortune." He smiled. "And she is half faerie, if I understood your wife correctly?"

His temples were throbbing. They had stripped his daughter of her clothing to examine her? They had probed her innocence? He blinked back the bloodred in his eyes, swallowed hard and said, "Yes, my lord. Her mother was a faerie woman called Ilona. She was my first woman, and came to me on a Midsummer's Eve."

"A most powerful time," Gaius Prospero remarked. "Now, John Swiftsword, are you willing to sell your daughter to me?"

This was the moment he had dreaded. Closing his eyes briefly, he nodded and said, "Aye, I will sell Lara to you, my lord." He wanted to weep. He wanted to run from the room where he now stood before the great Master of the Merchants. But he did not. He opened his eyes, and looked directly at Gaius Prospero.

"Excellent! And a most wise decision on your part, John Swiftsword. I am pleased to see you are not restrained by any foolish sentiments for the girl. I shall have Jonah bring the papers for you to sign now. You do write, don't you?"

"I both read and write," the mercenary responded, "as does my daughter."

The Master of the Merchants raised an eyebrow. "Then the girl is even more priceless," he said. "Magical beauty, innocence and an education." He rubbed his hands.

"I beg one boon of you, my lord," John Swiftsword quickly interjected.

"And that is?" Gaius Prospero asked. What could the man possibly want? He was being paid a fortune for his merchandise.

"Please, my lord, I will sign your papers today, but let my daughter remain with me until the time of the tournament."

So the mercenary loved his child. "You will need monies for your clothing, your armor and your weapons," the Master of the Merchants reminded John Swiftsword.

"I will ask only what my wife needs for materials," John said, "and a down payment to the armorer and the swordsmith. They are my friends, and will accept a final payment after the tourney ends."

Gaius Prospero considered the request. "The girl will not run away?" he asked.

"Nay, she is an obedient lass, and my wife and I will explain all the advantages this change in her circumstances will afford her. Lara is not a stupid girl. She will understand that this future we have planned for her will be a good future. Please, my lord. It is unlikely I shall ever see my child again once she leaves me."

The mercenary was right, of course. Crusader Knights were family men who generally cleaved to their wives, although he knew some who had the morals of alley cats. Still, it was unlikely this father and daughter would meet again. Gaius Prospero loved his own two daughters dearly, and this was an area in which he was disposed to be reasonable. "I will have it written into our agreement," he said.

Then he struck a bronze gong that sat on the table, and almost immediately the secretary Jonah was there, bowing to his master. The Master of the Merchants gave him his instructions. "And be quick. John Swiftsword will want to tell his wife and daughter of our agreement today, and he must walk across the City before dark. And I have promised my daughters that we are going to the farm for a few days. Send a message to my wife that we will leave within the hour, and have the traveling vehicle ready." Then the Master of the Merchants turned to John Swiftsword and said, "Perhaps you would enjoy waiting in my little garden. Jonah will come for you when the papers are ready for us to sign."

The mercenary bowed, turned and followed Jonah into the anteroom. When the secretary had disappeared in a cloud of his own importance John Swiftsword walked through the colonnade into the small garden. One day he would have a house with a garden like this. A garden where Susanna could sit at her loom, or with her sewing on the warm days. A garden where Mikhail could play in safety. And when he had that garden he would remember Lara with silent thanks. He sighed and sat down on a small marble bench, looking about him more carefully. There was a small fishpond in the middle of the walled garden. There was a miniature flowering tree at the end of each flowerbed. The beds were filled with blooms. Reds and pinks. Purples and lavenders. Yellow, orange and blues. And white flowers that perfumed the little garden with an incredible sweetness. It was so beautiful, and so perfect he felt near to weeping. Or was it the garden? He brushed the tears from his eyes.

He had no other choice. He knew with certainty that if he entered the tourney he would win a place for himself among the Crusader Knights, and in doing so he, Susanna and Mikhail would ascend to a higher social strata. They would never be poor again. Even if he were injured in his duties, and unable to serve his order further, he and his family would be taken care of. To remain a mercenary could only lead to eventual disaster. Susanna was right. His daughter was the only valuable thing he possessed. To retain Lara in his custody would be to doom them all to continued poverty and misfortune. He must put his sentiment, his memories, firmly aside and do what was right for all of them. He heard an impatient cough, and looking up saw the secretary, Jonah.

"My master is ready for you," the secretary said haughtily.

"Where are the papers?" John Swiftsword asked.

"In the antechamber outside of the library," Jonah responded.

"I will want to peruse the papers before I sign them," the mercenary said.

"What?" The secretary looked outraged. "Do you think my master is attempting to cheat you? Such a thing is impossible!"

"Restrain your outrage," John Swiftsword replied dryly. "I merely wish to see what it is I am signing. Would you sign an important paper without reading it first?"

"No," the secretary admitted, "but I would hardly think a man in your position would care. You are being paid a most excellent price for your daughter."

"Were I not in my position," the mercenary said low, "I should not sell the child I love. Now let me see the papers you have drawn up." He followed the secretary back into the antechamber where the parchments lay upon the round marble table. Picking them up, John Swiftsword scanned them carefully, his eyes widening at the price he was being paid for his daughter. Ten thousand gold cubits, half to be put with a goldsmith today that he might draw upon it, the other half to be turned over when he surrendered Lara to Gaius Prospero. The surrender date was to be, to his surprise, the day after the tournament was over. "Is this correct?" he asked Jonah.

"The master thought you might want your daughter to see you attain your goal, John Swiftsword. He is a family man himself, and loves his own daughters," the secretary answered in a gentler tone than he had previously used with the mercenary.

John Swiftsword nodded, and surreptitiously wiped his eyes again. Then he turned his attention once more to the parchment. All was exactly as he had agreed with Gaius Prospero. He handed the parchment back to the secretary. "I am ready to sign," he said.

Together the two men reentered the great library of the Master of the Merchants.

"I have the papers, my lord," Jonah said, spreading them before Gaius Prospero, who glanced at them carelessly before taking the inked quill from his secretary's hand and signing the two parchments. A copy for him. A copy for John Swiftsword. Jonah handed a second quill to John Swiftsword.

The mercenary closed his eyes but a brief moment, then opening them, took the quill and signed his name in a strong, legible hand. With a deep sigh he handed the pen back to the secretary. Then to his surprise the Master of the Merchants held out his hand.

"You have done a hard thing this day, John Swiftsword," Gaius Prospero said. "I shall look forward to your victory in the tournament in a few months. The Crusader Knights need men like you."

The mercenary shook the hand offered him. "Thank you, my lord," was all he could say. He had just sold the child of his heart into slavery.

"Come along now, John Swiftsword," the secretary said, ushering him from the august presence of Gaius Prospero. "Now tell me if you have a preference in goldsmiths, for I must send a messenger to he with whom you choose to open your account."

"I have no experience with goldsmiths," the mercenary said honestly. "Will you recommend someone to me?"

"With pleasure," Jonah replied, and a small smile touched the corners of his mouth. This man would soon belong to an important group, and while Jonah served one of the most important men on Hetar, it could not hurt to have a friend among the Crusader Knights. "Avram the goldsmith has his shop just outside the Garden District. He is honest, and has many of the order as his patrons. With your permission I shall open an account for you, and transfer the five thousand cubits to his keeping. If you will come with me I will give you a receipt for the gold."

John Swiftsword was suddenly in a daze. "Yes," he answered the secretary. Jonah, like his master, was assuming that he would gain one of the places open into the Crusader Knights in the coming tourney. The mercenary followed Jonah, waited while the receipt was made out, and then offering the secretary his hand, he shook it, took the receipt and departed the house of Gaius Prospero. Outside he found the transport awaiting to return him to the gates of the Golden District. The cart traversed the quiet parklike area once again, and then he was outside in the noisy, dirty streets of the City, the receipt for five thousand cubits clutched in his hand. He quickly tucked it into his doublet. Retrieving his sword from the guardsman at the gate he began walking back across the City to the Mercenaries Quarter where he lived. Where his wife, his son and his daughter awaited his coming.

The day was waning, and the streets grew dusky with the coming evening. John Swiftsword moved quickly. He was more than capable of defending himself, but he didn't want to have to bother right now. He reached the gates of the Quarter just before they closed for the night, nodding at the two old pensioners who guarded those gates, but not stopping to chat with them as he often did. Turning into his lane he stopped a moment. Then a deep sigh issued forth from him. He was a brave man, but he truly dreaded what was to come.

He could see the candlelight in the window of his hovel. Smoke rose from the narrow chimney. Straightening his shoulders John Swiftsword walked down the lane, opened the door to his hovel and stepped inside. Susanna was at the hearth stirring a pot from which arose a savory smell. She turned at the sound of his boot steps. Her face was serene with the familiar task she performed.

Looking up she asked softly, "Is it done, husband?"

He nodded. "Where is Lara?"

"Bathing Mikhail for me," Susanna answered. "The supper is almost ready. The butcher gave me several pieces of poultry that he would have otherwise discarded. I didn't even ask. I have made us a fine chicken stew, husband."

"Then the word is already about that I am entering the tourney," he replied, and he sat down at the table near the fire. "Of course it would be. Nothing is a secret for long in the Quarter. Give me something to drink, wife. I am parched. I have had nothing all day from the moment I departed our hovel."

She set a mug of cider before him. "Where is the gold?" she asked bluntly.

"With Avram the goldsmith. He has a shop outside the gates of the Garden District. Gaius Prospero's secretary, Jonah, deposited it, and gave me the receipt. I have made a bargain with the Master of the Merchants. Half down, and half on delivery of Lara. And she will remain with us until the day after the tourney's end."

Susanna came up behind him, slipping her arms about him. She kissed the top of his head. "It is a fair bargain, husband, and how proud your daughter will be to see you win your place among the Crusader Knights. When will you tell her?"

"Tonight, before I lose my courage," he replied. "You must leave us after the supper that Lara and I can be alone to speak on it."

She nodded, and then she smiled as her stepdaughter entered the room, her baby brother in her arms. "Here he is, all sweet and clean, stepmother. Will you nurse him now, or after our meal?" She handed the baby to its mother.

"Afterwards, I think. Put him in his cradle. He will be content to play with his toes while we eat," Susanna said, and she handed her son back to Lara, who put the baby boy down in the cradle.

"What?" John Swiftsword said teasingly. "No greeting for your old father, lass?"

"Where have you been all day, Da?" Lara asked, kissing his cheek and sitting down on the floor by his knee. She lay her head against it, smiling up at him.

He reached out to stroke that head. Her hair was a color he had seen only once. Lara had the golden gilt hair of her mother. And she had Ilona's lime-green eyes. In fact, everything about her was Ilona. Everything except her full lips, which she had inherited from him. "What have you been doing?" he asked, ignoring her query.

"Mistress Mildred watched Mikhail while my stepmother and I visited several mercers' shops in the Merchants Quarter. We wore our best skirts and bodices so they would not think we were beggar women," Lara reported. "Oh, Da, I have never seen materials such as I saw today. I never even knew such fabrics existed. And everyone was so kind to us! One of the mercers gave me a silver ribbon for my hair!"

His heart contracted. So they knew in the shops as well. Well, gossip was the meat and drink of the City. He should not be surprised.

"The supper will be cold if you two do not eat it," Susanna said briskly.

Lara scrambled to her feet and took her place, while her father swung about again to face the table. "I have put my ribbon away, but I will get it after supper to show you, Da," the girl said. "I shall only wear it on special occasions."

They ate the chicken stew that Susanna had ladled onto the worn wooden plates, tearing chunks off a small round loaf to mop up the gravy. They ate in silence. When they had finished, Lara quickly removed the plates and mugs from the table, taking them to the small stone sink outside the back door. Then she went to the hearth, and taking a kettle of hot water, poured it into the sink, refilled the kettle and replaced it on its hood over the fire. Adding a little cold water to the sink, she washed the wooden plates and mugs clean, dried them with her apron and replaced them in the bureau on the wall across from the hearth. Her father and her stepmother had been speaking quietly, but now Susanna arose, took Mikhail from his cradle and went into the garden to nurse her son.

"Come back and sit with me," John Swiftsword called to his daughter. "I must speak with you, Lara."

She rejoined him saying, "You look so sad, Da. What is it?"

"You know," he began, "that the tournament of the Crusader Knights will be held again this spring."

"Aye, Da, I know. You should be one of them! You should! Why have you not entered the tournament before?" Lara asked him.

"To enter the tournament a man must meet many requirements. He must know how to use certain weapons. He must be able to read and to write."

"You are a great swordsman, Da, and you can read and write," Lara said.

"But I have not been able to meet the third requirement, Lara. I do not look like I belong among the Crusader Knights," John said to his daughter.

"Why not?" she demanded.

"I must have a warhorse, and the beast must be well caparisoned. I must have beautiful armor and fine weapons. I need more than my skills, Lara."

"How silly," the young girl replied. "I would think your skills would be what counted most, not your appearance." She slipped into his lap and kissed his rough cheek.

"But my skills are nothing if I do not look like one of the order," he said. He put an arm around her, giving her a little hug. It was rare that he allowed himself to show her any real affection, but now their time together was growing short.

"And we are poor," she noted. "Have we nothing of value that we could sell that would allow you to enter the tourney, Da?"

"It is very costly, Lara, and I have not the means. Or so I thought until recently. I have one item, and one only, of great value. I have you."

"Me?" She said genuinely surprised, and a small tendril of fear rose within her. She pushed it away. "What value have I, Da?"

He smiled at her innocence. "Lara, you are extraordinarily beautiful, and you have your virginity, which has great value. As you have noted, we are poor. I have no dowry for you. I cannot make a match for you without one. It is all I can do to make ends meet. Now that my guild is receiving fewer and fewer assignments, there is less work for me, which means no coins in my pocket. I need to move up in the world, Lara, for all our sakes. What will become of you, of Susanna, of your brother if I do not? I know I can triumph in the coming tournament if I can but find the means to enter it."

"That is why Susanna took me to the house of Gaius Prospero, isn't it, Da?" she said thoughtfully. "That is why I was stripped naked, and why a physician probed my body, isn't it? The Master of the Merchants will pay a handsome price for me. He would purchase me."

"Ten thousand cubits, daughter," John Swiftsword replied.

Lara nodded slowly. "It is a great price, Da. Am I truly worth all that gold?"

"More," he told her, "for Gaius Prospero expects to make a profit from you, Lara. I think he will probably gain double or more when he sells you."

"What will he do with me, Da?" she asked. Suddenly she was truly afraid, and she trembled. Then swallowing hard, she fought back her fears, reminding herself that her father loved her. He would do nothing to harm her.

"I expect he will sell you into a Pleasure House," her father answered, his arm tightening around his daughter in a small gesture of comfort.

"Pleasure Women are admired, Da. They live lives of great luxury and privilege," Lara said. Then she reached out and patted his hand. "You must not be sad. What other future could I have? You have sold me then?" She had to be brave for her father's sake. She could see he was distressed. It wasn't a terrible fate, and actually a better one than she had considered, given their circumstances.

He nodded wordlessly.

"When must I go?" Her face was pensive. "Not right away, Da!"

"The day after the tourney, daughter," John Swiftsword told her.

Lara clapped her hands. "Then I shall see you attain your goal, Da! That is good. I will go with a light heart knowing that I have been able to aid you in this way."

"If there were any other way, Lara," he began, but she put a little hand over his mouth.

"If there were, Da, you would have found it for us," she said quietly. "The Celestial Actuary gives us each a talent. Yours is skill with a sword. I will make my way through life using my beauty. If I had been born ugly, you would have already put me into service in some magnate's house where I would be at the mercy of all. Nay. This is much better. I shall be a famous Pleasure Woman like Roxelana of the Rose. She bought her freedom, and now manages a Pleasure House. I would be like that. Charting my own destiny. At the mercy of no one."

"I had not expected such understanding from you, Lara," he told her gratefully.

"Sometimes I think my mother comes to me in the night, and whispers wisdom in my ear, Da. I am young, but there are times when I feel that I have lived a thousand years or more," she told him with a small smile.

"There are moments when you amaze me, daughter," John Swiftsword told his eldest child. "Thank you for understanding my position, for understanding what I must do. I did not make this decision that will affect all of our lives either easily or lightly." He tipped her from his lap, kissing her brow. Then standing, he said, "I will go and tell your stepmother of your courage now."

Lara remained where she was seated. Her life had stood still for
so very long, and she had always wondered what would happen to
her. She was fourteen, and grown. Many girls her age were already
wed, or in service, but neither would be her fate. She did not
mind. She had always wanted to know what lay beyond the City,
and now perhaps she would have that opportunity. She could be
sold into a Pleasure House in the Coastal Region. It was said the
coast was a rich and beautiful land. The Midlands were dull, just
farmers and their crops. Women in the Midlands Pleasure Houses
lived dull lives. It was unlikely any of them could purchase their
freedom one day. The land of the Shadow Princes was the one she
knew the least about. Few in the City knew a great deal about the
Shadow Princes. Did they even have Pleasure Houses? And as for
the Forest Lords, they kept to themselves, for they were the most
ancient of the clans on Hetar, with the purest of bloodlines—or so
they claimed. Their lives were guided by tradition.

But she was beautiful, her father said. Beautiful enough that the
Master of the Merchants would pay ten thousand gold cubits for
her, and then resell her for more. Lara had not a great deal of experience with life outside the Quarter, but she knew that if her
value was that great then her future could be even greater. Her
prospects were exciting and she eagerly awaited her fate. She was
half faerie, and now more than ever she felt that part of her stirring restlessly. Susanna said it was because Lara now suffered her
woman's blood flow each moon span that her mother's influence
was upon her more than it had ever been before. There was no de-
nying her faerie heritage, Susanna said.

Lara was happy that her going would help her family rise in the
social ranks, but she felt no sacrifice at what was to come. She saw
only great opportunity ahead, and the promise of a golden future.
Yet it niggled at her that her stepmother had been the one to pro-
voke the changes that were to come to them all. Should not John
Swiftsword have been the one to instigate these shifts in their lives?
Susanna had changed since the birth of Lara's baby brother six

months ago. Still, she did not envy her father's wife. The thought of being tied to one man as Susanna was tied to her father was abhorrent right now. Again her faerie blood spoke, but she had never confided any of these thoughts to anyone. Her stepmother, she suspected, would have been shocked. She had no friends her own age. The girls in the Quarter did not treat her well at all. Many were afraid of her faerie blood. She often wondered what they thought she was going to do to them. She knew no spells or magic. But now she realized that it was also her beauty that kept them at bay. Beauty, it would seem, was both a blessing and a curse. She must remember that in the times to come, Lara considered.

Chapter 2

SUSANNA WAS RELIEVED when her husband told her of Lara's reaction. She thought to herself that if she had been in Lara's position she would be very unhappy. But then the girl was half faerie. Who knew what she really felt? Susanna was glad that her stepdaughter would soon be gone. She was but five years older than John's daughter. She was young enough that she didn't want to share her husband with his beautiful child. But Lara had been so sweet and welcoming when she had married the girl's father that she was unable to be unkind, and could find no fault with her. Indeed, they were almost friends, odd as that seemed.

The next morning when John had gone out to see Bevin the swordsmith, Susanna called Lara to her. "Will you help me choose the fabric for your father's application clothing, and sew them with me? I cannot embroider half as well as you can, and your stitches are so fine as to be invisible."

"What will you do when I am not here to help you with your sewing?" Lara half teased her stepmother.

"What?" For a moment Susanna looked confused by her stepdaughter's words. Then Lara quickly said, "Will we return to the mercer today?"

"I think we must if we are to have your father's garments ready in time," Susanna said with a bright smile. "Now tell me which of the fabrics we saw last you favored?"

"My father's eyes are gray, and I think he must have a silver brocade. Silver brocade and sky-blue silk would suit him," Lara answered her stepmother.

"You did not like the gold brocade?" Susanna sounded disappointed.

"The gold was very fine, but perhaps a bit vulgar?" Lara replied thoughtfully. "I thought the silver more elegant with Da's eyes, ash-brown hair and fine features."

"Yes," Susanna reconsidered. Lara's instincts for fashion had always impressed her, considering the girl hardly ever left the Quarter. Yet she always knew what was right. It was very annoying at times, but still, best to listen to her. "Then the silver brocade it is," she agreed. "Run and ask Mistress Mildred if she will watch Mikhail today for if she will not we must have him with us. Take her one of the fresh loaves I baked early this morning."

Lara took the still-warm loaf and put it in a small market basket. Then she hurried to the hovel next to theirs where Mistress Mildred, a widow, lived with her son, Wilmot. "Susanna has sent you a nice warm loaf," she called out as she entered the room. "She wonders if you can watch Mikhail again today. We are going to the mercer's to purchase cloth for Da's application garments."

"So it's true then," the old woman said, coming forward and taking the loaf from the basket. "He's going to enter the tourney. Well, I'll be sorry to see you all go. He has been a good neighbor, and his mother before him. Where did he get the coin for such an expensive undertaking?"

"Are you so certain Da will win a place in the Crusader Knights?" Lara replied, avoiding the query neatly.

"Of course he'll win!" Mistress Mildred said. "He's the finest swordsman in the land, child. Did your grandmother not always say it? And everyone else?"

"Then you'll watch Mikhail?" Lara gently pressed her.

"I'll be over in just a few moments," Mistress Mildred responded, and Lara was swiftly gone out the door.

Warning Susanna of the old lady's curiosity, she and her stepmother were quickly on their way as soon as Mistress Mildred stepped into the hovel.

"We'll not be too long," Susanna promised.

"Take your time," Mistress Mildred called after them. "Remember you must chose the right fabrics and colors for your man if he is to make a good impression."

They left the Quarter and traveled through the City to the Merchants Quarter where the mercers were to be found. Why they should be recognized Lara never understood, but they obviously were as soon as they stepped over the threshold of the first shop. The mercer oozed with goodwill. His apprentices tumbled over one another to unroll bolts of fabric for Susanna. They snuck looks at Lara from beneath their lashes. The bargain struck between John Swiftsword and Gaius Prospero was publicly known now, for the Master of the Merchants was already seeking to drum up interest among the owners of the Pleasure Houses.

They looked at what the first mercer had to offer, and then moved on to two more shops, but Lara was not satisfied with the quality of fabrics being shown. Her grandmother had once been in the service of a magnate's wife as a seamstress. She had passed her knowledge of fabrics on to her only grandchild. And when they were in the Quarter's market square she had also instructed Lara in the fine art of bargaining. Susanna, a country girl, was not good at haggling for she had never had any experience in it as her father's daughter, and Lara still did most of the marketing for the household.

Walking on, they almost missed a small shop squeezed between two larger and more ostentatious ones. Susanna was not inclined to enter, for it looked a poor place with its dirty window, and a door that hung, but barely, from a single hinge. However, Lara gently insisted that until they found the perfect fabrics no establishment, even one so unfortunate looking, could be overlooked.

"You are probably right," she told her stepmother, "but we must look anyway."

The inside of the shop looked little better than the outside. It was dim and dusty, but when the ancient mercer hobbled forward Lara's instincts told her they had come to the right place. "We are looking for silver brocade," she said.

"I have precisely what you seek," the mercer replied politely. His voice was strong for one whose limbs were so frail. Reaching up, he brought a bolt of fabric off a shelf and unfurled it on the counter before their eyes. The silk brocade was cloth of silver, and its raised design was of sky-blue velvet. The quality was excellent, the finest they had seen this morning.

"It's perfect!" Lara breathed, turning to her stepmother. "Isn't it perfect?" She fingered the beautiful material.

"I have never seen anything so fine," Susanna agreed softly.

The old mercer smiled slyly, showing his worn and yellowed teeth. "It would make an applicant for the tourney more than presentable, my ladies. And I have a fine, matching blue silk that would sew up nicely into a pair of more than elegant trunk hose."

"And velvet for a cap?" Lara said quietly.

The mercer nodded. "And I know where you can obtain an excellent selection of plumes." The twinkle in his eyes was not quite human. His gaze met Lara's for a long moment while Susanna was murmuring over the cloth. Then he looked at her chain and its star, and nodded. "Ilona's star," he whispered.

"You knew my mother?" Lara murmured softly.

"Once, long ago," was the reply. "Like you, I am half faerie, though few live today who would know my heritage." Then he was all business once again. "Will you take the brocade, lady?" he asked Susanna.

She nodded. "And the silk and the velvet as well."

"You have not asked the price," he said.

Susanna blushed at her ignorance, and stammered. "I must have them," she said weakly. She looked nervously to Lara.

"And the mercer will be more than fair, stepmother, will you not, sir?" Lara quickly put in.

"If I am fair then the wife of the new Crusader Knight will patronize my shop again," the old man responded. "Your husband will need many fine garments, as will you and your little son."

"You know I have a lad?" Susanna looked surprised.

"Everything that can be known about John Swiftsword is known in the City, lady. We have been waiting for this day." He measured out the length of brocade she would need, and quickly cut it. Then he did the same for the pale blue silk, and the medium blue velvet. Wrapping the materials together in a piece of clean rough cloth he tied the packet shut with a bright piece of yarn, and handed it to her. "If the lady will wait I will write her a receipt," the mercer told Susanna. "A second receipt, signed with your mark, will be sent to Avram the goldsmith. The amount will be deducted from the credit your husband has with Avram."

Susanna was half in shock with the transaction. She had never bought anything in a shop like this in all her life. She looked helplessly to Lara.

"It is stuffy in here, stepmother," the girl said. "Go outside and take the air. I will sign the mercer's receipt, and learn where we may find feathers for Da's cap."

"Yes, I think I will go outside," Susanna replied. "Thank you, stepdaughter." Taking up her package, she departed the little shop.

Slowly the ancient mercer wrote out the two receipts. He pushed one forward, and handed the young girl the slender charcoal writing stick. It was almost entirely worn away, but Lara was still able to sign her name to the little parchment. Lara, daughter of John Swiftsword of the Quarter, she wrote in her best hand.

"Thank you, sir," she said, taking up her receipt as she pushed his toward him.

"Love and light be always in your path, daughter of Ilona," the mercer said, and he personally ushered her through the door of his shop. "You will find the feather merchant two lanes over. Choose a hawk's feather for it will bring your father additional good fortune. Your stepmother will want a more showy plume, but be certain your will prevails in the matter. One feather. No more."

"I understand," Lara responded, and then the shop door closed behind her and she rejoined her stepmother, who waited in the street. "Come," she said to Susanna. "He has told me where to find the feather merchant."

As the old mercer had predicted her father's young wife wanted the largest, whitest plume she saw. "Think how fine it will look with the blue velvet of your father's cap, Lara," she said excitedly, waving it about as the feather merchant grinned.

"It is beautiful," Lara agreed, "but do you not think it too big? It will draw all the attention away from Da. No one can compete with so wonderful a waving plume. The least breeze, and it will lift the cap from his very head." She laughed lightly. Her eyes scanned the tall glass canisters of feathers displayed. "I can see such a plume in your lovely hair one day, stepmother, but not, I think, on Da's cap."

The feather merchant scowled at her. "It is my finest plume," he said.

"Oh, it is very fair," Lara agreed, "but I think a feather that spoke more to my father's skills as well as his good taste would better suit. The plume is too ostentatious." She pointed. "Let us see that glass of hawk's feathers. Don't you think them elegant, stepmother?" She drew forth a long slender feather mixed with black, white and russet that was tipped with gold. "This one!" she exclaimed.

"It is very nice," Susanna agreed hesitantly, "but is not the white plume better?"

"The plume, I think, is the sort of thing every boy applying for the tourney will have jutting from his cap. Is that not so?" she directed her question to the feather merchant. "I will wager you have sold more plumes than anything else since the tourney was announced. I feel the hawk's feather will distinguish Da, and it will bring him luck, stepmother."

The feather merchant nodded reluctantly. "Your lass is right," he said. "I have sold nothing but white plumes to those applying. And I am the only feather merchant in the City. The hawk's feather she so carefully drew from the canister is the finest one I possess. It will indeed identify your man, and permit him to stand out among the others."

"Then I shall have it!" Susanna told him firmly.

"The hawk's feather is more expensive than the plume," he said.

"Wrap it carefully," Susanna instructed him. "My stepdaughter will sign the receipt. Our account is with Avram the goldsmith. Lara, I will await you outside." And Susanna swept grandly from the feather merchant's shop, her dignity restored.

Restraining her laughter, Lara stood quietly as the man first rolled the elegant hawk's feather in a length of gauze, then slipped it into a long, narrow wooden tube with a metal top. He wrote out two receipts, and pushed one forward for Lara to sign.

"So you're to be a Pleasure Woman," he said as he handed her the container and her copy of the receipt. He eyed her boldly.

"I know not what I will be," Lara said coldly. "That is up to Gaius Prospero." Then she turned, and left the establishment. The man was too forward.

"What is the matter?" Susanna asked her, seeing the anger on her stepdaughter's beautiful face. "Are you all right?"

Lara shook her head. "The feather merchant spoke out of turn," she replied. "It is nothing. Do you have the proper needles and threads we will need for this undertaking?"

Susanna nodded. "Aye, I do." When Lara got that particular look on her face it was best to leave her be, and inquire no further.

"Then we should go home, stepmother. We have much work ahead of us," the girl said in gentler tones. Then she smiled at Susanna. "We have been most successful this morning. You must speak to the cobbler in the Quarter. Da will need fine new boots to complete his attire, and the shoemaker must seek out the best leathers he can find."

"But, Lara, will that not be expensive?" Susanna said.

The girl laughed and patted her stepmother's arm. "Very expensive, but it will not make a dent in the credit Avram the goldsmith holds in Da's name," she said. "You are almost rich, Susanna, and I think it is time you got used to it," she teased the older woman. "When we have finished Da's garments we must make you a fine gown in which to attend the tourney."

"What of you?" her stepmother asked. "You should have a fine gown, too."

"I think that Gaius Prospero should supply me with such a gown," Lara answered. "I do belong to him now, do I not? If he wants to display his merchandise at the tourney I believe he should see that I have a proper gown to wear."

"How can you be so cold about this?" Susanna wondered as they walked.

"What else am I to do, stepmother? You are the one who suggested to my father that he sell me, and you were right. It was the only solution to his dilemma. Besides, what would become of me with no dower portion? No magnate's wife would have me in service in her house. I am too beautiful, I am told, although the most I have ever seen of my own face is what I can see when I gaze upon my reflection in a basin of water. You might have taken me to the public market and sold me there. But you did not. You sold me to the head of the Merchants of the Midlands Guild himself, which assures me a good fate. I am not cold. I have simply resigned myself to the fact that my childhood is over, and my future awaits. Did you not do the same when your father sought out the matchmaker? You did not know what kind of a man would take you, but you accepted that your fate was your fate. That is what I have done."

"I wish there had been another way," Susanna said.

"I do not consider becoming a Pleasure Woman a terrible fate, stepmother, but if your conscience troubles you, and I see it does, then before I go tell me what I must know of men and women. There is no shame to my virginity, but my ignorance distresses me greatly, I fear. I have heard you and Da at night in your bed, but I know not what you do to elicit such sounds. I can only account for the squeaking of the bedsprings."

Susanna's cheeks grew fiery with her stepdaughter's speech, but she managed to say, "Of course I will instruct you in all I know, Lara, but Pleasure Women know far more than I do."

"Of course they would," Lara replied, "but I certainly should have a grasp of the basics, shouldn't I?"

"I would think so," Susanna murmured, "but perhaps we should send to Gaius Prospero for his thought in the matter. As you have pointed out, he is now your owner."

"Let us go now," Lara said. "We are nearer the Golden District than we are to the Quarter, stepmother."

"Now? But he is not expecting us. And he has gone to the country, or so your father said. He had promised his children," Susanna replied.

"We can ask at the gate," Lara responded as they traversed the main square of the City. She then turned into the avenue leading to the Golden District. Behind her Susanna followed, helpless to her stepdaughter's strong will. Reaching the gates they sought, Lara strode up to the guard and said, "Is Gaius Prospero at home, sir?"

The guard looked her boldly over then replied, "You would be the new slave he purchased from John Swiftsword. But I did not think you due until after the tourney or so I was told. You are indeed a prime piece of goods, lass."

Lara glared. "I asked you a question," she said in icy tones. "If my master is in residence I need his advice on a matter that concerns me. I cannot act without his permission, and while I yet live with my father, I need my master's words to guide me."

The guard stood straighter now. "Aye, Gaius Prospero is in residence. His wife and daughters departed for the country yesterday, but he remained behind, for his son grew ill and could not travel. I will allow you through, but this woman must remain outside the gates to wait for you."

"This is the wife of John Swiftsword, but I will tell her to wait. Will you offer her a place to sit, and some water, please?" Lara said.

"The wife of Swiftsword? Then she may wait inside the gates. There is a bench beneath the trees, and I will bring her refreshment myself. Come!" He beckoned them.

Susanna was actually relieved not to have to accompany her stepdaughter. She reassured Lara that she was content to wait for her, and watched as the cart took the girl from her side, and down a smooth path. She thanked the guardsman who presented her with a wooden goblet of sweet watered wine, and sighed with pleasure at the greensward before her. The cart disappeared from her sight.

Like her father, Lara was enchanted by the parkland through which the cart traveled. She had seen it but once before when Susanna had brought her first to Gaius Prospero; how different and wonderful it was in comparison to the Quarter. She recognized the little road they now turned off upon. They were almost there. As her transport pulled up before the magnificent house a servant hurried out to greet it.

"The master is waiting for you," he said as he helped Lara from the cart.

"How did he know I was coming?" she wondered aloud.

"Faeriepost. The guard sent one from the gate," the servant explained. "They aren't like the one who bore you. They are tiny winged creatures, no bigger than a minute. Come this way, Mistress Lara."

Faeriepost. She had never heard of it before, but then there was much she didn't know about the world outside of the Quarter. The servant led her directly to Gaius Prospero, who was seated in the courtyard garden outside of his library. With him was a young boy Lara judged to be about eight years old.

The Master of the Merchants Guild looked up, and smiled. His fat hand with its several rings waved her forward. "I am told you would ask my advice," he said. "That pleases me greatly, Lara, daughter of Swiftsword."

"I am your possession, my lord," she replied, but there was no servility in her voice. "I am aware of my place in the scheme of things to come." Her lime-green eyes met his directly, and then she lowered them politely.

He nodded. The girl had spirit and intelligence. She would one day be a famous Pleasure Woman because he had been clever enough to see her worth, he congratulated himself silently. Then he said, "This is my son, Aubin. He will follow in my footsteps one day. You may speak to him."

Lara nodded graciously at the boy. "I greet you, young master," she said.

"She is beautiful," the boy said to his father as if Lara could not hear him.

"She is the most beautiful girl I have ever seen," his father told him. "Always seek out the best and the finest merchandise, my son. You will make no profit with the ordinary. Only the unique and the rare will be of benefit to you." He patted the boy's head and then turned to Lara. "Now tell me what it is you desire of me, my beauty?"

"First," she began, "I would ask your permission for my step-mother to educate me in the ways of men and women. I am totally ignorant of such things."

"Tell her she may explain the basics to you, but no more," Gaius Prospero replied. "A high-priced virgin should have certain knowledge, but only that she not be frightened by her first experience with passion. A man purchasing a virgin's first-night rights likes to lead the way. Surprised innocence has a great charm all its own." He smiled at Lara in almost paternal fashion. "What else?"

"I should like to see my father win at the tourney, but I thought I would need your permission to attend. And if you give it, should you not also give me a gown to wear that this beauty I am told I possess be displayed to your advantage?"

Gaius Prospero chuckled, and the chuckle grew into hearty laughter. The girl was amazing. Despite all her lack of advantages she had incredible instincts. She was a survivor. He pulled a large purple handkerchief from his sleeve, and wiped his eyes with it. He let his mirth subside, and then he said in calmer tones than he had thought himself capable of, "Aye to both your questions, my beauty. You shall go to the tourney, for I promised your father you should see his triumph—and you shall be displayed as the rare piece of merchandise I intend you to be. And I shall send two litters to your home that day. In one, your stepmother and half brother will ride. The other will be for you alone. You will be brought to my private box on the tournament field where all will see you, and many will desire you." He looked quizzically at her. "You have never seen yourself, your own image, Lara? This is true?"

"I have glimpsed my face in the basin, and the well bucket, but I see nothing out of the ordinary," she answered him.

"You must see yourself then before you leave us today." He stood up. "Come!" And he hurried from the garden with Lara and his son following behind. He led them into a gallery that was lined with mirrors on one side, and with windows that overlooked the vast parkland outside. "There, my beauty," he said triumphantly. "There is your image. The image of perfect beauty!"

Lara stared, not quite certain that what she saw was real. "Truly, my lord? I look upon myself?" The tall and slender image in the glass stared back. It wore a simple sleeveless dark blue gown tied at the waist by a twisted, natural-colored cord. Her graceful neck rose above the gown's round neckline. Her hair was pale with golden lights. Her lime-green eyes stared at her from a heart-shaped face with a straight little nose and generous lips. Her chin had just the daintiest of clefts in it. Her brows were dark in comparison to her hair, as were her eyelashes. "I see only a girl," Lara said.

"Remove your gown," Gaius Prospero said to her quietly.

"But the boy..." she began, and then she stopped. The boy was his father's heir in all ways. Lara undid the little ties at the shoulder of her gown and let the garment drop to the floor. There was a faint blush to her cheeks.

"You see, Aubin, the perfect breasts. Small yet, but perfect nonetheless. And the way her hips flare gently below her slim waist. Her limbs are most shapely, are they not? And see how full the golden bush so coyly hiding her sex is. Such is an indication of a very passionate nature. Everything is in perfect proportion on this girl. Touch her. The skin is like silk, and utterly flawless." He ran his hand casually down Lara's back, over her buttocks, and the boy imitated his motions. "You see, my son. A rare piece of merchandise. Lara, my beauty, do you not have a beautiful body? Do you now understand your value?"

She gazed at herself in the mirror with new eyes. She was beautiful. There wasn't a mark on her body to detract from her perfection. She wondered why Gaius Prospero wasn't desirous of her, but then she realized as their eyes met in the glass that her value to him was in her worth as quality merchandise. Nothing more. Profit was in his heart and soul. "Yes" she agreed, "though I have no other with whom to compare."

"But never allow that knowledge to overcome your common sense, my beauty," he advised her. He bent down and drew her garment back up, fastening the tabs at the shoulders. Then he touched her face gently. "Lovely," he murmured almost to himself.

"Thank you, my lord," Lara said quietly. "May I have your permission to withdraw now, and return to Susanna who awaits me?"

He nodded his assent, calling for a servant to lead her back through the house to where her transport was awaiting her. Lara was a glorious creature, he thought. He desired her himself, but she was simply too valuable to tamper with, and because he never allowed his own emotions to interfere with his judgment, he hid his desire well.

Her stepmother looked up, relieved, as Lara stepped from the cart. Together the two left the Golden District, thanking the guardsman on duty for his courtesy as they departed. Susanna was clutching their purchases to her ample bosom as they walked swiftly through the City. Finally she spoke. "What happened?" she asked Lara.

"Gaius Prospero says you are to instruct me in the basics of passion that I not be fearful," Lara began. "And he will give me a gown to wear so I am properly displayed. And he will send two litters for us. I am to ride alone in one, you and Mikhail in the other. We will be escorted to his box that we may see all."

Susanna almost dropped her packages. "How shall I ever make a gown for myself that will not shame your father?" she began to fret. "I know little of the mighty."

"I will help you," Lara told her stepmother.

"Perhaps we should return to the feather merchant tomorrow, and obtain that white plume for my hair," Susanna responded.

Lara swallowed her laughter. "I think perhaps a little less ostentation, stepmother, would serve you best. You must appear an elegant and proper young matron."

"It is true," Susanna worried aloud. "My appearance will be judged as well as your father's, and yours."

"Exactly!" Lara said. "So if you appear in too much finery it makes you look gauche and overproud. It would not, I suspect, sit well with the women whose husbands and fathers are Crusader Knights. Modest but fashionable is what you must be."

When they returned to the hovel they found Mistress Mildred with a very hungry Mikhail. Susanna immediately put her son to her bosom, realizing as she did so that her breasts were quite full. Their old neighbor was filled with curiosity, and Lara assuaged it by unwrapping the beautiful brocade, the silk and the velvet for her to see. Mistress Mildred touched the fabrics reverently and nodded. Satisfied, she told Susanna that Mikhail was a very good child, and she would stay with him whenever needed in these next busy months. Susanna thanked her, and Mistress Mildred went home to her own hovel, where her son would be expecting his dinner.

John Swiftsword returned home after sunset to find his own dinner awaiting him on the hearth. He told them of his search this day for a good warhorse with the help of an old Crusader Knight, to whom he had been introduced by Rafe the armorer. "We may have found one out at a Midlands farm today. He's four years old, and has had a good year of combat training," John said excitedly. "I rode him for a time, and we seemed to become friends. Sir Ferris says a man must feel kinship with his beast. We will go back tomorrow, and arrange to buy Aristaeus." He was very happy, happier than he had ever been in all his life. "What did you two do today?" he asked them.

"We went to find the perfect material for your garments," Susanna said. "I do not know what I would have done without Lara. Her taste is frankly better than mine, and she signed all the receipts, thus saving me the embarrassment of admitting I cannot read or write. We found the perfect feather for the cap we will make you. Lara visited Gaius Prospero, and then we came home," Susanna concluded.

John Swiftsword turned to his daughter. "You went to Gaius Prospero? Why?" He was still troubled by what he had done, but Lara, it seemed, was not in the least unhappy at the future ahead of her.

"I wanted to know if I might go to the tourney to see you win, Da. And I wanted to know if Susanna could speak to me of men and women. He is my master now, Da. I believed I needed his permission. He seemed well pleased that I came to ask him."

John nodded. "You were right to go to Gaius Prospero," he said slowly.

"He says I am to have a beautiful gown, and that he will send two litters that day. Susanna, Mikhail and I are to sit in his private box at the tourney, Da. Tomorrow Susanna and I will begin the process of fashioning your application garments. You will wear the most glorious brocade, Da!" Lara told him.

He could not bear it. His beautiful golden child would shortly be gone from him, and he did not know if he would ever see her again.

"Go to bed now, Lara," Susanna said softly, and the girl arose, kissing them both, and disappeared into the tiny chamber she shared with her baby brother. "She is content, John," Susanna said to her husband. "She looks forward to her future."

"She has no idea of what awaits her," he groaned. "She is so innocent. Her whole life she has lived here in the Quarter, rarely venturing out until now. How can she envision a future she cannot possibly understand?"

Susanna sighed. "You underestimate Lara, John. Your mother taught her a great deal more than how to keep a house and sew. You should have seen her today. I should have had little success without her. I was frankly intimidated by those with whom I was forced to traffic. Not Lara. She has the bearings of a young queen. The mercers actually deferred to her. She has a certain assured quality about her they recognized even as they recognized my hesitancy.

"And she treated me with such great and public respect, husband, suggesting I wait in the fresh air while she concluded our transactions. And knowing with the certain instinct that she has suddenly displayed that she should go to Gaius Prospero. And she wasn't one bit frightened. When I first took her to him I was terrified, but not your daughter. And not today. Nay, John, Lara knows precisely what she is doing, and you need feel no guilt in having sold her so you might have your chance. She has no regrets."

"What will you tell her of men and women?" he asked his wife.

Susanna laughed. "Now, husband, sooner or later this conversation between your daughter and me would have had to be voiced. I know what to say. She will know what she needs to know, and learn the rest as her life moves forward. Now tell me about this Sir Ferris you met today."

"Sir Ferris Ironshield," John began, "is one of the oldest and most respected of the Crusader Knights. He is sixty, wife, and still active. He is a client of the armorer's, and Rafe asked him if he would be interested in helping me. We met today outside the City on the road to a Midlands horse farm, but before he would take me on he said he had to test my mettle with the sword for which I have earned my fame. He warned me not to hold back, but to fight my best. He's the finest opponent I have come up against in years, but I beat him, Susanna. He laughed and said my reputation was justly come by, and he would be happy to sponsor me, for it seems I must have a sponsor's name upon the application. I have so much to learn, wife!"

"And you will," she encouraged him. "So you found your horse?"

"Aye. And while I am good with a sword and a spear, my skills with the axe and the mace need work. Sir Ferris says we will work on them over the next few months."

"Then all is as it should be now, husband," Susanna replied.

It was autumn and as the days lengthened Lara and her step-mother began the process of creating and sewing the garments that John Swiftsword would wear on the day of the applications for entrance to the rank of tournament goers. Lara carefully cut her father's tunic out from the beautiful silver brocade they had purchased. Then she cut the trunk hose from the sky blue silk. Only then did they begin the sewing. Susanna carefully stitched together the hose, taking her time, and working hard to make her stitches as fine as Lara's. An impossibility, she decided, but she tried anyway. Little Mikhail sat on the floor of the hovel playing with pieces of discarded material, and quite content to do so. He was his father's son in all ways.

Lara had returned to the old mercer's shop twice to purchase other materials as she considered how she would decorate her father's tunic. She had also found a lovely lilac cloth for Susanna's gown, which she would make only after the tunic was done. She had designed the tunic with a round neckline. Around it she sewed a wide band of cloth of silver she had embroidered with gold, silver and dark blue threads. She then added tiny gold and silver beads. The small straight opening in the neckline gave way to a short stretch of the same embroidery down the front of the tunic. The garment was slit on either side and the slits, as well as the hem of the tunic, were decorated with identical embroidery, which also curled about the cuffs of the full sleeves. Lara also made a wide embroidered belt to hang low on the garment. It was a labor of love that took weeks to accomplish. While she toiled over the tunic, Susanna made her husband's trunk hose, and the velvet cap with the hawk's feather he would wear. She had also gone to the cobbler and had a pair of soft leather shoes with turned-back cuffs made along with a pair of fine leather boots for her husband. Lara took the shoes and embroidered their cuffs to match her father's tunic.

And then to their surprise, one day Sir Ferris Ironshield arrived at the door of their hovel. "I have come to inspect the application garments," he said in his gruff voice.

"My husband is not here," Susanna said nervously.

"Of course he isn't!" Sir Ferris growled. "He is on the practice field where I left him with Sir Ajax and Sir Iven. He has improved tremendously under our tutelage, mistress. I have no doubt that in a few weeks he will be one of us."

"Come in, sir," Lara beckoned, giving her stepmother a moment to recover. "I will fetch Da's garments, which we have completed only yesterday."

"Yes," Susanna finally found her tongue. "May I offer you a bit of cider, Sir Ferris, while Lara brings my husband's clothing?" She ushered him to the bench by the fire. "Sit down, please." She bustled to pour the cider into her best wooden cup, and handed it to him quickly.

He drank it appreciatively. "It has been a long time since I have visited the Quarter," he noted. "Nothing here seems to change, I fear. It is still a poor place, and I hear the Mercenary's Guild is now taking a fee from its men to provide them with work. Shameful, but what can you expect with so much of their custom going to nonmembers?"

"I did not know," Susanna said softly.

"Nay, I expect your man would keep it from you. Well, not to fret, mistress. You'll soon be ensconced in the Garden District where you belong."

"Here are my da's garments, sir," Lara said as she brought forth the tunic, and held it out for him to see. "The trunk hose are sky-blue silk, and my stepmother will fetch his cap that you may see it."

Sir Ferris carefully looked over everything they displayed to his view. The tunic was quite magnificent, and the shoe cuffs were a nice touch. The application officers would be very impressed. Without a doubt it was the garment of a Crusader Knight. When he saw the velvet cap Susanna showed him, he nodded with a pleased smile. "Excellent, mistress. And you have been wise enough to avoid those damned white plumes almost every applicant feels he needs to put in his cap. The hawk's feather is elegant, and most manly. John Swiftsword would stand out with just the cap alone." He stood up. "You have done well, and I am content that with a good performance on the field John Swiftsword will soon become a Crusader Knight. I thank you for the cider." Then with a stiff little bow to them both, he departed the hovel.

"Imagine," Susanna finally managed to say, "he came to us. He must really like your father and think well of him. I am so proud. When we are settled in our new home I shall ask him and his two friends to dine with us."

"I must begin your gown tomorrow," Lara said.

"You would not show me the material you obtained," Susanna complained. "Will you show it to me now?"

Lara laughed. "Very well, but you must swear you will trust me to make the gown for you."

"I am in your hands," Susanna chuckled. "Now show me the fabric!"

Lara went to the chest on the far side of the room and lifted out a carefully wrapped packet. Bringing it to the table she undid it, and Susanna gasped.

"It's too beautiful," she cried. "I am not worthy of such loveliness!"

"It is perfect," Lara said. "I have planned a simple design, for a more elaborate garment would not be suitable for an applicant's wife."

"But the fabric itself…" Susanna held it up and against her. The lilac silk had a shimmering and iridescent quality to it. It was quite unique.

"The fabric," Lara told her stepmother, "is perfect with your dark brown hair and eyes. And your skin has a lovely rosy glow to it. When I saw it I knew it was for you."

Susanna began to cry, and Lara snatched the material from her lest her tears stain the fabric. "I wish you didn't have to leave us," she said, and thought for the first time that she actually meant it.

"My fate isn't with you and Da," Lara replied. "I do not know where it will be, but I know it isn't with you. Perhaps that is my faerie blood speaking."

And then the winter was over and Lara celebrated her fifteenth birthday with the spring. The day of the applications was upon them. Her father had risen early, and Susanna with him. He had bathed himself completely in the wooden tub, not just his body, but his hair as well. Susanna had shaved his handsome face smooth, being careful not to nick and bloody her husband. She called for Lara to come and put the tunic on her father when he was garbed in his sky-blue trunk hose, and the dark blue shirt whose sleeves would show from beneath the tunic.

Together Lara and Susanna drew the tunic over John's head. The garment fell, and Lara carefully closed the little silver frogs at the neckline. She stood back and smiled, pleased. "Da, you have never looked so grand. Sir Ferris told us that these are the garments of a Crusader Knight, and he was surely right." Fastening the embroidered belt about the tunic, she knelt and fitted the soft leather shoes to her father's feet.

Susanna handed her husband his velvet cap. He placed it on his head, drawing it to one side, and the hawk's feather jutted jauntily. He strutted about the hovel proudly, and then turning to his wife and daughter he said, "Thank you."

Lara went to the door of the hovel and unbarred it.

"Go now," Susanna said. "When you return I will have a meal for you."

He strode from the dwelling, and when he was out of sight Susanna turned to speak to her stepdaughter, but Lara was nowhere to be found. Susanna chuckled. Her stepdaughter, she had not a doubt, had followed her father that she might stand in the crowd in the City's main square and watch John Swiftsword as he made his application to the tournament of the Crusader Knights, and was formally and publicly accepted. She was entitled to this little triumph, Susanna thought generously, for it was Lara's sacrifice that had made this all possible.

Lara had snatched up a dark cloak so that she might remain anonymous as she hurried through the streets. Already the citizens were gathering to witness this rare event. Reaching the square she pushed herself to the front of the crowds, but no one seemed to mind. Her slender form was no more than a breeze as it brushed by them all. She saw her father standing in the long line that already stretched halfway across the square. Listening, she heard comments of the onlookers. They seemed to know most of the applicants either by name or by reputation.

John Swiftsword felt his heart pumping with excitement. Looking about him he decided that he was the best dressed of all the applicants, and he smiled at the prevalence of white plumes. Susanna had told him the story of shopping at the feather merchant's, and Sir Ferris's comment when he had visited the hovel. He tried to calm himself for the interview ahead. He didn't want to sound like a bumbling idiot. It wasn't just the honor of belonging to this order that thrilled him, it was the opportunity to truly serve Hetar.

The Crusader Knights were retained by the High Council as a deterrent against savages and chaos. They had always been, and they would always be. While there had been no great wars in many years, and Hetar was a peaceful kingdom, only the presence of the Crusader Knights protected Hetar from those in the Outlands. The Outlanders were barbarians with no rule of law, and he often wondered why the Celestial Actuary had created them at all.

The sun rose over the square, and the chill of the spring morning was warmed by its rays. Then suddenly John Swiftsword found himself facing a Crusader Knight, and his attempt to step into a better world began.

The knight behind the table looked him over very carefully. "Name?" he barked.

"John Swiftsword of the Mercenary Guild." Was his voice squeaking?

The Crusader nodded and wrote it down. Then he said, "Turn about, please."

John swung around slowly.

"Appearance, excellent," the Crusader Knight said, and checked off a small box on the parchment application. "Place of origin?"

"The Midlands."

"Father's occupation?"

"Farmer."

"How long a mercenary?"

"Since age fifteen."

"Your age now?"

"Thirty-one."

"Married?"

"Yes."

"Children?"

"Two."

"Have you sired sons or daughters?"

"A son with my wife, and a daughter with a Faerie woman," he replied.

"And you desire more sons?"

"Aye!"

"Who is your sponsor, John Swiftsword?" the Crusader Knight asked.

"Sir Ferris Ironshield," he replied. His throat was getting dryer by the minute.

"Any secondaries?"

"Sir Ajax and Sir Iven."

"First battle skill?"

"The sword," was the proud reply.

"Secondary skills?" the Crusader Knight demanded sharply.

"Lance, mace and axe." Was that sweat running down his back?

"You are a talented soldier," the Crusader Knight said with a small smile. "Your application is accepted by the tournament committee, John Swiftsword. What colors will you wear when you fight?"

"Green and gold," John said. Green for Lara's eyes, and gold for her hair. He would honor his daughter in this fashion.

The Crusader Knight marked it down on the application, and then wrote in large letters across the face of the parchment, AC-CEPTED. "I shall look forward to seeing you on tournament day. You will draw a number now to determine the day upon which you will do battle." He held out a velvet bag to the applicant.

John plunged his hand into the bag and drew out a tile. He handed it to the Crusader Knight. "It says one," he noted.

"Then you fight on the first day. That is good. You will have time to rest up for the final battle. Congratulations! Step aside. Next!"

He stepped away from the table half-dazed, and walked into the crowds pressing in about the square. Suddenly he felt a small hand slip into his, and he knew at once it was his daughter's. "Were you able to see?" he asked, not even bothering to look at her.

"I was right up front, Da. You looked so lordly, and your voice was so strong and sure. I was very proud. I'm sorry Mikhail wasn't old enough to see this day, but you will tell him about it when he is, won't you?"

"Aye, lass, I will. And I will tell him of his half faerie sister whose beauty made it all possible," John Swiftsword said softly. "I have not said it before, Lara. Thank you." Then stopping, he bent and kissed her smooth forehead.

"I am not unhappy, Da. I know my mother broke your heart. But the beauty I have inherited from her will atone for her sin, and we will both begin new lives. I am happy."

"You are certain of that, Lara? I could not bear if you were unhappy. Aye, Ilona broke my heart, but your loving sweetness has healed my hurt long since."

"I am happy, Da, I swear it! And besides," she teased him, "it is too late to go back now, for I doubt the mercer would accept your tunic in exchange for his cloth."

He laughed. Lara could always wheedle him from the deepest doldrums, and he had been very torn over these last months. He had fretted like an old woman, but now he must release all his crochets and fears. Lara was right. It was much too late to go back. He must clear his mind and heart of all darkness. In six days the tourney would begin. And while everyone was certain that he would win his place among the finalists, nothing in life, John Swiftsword knew, was ever a certainty.

Chapter 3

BUT HE DID WIN as they had all predicted. He had slept little the night before, but from excitement, not from nervousness. He rose early, bathed and then he had gone off to the tournament field where Sir Ferris, Sir Ajax and Sir Iven awaited him in a small tent. He had checked his weapons, and lifted each of Aristaeus's hooves to be certain they were clean, and free of stones that might impede the animal's performance. The three old knights had helped him to dress. The call to the joust had sounded, and he had mounted his warhorse, ridden out and prevailed over all his opponents. It had been, he thought, shockingly simple. There had been no time to look for his wife and family in the stands. He would not have known where Gaius Prospero's box was anyway.

When she awoke on the morning of the tournament, Lara had found her father already gone. Her stepmother was weeping softly in a corner by the fire. "What is the matter, Susanna?" she inquired anxiously.

"What if he loses?" Susanna said sobbing. "Then it has all been for naught!"

Irritation pricked at Lara's nerves, but she restrained from shouting at Susanna for even considering such a thing, and bringing bad luck on her father. "Da will prevail," she told her stepmother. "Do not think to bring ill fortune on him, Susanna. Now we must bathe quickly. Our litters will be here shortly, I am certain."

No sooner had they finished bathing than Mistress Mildred arrived to help them with Mikhail. She was dressed in her finest gown, for Susanna had invited her to accompany them. "Go about your business, my dears," she said. "I will dress the laddie and have him ready. You've nursed him, Susanna?"

"Aye, he's content," Susanna replied. She hurried to don the beautiful gown Lara had made for her. It was of lilac silk brocade with wide flared sleeves with dagged edges. The waist was high, and beneath the bosom Lara had embroidered a band with a swirling design of silver and gold. The neckline had a simple white silk collar. It was elegant, but not overdone. On her dark head, Susanna would wear a heart-shaped headdress. Her hair was done up beneath a crispinette of fine gold mesh.

A knock sounded and Mistress Mildred hurried to answer it. "'Tis too early for the litters," she grumbled, but opening the door she discovered a large woman with a basket.

"I am Tania. I was sent by my master to do the slave Lara's hair," she said.

"Come in! Come in! The girl is just out of her bath," Mistress Mildred said. "Lara, here is a woman to fix your lovely hair. Gaius Prospero sent her," she called.

"I was not expecting such kindness," Lara said, coming forward wrapped in a drying sheet.

"Kindness? Hah!" Tania scoffed. "You are being displayed to future buyers, girl, and nothing more. You must be shown at your best. Sit down at that table. I will need it to hold my tools. You will not garb yourself until your hair is fashioned. I have seen the gown, and since it fastens at the shoulders you can step into it."

Lara sat down, and Tania began brushing out the girl's long hair until it was a smooth thick sheet. Standing back she considered her next course of action. Reaching into the basket she drew out strings of beads. They were tiny gold, silver, crystal and pearls strung on almost invisible gold chains. Tania took a hank of Lara's silvery-gold hair and fashioned it into a thin braid. Then she wove several more narrow plaits into which she fastened the slender gold chains studded with their beads of silver and gold. These she interspersed with the strings of little pearls and sparkling crystals, weaving them into the tops of the braids which lay atop a background of Lara's thick hair.

"Let us get you dressed now and I will finish my work," Tania said.

The gown Gaius Prospero had sent for Lara was simple and virginal, yet sensual and exotic. It was sleeveless, fastening at the shoulders and having a round neckline that lay at the base of her collarbone. The material was of creamy silk, diaphanous and shot through with gold. Her entire young body was quite visible. Susanna brought the garment forward.

"Wait," Tania said, and she reached into her basket. "Her nipples must be rouged to draw the eye to them." She drew forth a small round container, removed its lid, and pulling away Lara's drying sheet briskly colored the young girl's nipples. "Give it a moment to dry and then we will put your gown on," she said.

Lara's pale cheeks grew rosy with her blushes.

"Should a virgin's breasts be so displayed?" Susanna asked nervously.

"The girl is to be a Pleasure Woman, mistress. Today our master will display her to her best advantage to gain the highest price. Already the rumors abound about her faerie beauty. And I can see that none will be disappointed. She has a lovely bosom and it must be shown. Come, they should be dry now. Quickly! The garment."

Lara could tell by the stunned looks of Mistress Mildred and Susanna that her gown was everything Gaius Prospero intended it to be. She wished there was a glass in the hovel as there had been at Gaius Prospero's home. She had removed the hair from her pubic mound, as her master had instructed her to do. Her mound seemed somehow plumper without its covering of golden curls. Tania set a small circular cap of gold and silver mesh dotted with crystals on her head. Then she placed a thin cloth of gold cloak about the girl's shoulders.

"You are ready now, and the litter should be waiting for you," Tania said. "I will see you in a few days when you come to the master's house."

"Thank you!" Lara said softly. "You have been kind."

"I have done my duty as I was instructed," Tania said gruffly, but the girl's simple gratitude pleased her. The attiring woman might be a slave, but she appreciated good manners. She had served many a girl like Lara for her master. Some were frightened and wept constantly. Others were aware of the opportunity being offered them and became proud and rude. This girl was different. Not only was she the most beautiful girl Tania had ever seen, there was something about her... Tania scrambled to find a word within her mind, but she could not. It had to be the girl's faerie blood, she finally decided. "Good day, mistress," she said to Susanna, and then she was gone, leaving the door open behind her.

Outside they saw the litters were indeed awaiting them. Susanna took her son from Mistress Mildred, who was helped into the vehicle by one of the bearers. It was constructed of solid ebony, striped with gold and hung with sheer red curtains. Mikhail turned nervously as he was handed to the older woman, and was about to cry a protest until his mother entered the litter. His little mouth closed even as he began to inspect his new surroundings with his bright eyes. Lara had made her baby brother a little tunic of the blue and silver fabric.

Lara entered her own transport, which was painted silver and hung with sheer turquoise silk curtains. She lounged luxuriously upon plump cushions of coral and gold as if she had always traveled in such a manner. She felt the litter lifted up, and the four bearers set off at a brisk pace. They quickly departed the Quarter, moving through narrow streets that eventually opened into broader avenues. They crossed the Great Square where Lara had watched her father's application be accepted for the tourney, taking an avenue that led through the Tournament Gate out to the large field where the tourney was held every three years. The gate itself was opened only for the tournament.

The litter bearers stopped, and the curtains were drawn aside. A plump, beringed hand Lara recognized immediately offered itself to help her out. Gaius Prospero beamed at her, nodding with approval as he lifted the cloak a moment to see the gown.

"Ahh," he noted, "I see Tania has rouged your nipples. The woman has incredible instincts. I could not do without her assistance. You look lovely, Lara. I foresee a golden future for my golden faerie girl," he chuckled.

"I am but half faerie, Master," Lara replied, "and I know no magic."

"Just as well," Gaius Prospero responded, "but you have the faerie look, Lara, and that is important, for none are more beautiful than your mother's race. Even the coastal peoples are not as fair. But come, and you as well, Mistress Susanna. I will take you to my private box. My wife and children are there today, for John Swiftsword's reputation is famous and today's jousts will be legend." He led them to the covered pavilion, whose awning shaded comfortable chairs with leather seats and backs, their wooden arms and legs decorated with gilded carvings. A woman, a man and three children were already there.

"My wife, the lady Vilia," Gaius Prospero said. "Here is the lovely Lara, my dear. Is she not perfect as I have said? And Lara's stepmother, Mistress Susanna, her son and the little lad's nursemaid." It did not occur to Gaius Prospero that poor people did not employ nursemaids for their children.

Susanna was about to correct his interpretation when she caught Mistress Mildred's eye, and the old woman shook her head in warning. Susanna smiled and said, "I am honored to meet you, my lady Vilia."

"And I you," the lady Vilia replied. She was an attractive woman not a great deal older than Susanna. "Ohh, I love babies," she cooed at Mikhail, who gave her a large and toothless smile.

A second wife, obviously, Lara thought silently. Wealthy men like Gaius Prospero were known to divorce older wives and take young ones, as if a young wife would keep them young, too.

"This is my secretary, Jonah," Gaius Prospero spoke again, but he was addressing Lara alone. His wife, Susanna and Mistress Mildred were already chattering like old friends. As for Aubin Prospero, he was looking as bored as any child would. He wanted the jousting to begin. His two older sisters looked at Lara, and giggled behind their hands.

"We are beginning to attract some notice, my lord," Jonah said. "I think it is time to remove the girl's cloak. May I?"

The Master of the Merchants nodded imperceptibly.

Jonah lifted the garment from Lara's shoulders, and laid it carefully aside. Taking her hand, he drew her forward so she might be seen in all her golden beauty. Across the tournament field where the mistresses of the Pleasure Houses and the Magnates sat, there was an immediate stirring of interest.

"Are the invitations out yet?" Gaius Prospero asked his secretary.

"Yesterday, my lord. The acceptances will come quickly now, I suspect." There was almost a smile on his narrow lips.

"Sit down now, Lara," her master said quietly.

She did, and took the opportunity to gaze about the field. Flags flew everywhere. To their left were the magnates and the mistresses of the Pleasure Houses. To their right sat the Crusader Knights, their families and their guests. At the opposite end of the field was the entry where the contestants would enter. Gaius Prospero's pavilion was but one of six at his end. There were few places for ordinary folk, but many managed to clamber up onto the low stone walls that surrounded the field.

The tournament began with a flourish of trumpets, and the combatants paraded into the ring and past the Crusader Knights, stopping to dip their lances to their leader, the Grande Knight, before riding off the field. Next came the pairing of contestants, and the jousting began. Lara cried out with delight as her father unhorsed his first opponent, then leapt from his steed to do battle afoot, but the young man yielded without a fight, amid the boos of the spectators. Several times more that day John Swiftsword rode forth to do battle, defeating aspirant after aspirant. At day's end he was the only one left standing, and was declared the winner of the first day. His place within the ranks of the Crusader Knights was assured. On the last day of the tourney he and the other four winners would battle symbolically with each other and members of the knightly order. Then they would be knighted in the arena by the Grande Knight.

Lara and her companions were returned home in the litters that had brought them. Susanna hurried to remove her beautiful gown and don a more sensible garment so she might prepare a fine feast for her husband's victory. Already word had spread throughout the Quarter of John Swiftsword's victory that day, and neighbors were pushing into their hovel to taste a small bit of his victory. Lara had slipped immediately into the tiny chamber she shared with her baby brother and removed the exquisite garment she had worn that day. It was not for inhabitants of the Quarter. She wiped the rouge from her nipples, and slipped on her plain round-necked gown of dark blue. Then she carefully removed the slender gold chains from her hair, undid the elaborate plaits that Tania had fashioned earlier and redressed her tresses into two simple braids. Then she went out to assist her stepmother. Except for the neighbors, life was as it had always been.

Her father arrived home on foot, for Aristaeus was already stabled in the Garden District. He smelled of wine, for Sir Ferris, Sir Ajax and Sir Iven had insisted they celebrate his victory—their victory—together. In just five more days he would be knighted and officially one of them. But as exhausted as he was from his physical travails, and as tired as he was from the strain of worrying if he was really good enough to win the day, he greeted his neighbors with charm and goodwill. What had begun as a small celebration given by his family now turned into a Quarter-wide fest. This was a great moment for the Mercenaries. One of their own had not reached the rank of Crusader Knight in over sixty years. Food was shared, ale and cider flowed, and it was well past midnight when the Quarter finally grew silent.

The next morning a page was sent from the Garden District to accompany the future Sir John Swiftsword and his family as they chose which house they would have among those currently available. Susanna was beside herself with excitement.

"Lara must come," her father said.

"But it will not be her home," Susanna said carelessly. She could think of nothing else but that she would soon have a real house.

"Where I am, my daughter will always have a home," John Swiftsword said sternly to his wife. "She has earned the right to see what her sacrifice has gained us."

Susanna's face fell as she realized how unkind her words had sounded. She turned to her stepdaughter. "Oh, Lara, forgive me!"

Lara laughed, and put her arm through Susanna's. "Let's go and see your new dwelling," she said softly. "I know you meant me no harm."

Outside they discovered a cart drawn by two pretty gray donkeys, with John's horse tied to the back of it. He mounted Aristaeus while the young page helped Lara and Susanna into the cart, which was white and had gaily painted wheels. They sat facing one another upon red leather benches. The page joined the driver at the front of the cart, and they were off, the soon-to-be Crusader Knight riding by their side. Reaching the Garden District, they were met by Sir Ferris.

"There are several fine houses just now available," he told them, smiling broadly. "I, of course, have my preference, but I will be curious to know which dwelling pleases my lady Susanna." He helped the two from their cart. "We'll walk," he said. "The day is fair, and most are at the tournament."

"Oh," Susanna said nervously, "should we have gone today?"

"Nay, my dear," the old Crusader Knight told her. "Your man has won his place, and now he is not expected back at the tournament field until his knighting day."

"I should not like to do the wrong thing," Susanna confided to Sir Ferris. "This is all so new for me, and I am, after all, just a farmer's daughter."

"So are many of the women you will soon meet among our stratum, although some have forgotten their humbler beginnings and occasionally need to be reminded," Sir Ferris chuckled wickedly. "I am very good at that."

Susanna laughed at the twinkle in his eye when he spoke. "I think, sir, you were a most naughty fellow in your youth."

"Still am!" came the quick reply.

They were shown seven homes, and Susanna marveled at the size and number of the chambers. She exclaimed at the wonderful light, and the privacy. Never in all her days had she seen such fine homes except on the day she had gone into the Golden District. These houses were smaller, of course, but they still had many of the same fine features. It was difficult, but she finally selected a house built around an inner courtyard with a shallow, narrow reflecting pool in its center. At first she considered if the pool might not be a danger to Mikhail, but Sir Ferris poohpoohed her fears.

"You will be given three well-trained household slaves, my dear. A maidservant to help you, a nursemaid for your children, for you will certainly have more, and of course, one manservant to do the heavy work and look after your little garden. You have chosen wisely, for this is the dwelling I would have chosen."

"We have a garden?" Susanna was surprised. The house itself with its inner courtyard seemed more than adequate.

"A walled garden behind your home," he answered her. "It has an apple tree."

Susanna began to weep softly. "There was an apple tree outside my bedchamber at home on my father's farm," she said.

Sir Ferris patted her arm, and smiled, well pleased. "Now that is settled I shall send you and Lara off to the Crusader Knights warehouse so you may choose your furnishings. Men are useless in such an endeavor. You may bring a few personal possessions from the Quarter, but nothing else," he explained. "We like our new knights and their families to fit right in. Your husband will meet you at home later, my dear."

They returned to the cart and were taken out of the Garden District to a large building on the edge of the City. There they were greeted by the manager, a self-important little man, who escorted them through the warehouse as Susanna made her choices of furniture, draperies and all manner of household goods, Lara at her side. When they had concluded their business the manager assured them all would be delivered on the morrow early, and if my lady would be there to tell the movers where to put everything it would certainly be helpful.

"Gracious!" Susanna exclaimed as they were returned to the Quarter. "I have never in all my life had such a day, nor could have even imagined one like this."

"We are both beginning new lives," Lara responded. The Garden District was lovely and the house Susanna had chosen was beautiful. Lara wondered if her new home would be as fine. But then the Pleasure Quarter was said to have some of the loveliest houses in all of the City. She had never been there, of course, but it was said, and if it was said, then it surely must be true.

The following day when Lara and Susanna arrived at the new house they found three slaves awaiting them. The trio bowed politely.

"I am Nels, and this is Yera and Ove," the man said, indicating the women who stood beside him. "We now belong to John Swiftsword, and are bound to obey him and his wife, mistress."

For a moment Susanna was speechless, but Lara quickly spoke up. "My stepmother, the lady Susanna, thanks you. Serve her well and you will be treated well. Serve her badly and you will be beaten."

Susanna now recovered. "Which among you is the nursemaid?" she asked. She didn't know what she was going to do without Lara, who seemed to have instincts beyond her knowledge and above her station.

"I am, my lady." The younger of the two women curtsied.

"And you are?" Susanna said.

"Ove, my lady."

"My son is called Mikhail. He does not yet walk, but he will in a few weeks. You must keep him from the reflecting pool at all times, Ove."

"Yes, my lady," the girl replied.

The furniture arrived, and the rest of the day was spent deciding where it would be placed. Yera took charge of all the household supplies, and began to set up the kitchen. Susanna was kept busy running from place to place, making decisions, while Lara quietly directed Nels in the hanging of the draperies. On the following day Nels arrived in a cart at the hovel to collect the few personal items they would be taking with them. When they departed on the day of the knighting they would not return again; a young mercenary and his bride-to-be had already been assigned their hovel. At the end of the knighting ceremony Lara would spend a final night with her family. On the following day she would be taken to Gaius Prospero's home, and after that she knew not what.

On the day of the knighting, the Master of the Merchants sent his litters for them as he had on the first day of the tourney. John had already gone ahead. Tania arrived once again, and this time she braided Lara's magnificent long hair into a single braid into which she wove fresh flowers. Lara and Susanna donned their fine gowns. Tania departed, and without a backward glance Susanna picked up her son, and hurried to the waiting litter, but Lara remained for several more minutes.

Looking about her she felt tears coming, and forced them back. This was her home. The only home she had ever known. She had been comfortable here with her grandmother Ina and her father.

And after her grandmother's death, and the passing of the initial sadness, she had never been lonely. There was dear old Mistress Mildred, her grandmother's best friend nearby, and then Susanna had come. She knew every inch of the Quarter for she had explored it over the years, but she had never had any friends. As a child she remembered playing with other children, but after her grandmother died there were fewer and then none of them. She had heard the word "faerie" murmured often enough as she passed by. Why did people hate her mother's race so much?

Her grandmother had said it was because they were so beautiful, and people were jealous of such beauty, but not just the beauty, Ina said. There was faerie magic to be feared. Faeries were different from ordinary folk. You never really knew what a faerie would do. They could be the kindest of all creatures, and the most vindictive. Their women seduced human menfolk out of spite because their menfolk seduced human women, who seemed to give them intense pleasure. More so, Ina said with a wise nod, than the faerie women who had cold hearts. Lara knew she looked like her mother for her father had always said so. But did she have a faerie's cold heart, she wondered?

With a final look around the hovel, Lara stepped through the door for the final time. There she found Mistress Mildred waiting. The old woman hugged the girl, and there were tears streaming down her face. Reaching up with a dainty hand Lara brushed some of them from Mistress Mildred's lined face, and smiled sweetly.

"Don't weep," she said softly.

"I've known you since the day your father came to his mother, my friend Ina, with you all swaddled in his arms."

"I wasn't born here?" Lara was surprised.

"Nay, you was born in an enchanted place, or so your da told his mother. You was six months old when the faerie woman who bore you left him. He awoke one morning to find himself, and you, on the edge of the forestland. He said that he had gone to sleep the previous evening in the magic place where he lived with the faerie, and you were in your cradle." Mistress Mildred shook her head. "Your da was barely fifteen when the faerie woman lured him away from his family's farm. Your grandfather had died during that time, and your uncle, who had inherited the farm, would not allow his brother to remain when he returned with you. He did not even want you in his house for you were half faerie and he feared you, but your grandmother's will prevailed, and he said you might remain until your father joined the mercenaries. Once that was accomplished your grandmother brought you to live in the City. She was so angry at her eldest son's behavior that she stayed to care for you rather than go back. Ina never spoke to him again, or even saw his children. I know he did not come to her departure ceremony after she died. I don't believe your father ever forgave his brother for it."

"How odd that I should know none of this," Lara murmured.

"Tonight, before you are separated from your father, ask him to tell you about your mother, child," Mistress Mildred said. Then she kissed Lara on the forehead, and gave her another hug. "The Celestial Actuary will protect you, I know."

"Thank you," Lara responded, kissing the old lady's withered cheek, and hugging her back. Then she turned and got into her litter. Drawing the curtains she settled back. She would not look again. She felt the bearers lifting her transport up, and they began to hurry through the City toward the Tournament Gate and to the grandstand where she would alight and enter Gaius Prospero's box once again. She could hear the murmur of the crowds as they drew closer to the tourney grounds. Now and again the litter bearers would slow until the mercenaries hired to clear their way could force people aside.

When the litter was finally set down it was Aubin Prospero who drew the curtains aside, and handed her out. "My father has sent me to escort you," he said. "I am learning his trade, and will one day be the Master of the Merchants myself."

"Who told you that?" Lara asked him as she exited the vehicle. "It is an elected office, young master."

"My mother told me," he replied. "And my mother is always correct. Come!" And he led her up the steps of the box.

"How old are you?" Lara asked him.

"I was eight on my last natal day," the boy responded.

"Do you not play games?" He was just eight and he sounded like an old man.

"Games are for those with no goals in life," Aubin Prospero answered her. "Games are for the poor. I have no time for games. There is so much to learn."

Lara shook her head. Poor child, she thought to herself.

"Ah, Lara, here you are at last!" Gaius Prospero was beaming at her. Reaching out, his grasp closed about the gold chain with its crystal star. "What is this?" he asked her, curious, fingering the star that seemed warm to his touch.

"It is the only thing other than life that my mother gave me," she answered him. "You will not take it from me, my lord?"

Gaius Prospero thought a moment, and then he said, "Nay, I will not. It burnishes your natural beauty. Each time I see you I am amazed at your beauty, my dear. Are you excited?"

"To see my father knighted? Oh, yes, my lord!" Lara said.

"Nay, I mean about tomorrow night. Tomorrow morning you will be brought to my house, and spend your day being prepared for display that evening, when I shall accept bids for your person, my dear. But only for a day's span. After that you must be sold promptly. It is not wise to hold choice merchandise for too long lest the excitement surrounding it wane, although I do not expect that to happen in your particular case." He smiled broadly. "Tomorrow night will be a very exciting one for you."

"I was not aware of how it was to be done," Lara responded. "I have never been to a slave auction."

"And you shall not be part of one, my dear child," Gaius Prospero clucked. "Nothing so common for you, my beauty, as a public display. Rare merchandise is offered privately. Only a choice number of guests have been invited to view you. The following day they will return in the morning to offer me their bids. You will not be there. It will not be necessary. When the bidding has ceased, and I have accepted the highest bidder, the agreement will be struck. Under our laws Pleasures Houses can only be owned by men, but they are managed by women. Both have been invited to your displaying."

"I see," Lara said. This was the most amazing new world she was about to enter.

The trumpets sounded with a grand flourish, and they all turned their eyes to the arena. A dozen trumpeters in red and gold livery, the sun gleaming off their shining brass instruments, were standing at the knight's entrance to the exhibition area. Several Crusader Knights and the new candidates galloped forth and did mock battle before the delighted crowds. When they had finished, a parade of the high officers of the Crusader Knights entered led by the Grande Knight. The five men who would be knighted this day and their opponents joined the great procession. Around the circuit they rode to the cheering of the crowds gathered.

Lara, Susanna and little Mikhail clapped wildly as John Swiftsword passed them wearing his fine armor. His horse was caparisoned in green and gold, and several ribbons of the same color flew from his lance. Finally the procession came to a halt. The knights all dismounted, their horses held by young pages. The Grande Knight took his place upon a raised dais, and each of the new knights came forward one at a time to kneel before him. They were bareheaded as they knelt, and each man clearly recited the oath of loyalty to Hetar before the Grande Knight tapped them with his sword of honor, and raised each one up to present the new member of the Crusader Knights to the citizens gathered.

Four of the men were known to come from Crusader Knight families. John Swiftsword, however, received the loudest cheers, for he was the everyman who had overcome obstacles to gain his rightful place among this high order of warriors. He was a popular hero today, and his companions were happy to allow him his moment. Each of the other men was secretly glad he had not been fighting on the first day of the tournament, for none of them was certain that they could have prevailed over John Swiftsword. He was a great asset to their group, and when it had become known that he was prepared to apply for this tournament the leaders among them had been greatly pleased, and were prepared to welcome him. It was not by accident he had fought the first day of the tournament.

The tournament was now officially over, and the crowds began to stream out of the arena and through the Tournament Gate which would, when all had reentered the City, be closed again for another three years. Lara told Gaius Prospero that she could easily share Susanna's litter with her baby brother. "I do not need to be paraded into the Garden District before all. Some of the knights might one day come to my Pleasure House, and it could prove embarrassing for them, and for my father."

He nodded understanding. "You will want to spend your last few hours with your family alone. I quite understand, my beauty."

Susanna was quiet as the litter made its way through the gates, and toward the Garden District. Mikhail had fallen asleep in Lara's lap, the slight rocking motion of the litter lulling him into slumber. "This is all a dream, but I hope I never wake up," Susanna finally said. "I cannot believe that I am not returning to our hovel, but to a beautiful house with a real garden. My sisters will be so envious of me. How they mocked me when I prepared to wed your father, scorning him because he was a humble mercenary. Now they shall see! He has risen high, and I with him."

Lara laughed. "Why, stepmother," she said, "I have never seen this side of you!"

Susanna grinned back at the girl. "They were very mean, Lara. They never saw what a good man your father was. The matchmaker gave me the choice of three men, but I wanted only your father. They said a mercenary would amount to naught."

"Do you love my father?" Lara wondered aloud.

"I do!" her stepmother said enthusiastically.

"I'm glad," the girl replied. "It makes it easier for me to go away."

Susanna sighed. "'Thank you' seems like two small words in light of what you have done for your father. For Mikhail and for me. I do not know if you will be permitted to come home once you have been purchased." She stopped, and then her eyes filled with tears. "It is not fair," she sobbed.

"Susanna, you are older than I, and should know that life is often unfair," Lara gently chided her stepmother. "You were wise to suggest I be sold. We will all have a much better life because of it, especially Mikhail. He will never remember the Quarter, or the hovel in which he was born. My father's soft heart will be the undoing of him but that you are there for him. I am glad for it!"

"I know I am five years older than you," Susanna said. "But sometimes you seem so much older. Even than your father."

Lara laughed. "I expect that is my faerie blood," she said. "I am told they are different from…from…well, you know what I mean, Susanna. Being both faerie and human I have no idea really where I belong. I always thought I belonged in the human world, but now with all this fuss being made over what is called my faerie beauty, I do not know at all where I belong."

The litter came to a halt and was set down. Immediately the curtains were opened up, and Nels helped Susanna from the vehicle.

"Welcome home, mistress," he said. "Ove! Take the little master from the girl."

"The girl," Susanna said sharply, "is Sir John's daughter and will be treated with courtesy, Nels. Help my stepdaughter from the litter."

Grudgingly, the slave man obeyed his new mistress. The girl was known to be half faerie, and would be shortly entering a Pleasure House. Faeries were not to be tolerated. He was glad the girl would be gone on the morrow. He was startled when Lara thanked him for his service, and wondered if she had put a spell on him.

Inside her new house Susanna began giving orders. Her husband would want a bath when he arrived home. They were to begin their preparations immediately. Mikhail was to be bathed at once, brought to her for feeding and then put to bed. Dinner, a simple meal she had discussed with Yera the day before, was to be served in the first hour of the twilight. Wine would be served as well, for they would be celebrating.

The new knight arrived just before sunset. He was slightly drunk, for the order had been celebrating the induction of its new members. His bath was waiting, Susanna ready with her scrubbing brush. Mikhail was already in his bed. Lara smiled at the splashing and laughter she heard coming from the bathing room. From the first day of the tournament when he had won all his matches she had seen a great change in her father. All the weariness and care that had been weighing him down lifted from his shoulders. He looked young again, and in these past months with the scarcity of work he had looked so worried and worn.

Part of Lara was happy that her life was taking this new turn, but another part of her was slightly apprehensive. She was leaving her family. She was leaving everything she had ever known. And for what? The unknown. She would be a vessel for a man's desires. Men, it seemed, got pleasure from putting their manroot into a female's body. This knowledge was hardly a secret among girls her age. She had listened, secreting herself about the edges of groups of giggling girls in the Quarter, learning what friends, had she had any, might have shared with her. Susanna had been willing finally to answer all her questions with Gaius Prospero's permission. Ignorance in such matters was not to be tolerated. Hetarian girls were supposed to be prepared to please their husbands and their lovers.

Finally her father and stepmother joined her in the garden where a table was set up for them to dine. John Swiftsword kissed his daughter's brow. "I am glad that we can have this evening together," he said as he seated her at the dining table.

"I have questions that I beg you answer me before I leave you," Lara said quietly. "Questions about my mother, and my birth. You have never spoken on it, but you must tell me now, Da. Mistress Mildred said things to me today before we left the Quarter, and she told me I must ask you before I could not. Will you tell me?"

"Aye, I will tell you all, but let us have our meal first," he responded. "And I will speak only with you, for Ilona warned me that should I ever speak of her before another woman I love, that woman would cease to love me, and so Susanna can hear naught of what I would say to you this night." He turned to his wife.

Lara looked anxiously toward her stepmother.

"I will leave you after the meal," Susanna promised. "I do not choose to hear of Lara's mother," she said. "But nothing you say, John, could make me stop loving you."

"You do not understand faerie magic, wife," was his cryptic reply.

Nels served them the meal Yera had prepared. They began with a delicate cold soup of pureed peaches and plums topped with sour cream. Next came a salad of baby lettuces and herbs to be followed by a juicy capon that had been roasted golden, and a platter of ham slices as well as fresh warm small breads that had been twisted into graceful shapes. There was sweet butter on the table and a small dish of salt. Salt had always been a rarity in the Quarter. When the fine pottery plates had been cleared away smaller plates were placed before them, and a bowl of fruit was set in the center of the table. Lara had never in her life seen fruit other than oranges. Fruits were reserved for the privileged classes. Nels, to his credit, had explained everything to them as they ate.

The wine in their crystal goblets was sweet, and heady with the aroma of its grapes. Lara felt sleepy, but she forced herself back from the brink, remembering that Gaius Prospero's people would come early for her, and she must speak with her father before she slept. "Da?" she said softly.

John Swiftsword was looking at his nubile wife, and considering how much he was going to enjoy futtering her in that fine new bed in their bedchamber very shortly. His first act as a Crusader Knight would be to get Susanna with child again. Another son for the order. And then his daughter's gentle voice pierced his consciousness. "I have not forgotten," he told her.

Susanna arose from the dining table. Walking around the table she kissed Lara tenderly. "Good night," she said simply, and left the room. She could not bring herself to say goodbye.

"Let us walk in the garden," the new knight said to his daughter. "What I have to say is for your ears alone, daughter." He led her not to the inner courtyard, where someone might have secreted themselves in the shadows of the portico, but rather out into the small walled garden with its apple tree. There they sat upon a rustic wooden bench. "Now tell me what it is you would know, Lara, and I will answer."

"Begin at the beginning," she replied. "I would know all."

"There is really not that much," her father answered her. "It was shortly after my fifteenth birthday. Midsummer's Eve. My friends and I were gathered about our fire flirting with the girls we knew, dancing and drinking, and lying about our adventures with those same girls. And then, for the briefest moment, it seemed as if the whole world was frozen in time, and I saw Ilona, standing in the shadows at the edge of a woodland. I remember my mouth falling open. I had never in all my days seen such beauty. The long golden gilt hair. The eyes as green as new leaves in springtime. A body so tempting and lush that I knew she was magic, and I was afraid. Then she beckoned me, and I could not help but go to her. Suddenly I could hear my friends behind me calling me back. I could hear the crackle of the fire, but I could not for the life of me turn away from the vision who called me so sweetly and so silently.

"I reached out to her, and she took my hand in hers, leading me away to her secret bower in the Forest. I should have been afraid, but I wasn't. I knew the tales of those bewitched, and I had always wondered why they allowed themselves to be taken by the faerie folk. Now I knew. Ilona was utterly impossible to resist. I didn't care what happened to me as long as I might be with her. You were conceived that very night, Lara. It amused her that I had never known a woman in the fullest sense before. At first she was tender and gentle with me. Then she began to teach me what pleased a lover. Later she said I was the best pupil she had ever had. It was because of my innocence that she let her guard down that night and conceived you."

"I don't understand, Da," Lara said to him.

"Faerie women conceive children only when they want them, Lara. If they do not want them, they do not have them, unlike human women who conceive more often than not when their lovers mount them and spill their seed. Remember that, for I do not know if you have that ability of your mother's. I pray that you do. I stayed with Ilona during the months in which she carried you. I thought not of the morrow, but only of how much I loved her—and I did, from the moment I laid my eyes on her. I love her still in spite of it all. But I love Susanna, too, and I am wise enough to know I shall never have a love like the one I had for Ilona again. So I content myself with my good wife, and am glad the matchmaker found her for me.

"When I was with your mother, everything I did, every thought I had, was for her and her alone. She consumed me entirely and I did not care what happened to me as long as I was with her. And then you were born. She birthed you quickly and easily, and once she had seen you she lost interest in you. I was stunned, for from the moment you entered the world I loved you. But for Ilona the mystery and the excitement was over. And she began to lose interest in me."

"Where did you live during this time, Da?" Lara asked her father.

"In her bower in the woodland," he said. "I can't really describe it to you, for it seemed to have no walls or roof, but we were warm in the winter and the rain never touched us. Our bed was made of moss and covered in a downy quilt. You slept in a cradle that I made you, which hung from a tree branch."

"If my mother ignored me, how did I survive? Who fed me? What did I eat?" Lara wondered.

"Your mother bewitched a young girl she found lost in the wood one day, and by magic put her milk in the girl's breasts. She fed you several times a day, and then would fall into an enchanted slumber. But as the next Midsummer's Eve approached I saw your mother less and less. She began to wander. I no longer held her interest. In desperation I told her I intended to take you and return to my family. 'Oh,' she said, 'you understand, don't you? You are truly the most unique human I have ever had as a lover, John. Thank you! Yes! Yes! Go, and take Lara with you, for she will not be accepted in my faerie world. You have my blessing, which will one day bring you good fortune, and Lara will have my blessing as well. I have loved you both.' And then I found myself growing weary, and when I awoke I was on the edge of the woodlands, and you were carefully and neatly swaddled, and lying next to me. You were but three months of age." He paused, and wiped a tear from his eye.

"So my mother abandoned us both, Da," Lara said. "If she loved me, but then she didn't love me. Not really. Not the way Susanna loves Mikhail."

"I am sorry to hurt you," her father said, "but you would know all. Shall I go on?"

Lara nodded. "Aye please, Da."

"It was early morning," he continued. "The grass and flowers were wet with dew, yet we were not, nor was the ground beneath us. There had been a midsummer bonfire nearby in almost the exact same place as the previous year. I recognized several of my friends asleep about its warm embers. I picked you up, and walked past them back to our farm. The first person I saw was your grandmother. She was drawing water from the well, and seeing me she dropped her bucket to come running. When she saw you she knew immediately who your mother was, and she wept."

"Why, Da?"

"Because you were a faerie's daughter. You would not be accepted by my family. She brought us into the farmhouse and sat me down to learn the whole story of my disappearance. And when I had related all to her, she told me my father had died in the winter, and my oldest brother was now the head of the family. Dorjan has never been an easy man. He is the first of my parents' children. I was the last. We had seven sisters between us. He was already grown when I was born. I was scarcely a welcome addition in his world. The first words I ever recall him saying to me were 'the farm is mine.'

"That morning when he discovered I had returned he was not pleased at all, and when he learned I had brought my half faerie child with me he grew angry and accused me of drawing disaster onto his house. I would have to go, he said, and take my faerie brat with me. It was then your grandmother spoke up. Indeed, she said, I would have to go to the City and join the Guild of Mercenaries to earn my living, but first she would have me rest myself a few days, for my sojourn in the woodland would have weakened me. And her granddaughter would remain with her after I departed for the City.

"'Your brother can scarce apply for the Guild carrying a child in one arm. Lara stays with me, and I will care for her,' your grandmother said. 'When John is settled, then his daughter shall join him.' 'And who shall care for the babe in the City?' my brother, Dorjan, demanded to know. 'I will,' your grandmother replied. My brother was astounded, but she went on, 'You have a wife who has resented my presence since the day your father died. Now she will be sole mistress of this house.' It was then my brother, who often spoke before he thought a matter through said, 'If you leave my house, Mother, you will not be welcome back. If you leave you choose the faerie over your real grandchildren. I cannot abide such a thing.'

"I can still remember the cold smile that touched your grandmother's lips at his words. But she said nothing, and he, foolish man, did not know what he had done. I did, though. I knew that the day she left her comfortable farmhouse to live in a mercenary's hovel in the City, she would never return. She was mistress of that great farmhouse. Dorjan's wife was a meek creature who harbored all manner of resentments, but was lazy. She might be annoyed having her mother-in-law as mistress of the house, but my mother kept that house in perfect order. I can but imagine what happened when your grandmother left them to come to the City." He chuckled. "Dorjan's wife was no housekeeper."

"So you came to the City and joined the Mercenary Guild," Lara said. "How did you become so proficient with the sword?"

"A young fellow joining the guild is sent to training school, which is one reason I couldn't send for you as quickly as I would have wanted," John explained. "The old swordmaster running the school saw I had a knack for the sword for I had begun to learn its use from a retired mercenary at home. The swordmaster drilled me mercilessly in its proper use. He had been famous in his day. When I finally beat him in a mock combat he said he could teach me no more, that I was better than he had ever been. It was quite a compliment.

"On his recommendation I was hired to fight in several small wars between local bandits and the Province rulers. My reputation grew. I have escorted caravans of Taubyl Traders from the City into all the other provinces, for once I gained my reputation as a ruthless warrior few would take me on. I know how to impose Hetarian order, Lara. As a society we cannot allow discord to disrupt our lives."

"Why did my uncle not come when grandmother died?" Lara asked.

"My brother is a stubborn man, daughter," John Swiftsword said. "He never forgave her for leaving him, for leaving his house. For a time she kept in touch with old friends in the Midlands, but eventually there was no point in it. He always blamed me for stealing her from him. He said I brought back faerie magic with me, and used it against him. It was never true, of course."

"Did you ever see Ilona again?" Lara asked her father.

"Once," he replied. "When I came to take you and my mother to the City I went first to the edge of the woodland and called her.

I was not certain at all she would appear, but to my surprise she did. I told her what had happened, and how I was now a mercenary, and would be taking you into the City."

"Did she ask about me?" Lara wondered hopefully.

Her father shook his head. "She gave you life, child, and for her it was enough. I told her how you possessed her beauty, and she smiled for she always enjoyed a compliment. I told her I would probably not see her again, and she laughed. That is up to me, she said. I might marry, I replied. Do not, she said, ever discuss our love, or our time together with another woman you love but for our daughter. If she asks you one day, you may tell her of me, and our life that year. But no other, or bad fortune shall befall you. And then we parted, Lara. I have not seen her since. I have watched as you grew into her image, and sometimes it hurts me to look at you, for you are so like Ilona."

"Then it is a good thing I am going," Lara responded softly. "You have been a good father to me, and I would not hurt you, Da. The world of the Crusader Knights is where you belong, and now you have entered it. Susanna is happy." Lara giggled. "She told me she cannot wait to brag on your latest accomplishment to her sisters who were always mean to her, and mocked her for marrying a poor man. Perhaps in that way your own brother and his family will learn of it, too, and you will have a small revenge."

John Swiftsword chuckled. "That is something your mother would have said. She did not easily tolerate a fault she felt was directed at her."

"Is that all, Da?" Lara looked closely into her father's face.

"Aye, that is all, daughter. There is no more to tell you. From the time you were six months of age you grew up in the City."

"The necklace I wear around my neck, Da. My mother gave it to me, grandmother once said."

"She put it about your neck the day you were born, Lara," he responded.

"Do you know that the chain has grown in length as I have grown?" she asked.

He nodded his head. "There is magic in the chain and pendant, but of what kind I do not know, Lara. All I can tell you is that your mother said it would always protect and guide you."

"What if it is taken from me?" Lara fretted.

"Gaius Prospero has promised it will not be," he reassured her. Then he arose, drawing her up with him. He kissed her on the forehead. "I have told you all I can now, Lara, and I would go to bed. Good night, my daughter, and a final time my thanks for all you have done for me, and for my family. You are to be collected early, and I will not see you again. May the Celestial Actuary guard and guide you." He kissed her a final time, and then, turning, left her in the garden.

Lara stood quietly in the still night air. Everything was silent. A sliver of the new pale blue moon hung in the dark skies. Hetar had four moons, one for each province, and the only place they could all be viewed at once was in the Outlands. She wondered what the four moons would look like together, but she was unlikely to ever know. In just a few hours Gaius Prospero's people would come to get her, and her new master had promised that tomorrow would be a very exciting day. Lara hurried back into the house and, going to the guest chamber, took off her clothing and lay down to sleep. But before she fell into her slumber she touched the crystal star about her neck, and the tiny flame within flickered encouragingly.

Chapter 4

THE SLAVE WOMAN, Yera, woke her just before dawn. "A faeriepost has just arrived from the gate, young mistress," she said. "Your transportation has just arrived, and will be here shortly. Come with me to the kitchen. I have fresh bread and milk for you before you go."

Lara arose sleepily, and Yera pulled a chamber pot from beneath the bed.

"There is water to wash with, and I will be in the kitchen," the slave woman said. "Do not dally. They will be here soon and will not want to wait."

Finishing her ablutions, Lara hurried to dress, then went to the kitchens where Yera gave her a cup of fresh milk and a slab of buttered bread just warm from the ovens. There was also a dish of cut-up fruit. Lara ate it all down.

"You have a good appetite on you for such a slender girl," Yera noted dryly.

"So my grandmother always said," Lara replied with a smile.

"The conveyance is here." Nels had come into the kitchen.

Lara arose. "Thank you for your kindness," she told Yera and then turning, she followed the male slave.

He led her to the front door of the house, beyond which she could see a beautiful litter, well curtained. Drawing a deep breath

Lara walked outside, waiting while Nels drew the draperies aside, and then helped her into her transport. As he closed the curtains with a snap Lara called out, "Thank you, Nels." The litter was lifted up, and she was finally on her way. She was sorry she had not seen her father, or Susanna or little Mikhail before she left, but she knew they had done her a kindness in saying their goodbyes the previous evening. It really was better this way, and she could be strong for whatever lay ahead. Reaching down, she raised her star pendant to her lips and kissed it. The tiny flame flickered for a brief moment. She was safe. Had her faerie mother not said the necklace would always keep her safe? Her father had told her so, and Lara believed him. The bearers moved quickly, and before she knew it she heard the hail of the guard at the gate to the Golden District. He opened the curtains a moment, winked at her and then closed them. The litter moved off again, finally stopping for good. The curtains were opened gently and fully.

"Welcome, Lara, welcome!" Gaius Prospero's fat hand helped her from the litter. "We have a busy day ahead of us. Have you eaten yet?"

She nodded. "My father's slave woman fed me," she told him.

"Excellent!" He beamed his approval. "Then come with me, my dear. There is much to do, and you must get started. The northern wing of my house is for the special slaves that pass through my hands. Tania is waiting there for you. She will prepare you for this evening. I am giving a dinner for the owners of the finest Pleasure Houses in the City, and the Pleasure Mistresses who manage these houses. Many began as you will, as simple Pleasure Women. You are to be the final course of the meal, the sweet if you will," he chuckled, well pleased with himself. "I will display you to them so they may inspect you thoroughly. The bids on your person must be brought to me in writing between sunrise and sunset tomorrow. This permits me to weed out the serious buyers from those who do not have the wealth it will require to purchase you. There will then be one more viewing of you at which point those remaining may bid on you in a formal auction. At its conclusion you will be consigned to your new owner, and I shall have you delivered to his premises. Do you understand?"

"Yes, my lord Gaius," Lara said.

He took her little hand in his plump one, and patted it comfortingly. "It all sounds very complicated, I will admit, but it is actually quite a simple process. And after your first-night rights have been taken, you will be very well trained to service the men who come to take their pleasure of you."

"What are first-night rights?" Lara asked him.

"You have three virginities," Gaius Prospero told her. "Each of them will be sold for a fabulous sum to the men who want them the most. Since you have never known intimacy, your reactions to these men, and their knowledge that they are the first to possess you, are valuable. Innocence has great charm, but afterward you will need to be taught the complexities of offering varied pleasures to a man. Ah, here we are! Tania, here is the lovely Lara. She is in your charge until she leaves us. See she is well prepared. Until tonight, my dear," he purred, and turning was gone.

"Let me see your hands," Tania said, and then she exclaimed, "What have you been doing, child? A Pleasure Woman must have the softest hands, and yours are all rough, and your nails are broken. And to think I have only until tonight to make you presentable! Come along! Come along!"

Lara followed Tania, and during the next few hours her world was expanded as she learned the secret of how Pleasure Women were treated. She was seated, and a slave woman began to pare and shape her nails. Her hands were first soaked in a mixture of hot water and soap, then her nails were cleaned, and each hand massaged before being put into a separate bowl of warm scented cream. While her hands were being treated, another slave woman began on her feet, tsking at the rough heels and soles she possessed.

"Make them like silk," Tania ordered.

"It will take days to make these feet presentable," the slave told Tania.

"She is being shown tonight," Tania said. "You don't want the master displeased, do you? Do you remember how long it took the welts to go down on the last slave who made him unhappy? He has a great investment in this girl."

"Then he should have taken her from her family sooner, and not left it to the last minute," the slave at Lara's feet huffed. "I'll do my best, but I'm not promising anything, and threatening me with a beating isn't going to change a thing. The girl has feet like a farm worker, although I admit their dainty size will work to her advantage."

Lara remained silent as the slaves worked on her. She was bathed next, slaves washing her all over with large sea sponges filled with scented soap. Then she was scraped and rinsed to be certain the dirt was removed from her body. A sweet-smelling paste the color of almond blossoms was smeared on her legs and her pubic mound. It burned slightly, and she complained as it was quickly rinsed away. She was then washed again, this time by Tania, who pushed the cloth she used into the most intimate areas of Lara's body, causing Lara to blush furiously.

Tania snorted with impatience. "Every part of you must be fresh and sweet-smelling for your lovers," she explained. "You'll get use to this." She rinsed Lara with basins of fragrant warm water. "Now, get into the bath pool and sit down while your hair is washed, child."

The bathing pool had a bench that circled the entire pool. Lara sat down. The water was warm and very relaxing. She waited for someone to get into the water with her to wash her hair, but instead she was instructed to put her head back, and a slave woman washed her long tresses from the outside of the pool. Her pale gold locks were twice soaped, twice rinsed and then rinsed a third time with lemon juice and water.

"It makes golden hair even more golden," Tania told her. "Are you hungry?" She busily toweled Lara's hair dry first with a drying cloth, and then with a silk one.

"A little," Lara admitted. She had been pampered for several hours now.

"Then I will have something brought to you before we continue," Tania said. "It will be light, and you will not eat again until after you have been displayed." She gave orders in a brisk tone, and shortly Lara was served a dish of yogurt flavored with berries, a piece of flat crisp bread with a thin slice of cheese, and a small goblet of wine.

When she had finished Tania handed her a goblet of minted water with which to rinse her mouth. Then to Lara's surprise her mouth, her tongue and teeth were brushed with a boar's bristle brush, and she rinsed again.

"A woman should always have sweet breath," Tania said.

Lara was then laid out on a padded table. Her face was cleaned and creamed. Her body was thoroughly massaged until she felt as weak as a newborn kitten, and could barely stand on her own two legs. She was then led to a soft mattress, and a silvery curtain was drawn around it.

"You will sleep now," Tania said. "When it is time I will come and get you."

Lara needed no encouragement, and when she was awakened several hours later she realized that she felt better than she had ever felt in her life. Instinctively she touched the pendant. She had not allowed them to remove it from her neck while she was being prepared for display. Tania offered her a small goblet of water, and thirsty, Lara drank it down. Then at the older woman's suggesting she relieved herself and was washed in that private place once again.

"What am I to wear this evening?" she asked Tania.

"You will be displayed naked but for your pendant and some flowers," Tania said. "You understand that you will be touched by both the men and the women at the table? You must show no emotion at all, no matter how intimate a gesture it seems to you. Fear or repulsion will irritate the master's guests. There are also some among the guests whose houses cater to those men with odd or brutal tastes. You do not want to end up in one of those places, child. Remain emotionless at all costs."

Lara nodded. "I don't understand, but I know your advice is sound," she told Tania. "What is it these men like that is so strange?"

"Pain and degradation," came the answer. "Your first-night rights would be sold to men who would rape you instead of enjoying your sweetness and innocence. These men like inflicting punishment on women. They whip them with all manner of cruel instruments. They beat them with their hands and make them beg for mercy before using them in vile ways you should never hear from my lips. Show no emotion, Lara, lest you fall prey to one of these Pleasure Houses."

"But surely Gaius Prospero would not permit me to be sold to such people?" Lara cried. "He seems a kind man."

Tania laughed bitterly. "Child, remember, Gaius Prospero cares only for profit. If one of these creatures should offer him the highest price for you he will take it, and you will be lost. Remember what I have told you. Come now, I must place you." She led Lara to where a large round golden tray was placed upon a small table. "You are to sit upon this. On your side, on one hip." And when Lara had placed herself according to instructions, Tania brushed the tangles from her long hair, spreading it out. Then she placed a crown of small white flowers upon the girl's head. Next she decorated the tray with the same white flowers and, standing back, surveyed her handiwork and nodded, pleased. "Are you afraid of being enclosed?" she asked Lara.

"I do not know," Lara replied.

"Well, it will only be for a few moments," Tania remarked. Then she clapped her hands, and two ebony-black men slaves stepped forward.

They were muscular and their beautifully formed bodies were oiled. They were completely naked, and their male organs had been painted with gold paint to display them. They seemed very large to Lara, but then she had never seen a male organ except her baby brother's. About the necks of the men were twisted gold torques.

"You are to be carried to the dining room," Tania explained, and then she lifted a large gold dome which she placed over Lara and her tray. "Take her to the master!"

Lara felt the tray lifted up. She struggled a moment to maintain her balance, but once she found it she had no more difficulty. The two men hurried with a measured step from the north wing of the house through the halls, and finally they stood outside the dining room where Gaius Prospero was entertaining his special guests. Lara heard the doors to the room open wide, and then she heard the voice of her master saying, "Ahh, here is our dessert, my friends. A most special treat, I assure you," and he chuckled richly at his own humor.

"If it's as good as the rest of the meal," Lara heard a man's voice say, "we will surely have no complaints," and laughter erupted about the room.

"Oh, I think you will find this a most special and rich dish. One such as you have never had before," Gaius Prospero said. Then he nodded to his majordomo who quickly lifted the lid to reveal Lara.

The guests gasped as one, surprised and delighted. Laughter rippled around the dining room.

Where the instinct came from she never knew, but she looked coyly at the guests about the table, her head moving slowly to take them all in. The impression she gave was of utter elegance and pride.

"Now, my friends, I will give each of you the opportunity to inspect this truly rare and, you will agree, unique piece of merchandise. She is a virgin. Every orifice is intact, untouched by man or woman. She is ready to be trained as the most perfect of Pleasure Women, but before that her first-night rights will bring her owner a fortune. Who among your clientele will not lust after this exquisite beauty?" He stood before Lara on her tray, and offering her his hand helped her down from the table, and up onto a small dais of polished wood. "Look at this skin. Silken to the touch." His hand swept down Lara's graceful back.

She was startled, but she remembered Tania's warnings, remaining still and without expression. No matter what happened she would show no emotion.

"When did you last see breasts like these? A bit small, perhaps, but perfect in every way, and she is young. They will grow with loving handling," he chuckled. "And have you ever seen hair like this?" His fat hand ruffled through Lara's hair and it cascaded about her like a waterfall of golden gilt. "I have never had a finer piece of merchandise to offer you, and I will expect your bids to echo my expectations by this time tomorrow night."

"Is it true she is faerie?" one of the men asked.

"Her mother was faerie, none will deny it. You know her father, Sir John Swiftsword," Gaius Prospero said. "A fine lineage."

The guests now arose from the table, and came forward to get a closer look at Lara.

"Open your mouth," one woman said.

Lara complied.

"She has all her teeth, and there is no rot. The breath is sweet," the woman remarked. "Her eyes are beautiful. They are green but the lashes are dark. A most striking contrast."

Lara felt a hand fondling her bottom. She swallowed as discreetly as she might, but the expression on her face remained impassive.

"The skin is soft, and firm," the fondler noted. He ran his hand down Lara's calf. "Very nice, Gaius. She isn't mushy like many, but rather nicely tight."

"My lord, this is the best slave I have ever had for sale," the Master of the Merchants said proudly.

"I would see her more important attributes," another man said.

"Yes," agreed a woman. "Draw your nether lips apart so we may inspect your treasures, girl, if they may be called that. We'll know soon enough."

Lara reached down, and opened herself to the prying eyes. The woman put out her hand touching a small plump nub of flesh that had been revealed. Almost immediately a tiny pearl of liquid appeared. A man reached out, and wiped the bead of moisture onto his large finger, putting it in his mouth.

"Ahhh," the guests breathed.

"She is perfect, as I have said," Gaius Prospero murmured.

"Yes," the man agreed, "and sweet as honey." He took a strand of her hair between his fingers rubbing it as did several of the others.

Gaius Prospero then helped Lara down from the little dais. "Go now," he told her. "You will find Tania outside the door waiting to escort you back to the north wing."

Lara ran quickly to the door, and was gone.

The guests sat back down again at the table.

"It's no wonder you have remained the head of the Merchants Guild for so long," one of the men said to Gaius Prospero. "So that is how John Swiftsword managed to get the wherewithal to finally enter the tournament. Could you not have just lent him the monies, and taken a usurious share of his profits for the next ten years, Gaius?"

"I could have," the merchant replied, "but I would have had to wait for my profit if I did that, wouldn't I?"

There was laughter about the table at his remark.

"Believe it or not, I did not seek the girl out. Her stepmother brought her to me and asked if I would have her. A pretty girl not much older than Lara, but obviously ambitious for her husband, and happy to have a beautiful stepdaughter out of the house," he chuckled. "It was too good a chance to pass up, and when the father agreed I could not turn away from such an opportunity.

"Now you all know the rules. You have between sunrise and sunset to post your bids with me in your own hand. Go now and talk among yourselves, owners and Pleasure Mistresses. The sale must be in gold, and presented the day you take possession of the girl." He stood up again. "Thank you all for coming. I hope it has been worth your while." And then Gaius Prospero, the perfect host, ushered his guests from his house to their waiting vehicles. Returning into the house he sought out his wife, Vilia. "Well?" he said. "You were watching, weren't you?" He sat down next to her on their bed.

"Aye," Vilia answered. "Your presentation was masterful, my dear Gaius. If you had allowed it they would have taken the girl on your dining table." She laughed. "The lust was palpable. She will bring you a fortune. I cannot wait for the bids to begin coming in. You must let me open them! Not all will be able to bid, but most will even if they cannot afford it."

But by sunset of the following evening no bids for possession of the slave, Lara, had been delivered to Gaius Prospero's door. The Master of the Merchants was sick with anxiety and concern when his majordomo announced a visitor.

"The lady Gillian, my lord," he said as he ushered in the Head Mistress of the Pleasure Mistresses' Guild into his master's library.

"You look pale, Gaius," she said by way of greeting. She was a tall imposing woman with dark hair and bright blue eyes. Her simple gown of burgundy red silk hung in graceful folds. It had long, wide pleated sleeves, and a square neckline that revealed her fine large bosom. Her hair was piled upon her head, and covered with a sheer veil.

"Why have there been no bids?" Gaius Prospero managed to gasp out.

"Yes, I will sit down and have a goblet of wine," the lady Gillian answered him pointedly.

The majordomo quickly handed the lady the requested goblet, and then departed the library, but he remained on the other side of that door listening.

The lady Gillian sipped at her wine. "It is always a pleasure to visit you, Gaius," she said. "You never stint on the vintage."

"What has happened?" he ground out in a harsh voice. He was becoming calmer, for if Gillian was here he would get the truth.

"There will be no bids for the slave girl, Lara, Gaius," she began. "She is simply too beautiful, and of course there is the matter of her faerie blood."

"Faerie blood never bothered you before," he snapped. "At least three very well-known members of your guild possess it, and so do a number of Pleasure Women. And what the hell do you mean she is too beautiful? What is wrong with beautiful?"

"Not just beautiful, Gaius," Gillian told him. "*Too* beautiful. Exquisite. She is perfection, and therein lies the problem. No sooner had you ushered us from your house last night than two owners got into a physical quarrel over the girl. And the Pleasure Mistresses were no better. There was at least one incident of hair-pulling. And when they all returned to their Pleasure Houses most found their women in a disturbed state at the thought of Lara joining them. They fear her great beauty will rob them of their clients, and if they protest, her magic will harm them. No one believes a girl this beautiful does not have faerie power. I know she does not, for if she did she would not be in the position she is now in, but convincing the others is impossible. Ignorance is a dangerous thing, Gaius. By this morning, regular patrons were offering the owners additional coin to help purchase the girl. Others were attempting to book time with her for you displayed her well at the tourney. Several of my guild have been threatened with bodily harm if they are not given the girl's first-night rights. I have no choice but to forbid this girl's sale into any of our houses. It is too risky. I am sorry." She sipped again at her wine goblet. "Nor can I permit an untried girl to be sold as a Pleasure Woman to one of the magnates. Whoever purchased her would find he had bought a most dangerous possession. He would be envied by all, and therefore find himself in peril of his very life. Lara is the kind of girl that men see, and must have at all costs."

Gaius Prospero was stunned by her words. His investment was suddenly gone. The Head Mistress of the Pleasure Mistresses' Guild and its satellite, the Guild of the Pleasure Woman, was no fool. And her word was law among the owners and the houses. "What am I to do with her then?" he asked helplessly. "I cannot give her back to her family, and ask for my gold to be returned." He ran a nervous hand through his thinning hair. "I am ruined! How could I not have seen it?"

"Oh, Gaius," she told him, "do not be so melodramatic. You are not ruined, and your eye for a fine piece of merchandise simply blinded you to the fact the girl was too beautiful to not cause difficulty. You have a cousin, Rolf Fairplay—a Taubyl Trader, I believe. Am I correct?"

"Yes," he said. He was listening intently. Gillian was an intelligent woman, and might have been a merchant herself had she not been of the female sex.

"Cut your losses now, Gaius," she told him. "Give the girl to your cousin to sell in one of the provinces. You can make a small profit on her even with the percentage you must give your cousin. The provinces are not as sophisticated as the City, nor do they have our refined tastes. She will still be beautiful beyond compare, but that will just make her unique there, where here it will cause problems. The Coastal Province would probably be best, for there are so many there who are fair she will not stand out as much. What did you pay for her?"

"Ten thousand gold pieces," he groaned. "I expected at least thirty for her."

Gillian laughed. "And you might have gotten it had she not been so perfect, Gaius. But if I understand she only came into your possession a few days ago. You can hardly have expended a great deal on her but for that outrageous gown she wore to the tourney. I am certain you can get at least fifteen for her in the provinces. Your cousin will have heard of what has happened, so offer him not the usual fifteen percent of the girl's sale, but a full quarter share of the profit. You will at least break even."

"If she goes to the coast I can ask for a minimum of twenty thousand," Gaius said almost to himself. "The Coastal Kings are wealthy men. They would pay that or more for Lara. At twenty thousand I should make a profit of at least five thousand. I had the gown made by one of my slave women, and the material was purchased several years ago. It was just lying there in my storerooms waiting. I have actually expended little in this endeavor." He was beginning to feel better. It was a disappointment, of course, but all was not lost after all.

Gillian laughed. "Gaius, Gaius, trust you to find a bright side in a dark matter. Yes, I think you are right. Have Rolf Fairplay take her to the Coastal Province. It is the perfect place for her." She drank down the remainder of her wine, and stood up. "You have not been to my house in some time now. You should come again. Your young wife cannot keep you all to herself."

"I came only to see you, Gillian," he told her.

"Then come again," she purred at him smiling. "I have a new girl, Anora."

"I thought you did not entertain any longer," he responded, eying her breasts. Gillian had always had the finest bosom.

"I don't, but for old friends," Gillian murmured, touching his cheek with her elegant long fingers. "I am glad I was able to help you solve this little problem, Gaius." She put her hand on the door handle. "My felicitations to the lady Vilia. Good evening." And then opening the door she glided through it, smiling in amusement at the majordomo, who had had little time to vacate the spot where he had crouched, listening. He ran ahead of her now to open the front door, and she playfully waggled her finger at him as she passed through to her awaiting litter.

Gaius Prospero sat for several long minutes reliving his conversation with the Head Mistress. Silently he chided himself for not seeing the problem with Lara himself, but then he had always been a connoisseur of beautiful things. He simply could not help himself. He bought only the best, as his many clients knew, and Lara was the best. Alas, she was too perfect. He called out for his secretary whom he knew was nearby, for Jonah was always nearby.

"My lord?"

"You heard?"

"Yes, my lord."

"All of it?"

"Yes, my lord."

"Go the Traders Guild and learn where Rolf Fairplay is. If he is out of the City, find out when he will return."

"Yes, my lord," Jonah said.

"Do you think she is too beautiful?" Gaius Prospero asked his secretary.

"What is too beautiful, my lord? I thought your instincts were perfect as always. It is not your fault that the minds of others are narrow and unseeing."

"Do you always say the right thing, Jonah?" the merchant asked.

"I try, my lord, having you as my example," came the clever reply.

Gaius Prospero laughed. "One of these days I shall have to free you," he told Jonah, "but only if you agree to remain with me."

"You will have to free me eventually if I am to realize my goal in life," Jonah told his master. "And I have the gold to purchase my freedom now."

"And what is your goal?" Gaius Prospero asked.

"To be Master of the Merchants, my lord," was the startling answer.

Gaius Prospero laughed heartily, nodding. "Be patient, Jonah," he counseled his secretary. "You have the right attitude. Now go and find my cousin." He waved the man away, and hurried from his library to tell his wife of what had transpired.

Vilia was not pleased. "They are fools! Fools!" she cried. "Now I shall not get my new travel cart, and I had already decided upon the one I wanted."

"You shall have it, my dear," her husband promised.

"But I wanted it *now,*" Vilia said, and she began to sob.

"We shall go tomorrow and purchase it, my love," he said.

"But can we afford it as you have expended so much coin on that worthless girl? I want the one with the soft leather seats, and the crystal lanterns, and flower vases, Gaius. It is very, very expensive. The wheels are hand-painted and gilded. And I wanted new horses to draw it as well. I saw the prettiest pair of black-and-white animals at the horse yards. But then there was also a golden pair with creamy manes. I just can't make up my mind. They are very expensive, too." She pouted prettily at him.

"You may have anything your little heart desires, Vilia," he promised her. After all, Gaius Prospero thought to himself, he couldn't have anyone thinking that this unfortunate incident with Lara had weakened him financially. Yes! It was absolutely the right thing to go out tomorrow and purchase Vilia her new travel cart, and a pair of lovely horses to draw it. Kissing his wife he told her to go to bed. "I will join you after I have spoken with Jonah, my love. You will want to thank me for my generosity, I am certain."

"I do not have my new cart and horses yet, Gaius," she told him. "Have you not taught me never to pay for what I do not possess?"

"We will consider it a down payment, then," he chuckled, and left her.

He waited for close to two hours for Jonah, and was about to join his wife when the secretary returned with Gaius' cousin in tow.

While Gaius Prospero was a round-faced man of medium height and comfortable girth whose very appearance exuded prosperity, Rolf Fairplay was tall and rangy with a long narrow face. But his gray eyes were intelligent and alert. Those eyes now looked directly at the Master of the Merchants Guild.

"How may I serve you, cousin?" Rolf asked.

"Jonah, get my cousin some wine, and then join us," Gaius said.

"No wine," Rolf replied, "but I appreciate your hospitality, cousin. I must depart in the morning with my caravan, and I need a clear head, you will understand. This is a long trek I have ahead of me. I'll be going through the Forest and Desert provinces, crossing into a portion of the Outland, and then heading for the coast before I return to the City. I will be gone for almost a full year. You caught me just in time."

Gaius nodded. His cousin was probably the best trader of them all. He might have even been their leader, but he had turned the opportunity away, preferring to travel with his caravans the length and breadth of the four provinces. "You have heard of the purchase I recently made? Lara, the daughter of Sir John Swiftsword."

Rolf Fairplay nodded. "She is to be a Pleasure Woman. A most sound investment, cousin. When is the auction?"

"The owners and the Pleasure Mistresses came last night to view her. They were to place their bids between sunrise and sunset today. The auction was to have been held tonight. But no bids were received, and earlier this evening I was visited by the lady Gillian who told me because of the girl's beauty, and the dissension it was already causing among the house owners, the Pleasure Mistresses, the Pleasure Women and even their patrons, no bids would be offered me. She has, in her position as Head Mistress of the Pleasure Guilds, forbidden the girl's sale here in the City. She suggested I consign Lara to you for sale in the Coastal Province."

"What if I can sell her before I reach the coast? 'Tis the last stop on my trek, cousin. It would be better if I could. If word gets out that I am carrying such a valuable piece of merchandise my caravan could be attacked. If I agree to take her I will need at least six more mercenaries, and you must pay for them."

"Nay, Rolf, you will pay for them, but if you take her I will pay you a quarter of the profit, and not the usual fifteen percent the traders get. I want twenty thousand in gold for her. She is worth more, but unfortunately the market here is closed to me. Think of it, cousin. Five thousand to you for selling her. She cost me ten. I shall have little profit from it as you can see, but as Gillian has pointed out, it is best to cut my losses as quickly as I can."

"I want an agreement in writing," Rolf Fairplay said.

"Of course," Gaius Prospero agreed. "But remember, twenty thousand, cousin, and you get a quarter share. Less, and you will just get fifteen. An additional ten percent should certainly make it worth your while. Are we agreed then?"

"I'll get you your twenty thousand, Gaius, possibly more if I can," his cousin promised. "The Shadow Princes like their women fair and young."

"Jonah," his master called, "draw up the agreement."

"Two copies, Jonah," Rolf Fairplay said smiling at Gaius Prospero. "When can I have the girl? I want to leave at dawn, and everything else is ready."

"As soon as we sign the agreement you may take her, cousin. She is a virgin, and I need not tell you that her value is not just in her beauty, but in her innocence as well. See that she remains pure and untouched."

"Of course, cousin," Rolf answered. "We want your little investment to bring the highest price for us, and she will—I guarantee it."

The agreement was a standard contract between the Master of the Merchants Guild and a Taubyl Trader, with the exception of the fee. It took an hour for the secretary to draw up the two identical contracts, but finally the parchments were ready to be signed. Carefully he spread them on his master's desk and handed Gaius Prospero an inked quill. When both contracts had been signed by both men he sanded their signatures, and rolling up the parchments handed one to each man.

"Go to Tania yourself, and have Lara dressed for transport," Gaius instructed Jonah. "Tell her briefly what has happened, and see the girl has a small pack of necessities for her travels. Nothing elaborate, mind you," he warned.

"At once, my lord," Jonah answered, and hurried out. He reached the north wing, knocked, and was admitted by Tania.

"What has happened?" the woman demanded. "He did not send for Lara for the final auction. It has gotten so late I have put her to bed. She was so nervous I gave her some wine with a bit of poppy in it."

"There will be no auction. There were no bids for her, and tonight the Head Mistress of the Pleasure Guilds came to tell him she had forbidden the girl's sale to any in the City. They say she is too beautiful. That after last evening's display the owners and the Pleasure Mistresses began to quarrel over her. Patrons who had seen her at the tourney were threatening the houses if they were not given the girl's first-night rights. There was too much dissension being caused, and so the lady Gillian called a halt to the proceedings." He stopped, waiting for her to say something.

Tania shook her head. "What will happen now?" she asked him.

"He is consigning her to his cousin Rolf Fairplay, the Taubyl Trader. He thinks she is good for one of the Coastal Kings, but Rolf says she will appeal to the Shadow Princes. It matters not, Tania. Awaken the girl. She is being put into the trader's care tonight. His caravan leaves on the morrow at dawn. The master says you are to give her a small pack for her travels. Nothing elaborate."

"Go back to him, and say because of the poppy juice she will not awaken for several hours. I will make certain she gets to the caravan before Rolf Fairplay leaves, but I cannot awaken her now."

Jonah left Tania, who began to prepare for Lara's departure. She was not surprised when Gaius Prospero angrily entered the room several minutes later. She knelt quickly saying, "Forgive me, master, but the girl was becoming unmanageable. When it grew so late I did what I thought best for all concerned."

He grimaced. "You are certain you can awaken her in time? I do not want the additional expense of sending her along in a separate transport to catch up with the trader. Are you preparing a pack?"

"Yes, master, and I swear I will get her to the caravan on time!"

"You have recently acquired the habit of getting above your station, Tania," Gaius Prospero said threateningly. "Attempt to curb this habit, or I will have to send you to the country. I know how much you love it there, Tania." And he laughed nastily as he left her, knowing that Tania hated his country estate. There she would be forced to do farm labor under the eye of his estate manager, Creager, who was not above putting a woman slave on her back to service him. Gaius Prospero overlooked Creager's lustful nature because he did his job well. And after all, the women were only slaves.

Tania arose from her knees, resentment burning in her breast. She might be a slave, she thought, but she worked hard and was honest. Well, she thought, for once she would not be quite so honest. She would give Lara more than her master wanted, but he would never know. Gaius Prospero had so many possessions he could not remember half of them. And the poor girl should not be penalized for what had happened. Who knew how long and how far her travels would take her? Tania packed two simple gowns with round necks, full long sleeves and long pleated skirts. One of silk was light blue, the other a mixture of tawny orange wool and silk. She packed four white cotton chemises and two pairs of stockings, one a light wool for cold weather. She wrapped all of these items up tightly so Lara's pack would not look excessive. She put in the pearwood brush with which she had been brushing Lara's hair, and a small lacquer box of hairpins. She lay out a plain, dark green gown for her travels, another chemise, stockings, a pair of leather boots and a long veil to cover Lara's hair. Satisfied, she lay down on her mattress and slept for exactly four hours as she had trained herself to do.

Awakening, Tania arose to fetch a basin of warmed water and a small cloth. Then she drew the silvery curtains around Lara's sleeping place and shook the girl gently but firmly by the shoulder. Lara stirred sleepily. "Wake up, child!" Tania insisted. "It is almost time for you to go."

Lara's green eyes opened slowly. Her wits felt dull, and she could scarcely move. "Go where? Is it time for the auction?" She found herself growing stronger, the mists clearing from her brain as she spoke. "Tell me who has bought me? I hope it isn't the woman who wanted to see my teeth. I thought her rude."

"No one has purchased you. Get up, Lara, and bathe quickly. I will tell you all," Tania said. She poured out a goblet of pomegranate juice from a decanter and shoved it into Lara's hand. "Drink this! It will help."

Lara drank down the entire portion. She had been very thirsty. Relieving herself, she washed as quickly as she could. While she did, she listened to Tania's explanations of what had happened, and what was to happen to her.

"I am to leave the City?" She was astounded, and perhaps a bit afraid.

"It could be worse, child," Tania said.

"How?" Lara asked. She brushed the fuzz from her teeth and tongue, rinsing with minted water. "How could it possibly be worse?"

"Your father could have failed in his attempt to become a Crusader Knight. Or you might have been bought by one of the cruel owners to be used for the pleasures of depraved men and women. All that has happened is that you are considered too beautiful, and that men and women are already fighting over you. The trader who has you in his care is the master's distant cousin. His reputation is a good one, and he is a kind man. He will see you come to no harm, Lara, and it is in his best interest to see you fetch the highest price, for the higher your price, the greater his profit. His blood runs as cold as that of Gaius Prospero, and like our master, his only goal is for profit. Come now, and dress. I have laid out your clothing. We must reach the caravan before it departs at dawn."

Looking outside, Lara realized it was still dark. She pulled the stockings on, the clean white chemise and the dark green gown. Tania then brushed her hair out quickly, braiding it into a single thick plait and pinned on the veil, part of which she drew over Lara's beautiful face. Then she fitted the short boots onto Lara's feet, and draped a dark cloak over her shoulders. "Come, we must hurry," she said, and together the two walked from the north wing to the front door of the house where Jonah was awaiting them with a small transport he would be driving himself.

Climbing into the vehicle, they moved off, hurrying down the narrow private road onto the main avenue of the Golden District, escorted by the six mercenaries on Gaius Prospero's payroll. Things might not have turned out quite as the Master of the Merchants had expected, but Lara was still very valuable merchandise. When they reached them, the gates were opened without comment, and they drove out into the City. Lara had never been up this early, nor had she ever known the streets to be so empty or so silent. It was a little frightening. They passed by the closed gates to the Quarter, and for a moment she thought that she would cry. She reached for her star pendant, and the tiny flame within flickered as if to give her new courage.

"Master Jonah," she said politely, "I have nothing to give you but a faerie blessing, but will you tell my father what has happened to me so that he does not worry? Not my stepmother. Susanna would not tell him, for she overprotects him. My father. And tell him I am not unhappy or afraid, for I know I am shielded from harm." She felt almost guilty telling Gaius Prospero's secretary that she would give him a faerie blessing. She hadn't the faintest idea of how one would do that, but she needed his aid, and she had seen he was not a man who did something for nothing.

"A faerie blessing is a valuable gift, young Lara," the secretary replied. "I am happy to accept it for I need all the luck I can muster if I am to be free one day."

"You will be," Lara told him, amazed as the words came from her mouth. Yet she knew them to be the truth. What was happening to her?

"I will tell him, young Lara. I will also tell him he has a daughter to be proud of," Jonah said. "You are a brave girl, I think."

"Will you give me a faerie blessing?" Tania asked anxiously.

"I will give you two." Lara smiled. "You have been more than kind to me."

"I put the pearwood brush in your pack," Tania whispered.

"Thank you, and blessings on you, Tania. And you, Jonah." How odd, Lara thought, at the sight of their suddenly smiling faces. She knew little of her heritage or its customs, but faerie blessings were obviously highly prized. It was a piece of knowledge she would retain.

They reached the Place of the Traders, where Rolf Fairplay's great caravan was even now preparing to get under way. Jonah jumped down from the cart and sought out his master's cousin, bringing him back to where Lara and Tania waited. The trader lifted Lara down from the traveling cart and unfastened the veil.

"They are right," he said softly. "You are beautiful." Then he re-fastened the veil. "Keep your face covered when in public, Lara," he warned her. "I don't want you stolen away when you can bring my cousin and me such a fine profit." He turned to Jonah. "I will take her from here," he said. "Return to your master and say you have delivered the merchandise."

"Here is her pack, sir," Tania said, holding it out for him.

"Take your possessions, Lara, and follow me," Rolf Fairplay said.

"Goodbye," Lara told Tania and Jonah, and then she hurried after the trader.

He led her to a large covered cart. "You will have several female companions for some of your journey," he explained as he helped her into the conveyance. Then he was gone.

Lara looked about at the half-dozen sleepy girls. They were silent, and so she remained silent, too. Outside of the cart the sounds of the caravan getting under way could be heard. A flap had been drawn down, but she could see through the crack along the sides of the canvas. Their cart began to move. Lara watched as they exited through the Traders Gate, as was the law for all caravans. She watched for some time as the walls of the City grew smaller and smaller and finally faded from sight. One of the girls began to weep.

"Why are you crying?" Lara asked her gently.

"I have never been a slave before," the girl sobbed.

"Neither have I," Lara told her. "Tell me your name. I am Lara."

"I am Noss." The girl hiccupped.

"I know who you are!" one of the other females said. "You are the daughter of John Swiftsword. Your father sold you so he might enter the tourney. You are a faerie child," she said, drawing her cloak around her with a sneer. "I thought you were to be a Pleasure

Woman in one of the great Pleasure Houses, and yet here you are in a wagon of common slave women trekking off to who knows where. Why?"

"Like you," Lara said softly, "I am a slave. Slaves are not given reasons why."

"Humphh!" the woman replied, but she grew silent.

Lara smiled to herself. The woman was looking for trouble. She could just imagine what she would have said to the explanation that Lara was considered too beautiful to enter a Pleasure House.

"Are you really a faerie child?" Noss whispered. Her soft brown eyes were wide.

"My mother was faerie, but she deserted my father and me when I was only three months of age. While her blood runs in my veins, I know nothing about the faerie kingdom from whence she came. I was raised to be human just like you, Noss."

"My father was a mercenary, too, but when he was badly injured he could no longer find employment. I was sold so they might live," she told Lara. "Our hovel was taken from us, and we were homeless. We last lived in a tunnel beneath the City walls, but my mother was violated by some soldiers who found her there. She heard them coming, and hid me. I saw it all, Lara. Afterward she swore me to secrecy, and told my father that she had fallen while he was out begging so we might buy bread." Noss sighed. "They hoped by selling me they might escape the City, and buy a bit of land to work in the Midlands. I hope they can," she finished sadly.

"The life of a mercenary is difficult," Lara agreed. "I hope your parents find a new and better life. My father and stepmother did, and I am glad. My baby brother, Mikhail, will never know what it is like to be a mercenary's child."

"What do you think will happen to us?" Noss asked.

"We're going to be sold to the highest bidder, you stupid little bitch," the woman who had earlier attempted to quarrel with Lara said. "All of us are a special consignment for the Forest Lords. They have quite an appetite for female flesh, given how many women are sold into the Forest province nowadays. I guess their own women don't satisfy them," she said and laughed out loud. "I won't mind one of those big brutes foraging between my legs, girls. I have heard they are the lustiest men on Hetar."

"You talk too much, Truda," another woman remarked. "I have heard the Forest Lords only mate with those of pure Forest blood. If we're going to be sold to them, it will be as servants who cook, and clean, and sew, and slop the pigs."

"Don't tell me any man is true to his wife all the time, Belda," Truda snapped back sharply. "Men are like dogs, always sniffing at a new tail, and I intend wagging my tail prettily in my new master's direction. But I don't suppose Lara is meant for the Forest," she sneered.

"My master, Gaius Prospero, suggested I be sold in the Coastal Province, but Rolf Fairplay said he thought one of the Shadow Princes might like me," Lara murmured.

"I'll wager a Forest Lord would enjoy your favors greatly,"Truda said meanly. "Being a hall whore is quite like being a fancy Pleasure Woman except for the niceties involved," she said with a chuckle.

"Don't pay any attention to her," Belda said. "Truda is angry because her last master's wife caught her fucking one of the house's sons, and insisted she be sold. She was a servant in the Garden District."

"And what about you?"Truda demanded angrily.

"I am no better than I ought to be," Belda laughed. "My husband sold me to pay his debts. Debts he ran up with another woman. But then, I was in bed with his brother when we were caught, and I was condemned to slavery by the courts."

"Was your husband not condemned too for his lechery?" Lara asked.

"Nay, the law considers it a man's right to have any woman he desires," Belda said. "Do you not know this?"

"I lived in the Quarter my entire life," Lara answered. "I suppose I was sheltered. My grandmother raised me, and after she died and

Da remarried, my stepmother, Susanna did. We were friends, but we never spoke on things such as these."

"It is a hard world in which we live, Lara, daughter of Swift-sword," Belda said.

They were silent again for the rest of the morning. When the sun had reached its zenith the caravan stopped briefly. They were herded from their wagon, fed bread and water, sent into the bushes to relieve themselves and then returned to the wagon. Their trek began again. Finally at dusk they stopped once more. Mercenary guards were posted about the encampment. A fire was built and food cooked. The women were each given half a trencher filled with a rabbit stew, and a wineskin was handed them to share, but Truda drank the most of it, growing more belligerent by the minute. When she attempted to attack her companions physically, Rolf Fairplay had her strung up naked between two trees. Then he strapped the woman's bottom until it was red and welted while the entire camp looked on as Truda shrieked more with outrage than pain.

"I'll not have my merchandise damaged, woman," he growled in her face as she hung there between the trees. "Do you understand me?" Then cutting her down, he shoved her toward a group of mercenaries. "She's yours for the night. I want no bruises on her in the morning. She's one of the Forest consignment." He walked away.

"What will they do to her?" Noss whispered fearfully.

"Fuck the ears off of her, " Belda laughed. "Serves her right, the bitch. That'll sober her up quick enough. Come along now, girls. It's time for us to get our beauty rest." And she cackled once again as they walked back to the wagon. Inside there were thin mattresses that were rolled up. "Rolf Fairplay told me earlier that Lara and Noss are to sleep in the wagon. The rest of us will spread our mattresses beneath it for protection from any rain in the night."

"I am happy to sleep out of doors," Lara said, not wanting to appear as if she were privileged. She smiled at the other women with them. They were Adda, Wilda and Jael.

"Nay," Belda said quietly. "You are to be in the wagon, for we all know you are the most valuable among us by far. And Noss is the youngest, and still frightened. Without Truda complaining and causing dissension we will have a good night."

The mattresses were spread out, and Lara climbed into the wagon with young Noss to spread theirs. "How old are you?" she asked Noss.

"Twelve," Noss replied. "How old are you?"

"I am just fifteen," Lara told her. "My mother mated with my father one Midsummer's Eve, and I was born with the next spring." She smiled, laying down next to the girl, and drawing up the coverlet they had been given over the both of them.

"I am so afraid," Noss whispered to Lara.

"Then I must give you a faerie blessing to take away your fears, Noss. Go to sleep. I am by your side, and come the morning you will no longer be afraid."

"Really?" Noss quavered.

"Truly," Lara said, putting a comforting arm about the younger girl, and soon Noss was sleeping peacefully. Lara, however, lay awake for some time considering how quickly everything had changed in her life. Three nights ago she slept in her father's new home in the Garden District. Two nights ago she stood displayed for sale to the powerful of the City. Last night she waited to learn her golden fate. And tonight she lay on a thin mattress, in the bottom of a wooden wagon, with absolutely no idea of what was to happen next. She sighed, and picked up the pendant between her two fingers. *What is happening?* she asked silently.

Everything, the voice replied as silently.

But where am I going? Lara demanded.

Straight ahead, the voice answered, and then the flame flickered bright for a moment, and died back.

Lara closed her eyes and slept. There was nothing else to do.

Chapter 5

THE CARAVAN'S ROUTE led through the Midland province, which was the largest of the four civilized precincts on Hetar. It was from here that those men and women no longer needed on the farms emigrated into the City. The region was made up of a large flat wide valley sandwiched between two long ridges of gently rolling hills, some with vineyards of growing grapes. The farms were comfortable places growing all manner of edibles, some with orchards as well. The cart rumbled past green meadows and fields of hay being baled. The houses they saw were all sturdy and substantial. Lara, having never before been out of the City, had never seen their like. She watched thoughtfully, young Noss pressing against her side as if for protection.

Truda had rejoined the women the second morning, but her harsh punishment had done nothing to sweeten her disposition. The others did their best to ignore her, taking silent pleasure in the fact that sitting was obviously painful for Truda after her beating last night. She had brought whatever she got on herself, Belda insisted. A slave kept her mouth shut unless it was required she speak. Truda knew better. Fairplay was known to be good to the slaves he transported. The wine that she had so freely swilled had been a generous treat meant for them all, and her greed had spoiled it. It was unlikely they would see wine again.

The day passed without incident, and the next morning they turned off the main track into the hills. The women learned from one of the mercenaries that their first stop was to be in the Forest province at the Great Hall of the Head Forester. The six women traveling with Lara were a prepaid consignment for the Forest Lords. They would be delivered, and the caravan would move on toward the next destination—the Desert kingdom of the Shadow Princes.

"The Forest Lords are not easy masters, I've been told," Belda said.

"Are they kind?" Noss quavered, her eyes wide.

"To those who work hard, aye, I'm sure they would be kind," Belda responded. Poor little Noss was afraid of her own shadow. She would have to toughen up, or it was unlikely she would survive.

"They're lusty as buck deer in all seasons I've been told," Truda said with a smirk. "They will just love mounting a fresh little virgin like you, Noss." And she laughed.

"Be quiet!" Belda snapped. "Do not frighten the child with your gossip, which is more than likely wrong. If you do not shut your mouth, Truda, I will tell Rolf Fairplay. Perhaps you would like another beating with his strap? You are still having difficulty sitting, and it has been several days since you felt his wrath."

Truda glared darkly at Belda, but she said no more.

The road wandered through hillsides of lowing cattle, and fat woolly sheep. Lara was enchanted with the beauty of it all. She had never imagined that such a world existed outside of the City. Ahead she could see trees, and with each step the donkeys took their cart closer and closer. Two mornings later they stopped at the border post between the Midlands and the Forest Kingdom. Officials from each province were there to inspect Rolf Fairplay's papers. His cargo was thoroughly checked to ascertain that he carried no contraband, and that the number of slaves listed was exactly the number in the caravan.

The border official from the Midlands province knew that all of Rolf's papers would be in order, for the trader's reputation was sterling. But the official from the Forest Kingdom carefully inspected everything on the roster, checking each item off as he came upon it. Foresters were very tradition-bound peoples. When finally both sides of the border were satisfied that everything was in order, the caravan was waved through into the Forest.

Lara had never seen a Forest, let alone been in one. There were so many trees, and in some places they were so thick that the sun had difficulty getting through. Even the City was lighter, she thought. But it was also very beautiful, yet still but for the birds singing in the trees, and the rippling of water from the streams and brooks. The green, she thought, was a very soothing color. Now and again the road led through a flower-filled meadow. Sometimes browsing deer, startled by their passage, would leap away into the safety of the tall trees.

They stopped at midday to rest and water the pack animals. Rolf Fairplay came to the wagon, where the women were now milling about. Taking Lara aside he said, "You will remain in the wagon when we reach the hall of the Head Forester, my girl. You are not for these rough crude men, but for a Coastal King. Foresters, however, are lusty and greedy. If they see you they will want you, and I shall have great difficulty convincing them otherwise. It is better if you remain hidden. I will see to your comfort while we are here, but you must remain out of sight. Do you understand?"

"Yes, my lord," Lara said. Then, "Would it be possible for Noss to remain with me? She is very frightened, and so young."

Rolf Fairplay patted Lara's hand. It was a gesture that reminded her of Gaius Prospero. "You have a good heart, Lara, but the girl has already been bought and paid for. She belongs to the Forest Lords. I will suggest to the Head Forester that she be put with a kind mistress. It is the best we can do."

"Yes, my lord," Lara replied.

They were fed, and took their relief, and then the caravan moved from the meadow back onto the dark Forest track. Because it was summer, the day was a very long one, and they reached the hall of the Head Forester before dusk. As the caravan stopped, Lara peeked out, but she saw nothing but trees.

"Where are we?" she asked Belda, who seemed to be relatively knowledgeable.

"Look up," Belda whispered back. "Their halls are in the trees themselves. See the staircases winding about the great trunks? It is impossible for an enemy to break into their halls because of it. The stairs are steep and narrow."

Lara looked up amazed. She could see the lights from a great hall twinkling amid the leaves and branches. And smoke! There was obviously a fireplace in this odd building as well. She could never have imagined such a thing, and realized now that beyond the City a great and varied world existed. She could not wait to see more. She bid her companions farewell, advising Noss not to cry and appear a weakling lest she be victimized by others. She thanked Belda and the others for their kindness and company. Then she watched as they were led up into the hall in the trees, praying that they would have kind masters. Instinctively her hand went to her star pendant for comfort, and she smiled at herself for her own foolishness.

A mercenary brought her a slab of bread, meat and cheese. He poured some wine from his own skin into a little cup for her. "Thank you," Lara said softly.

He nodded, saying in a gruff voice, "You are one of our own, Lara, daughter of John Swiftsword. We will guard you on your journey, never fear." Then he moved quickly away.

Lara ate her cold meal, and then curling up on her mattress she drew up her coverlet, and settled down to sleep. She wondered what was happening in the great hall in the trees above her, and peeped a final time through the canvas flap. She could hear singing coming from the trees. Or was it the sound of voices raised in protest? She shivered and dropped the flap, settling back on her mattress.

Far above her, the Head Forester was arguing with Rolf Fairplay, though Lara could not hear the rough voice who shouted, "I was promised six women slaves!"

"I have delivered you six," Rolf said.

"You have brought me five, and a whining, frightened girl. I paid for six *women,*" Durga, the Head Forester snarled.

"I have brought the six females consigned to me by the trader with whom you placed your order. Take the matter up with him, my lord. I only agreed to deliver these women as a favor to my guild. I am receiving naught for my trouble, I might add."

"I need six strong women. Women who can work the day long and be used for pleasure by the lower lords at night. Even I can see that the child is too young to be mounted." He glared at Noss. "How old are you?" he demanded of her.

"Twelve, my lord," Noss quavered.

"Are you moonlinked yet?" Durga persisted.

"No, my lord," the girl whispered. She had begun to shake with her fear. Belda put an arm about her to keep Noss from collapsing.

"I will not accept her," Durga said firmly.

"That is your decision, my lord," Rolf Fairplay said. "I am content to refund you your coin for the girl, or send back to the City for a stronger, older female for you. The bill of lading says the little lass was but five gold pieces. I can take her along with me to sell in the Coastal Province. As I have pointed out, I did not take this order from you myself. I did not choose the women in the consignment. I have only made the delivery." He stood tall and firm before the Head Forester.

"I wanted six young women," Durga grumbled.

"I offer you my most abject apologies, my lord. Had you placed the order with me there should have been no difficulty. I am aware of your tastes. I will bear the extra cost above your five gold pieces for another woman in an effort to regain your favor," Rolf Fairplay said smoothly. "It is the least I can do for the inconvenience caused you."

"Well," Lord Durga said sourly, "I suppose if that is the best you can do I must be satisfied, Rolf Fairplay. Your reputation for honesty is well known throughout Hetar."

The Taubyl Trader felt an easing of the tensions in the hall with Durga's words. But suddenly the slave woman Truda broke away from the other women and fell to her knees before the Head Forester.

"He has another woman in his caravan, my lord!"

"What is this?" Durga growled fiercely. He stared down at Truda, deciding he liked her large pillowy breasts. He would mount her later, and take pleasure of her. Then he looked directly at Rolf Fairplay. "Is this true? Is there another woman with your party? Have you attempted to cheat me by palming off this child on us while you keep the woman meant for us?" His hand went to the dagger at his waist.

If he had had a weapon he would have slain Truda where she knelt, Rolf Fairplay thought angrily. Instead he said, "I do indeed have another woman with my caravan, my lord. She is a consignment for one of the Coastal Kings from my cousin, Gaius Prospero." He smiled a quick smile, but his eyes were cold and cautious.

"I would see her! Bring her to me now, Rolf Fairplay," the Head Forester said.

"My lord, she is already consigned to Arcas, a king's son," the trader lied.

"Give him the girl, Noss," Durga replied.

"My lord, this girl is a very rare and expensive slave. The plain truth is that you could not afford to purchase her even if she were for sale, and she is not."

"She's half faerie," Truda murmured wickedly.

At this both the Head Forester and his younger brother cast a meaningful look at one another. "Leave us," Durga said waving them all from the hall. "Rolf Fairplay, await me outside the hall. He turned to his wife who had been sitting quietly at his knee. "Sita, take these new slave women to their quarters. Return the girl, Noss, to the caravan."

Bowing her head in acknowledgement Sita gathered up the slave women and hurried them from the hall, which was quickly emptying. Rolf Fairplay was the last from the great chamber. He hoped the Head Forester, a rather dull-witted man, would not attempt to steal Lara from his caravan. He was well guarded for travel purposes, but not enough to fight off a small army of Foresters. He touched Sita's arm as she passed him.

"Beware Truda, the one who spoke. She is a troublemaker," he said softly.

"I saw it at once, Rolf Fairplay," Sita answered. "My thanks." And then she moved away with the slave women.

Inside the empty hall Durga turned to his brother. "A half faerie girl," he said thoughtfully. "Is it possible if we breed her we can somehow remove this curse that hangs over us, Enda?"

"I do not know," Enda replied. "Who has studied what breeding can do or cannot do, Durga? I just enjoy mounting a woman, and pleasuring myself on her body." He was a tall, handsome man with a ruddy, outdoor complexion, dark auburn hair and brown eyes. He looked nothing like his elder brother although they shared the same parentage.

Durga was a stocky man of barely medium height with small black eyes and black hair. He disguised a rather bad complexion with a bushy black beard. The Head Forester looked just like his late father whereas his brother looked like their mother. That woman had died birthing Enda, who had been a large infant. Her fortuitous death had saved her master the trouble of disposing of her.

Durga considered. "It was a faerie who brought this disaster on us in the first place," he said. "Why can a faerie not remove the scourge?"

"The slave woman said she is but half faerie, brother. I doubt her magic is strong enough. The curse has been on us for over seventy years now. Only the faerie queen who spoke it can remove it, and the faeries are gone from the Forest thanks to our foolish grandfather and his stubborn pride," Enda remarked.

"The faeries were just as obdurate," Durga insisted. "Was it not one of their own who led the hunting party on that day, and then mocked them?"

"Was it necessary for that hunting party to violate the faerie, and then kill her?"

"The faerie girl was asking for it, taunting the men with her charms. What did she think would happen? Besides she might have vanished away if she chose. She wanted those men between her legs, brother," Durga said crudely.

"You know as well as I do, brother, that a faerie having spent a day shape-shifting as that one did would be weakened when she took her own form once more, and unable to act in her own defense. So did our men. Did we not in those days rule the Forest along with the faeries, and the giants? We knew each other well once. But now we have driven our allies away and are cursed for it," Enda said.

"The faerie girl could help us regain our purity, Enda, I am certain of it," Durga insisted. "And our children would have faerie blood in their veins. The girl would help to bring her queen to us to remove Maeve's curse on the Forest Lords. Each generation born to our breeders grows less pure, no matter they are raised in our traditions. Our women are also of impure lineage now. Only two of the pure blood remain among our clans, Enda. We must reverse the tide of our destruction before it is too late. Mayhap the half faerie girl will not be the answer, but she suddenly has been placed in our midst, and so we must try. It is surely good fortune that has brought her to us, brother!"

"She is consigned to a Coastal King," Enda said. "We do not want difficulties with the coast, Durga. We are no longer as strong as we used to be. If the faerie girl has been paid for we must let her go on with the caravan, and we will seek another half faerie girl for our purposes. But if this girl is to be paid for upon her delivery, which I suspect is the case, then we must pay Rolf Fairplay the amount agreed upon ourselves. As long as Gaius Prospero receives his monies he will not care, and another girl can be found for the son of that Coastal King. First, however, we must learn her price. And if it is as high as I suspect it is, where is the coin to come from, Durga?"

"We have wealth," the Head Forester said. "Our hidden wealth, Enda."

"But will it be enough?" the younger man asked.

"You and I will pool our resources," Durga responded.

"Agreed!" Enda replied. "But you must agree to allow me first rights with the girl. You are too rough, and lack finesse to deal with so delicate a creature as a half faerie girl. If you didn't kill her outright with your wooing, you would likely frighten her to death. She will be a virgin without a doubt, else her price would not be so high."

"Our mother always said you were too greedy," Durga grumbled.

"You are impatient with virgins, brother. I have seen it before. We do not want to ruin our investment. I will woo her gently, and when she finally enters your bed she will be well trained and eager," Enda tempted his elder.

"What if you get her with child right away?" Durga asked.

"When she has spawned her child then you will have her next," Enda said reasonably. "Besides, I saw you looking at that big breasted wench among the new slave women, the one who spoke up in an effort to gain your favor. Don't tell me you didn't intend getting between her legs tonight," he chuckled. "She's a healthy-looking wench, and will give you a good ride. She could breed you up a healthy son before you dispose of her."

Durga grinned. "Aye, I could see immediately that she's a hot-tempered one. I imagine I'll be beating her as much as I'll be fucking her, and I'll enjoy both. Very well, 'tis agreed. We will purchase the faerie girl together, and you will have her first."

"Shall we call the trader back into the hall?" Enda asked.

"Nay, we shall go down to his encampment, and settle the details of the matter," Durga said. "If we meet his price he'll not refuse us."

Outside the hall the two brothers found Rolf Fairplay waiting beneath the treed portico. He looked up as they came forward. "Do you want your monies refunded, or shall I send back to the City for another woman to complete your consignment?"

"We want to buy the faerie girl," Durga said. "Come, and let us descend to your camp so I may examine her, and see if she is worth the outrageous sum you say you can obtain for her on the coast."

The trader swore silently to himself. Not only did Durga resemble a wild boar, he had the intellect of one. Well, there was nothing for it but to tell him the price, and end it here. His cousin had wanted a minimum of twenty thousand gold coins which he knew the Head Forester would not be able to pay, but to make it entirely impossible he said, "The king's son is paying twenty-five thousand gold pieces for the girl, my lord."

There was an audible and sharp intake of breath from both of his companions, but then Durga said, "We'll want to see her. She is a virgin? Guaranteed?"

"Of course," Rolf Fairplay answered. There was no chance that the Head Forester could meet his price, but he would show them Lara to torture them a little bit, as Durga had given him so much difficulty this evening.

They reached the ground and walked across the clearing to where his caravan was settled for the night. A mercenary guarded the wagon where Lara was housed. He had not ordered it, but they all knew who she was. They would consider her one of them, and watch over her with great and tender care, the trader realized.

"I will go in and speak with Lara before bringing her out," Rolf Fairplay said, and then he climbed into the cart. Noss gazed at him, startled. He put his finger to his lips warning her to silence, and turned to Lara. "Listen to me, Lara," he began, "thanks to Truda, the Head Forester would see you. I have told him that you are promised to the son of a Coastal Province king who is paying twenty-five thousand gold pieces for you. I know Durga cannot afford such a price, but he must still see you now in order to preserve his dignity. He will find fault with you, and then the incident will be concluded."

"I understand," Lara said.

"Good, then let us go out. Do not speak unless spoken to, girl." Climbing back out of the cart, the trader lifted Lara down, and brought her over to where the two men waited. "Her name is Lara," he said.

"I would see her naked," Durga said leering. "I want to know that this treasure you have is worth the outrageous price."

Reaching up, Lara unfastened her gown at its shoulders, and let it fall to the ground. She said absolutely nothing, but turned slowly that the two men might look their fill. The younger, handsome man reached up and pulled the pins from her hair so that it fell like a swath of silk down her back. He rubbed a coil between his fingers and smiled slowly into Lara's green eyes. It was a cruel smile, and his brown eyes remained cold even as his mouth turned up at its corners. He reached out and fondled one of her breasts. She wanted to slap his hand away, but she remained motionless.

"Spread your legs, girl!" His command startled her, and she looked anxiously to Rolf Fairplay.

The trader nodded.

The young man knelt before Lara, and opening her nether lips with the fingers of one hand, he slowly pushed a thick finger from his other hand into her body. "She's a virgin without a doubt, Durga," he said in a hard voice. He withdrew the finger sucking it as he stood up. "And sweet as honey."

"We will take her," the Head Forester said.

"My lord, she is twenty-five thousand pieces of gold, and she is promised to the Coastal King's son, Arcas," Rolf Fairplay said nervously.

"Is she paid for?" Enda demanded to know.

"Well, no, but the order was given me last time I was in his domain. I promised that I would bring him just such a girl as this one. He wanted a half faerie lass for a wife. He does not have one among

his wives. My cousin, Gaius Prospero, found the girl, and not without difficulty I can assure you. I simply cannot let her go, my lord
Durga." Rolf Fairplay was growing nervous. These Foresters were
cruel men.

Lara was still half in shock from having had her body invaded in
such a startling manner by the younger of the two Forest Lords.
Although he looked calm and in complete charge, she could sense
that the trader was growing frightened.

"We will pay you thirty thousand gold pieces, Rolf Fairplay,"
Enda said. "Such a sum should make it easier for you to overcome
your qualms. If Arcas has not paid you, you can tell him you have
not yet found a girl to suit his requirements. He will not doubt you
for you are a man of the highest repute. My brother and I want this
girl." He smiled his cold smile at the trader, showing his teeth and
reminding Rolf of a feral animal. Then he heard Lara's soft voice
murmuring in his ear.

"Say yes."

"It is not my custom to bargain in the open like some common
trader," Rolf said to the two men. "I will put the girl back in the
wagon, and then we will speak on it. Shall I return to your hall, my
lord Durga, so we may seal the bargain with a goblet of your fine
wine?" He drew Lara's gown up and fastened it at the shoulders.

"Agreed!" the Head Forester said, jovial once more. "Come,
Enda!" He turned and began climbing the steps to his hall again,
his brother behind him.

Rolf helped Lara back into the wagon. "Are you mad?" he asked
her. "These are brutal men. They will not treat you kindly, and they
are as likely to steal back their gold as look at me once they possess you. May the Celestial Actuary help us all now!"

"Listen to me, my lord," Lara said. "From the moment I knew I
was to leave my family something strange happened to me. Instincts
I never knew I had began to boil up within me. That is why I have
been so composed. While I do not believe I possess any real faerie
magic, I think these new feelings may be due to my faerie blood.

These two men, whatever their reasons, want me for some purpose I cannot yet divine, but they will indeed consider violence if you refuse them.

"You will be allowed to depart their hall, and your caravan will begin its trek again, but then something will happen, and whether you are ever heard from again is another matter altogether. They will claim they have no knowledge of what has happened. Take their gold, my lord, but refuse to consummate the sale until you stand on the border between the Forest and the Desert. Only then will you turn me over to them. My grandmother, Ina, taught me the history of this land, and I know that the Forest Lords will not dishonor themselves publicly. It is the only way to save yourself, and I would not have it said that Lara, daughter of Swiftsword, brought you ill fortune."

The trader shook his head. "It must indeed be some faerie magic that gives you such wisdom, Lara. I shall do exactly as you have suggested, and I am grateful to you for your advice. I am sorry I must leave you with these people. You deserve a better fate than this."

"This is only the beginning of my journey, Rolf Fairplay," Lara told him, and he climbed from the wagon.

"This is all my fault." Noss began to weep.

"Nay, it is the fault of the trader who purchased you for this consignment despite knowing better, which I am certain he did," Lara soothed the girl. "Some traders are good and honest men. Others are not. The one who bought you thought to gain a few more coins in his pocket. I do not doubt Rolf Fairplay will have them from him eventually."

"What will happen to me now?" Noss asked Lara.

"Rolf will sell you to one of the Desert people, or you will have a master from the coast. He is a kind man, and will see you are placed with a good master, I am certain," Lara reassured the frightened girl.

"I will be alone now," Noss said.

"I would have been alone if you remained here," Lara replied. "I will ask my mercenary friend to look after you."

"You are very important, Lara, aren't you?" Noss asked, her eyes wide.

Lara laughed. "No, I am not important at all. The mercenaries watch over me because my father was a mercenary once. Now he is a Crusader Knight. They are proud of him for being able to gain such heights. I am, too."

"But if your father is a Crusader Knight, why were you sold?" Noss wondered.

"To become a member of the Crusader Knights one must enter the tournament which is only held every three years. An applicant must be beautifully garbed to offer his applications, and he must be outfitted with the finest armor, and the best weapons. All of this costs much gold. My father is a great swordsman, but he was also a poor man. My stepmother suggested I was the only possession he had of any value, and she was right. So I was sold to Gaius Prospero for a great price. My da was able to enter the tournament and win one of the five places available to the applicants. And that is my story," Lara explained.

"But you are very beautiful," Noss responded, "and beauty always wins a place of importance in the world. And you are half faerie, it is said."

"My faerie mother deserted me when I was an infant," Lara said. "I know naught of faerie magic."

"But you gave me a faerie blessing," Noss reminded the older girl, her lip beginning to quiver.

"I did, and I meant it." Lara smiled. Then reaching out she ruffled Noss's brown-gold hair. "Go to sleep, youngling. We leave tomorrow for the Desert."

Noss obediently lay down, and was soon asleep.

Lara touched her star pendant. The flame flickered within the crystal. *This is my fate?* she asked it silently.

Nay, but you have a task to complete here, the voice responded.

What is it?

You will know soon enough, the voice of her magical guardian, Ethne, replied. *You will have to sacrifice yourself, but we will help you. Be brave!*

Lara closed her eyes. *Be brave.* She would have to be. She had been horrified when the Forest Lord pushed his finger into her body, but she had somehow managed to remain silent and still. Soon, she knew, he would push his manroot into her as well. She had seen the look in his eyes as he probed her innocence so boldly. And the other man, The Head Forester. He had licked his lips in open anticipation as the younger one examined her with rough hands. What purpose was there in all of this? Ethne, her guide, said this was meant to be so it must be. The flame within the pendant had always been with her, and she couldn't even recall when it had first spoken with her, so familiar had the voice become. She wondered how Rolf Fairplay was doing in his negotiations with the Forest Lords. They wouldn't be happy with his decision, she knew.

And they were not.

"You will sell her, but only when we reach the border? Do you take us for fools, Rolf Fairplay?" Durga demanded.

"My reputation is gold," the trader said in icy tones, "but I must protect myself, my lord Durga. You have agreed to pay me a small fortune. But I do not see it, nor are your Forest clans noted for much wealth. Lara is an extremely valuable piece of merchandise. She was meant for a king's son. I know her owner, for he is my own blood. Arcas has agreed to pay twenty-five thousand pieces of gold for the girl. You offer thirty thousand. I would be a fool not to sell her to you. My cousin would chastise me for such foolishness. But I have not seen your gold, and until I do there can be no agreement between us, my lord. And if indeed you pay me this great amount, and take the girl, what is to stop you from attacking my caravan before I reach the next district? My route for this journey, as for all the journeys I make, is public knowledge. Each trader must publish with the Guild the route he is taking, the stops he is making, the merchandise he is carrying. You could steal your gold back and murder me, yet claim no knowledge of me after I left your hall. I think not, my lords.

"I have agreed to sell Lara to you, but the transaction will not take place until we reach the borders between your land and the Desert region. The border guards will witness the compact between us. You will count out your coin, and when you have, I will turn the girl over to you. That is how I desire our agreement to be. If you choose not to do it my way, then I will depart, but you have my word that I will have a suitable slave girl sent to you as quickly as possible."

"You offend us by suggesting we would betray you after we have the slave," Durga said. His black eyes were narrowed in irritation. "And what makes you think we couldn't take the girl now, and dispose of you and the rest of your caravan?"

"You live by a certain code, my lord. It would not be the honorable thing to do, and so I can trust you will not do it. If you give me your word this night, and we shake hands, I know you will keep your word, and all who bow to your authority will as well."

"Very well, I give you my word," Durga finally said.

"Then give me your hand," the trader replied.

"Is my word not good enough?" Durga roared angrily.

"Nay, it is not!" Rolf replied just as loudly. "Give me your hand, or the agreement between us is null and void. I know your ways, my lord. The members of my guild have not traveled your lands all these years in safety because they are fools."

Durga held out a fat broad hand, and shook the trader's thin hand grudgingly.

"And your brother as well, my lord?" Rolf Fairplay said quietly.

Enda laughed, and offered his hand to the trader in a firm grip. "Then we are agreed, Rolf Fairplay?" he said. "I am eager to have the beautiful Lara beneath me."

The trader nodded reluctantly. "We are agreed. I will leave at dawn. We should reach the border in two days of travel—I shall meet you there. The gold will be counted, weighed, and the girl will be yours." Then he added, "While my cousin will certainly be pleased with this transaction, Arcas will be quite disappointed. I wonder if I should not send a faeriepost messenger to the coast, and perhaps you might bid against one another." It did not hurt to keep up the pretense and worry the Forest Lords, Rolf thought. He was not happy leaving a girl like Lara with them. After all, her father was a Crusader Knight, and famous even before he won his spurs in the recent tournament.

"We have agreed verbally, and I have given you my hand," Durga protested. "You cannot break our agreement now, trader."

Rolf pretended to consider. "I suppose not, and why waste the time? After all, in my business time is always money. Oh, one thing. The girl wears a thin gold chain with a tiny crystal star about her neck. Her faerie mother put it there. Gaius Prospero requests that it remain with her. Who knows what magic it possesses?" He smiled at the two men, and then with a neat bow left them to ponder his words.

"The girl possesses faerie magic," Durga said. "I knew it! She will be worth every coin we give the trader. And they say that faerie women are passionate beyond all other women. Take her virginity, brother, and teach her a few tricks, but then I want my turn, and I do not choose to wait. Was her sheath tight when you put your finger in her?"

"I have never known a virgin's to be tighter," Enda said wickedly, and then regretted his words immediately.

His brother's black eyes gleamed in lustful anticipation. "I have said I will leave her to you, and I will—but the night you take her virginity I must have her, too, so I can also experience that virgin denseness. It is only fair, Enda, for I have put up much of my gold for this purchase, too."

Enda laughed. "Mother always said *you* were greedy, too, Durga. The girl will receive a full measure of our lust that night. And if she conceives then it matters not which of us is the child's sire, the infant will have her faerie blood. We should have thought of this before. We must find more like her so all of our men may breed sons on faerie women. The curse will finally be lifted from us."

"You must marry Tira as soon as possible," Durga said. "She must be ready to receive her son from the faerie girl."

"We cannot kill her as we do the others," Enda told his brother. "This disaster came upon us because our men murdered a faerie woman in the first place. This faerie, and the others we find, must be treated well, for their wombs hold our future.

"I am ashamed that my blood is tainted by that of a Midland woman. Once our seed was pure, and we wed only with each other. We did not have to bring strangers into our midst in order to breed up our sons."

"At least the same breeder gave us life," Durga said. "She must have been a clever creature to lure our sire back into her bed when she was nursing me. None before her had done so. They suckled their nurslings like good little ewe sheep, never knowing that when their children were weaned they would be taken away and given to their real mothers. Never suspecting, poor little lambkins, that the men who filled their wombs would strangle them, and bury their bodies in the darkest part of the Forest." He laughed.

"It will not happen in our generation," Enda said, "but possibly in our sons' time, or our grandsons'? One day we will produce sons on our own women again. One day our women will not weep with the curse of their infertility because the men of our grandfather's generation murdered a faerie woman, and then refused to atone for their crime. This is a new beginning for us, Durga. We will be hailed as heroes by our descendants."

Durga nodded and then, swilling down his goblet of wine, he arose from the high board. "I am going to bed," he said. "I have a fresh and juicy woman to give me pleasure this night. The trader may depart tomorrow unharmed. 'Tis only a day's ride to the border by horse, though the caravan travels slower. I intend plugging the fiery Truda until her legs can no longer hold her up—the memory of the beautiful Lara will encourage me onward," he chuckled.

"I will tell Sita you are to wed her sister, Tira, soon. I think the autumn is a good time, eh?"

Enda nodded. "Why not?" he agreed. "We will plan the date for a time when Lara's moonlink is broken. She is unclean then, and I will need a pretty outlet for my lustful nature. Tira will be a good substitute. Now that I have a breeder to get a son on it is time I wed."

The brothers parted, Enda remaining in the hall drinking. He considered taking one of the new slave women for his amusement, but he knew now he would never be content knowing that Lara lay sleeping below the hall in the trader's wagon. He licked his lips in anticipation of their first night. She would be afraid, of course, but he would soothe her with kisses and caresses. And when he had convinced her she had no other choice but to sweetly yield herself to him, he would fill her tight little sheath full with his manroot, leaving her breathless with his skill. And while he plundered her virginity his brother would watch, his own need for Lara swelling. When Enda had finished with her that first time, Durga would cover the girl's fair body with his own. He would howl with his satisfaction, for Durga was a noisy lover. How Lara's eyes would widen when his brother's thick manroot filled her sheath! He fully admitted his elder sibling had a bigger mass of man flesh; but Enda had a much longer organ. He would push it right to the mouth of her womb, and she would cry out when he filled her full with his potent seed. Then Enda grinned, looking down to see his manroot engorged and poking up beneath his tunic. The mere thought of the beauteous half faerie girl set more than his pulses racing. He was afire with need for her. Standing up, he walked slowly from his brother's hall and stood on the treed portico looking down at the trader's encampment, where the object of his intense desire slept her innocent sleep. Or was she thinking of him, and tossing with her own thoughts?

SHE COULD FEEL HIM. He was somewhere near, and his very presence was disturbing. *I don't want this,* she murmured silently to the crystal. *You have a fate to follow, to live out,* the voice said back to her. *They repel me, these Forest Lords,* she replied. *You will not be long with them,* Ethne promised her. *Just a little while. Be brave, child. You are protected.*

The caravan awoke before the dawn. Noss gently shook Lara awake, and handed her a piece of flat bread with cheese. The older girl nodded her thanks, and began to eat slowly. She had not slept well at all, but she knew she would need all her strength and her wits about her if she was to survive what was to come. She smiled suddenly, remembering Rolf Fairplay's lies yesterday as he attempted to save her from the determination of the Forest Lords to have her for themselves. What made them want her? Surely it was not just her beauty. If it was, then her beauty was an anathema, and she didn't want it. But no, she sensed it was something more. But what? She hoped the revelation would not be too awful.

Noss brought her a basin of warm water.

"You don't have to wait upon me, Noss," Lara told her.

"You saved me from those men," Noss whispered. "I shall be forever in your debt, and must do what I can to serve you while we are yet together, Lara."

"Thank you," Lara said, quickly washing herself. Then she grew serious. "In two more days I will leave you, Noss. You will be protected by my mercenary friend, but you must stop being afraid of life, little one. It is an adventure to be lived. Promise me whenever you think you are growing frightened to remember those words and me."

"You are braver than I," Noss said.

"Until a few days ago I had lived all of my life in the Mercenaries' Quarter of the City, Noss. I have no deep well of experience to sustain me, and I am only three years older than you," Lara replied. "We are on a journey, you and I. How we travel our journey's road is up to us. If we choose to live in constant fear, the journey will be an unpleasant one. But if we live it with enthusiasm, taking each day as it comes, enjoying the surprises and appreciating the quiet times, then we will travel a far less bumpy road."

"Aren't you afraid of being left with the Forest Lords?" Noss asked Lara.

Lara sighed. "Afraid? Perhaps a little, but I will master my fear, for to be afraid of these men will give them power over me. I do not want that. They have some plan in mind for me, but I sense I will not be with them for long. My road does not end here in the Forest. It is longer and more complex." She smiled at the girl. "Come, let us roll up our mattresses and fold our coverlets. It is almost time for the caravan to depart. We have a long day ahead of us."

Noss shook her head. "You are so brave," she said.

"Will you try to be brave, even when I am gone?" Lara replied.

"I will try," Noss promised.

They left the Head Forester's compound just as the first rays of the sun crept over the horizon, traveling at a steady pace as they had since leaving the City. At midday, the wagons stopped to allow the animals a small rest. They ate and then were on their way again, not stopping until the summer twilight had almost faded into night.

Rolf Fairplay came to see how the two girls were doing. He patted Noss's cheek telling her, "I will only sell you to a kind master, little one. I have promised Lara."

"And I have promised her to try not to be so fearful," Noss said.

The trader chuckled. "Excellent!" he said.

"Will we reach the border tomorrow?" Lara asked him.

"Late, probably. The exchange between the Head Forester and myself will take place the following morning. Lara, I could slip over the border and refuse the sale. One of the Coastal Kings will pay just as much for you."

"You would make a fearsome enemy, my lord," Lara told him. "One who would complain to your Guild, who would probably attack any trader's caravan that entered his precincts from now on. Even Gaius Prospero would disapprove of such behavior, and your good reputation would be ruined. You have agreed to the bargain, and you must keep it, but I thank you for your kindness."

"It pains me that a slave as fine as you should be condemned to life with the Forest clan," Rolf Fairplay answered her. "You are meant for a better master."

Lara laughed. "Do not compliment me so, my lord. I might begin to believe you. I did not know my mother, but believe me I am protected by her faerie magic. This star I wear about my neck is proof of it. I will be fine."

"Lara says she will not be long with the Forest Lords," Noss spoke up.

The trader looked askance. "What is this?"

"An instinct, my lord, nothing more," Lara told him softly.

"Faerie magic," he said, nodding. "Only those with it know such things. It sets my heart at rest, Lara. I am a trader by profession, and commerce is in my very veins. But I am also a man like my cousin, who likes to see fine merchandise with fine people. This sale I have made is grand in scale, but far less than I had hoped for— although I must admit to you that I have made an outrageous profit, and obtained more for you than my illustrious cousin would have dared to dream." He chuckled. "I intend to send the gold directly back to him from the Desert Kingdom."

"Is that not dangerous, sending so much coin by another caravan?" she asked him.

"Nay. I will give the gold to one of the Desert men who acts as a banker for the Shadow Princes and traders like me. The banker will send a faeriepost to the City crediting my cousin's account for the amount. He, in turn, will have his banker credit my account for the commission. I would not travel a step farther than I must with all that gold. It is not likely I will see the City for another seven or eight months."

Rolf bid them goodnight then, and the two girls unrolled their mattresses and their coverlets, and slept again that night in their wagon transport. The next day was very much like the previous, but the landscape began to change as they traveled. The Forest thinned out, and then was gone entirely. During the last few hours of daylight they traveled across a flat terrain of scrubland with stunted trees and bushes rising from an increasingly sandy soil. Finally, as darkness was falling, they reached the border station between the Desert and the Forest.

Grumbling, the border inspectors from the Forest painstakingly inspected the bills of lading. "Why do you carry two slaves instead of only one?" one of the guards demanded.

"One slave was considered unfit. I only delivered the order, but I agreed to see the inferior one was replaced. I am taking her for sale elsewhere," Rolf explained.

The guard grunted, satisfied with the answer. Content with his inspection, he passed the caravan through into the Desert realm. There Rolf Fairplay requested permission to camp for the night.

"The Head Forester from the Forest District will be here on the morrow to complete a sale," he explained to the Desert official. "I expect he will arrive shortly after the sun is up. There is much involved, and I thought it better to finish our transaction here rather than at his hall. Have you a banker nearby?"

The official nodded. "I will send one of my men for him at dawn. You need not depart until you have put your monies with him for credit in the City."

They ate, and prepared for bed once again. The sky above them was darker than any Lara had ever seen, and filled with bright crystal stars. While the blue moon of the Midlands had been new when she left the City, the deep red-orange Desert moon was a full glorious globe. The Forest moon, a first quarter the previous night, was a pale green. She wondered what hue the coastal moon was, and whether she would ever see it. Or if one day she might stand somewhere in the Outlands and see all the four moons of Hetar.

"Come to bed, Lara," Noss called to her.

"In a moment," Lara responded. She wanted a few last minutes alone in the night to enjoy her freedom. She knew that once she came into the possession of the Head Forester and his brother, she would not find much time if any to be alone again. She had always enjoyed her solitary time. She looked down into the crystal that hung around her neck. The little flame flickered and grew brighter.

What do you want? Ethne asked.

To remain brave. To not show fear before the Forest Lords.

The strength is within you, came her reply. *You have but to use it.*

Lara dropped the crystal, and it fell to lie in the valley between her breasts. She felt its subtle warmth against her skin. She wondered once if the voice she heard was her mother's, but her father had said no. Ilona had given her the chain and pendant from her own neck. She, too, had heard the voice, for so had she told him when she first showed him the crystal star. Still it was faerie magic, and Lara was glad to have it. It was odd, but she did feel strong. It was a sensation she had never truly experienced until recently. With a final look at the sky she returned to the cart to sleep. Too soon morning would come. Climbing into the cart, Lara sighed softly. Noss was already sleeping, no doubt relieved that she would not go to the Forest Lords tomorrow.

Yet the next day Noss was awake early, and again she brought food for Lara, and water for her to bathe in before she left them. Lara thanked her once more, and when she had finished her food she washed her face and hands in the warm water even as the Forest Lords arrived at the border. Hearing the approaching hoofbeats, she brushed out her hair and plaited it into one braid, knowing that she would be sent for when it was time. Rolf Fairplay would not let her go until he had counted and weighed every coin.

In the end, it took several hours, for the trader was a suspicious man where transactions of this sort were involved. Each coin was checked to be certain it was pure gold, and not a baser metal merely gilded. Some coins weighed a bit more, and others a bit less, but the final weight was exactly what it should be.

The Desert banker was standing by on his side of the border to take the gold that the Head Forester passed over. Lara was called to come. Hugging Noss, she reminded her to be brave, and kissed the girl's cheek. Then the papers transferring Lara's ownership from Gaius Prospero through Rolf Fairplay to Durga and Enda of the Forest Kingdom were signed. And finally, Lara, daughter of Sir John Swiftsword, stepped across the border separating the Desert from the Forest, and into the custody of her new masters.

Chapter 6

"CAN YOU RIDE?" Enda asked Lara.

She shook her head in the negative. "But I can learn," she told him.

Reaching down, he pulled her up and settled her before him on his saddle. His free hand smoothed over her breasts. "Sweet," he murmured in her ear.

She probably should be afraid, Lara considered, but she wasn't. It was a childish display of ownership. She said nothing as he drew her back against him, his sinewy arm clamped about her slender waist.

"We won't go very fast," he told her.

"If you expect to return to your hall tonight you will have to eventually," Lara said. "If it took Rolf Fairplay's caravan two days to reach the border you must have ridden quickly to reach here in just a day."

"You are educated?" He was surprised.

"Enough to understand time and distance," she told him.

"You have not been raised a slave?" His voice was hot in her ear.

"No," Lara replied shortly.

"Tell me," he said, curious now.

"You know my mother was a faerie woman. She deserted us when I was an infant. My father was a member of the Mercenary Guild," Lara said. "My father's mother raised me, and then my stepmother, Susanna. My father is a great warrior, and very much wanted to join the Crusader Knights, but he had not the means until it was suggested that he sell me to Gaius Prospero. And so I am now in your possession."

"Did your father at least win his place among the Crusader Knights?" Enda asked.

"Yes," Lara said. "I saw it all, and he fought well."

"Why did not Gaius Prospero sell you to one of the Pleasure Houses? You are obviously meant for one," Enda probed.

"That was his plan, but the Head Mistress of the Guild of Pleasure Women would not permit it. My beauty was already causing dissension among the women, the owners of the Pleasure Houses and their patrons. And then there is my faerie heritage. Some feared it," Lara concluded.

"I do not fear it," he said softly, and she felt his hot mouth on the back of her neck. "For centuries the Forest folk and the faerie folk have been allies. We enjoy making love to faerie women." His teeth nipped her flesh.

"I am not a faerie woman," Lara protested softly. "I only had a faerie mother. I know nothing of magic or spells. If you have purchased me for that reason you have cheated yourselves. There is still time to catch Rolf Fairplay, and have him return your gold. He will do so, and the Coastal King's son will not be disappointed."

Enda laughed. "No, we will not return you, and poor Arcas will never know what he has missed. The trader is satisfied with the transaction, and the banker who took our gold has already sent a faeriepost to the City to credit Gaius Prospero. You belong to me and my brother now, Lara. Best to get used to that fact." The hand fondling her breast pinched the nipple sharply, making her gasp in surprise.

He laughed, and they continued on their way. After a short while their pace increased until they were cantering along a barely discernible trail, and the Forest around them was deep and dark. The caravan had not come this way, Lara realized, but it occurred to her that the traveler's route might not necessarily be the fastest route, but the easiest. Their path led up hills and across meadows. The horses never seemed to flag, and Lara wondered if they would stop before they reached their destination. But as the sun reached its zenith in the summer sky the brothers drew their mounts to a halt in a small clearing with a stream.

Durga was off his mount first, and coming over, lifted Lara down from her perch on Enda's saddle. He tipped her face up to his, saying, "Do not be fearful, faerie girl. We will treat you well, and you will do our bidding obediently, eh?"

"Yes, my lord," Lara told him. His black eyes were small and piggy.

"Restrain your lust, brother," Enda said joining them. "Remember your promise to me." And he chuckled.

"Do not take long, then," his elder replied. "If you were not so delicate in your manner we could have her here and now on yon mossy bank. Think of the pleasure we would gain, and 'tis a fine day for it," Durga concluded.

Enda laughed aloud. "No," he said. "Our seed will grow more potent if we wait." Then he turned to Lara, who had been listening to them and struggling to restrain her aversion. "Go into the bushes, girl, and relieve yourself. We will be doing the same. Are you hungry?"

"Aye."

"Do what you must, and then we'll eat," he told her.

Hidden behind the greenery Lara obeyed him, for it was the only sensible thing to do. She gazed down at her pendant. The little flame glowed steadily. She drew a deep breath, and stepped out into the clearing again, where the two men were awaiting her. Enda handed her a chunk of bread spread with the most delicious cheese she had ever tasted in all her life. It was soft and creamy, and had bits of mushroom in it. Lara gobbled it down none too delicately, and Enda, eyes dancing with amusement, handed her a second piece.

"My betrothed wife, Tira, makes the cheese," he said. "It is good, isn't it?"

"You have a wife?" She was surprised.

"We wed in the autumn. She is the younger sister of Durga's wife, Sita. My brother and I are members of the ruling family. It is tradition that our wives come from one particular family."

"What if a particular generation had no females?" Lara asked him.

"It has never happened," Enda said. "Our bloodline is pure, and goes back to the days of the Creation. The Forest clans are the oldest families on Hetar."

They gave her a little wine to drink, and then they remounted their horses and were on their way again. It was very late afternoon when they arrived back at Durga's hall. Sandwiched between her two owners, Lara mounted the narrow, winding staircase that led to the treetop structure. She was amazed by it all. There was nothing like it in the City.

"I have my own quarters here in the hall," Enda told her as he led her away. "Although my brother and I both own you, you will remain with me for the interim." He opened a door at the end of a dim passageway, and led her inside. It was different from anything she had ever known, but it reminded her somehow of the hovel. Yet it was not. The large chamber was dark because of its rough wood walls and ceiling. A big stone fireplace with a blazing fire gave the room a pleasant warmth. The floors were covered with sheepskins to keep out the cold. The furniture, a large table and several chairs, were rough-made of heavy wood. There was no decoration of any kind. She did not know if this was because it was a man's quarters, or because the Forest clans did not have such finery.

He walked across the chamber, and flung open another door. "This is where you will spend a great deal of your time, Lara. Here, in my bed. When Tira and I are wed I will not live here, but rather in my own hall. You, however, will remain here, waiting on the pleasure of your masters." He slid an arm about her. "Are you afraid?"

"Of what?" she asked him striving to seem unconcerned. Yes! She was afraid. Afraid of this dark place. Afraid of the knowledge that it would be her task to give pleasure to both of these brothers who called themselves her masters. But she would never admit it. Never!

"Of what lies ahead for you," he said turning her about to look down into her beautiful face. "Of me." His lips brushed hers gently.

She felt nothing, nothing but icy disdain, and she was surprised. "I should be a fool not to know that you and your brother have purchased me to be your Pleasure Woman, but I know naught of what you desire," Lara told him. "In the City a virgin who enters a Pleasure House has her first-night rights auctioned off to the highest bidders, for I am told every girl has three virginities to take. After that first night she is trained in the arts of pleasing the men and the women who visit her. Since the Pleasure Guild refused to have me among them, I have had no training in the pleasure arts."

"My brother and I will teach you how to please a man," he told her, "and we shall enjoy taking your virginity. I shall go first, for it was my extra gold that allowed my brother to pay what he did for you. But he shall be with us that night in our bed, and he shall enter your body second, that same night. It is only right, as he is the elder."

"Why did you pay such an outrageous sum for my person?" Lara asked him.

"Our reasons are our own. You would not understand," Enda told her. "Do not ask me again or I will personally whip you. I would dislike marking that lovely skin, but I will be obeyed, Lara, lest anyone think me weak. Do you understand me?"

"Yes, my lord," she replied softly.

"Then we shall not quarrel," he said, his fingers caressing her arms as he spoke. He could feel his lust for her rising. Durga was right. They would not wait long. Not tonight, for he could see the girl was tired. But perhaps tomorrow. If she had no knowledge, then it was probably best to begin her schooling as soon as possible.

"Is there somewhere I may wash, my lord?" her soft voice made the request.

"There is always water and a basin in the bedchamber," he told her. "You will want to rest until the evening meal. I will have food brought to you. You will be left in peace tonight. I will have one of the women bring you your belongings. You will not leave these rooms unless I come for you, Lara."

"Yes, my lord," she agreed, and watched as he turned and left her.

When he had gone she looked about her more carefully, but her first impressions were only confirmed. Durga's dwelling was a comfortable but rough place. She went into the bedchamber and looked about. The wooden bed, of course, was huge, with four carved pillars and a wooden canopy. She wanted to see what covered it, but she also wanted to bathe the dust of the road from herself. She hadn't had a bath since leaving the City. There would be time enough to explore if she was truly to be left alone tonight.

She found a pitcher of water in the coals of the bedchamber fireplace exactly where it should be. She tipped the water into the basin on the little table that stood against a wall. Loosening her gown she let it slip to the floor, and taking up the cloth that had been in the basin, she washed herself all over. When she had finished she shook the dust from her gown. She disliked donning it again as she thought it dirty, but there was no other choice. She did not yet have her pack. Then she went out into the other room, and sat by the fire.

It felt good to sit still and quiet. The warmth of the hearth took the Forest's dampness from the chamber. She was certain that Durga's hall was filling up with his family, his friends and retainers as the evening came on, but she heard nothing. And then the door to the chamber opened, and two women entered. One carried a tray, and the other her pack. Lara recognized them at once.

"Belda! Jael!" she cried.

"We're not supposed to talk to you," Belda whispered.

"Durga's orders," Jael added, putting Lara's pack on a chair.

"Are you all right?" Lara said low.

They both nodded.

Belda put the tray on the table. "We'll find a way," she murmured, and then she and Jael hurried out of the chamber.

On the tray Lara found a bowl of venison stew, fresh warm bread, a piece of cheese and a small cup of ale. Never a fussy eater, she wolfed it all down, leaving not even a crumb for a mouse. Going to the chamber window she looked out, but in the twilight saw nothing but thick green leaves. She wondered if she should bar the door, but there was no lock. Shrugging, she walked back into the bedchamber. She was very weary with all that had gone on in the past weeks. Enda had said she would be left to herself tonight, and she suspected it would be a good time to catch up on her sleep. To her surprise there was a glimpse of the green Forest moon through the trees outside this chamber's window. She added a bit more fuel to the fire, and then fetched her pack.

Setting it on the bed, she opened it and drew out a clean chemise. She removed her dusty travel gown and put on the clean one. Then digging down in the packet she pulled out the pearwood hairbrush that Tania had given her and began to brush her long gilt hair. Her hair needed washing, but the morning would be time enough, Lara thought to herself. She slowly rebraided her hair as she considered that, for the first time since her grandmother had died, she was completely alone. It was both comforting and frightening. The light had now faded completely, and Lara drew the coverlet from the bed, surprised to find it made with rough but clean linen. Climbing in, she settled down, reaching for the crystal about her neck.

Am I really where I should be? she wondered silently.

You are exactly where you should be, the flame flickered its answer.

These men frighten me. They are so different from those I have known.

Men are men, the fiery voice murmured. *These are simply less civilized than many, and yet they are the proudest on Hetar.*

Why must I be sacrificed to them? Lara asked, suddenly rebellious. *I shall hate it when they touch me. I already do! I shall feel nothing! It is the only way I will survive.*

No! You must feel everything, for to understand passion and to control it you must know it most intimately, Lara. Your faerie blood will protect you, believe me.

What is it they want of me? And why me? she begged the guardian of the crystal.

You will know when the time is right. You will find a true friend here, one of the best you shall ever have, Lara. That friend will reveal all you need to know when you need to know it. Why do you refuse to understand that you are protected?

By whom? Lara pleaded desperately.

By me, the voice said softly. *By those who arranged for your creation on the body of a faerie woman by a young human warrior. You will serve us in a special way, and then we will serve you in gratitude for the remainder of your life, which I can tell you will be a very long one. Tomorrow night the Forest Lord brothers will take your virginity from you. Accept it. Learn what they can teach you, for though they are rough and crude they possess the rudimentary skills of lovemaking. Do not fear the pleasure you will experience at their hands, Lara. You need to know it, and you were never meant for an ordinary life as an ordinary woman. Now, sleep, child. You will need your strength in the days to come.*

Are you my mother? Lara asked.

Nay, you know I am not, the voice from the crystal flame replied.

Then who are you?

One who loves you, came her answer. *You know my name. I am Ethne.*

And with the words echoing softly in her head Lara fell asleep, and slept until the sun was well up the following morning. She opened her eyes to see the dappled sunlight coming in through the leaves outside of her window. She felt both well rested, and strangely calm. She had never spoken so familiarly or at such length with the guardian flame in the crystal before last night, but then her life until just a few weeks ago had been quiet and predictable. She had never considered that she was growing up, and that her life would have had to change in some way. She had assumed that despite her father's poverty someone would have her to wife, and she would go on as she always had, but serving a husband instead of her father. She sighed, and rolled over to gaze out the small window at the green leaves blowing in the summer breeze, the patches of blue sky beyond them. Then resigned, she arose, and pulled a clean gown on over her chemise.

Going into the dayroom she discovered her tray from last night was gone, and in its place was another with a thick slice of brown bread, a wedge of hard yellow cheese, a hard boiled egg and a peach. There was also a carafe of clear spring water to drink. She ate, and then opening the window of the chamber, leaned out to see what she could see in the light of day. The air was warm, and the scent of the Forest was fresh and entirely different from the smells of the City. But she could see naught but leaves. Turning, she looked about the room for something to do. She was bored, and the thought of spending the entire day penned up here was not a pleasant one. Exploring the room she discovered a trunk full of Enda's clothing, much of it in need of mending. Didn't his bride-to-be keep his clothing in good repair? She slammed the trunk lid shut. In desperation she took some of the water from the carafe, and her bathing cloth, and cleaned the two little windows in the two rooms.

In midmorning the door opened, and Belda slipped inside, finger to her lips in warning. She beckoned Lara into the bedchamber. "We can talk here," she said in a low voice. "I came for the tray, so I don't have a great deal of time. How did you come to remain here? Surely you were meant for a better place in life, Lara."

"For some reason I neither know or understand the Head Forester and his brother would have me. They paid Rolf Fairplay thirty thousand pieces of gold for me. The trader did all he could to discourage them, even saying I was meant for one of the Coastal Kings. But they were adamant, and would not be denied. But I do not know why they would pay such a sum, Belda."

The woman shook her head. "Truda says they mean to sacrifice you to one of their Forest gods because you are a high-born virgin."

"Truda is a fool. I am a mercenary's daughter, although my father is now a Crusader Knight. I have been poor my entire life. And tonight my virginity will indeed be sacrificed, but to no god—rather it will be sacrificed to the lust of both Enda and Durga. One does not spend that kind of wealth for a religious sacrifice, but let Truda think what she will," Lara said with a small smile.

"Durga has used her for pleasure already. She thinks that makes her special, and has tried to lord it over us, but Durga's wife, the lady Sita, slapped her for her presumption," Belda said. "Now I must go. I was to ask if you needed anything."

"Two things, if I might be indulged. A real bath so I may wash my dirty hair, and a needle and some thread to do some mending," Lara told Belda. "I am not used to being idle, and I am bored."

"I'll tell the lady Sita. They are not bad, these Forest folk. I'll be back if I can," Belda promised, and picking up the tray, left Lara alone again.

To Lara's surprise, however, Belda returned shortly, bringing with her a small basket containing needles and thread. "The lady Sita sends you this with her compliments. She says she must ask her husband and lord Enda if you may bathe, for you would have to be escorted to the bathhouse."

"Do they all live in the trees?" Lara asked Belda.

"Nay, only the few lords among them. There is a village below, but you could not see it from the caravan. The trees are like the great walls of a town, or the City." Then she hurried from the room again.

Lara went to the trunk, and pulling out the most damaged of Enda's garments, set to work repairing them. The day did not seem so dull now as she sat by a window for light, plying her needle industriously. By late afternoon she had finished the worst of his clothing, and was making minor repairs on the rest of them. She did not hear the door to the chamber open and close, and jumped at the sound of his voice.

"What are you doing? Are those my clothes?" Enda asked her in a hard voice. "Where did you obtain your sewing supplies?"

Lara looked up, calmer now. "You could not expect me to remain here all day without something to do. I found your garments, and asked the woman they sent with my meal for needle and thread. She returned with this basket and the lady Sita's compliments. Surely you are not displeased with me? I would have thought your betrothed wife would have done this, but perhaps you have not asked her."

"Tira is the daughter of a great family like mine. She does not do slave's work," he answered Lara. Then he picked up one of his shirts, examining it carefully. "This is very good work. I cannot see the stitches," he complimented her.

"Thank you," Lara told him. "I am glad if I have pleased you, my lord."

"There are other ways in which I would have you please me," he said drawing her into the circle of his arms.

"And so you shall, my lord, I have not a doubt," Lara said. "I am told I am a good student. I hope I shall prove worthy of your teaching." She looked up at him but briefly, and then down again, her dark lashes set off by her fair skin, and in vivid contrast with her hair.

"I have not your skill with words, my fair slave girl, but I shall teach you better ways to entertain me. That little tongue of yours will soon discover other talents than speaking cleverly." He tipped her face up to his. "I am told you would bathe."

"Aye." His deep brown eyes were very beautiful, and even mesmerizing. *Do not fear the pleasure,* she heard the echo of the crystal guardian's voice.

"You look clean enough to me," he said.

"I am used to bathing regularly," she told him. "At least several times a week, my lord. And my hair is filled with the dust of my travels."

"If I take you to the bathhouse I will remain to watch you," he replied.

"It is your privilege, my lord," she answered sweetly.

"Are you always so amenable and mild-tempered?" he wondered.

"Not always, my lord," Lara said.

"Are you not in the least fearful of losing your virginity tonight?" he demanded.

"I am anxious, aye," she responded quietly. "What virgin is not? But it is a natural thing, which must happen to all girls, mustn't it? It is a part of life, my lord. You have said you mean me no harm, and so I have hope that you will be patient and gentle with me." She gave him a faint smile.

"My brother and I love differently. That is why I have insisted upon being the first with you," Enda said. "I will be gentle, and I will be patient. I have great hopes of you, Lara. But Durga is a bull of a man. He is likely to be rough and impatient with you in his lust. But remember, I will be by your side, too, and after tonight he must wait several months again before I will share you with him."

She wanted to ask why he wanted her. Why his brother wanted her. Why they would share her body between them. But he had already warned her away from the subject, and even her crystal guardian had said it was too soon for her to know all. She looked up at him, her green eyes unwavering. "May I have my bath, my lord?"

He nodded. "Yes, come, and I will take you," he said. Then grasping her small hand in his larger one he led her from his rooms, and from his brother's great hall. They descended the winding stairs, but this time they stopped at a small landing, and he led her down another flight of steps that went around the huge tree until Lara found herself in a pretty village. The houses all blended into the landscape. They were wood with thatched roofs, which she recognized from her grandmother's description of country houses. In the central square was a great stone fountain where women were even now drawing water. They looked briefly at her as she passed with Enda. Finally they arrived at a square stone building.

"Og!" Enda shouted. "Where are you?"

"I am here, my lord," came a voice, and a huge creature shuffled from the dimness. When he straightened himself up, Lara gasped. He had to stand at least six cubits tall. "How may I serve you, master?"

"Stoke the furnace up. My new Pleasure Woman would bathe herself," Enda said.

Og shuffled away, bending to pass beneath the stone archway.

"I have never seen a creature like that," Lara admitted. "What is he?"

"The last of the Forest giants," Enda told her. "They have served us for centuries." He drew her down upon a stone bench. "He will tell us when your bath is ready." His hands began to fondle her breasts. "I am told a maid's breasts grow with loving," he said, and brushed her lips with his. "Tira has almost no breasts at all. I shall have a great deal of work on my hands," he chuckled, "to give her pretty tits. You, however, have two nice little fruits about the size of summer peaches. I shall attempt to grow them to nice large apples by autumn." He undid her gown, and slid his hand beneath her chemise, touching her skin with easy fingers. "Do you like it when I touch you, Lara? You must not be afraid to tell me what pleases you as I tutor you in passion." His thumb rubbed a nipple, and he smiled as it puckered. "Ah, you do like it, don't you?"

She hid her face in his shoulder. His hands were invasive, but it was exciting.

"They say daughters are like their mothers. If that be true then you will have a deliciously licentious and lascivious faerie nature. They say faerie women enjoy humans because they are more passionate. Is that so, my girl?" he murmured in her ear, nipping the lobe, and licking at it seductively as his fingers tightened about her breast.

"I do not know, my lord," Lara half gasped. "I have never had a lover." Why did her blood feel like it was beginning to boil?

"No, little virgin, you haven't, have you? But tonight I will instruct you in the joys of passion. You are going to like it, I promise you."

But to what purpose, Lara wondered once again, and then she sighed, which seemed to please him greatly.

"The water is growing hotter by the minute, my lord." The giant, Og, had returned. He seemed able to stand within the bathhouse, but for the arches.

"There is soap? Drying cloths?" Enda demanded as he loosened his grip on Lara, and drew his hand from her chemise.

"Everything is as you would have it, my lord," the giant replied.

"Then get out, and do not return until you are certain we are gone. Go and ask for food at my brother's hall. Tell them I said you were to have it."

"Thank you, my lord, you are generous," Og said, bowing, but Lara heard the hint of sardonic rebellion in his voice. The giant withdrew from the bathhouse.

"He sleeps here," Enda said. "It is the only place in the village large enough for him. Come!" He led her into a room with a great stone tub in the floor. "Take off your garments, but do not enter the water until I have had my fill of looking at you."

Lara complied with his request, feeling shy, but refusing to show it. Enda and Durga had seen her naked when they had inspected her, but that was somehow different. She slipped slowly from her gown and chemise, standing quietly beneath his gaze.

He stared hard, and then said, "The hours until I can couple with you will be long, Lara. Get into the water, and do what you must." He sat down on a single stone bench in the bathing room, and watched as she bathed herself thoroughly. He almost wept at the beauty of her body, and the long hair she now washed. Even dirty, it was glorious.

When she had finished she said quietly, "Would you not like to bathe, too, my lord? I have been taught by my stepmother how to wash a man."

He couldn't resist, stripping his clothing off so quickly she had no time to look at his masculine attributes, but she noted that his arms and legs were hairy. Well, she thought, soon enough she would be most familiar with them. He slid into the warm water and placed himself in her capable hands.

He would have never admitted it aloud, but this custom of the City's was a most enjoyable one. Her soft hands moving the washing cloth over his shoulders, his back, his chest, was not simply pleasant, it was seductive as well, although he could see she was working hard not to entice him.

"I'm going to wash your hair," she told him, and before he might protest she did just that. And then she washed his face, his neck and his ears as well. "There!" she said finally. "We are done, my lord." And she climbed swiftly up the tub's steps, and wrapped herself in a drying cloth, while holding one out for him.

He entered it meekly, and sat quietly as she dried him efficiently. Then he watched as she dried herself off, and toweled her long hair damp.

"I'm sorry you must wear dirty garments," she said. "Mine were clean this morning. I should have thought to bring some. Next time, then." She handed him his clothing while quickly donning her own. "Did you like it?"

"I did, and Durga will be most jealous when he learns of this interlude. But then, if he had come with us he would have not been able to restrain himself, and would have taken you upon the floor. But we will bring him next time, eh?"

"It is your right to command, my lord, and mine but to obey," Lara responded.

Enda laughed. "Why is it I sense you are not as meek as you pretend?" he asked her. "But I shall soon teach you that a man is the master." He caressed her beautiful face with his hand. "And when I have taught you the beginnings of passion, I shall make you beg me for the pleasures a man and woman can give one another when his manroot is buried deep in a woman's hidden garden." Then he yanked Lara into his arms, and kissed her surprised mouth hard. "Tell me you want me," he groaned.

"Not yet," Lara heard herself say, and wondered where the answer had come from. She was amazed at her calm in the face of her situation. She felt an odd strength filling her, and knew that she was indeed protected, as the guardian of the crystal had told her.

"Tonight you will," he said curtly, ashamed to have shown her even the slightest moment of weakness. What was the matter with him? This faerie girl was intoxicating, and he began to wonder if they had not made a mistake in purchasing her. "Come," he said. "I must return to my brother's hall, and you to my rooms. You will not yet be allowed to speak with our women."

Back in the dayroom Lara found her supper waiting. She had been given a portion of broiled trout, a ham slice and a roasted capon's wing. There was bread, and cheese, and another peach. And wine, a large carafe of it. She ate everything and drank sparingly. Then, finished, she washed her hands and face, and cleaned her teeth. Removing her clothing she climbed into the large bed. She instinctively knew he would want her naked, and she had few garments as it was. Tonight she could hear singing from Durga's hall. She finally fell asleep, only to awaken at the sound of a footfall in the other room. She heard wine being poured into the silver goblet that had arrived this evening with her meal.

Enda entered the room and slowly pulled off his garments, folding them neatly and laying them upon the chair. Then he moved to the hearth and added some fuel to the fire. Lara noted his buttocks were nicely rounded and firm. Finally he turned to her, pausing to allow her a full measure of his manliness. Men's bodies, Lara decided then and there, had not the beauty of a woman's. Enda was big-boned, as were all the Forest people. He walked to the bed and, lifting the coverlet, climbed into it, reaching for her as he did so.

Lara tensed as he pulled her atop him so that their bodies were matched breast to breast, belly to belly, thigh to thigh. Her flesh seemed to melt into his hardness. She swallowed hard as a big hand caressed her from the nape of her neck to her buttocks, but she was unable to restrain the shudder that overcame her. The touch was so possessive.

"Easy, girl," he said softly as if he were speaking to a frightened animal. The hand encircled her bottom slowly, slowly, slowly. "That's right. Get used to your master's touch. Be good, and you will be rewarded." The hand fondled her again.

Just as she was getting used to it, his two hands clamped about her slim waist and lifted her up just enough to put his face in the narrow glen separating her little round breasts. She felt him breathe deeply, inhaling her scent. Then raising his head, Enda deliberately licked the flesh between her breasts. Lara's eyes widened with surprise, and when he shifted her position just slightly to clamp his mouth over a nipple, she felt her heart skip a beat.

The brown eyes stealthily observed her every little reaction. He suckled on her nipple and was rewarded with a startled gasp. He sucked harder, his teeth gently worrying the tender nub of flesh, and she cried out softly. She was utterly charming in her surprise. He released his hold on her breast and quickly rolled Lara onto her back within the curve of his embrace. "Did you like that?" he asked her.

She hesitated, but then remembered Ethne's advice. "Aye," she admitted. "I did."

"There is more to mating than the coupling," he told her, "although with Durga you will simply be mounted and used. My brother is not a subtle man. I, on the other hand, find women who enjoy passion more enjoyable as lovers. Durga does not understand why the slave women prefer my attentions to his, except for women like Truda, who think by lying beneath him they can gain power and status for themselves."

"But they cannot," Lara noted quietly.

"Of course not. She is not of the pure blood," he answered her. Then he tipped her face up to his, and kissed her. "How clever of you to see it so clearly, and so quickly, Lara." His knuckles grazed her cheekbone. "Now enough talking, girl. If we do not get on with this business of deflowering you soon Durga will be here, and eager for his share." He kissed her harder now.

He was the first man to ever kiss her, Lara thought. She let her mouth kiss him back, tasting him, sensing the rising desire in those kisses. What would it be like to love and be loved? she wondered briefly. Then she put the thought from her mind. Love was a luxury available to a very few, if indeed it even existed. It was not her fate to be loved.

Enda now rolled Lara beneath him, growling in her ear, "Open your legs for me, girl! I am almost ready to have you."

Obediently she spread herself for him. This much she understood, for Susanna had explained it. She felt his fingers playing with her most intimate flesh, which sent a bolt of sensation through her. What was this? Susanna had said nothing of reciprocal feelings, but perhaps she was not allowed to speak on such things. The tingling in her nether regions made Lara uneasy, and she squirmed restlessly.

"Ahh, yes, girl, you are almost ready for me." The fingers swirled expertly between her nether lips, playing with the sensitive nub. He half rose, putting her between his two sinewy thighs. He leaned forward, moving carefully toward his ultimate goal.

Lara watched him, fascinated, through half-closed eyes. The play of emotions across his face was most revealing. She sensed the tip of his manhood touching the entry to her body, felt him pushing his manroot into her, stopping, and then with a cry of undisguised triumph bursting through her maidenhead to fill her entirely. Lara cried out, for the momentary fork of pain caught her off guard. She struggled to unseat him, scratching and clawing at him even as the pain subsided quickly and was gone.

Enda caught at the dainty hands that fought him, pinioning them at her sides as he found his rhythm, and began to pleasure himself within her tight sheath. He groaned with his enjoyment, relishing her compactness as he was filled more and more with hot desire. Never had a woman given him such delight. He actually wept with the feelings consuming him, and realized he craved far more of her than he had any right to want. He brushed her lips tenderly, and was startled when their gazes met.

Lara looked at this man laboring atop her, and for a brief moment she felt sorry for him. His need for her seemed so genuine and so desperate. She didn't understand why. "Free my hands, my lord," she whispered to him. "Tell me what to do."

He released her immediately. "Put your arms about me, and close your eyes," he instructed her in a tight voice.

She did, drawing him down against her breasts, her fingers caressing the back of his thick neck. With her eyes closed she was more acutely aware of him inside her. She sighed and, catching his rhythm, matched it. He told her to wrap her legs about his torso, and when she did so she felt him slip deeper. She began to gain a certain pleasure herself now that she was no longer afraid or in pain.

Enda could not hold back any longer. She was too delicious, but he hadn't had enough of her yet. Still his juices exploded forth with a ferocity that left him breathless, and Lara, surprised at another revelation Susanna had not mentioned. But when he collapsed upon her, she held him as she would have held a fretful baby, and in that moment Lara understood the power that women held over men. Men might think whatever they chose to think, but in the end women would rule the day. She almost laughed aloud. To take a man between your legs was nothing at all.

Finally his breathing grew normal, and he rolled off of her. "You show promise," he said to her.

"I am glad if I have pleased you, my lord," Lara told him dryly.

"I must summon Durga now," Enda said. "He will want his share of you tonight before I may have you to myself again. Do not let him frighten you. He will be rough, and he will be quick if he is up to his usual form." He laughed as he arose from the bed.

She lay quietly as he left the room, returning several minutes later with his older brother.

Durga viewed her with contemplative lust, his piggy black eyes bright. "Has she washed your scent off of her?" he demanded of his sibling.

"She will do so now," Enda said. "I arose from her body immediately to fetch you, brother." Reaching out, he pulled Lara up from
the bed.

She hurried to the hearth, where the bowl of warmed water and
a cloth was waiting. Susanna had advised her to always wash one's
private parts after passion. She winced, however, as she bathed herself, amazed at the amount of blood that had been shed in the taking of her virginity. When she turned back to the bed she found
both men were already in it. Durga had drawn off his clothing, and
she saw that while he was a big man, he did not run to fat. Lara approached the bed slowly.

"Hurry up, now," Durga snapped. "I've waited for you long
enough, I think." Reaching out he yanked her atop him. "Sit up now,
faerie girl, and let me play with your titties. They have a ways to
grow, but they're the prettiest I've ever seen!" His two big hands
sat her up and grabbed at her breasts, crushing them and making
her cry out.

"Gently, brother," Enda said, laughing. "Lara is a delicate little
creature, not like that big healthy cow, Truda, you've taken to
your bed."

"Truda knows how to give a man a good ride," Durga answered.
"You should try her sometime. She can suck a manroot better than
any I've ever had."

"I think I'll keep my little faerie girl for a while," Enda replied.
"She gave me much pleasure tonight, and will give me more when
you have had your turn, brother."

"All right, wench," Durga said, looking directly at Lara, "the time
has come for you to give me a bit of that same pleasure." He removed her from his torso, and put her on her back. Then climbing
atop her he lifted his engorged manroot to her eyes, and pushed it
between her two breasts, closing his eyes for a long moment.
"What do you think of this one?" he demanded of her.

Knowing she was expected to comment, Lara said, "'Tis a very
fine manroot, my lord. Quite different from the lord Enda's."

Durga laughed heartily. "Aye, mine can split a girl in two, and leave her wanting more than she ought to have." And he roared with laughter once again. Then withdrawing himself from between her breasts, he pulled her beneath him, and without another word thrust hard into Lara's body, groaning with delight at her denseness. His black eyes closed, a look of rapture blooming on his face as he pumped her vigorously over and over again.

She had not been ready, but he hadn't cared. Didn't even notice. All he had wanted was her body for his pleasure. At least Enda had made the experience a pleasant one. But Lara knew what was expected of her with this man. She cried out as if she were actually enjoying his attentions. She wrapped her legs about him, whimpering. But she felt nothing but anger at his cruelty.

With a roar and a howl he released his seed into her body. For the briefest moment he lay atop her, crushing her, but then he arose. "She's good, brother, and with your careful schooling she will eventually be perfect. I've had my fair taste, and I wish you much enjoyment of her. You may have her to yourself for the autumn, but come the winter I will want her again. But I am willing to share as we have this time. Good night." And gathering up his few garments he left them to find Truda, for if truth be known, it was Durga this night who wanted more than he ought to have.

Lara arose and bathed herself again. She was sore now, and where Enda had taken care with her, Durga had left her feeling dirtied. Returning to the bed she lay down, and waited for Enda to claim her again.

Instead he said, "Sleep now, Lara. I will stay with you, and later I shall have my pleasure of you again." He rolled away from her, and was quickly asleep.

She was surprised, but grateful. She doubted he would be as thoughtful in the nights to come, but this was tonight. She reached for the crystal to reassure herself. *Well it is done,* she told the guardian silently.

Yes, it is done, Ethne returned as silently, and the flame flickered. Lara closed her eyes and slept.

When she awoke she could see a sliver of light coming through the leaves outside the window, and Enda was covering her face with his tender kisses. "You wish more pleasuring," she said quietly, looking at him directly. She supposed he could be called handsome. He was tall, and big-boned, his skin ruddy from being outdoors. Durga, however, was stockier and shorter than Enda, although just as big-boned. And Durga's features could not be called pretty by any means, though his black beard was attractive. His dark eyes were small, and his nose large. Yet they had the same mother. It was curious, Lara thought.

"Aye," he agreed, "but first you need a little bit of soothing. Open your legs for me, Lara," and when she had he slid between them. Drawing her nether lips apart with two fingers, he let his tongue begin a journey of exploration about the coral shell of her womanhood. He licked her slowly, first the inside of the lips themselves, and then moving deeper into the more hidden regions of her body.

Lara murmured with surprise at his actions, but it was so nice, and he was soothing her newly opened flesh. The pointed tip of his tongue swirled gently about the opening to her sheath, and her eyes closed to better savor the sensations he was now arousing within her. She was almost purring. The tongue touched the sentient nub within her flesh, and began to tease at it. She moaned and moved restlessly as her body grew hot, and she experienced a longing she had never before felt. She could feel her own wetness as the nub tingled.

He raised his dark auburn head, his brown eyes glazed with his desire for her. Then slowly he moved his big body up and over her, his manroot sliding into her smoothly in a single motion. And then he lay quiet. "Do you feel me within you, Lara?"

"Aye, I do, my lord." He seemed thicker and longer than he had earlier.

"Tell me," he murmured hotly in her ear.

"You are hard," she whispered. "Harder and bigger than before. I feel the heat from you. I am almost afire."

"You are beginning to experience passion," he told her, "and you could not have a better teacher, my little faerie girl, for I am a master of passion. Tonight I shall begin teaching you all you must know to please me, and thereby any man you take between your legs. But now I must release my lust for you for it but weakens me." He began to move on her, and shortly she felt him filling her with his seed again. And when he had finished he arose from the bed they had shared, gathering his garments. "Remain in bed to rest," he told her. "I will send a woman to you with food and water."

"I want to bathe again," she said.

"Will you do this every day?" he asked her, amused.

She nodded. "I like being clean, and I can smell both you and your brother on my flesh. Besides, I am more pleasant for you when I smell fresh." She gave him a small smile.

"I will tell the woman she may escort you to the bathhouse," he agreed, and then was gone out the door.

Lara slept, awakening when Belda entered the bedchamber calling her name.

"I have brought you something to eat. Gracious! That bed looks well used."

Lara slid from beneath the coverlet. "I am well used, and the prize of my virginity gone in the night," Lara told her, stepping from the bed.

"You bled heavily," Belda said, pointing. "Was he pleased?"

"Well satisfied, and his brother as well," Lara replied.

"Both of them?" Belda's eyes grew wide. "You poor girl!"

"First the lord Enda, and then his brother who came, conquered and departed. Lord Enda is not a bad sort I suppose. He was not unkind last night when he breeched me, or this morning when he took his fill again." Lara pulled on her chemise. "He says I may go to the bathhouse."

"Aye, so I was instructed by the lady Sita. Do you want to eat first?" Belda inquired. "I've brought a meal."

"First I need to get the stink of those two men off me," Lara told her. She picked up her cloak and started for the door. "Have you see the giant, Og, who lives in the bathhouse? Lord Enda says it is the only place other than the out-of-doors where he may stand up." She followed Belda down the stairs through the hall and outside.

"They say the Forest giants were servants of the Forest Lords until some plague wiped them out. Og was an infant, and the only survivor," Belda said. "Imagine an entire race being extinguished like that. Poor fellow must be lonely."

They hurried through the village which was busy this morning. Lara noticed that some of the women pointed toward her, and others made signs as if to ward off a hex. Reaching the bathhouse they went inside where Og greeted them, bowing low.

"The lord Enda sent ahead to say you would be coming, lady," he said.

"I am Lara," she told him. "A Pleasure Woman, and nothing more, Og. Please call me by my name. And this is Belda, a slave woman."

"The water is hot, Lara," Og said to her, and he smiled a sweet smile. He had very light blue eyes, and short cropped red hair. "Go in, go in."

"I'll come back for you," Belda said. "Do you know how long you will be? The lady Sita doesn't approve of idleness, and so I must return to the hall now or be punished."

"Perhaps a half an hour," Lara said. "I washed my hair last night."

"I'll tell my lady, and someone will return to escort you back," Belda said, and then she hurried out.

Og ushered Lara into the bathing room, and then withdrew, closing the great oaken door behind him. Alone now, the girl shed her enveloping cloak, slipped out of her chemise and stepped down into the water, pinning her hair up as she did. It was hotter than last night, and perfect to take the soreness from her body. With a sigh she closed her eyes. The worst, she hoped, was over, although she still didn't understand what it was they wanted of her. After a few minutes Lara stepped onto the lower step of the tub and, taking up the washing cloth, dipped it into the stone jar of soft soap. She washed herself thoroughly, removing the soap with the rinsing shell by the bathing tub's edge, and then returning to soak for a few more minutes.

Finally remembering that someone would be coming to escort her back to Durga's hall, she stepped from the water and wrapped herself in a large drying cloth. A long dull day stretched ahead of her, but at least there was more mending to do. She had not finished repairing Enda's garments yesterday, but she probably would today. And what would she do tomorrow, penned in those two rooms? She would ask him tonight for a little more freedom. Even in the City she had been permitted to roam. Pulling her chemise back on and covering herself with her cloak, Lara came from the bathing room. But no one was waiting for her. She sat down on a bench within the waiting room where they had waited last night for Og to stoke the fires heating the water.

The giant shuffled into the chamber, ducking his length beneath a stone arch in order to do so. "I would take you back myself, but they are very bound that things be done a certain way. Your desire for a bath has discommoded them. They will make you wait here to punish you."

"If they would permit me to speak with the lady Sita I could schedule my visits here to coincide with their tasks," Lara said.

"Yes," he agreed, "that would be the sensible thing to do, but the Forest folk don't always do things in a sensible manner. They have their traditions, their ways, and will change nothing. You are part faerie?"

"Aye, I am. And you are the first to understand that half faerie is not all faerie," Lara told him with a smile.

He chuckled. "If any of them had ever seen a real faerie they would know the difference," he told her.

"You have seen them?" Lara was intrigued.

"You must not tell," he said, and was suddenly frightened. "I should not have said it, Lara."

"I will keep your secret," she promised, reaching out to pat his huge hand with her tiny one. "I am good at keeping secrets. I thought the Forest Faeries were the allies of the Forest Lords."

"Once," Og said, "but no more. They work hard to keep that fact unknown lest any think they have lost their powers as the oldest clans on Hetar."

The door to the bathhouse opened, and Truda stepped inside. "I'm to escort you back to my lord Durga's hall," she said sourly.

"Goodbye, Og," Lara said, rising and following after Truda.

"Goodbye, Lara," he called after her.

Chapter 7

"YOU TALK with that dirty giant?" Truda wanted to know.

"He is the bath keeper," Lara said. She didn't want to talk to Truda.

"My master, lord Durga, came right to my bed from yours," Truda said. "You obviously didn't give him much pleasure."

"But you do," Lara answered sweetly. "I am glad."

Truda looked confused. She had just bragged on her allure, practically saying that hers was obviously greater than Lara's, and yet the faerie girl had simply agreed, and she had even been pleasant.

Lara could see the puzzlement on Truda's face. Good! She didn't want to speak with the woman to begin with, and now she had rendered her speechless. They climbed the winding staircase up the tree and entered the hall. "Thank you!" Lara told Truda cheerfully, and ran into the corridor where Enda's chambers were located. Safely back in those two rooms she opened the trunk, and took out the two garments that still needed mending.

Suddenly the door to the chamber opened, and a woman stepped through. "I am the lady Sita, Lord Durga's wife," she said. "I came to see if you were all right after your ordeal last night." She was a tall woman with sad eyes, but an air of command.

Lara arose, and bowed from the waist. "Thank you, lady, I am well. Tired, perhaps, but well."

"You are mending Enda's garments?" There was surprise in Sita's voice.

"I am not used to being idle," Lara told her. "That is why I asked for needle and threads yesterday. Thank you for sending them."

"I did not know Pleasure Women were able to sew," Sita replied.

"I am not a Pleasure Woman, lady. I was supposed to be, but I wasn't sold to a Pleasure House. I was sent to the coast. Virgins entering the pleasure houses have their first-night rights auctioned off, and not until after that night are they taught their craft. My father was a mercenary until he became a Crusader Knight at this last tournament just held in the City, and I helped my stepmother keep his house clean and his garments mended. I am just a girl, no more," Lara told her quietly.

"Then why did they buy you from the trader?" Sita asked.

"I do not know, but I believe it had something to do with the fact that I am half faerie. They seemed quite interested in that," Lara responded.

"Who told them that?" Sita said.

"The slave woman, Truda," Lara answered.

Sita nodded, and then she said, "You will tell no one of this conversation between us, girl. Do you understand me? Sometimes it is better a wife know things that perhaps she should not for the protection of her family."

"You are the mistress of this hall, lady, and I will obey you. In return I beg your permission to bathe at the bathhouse each day. It is my habit."

"You dare to bargain with me, girl?" Sita did not know whether to be angry or amused by Lara's simple request.

"Nay, lady, I but humbly ask your permission," Lara quickly said.

"Displease me, and you will die of your own stink, girl," Sita said by way of acquiescence. "You know that my younger sister will wed lord Enda in autumn?"

"Aye, lady, I do."

"And that Forest folk do not mix their blood with those of outsiders?" Sita continued.

"Aye, lady, I have been told."

"I will tell Enda you may come to the hall, then," Sita said, and turned to go.

"Thank you, lady," Lara responded to the retreating figure.

The summer came to an end, and all around her the Forest grew bright with color. The trees were dazzling in their brilliant display of hues. Lara had never seen such glorious shades of reds, purples, oranges, yellows, gold and russets. In the City, the vines on the walls of the Quarter had gone red or purple. The trees about the Great Square turned a pale yellow and their leaves were quickly gone, blown away in the winds that began to come from the north. Here, however, the display seemed to go on forever.

On the last night of the year Enda married his betrothed, Tira. The following morning their bloodied bedsheet was offered as proof of Tira's perfection. After that Enda spent part of each night with Lara, and the remainder of the night with Tira. Lara did her best to stay in the background as much as possible. Having discovered her skills at sewing, Sita saw that all mending needed by the household was brought to Lara for repair, and she was grateful to be busy.

Enda and Tira had not yet moved into their own hall. It would not be ready until the spring. Lara caught Tira staring down at her several times from her place at the high board. The look was filled with venom. After it had happened for the third time, Lara began taking her meals from the hall and retreating to the two chambers, which were now hers. One evening Durga caught Lara by the arm as she attempted to make her escape with some bread and cheese.

"Why are you departing the hall, faerie girl?" he asked her roughly.

"My lord Enda's wife does not like me, and I would not disturb her," Lara said.

"She hates you," Durga said with a grin. "She is young, foolish and jealous. She knows her husband gains more pleasure between your legs than hers. Go on, then." And he released her arm, still grinning.

That night as Enda pushed himself eagerly into her he said to Lara, "Are you not with child yet, Lara? I have seeded you almost every night for the last four months."

"Why would you want a child with me?" she asked him candidly. "You Forest folk do not mix your blood with outsiders. I have been told it often enough. Seed your wife as vigorously as you have me, and you will have a fine son."

"But I want you to give me a child, my faerie lover," he murmured low in her ear. "If you do not, Durga will take you into his bed and he will seed you vigorously until his child grows in your womb." He held her hips firmly in his two hands, and pumped her until she was crying out with the pleasure they had come to share.

"I don't understand," Lara moaned, wrapping her legs about him. She had come to crave the pleasures their bodies could give one another.

"You don't have to understand. You have but to obey me," he told her, thrusting hard and smiling wolfishly at her whimpers. The rumors had been right. Faerie women were the finest lovers on the face of Hetar.

After he had left her Lara took up her crystal. *Why does he crave a child of me so badly when the Forest folk do not mix blood?* she demanded of her guardian.

Ask the giant, Og, and tell him that Ethne says he may speak the truth to you, the guardian of the crystal replied in her silent voice.

In the morning Lara went to the bathhouse for her daily ablutions. She was now allowed to go alone, as she had shown no desire to escape the Forest folk. Og was expecting her and greeted her with a smile. He was her only friend now that Belda and the other slave women with whom she had come—except for Truda, alas—worked in other halls. Few spoke with her, and then rarely.

"The water is hot, Lara," he told her.

"We must speak where we cannot be overheard," Lara said softly.

He nodded, and led her into the bathing room. "I expect no others, for they are afraid to come when you are here," he told her.

"They fear the faerie," she said, resigned.

Og grinned. "Fools," he said. He always spoke freely with Lara though with others he answered their queries but simply, or with a grunt. Many thought him a lackwit.

"You see the crystal I always wear about my neck," she began, and he nodded again. "It was put there by my mother. See the flame within it. That is my guardian, Ethne. She says you are to speak the truth with me and answer all my questions, Og."

"Ethne?" A smile lit his face. "Aye, I will answer as best I can, Lara."

"How do you know her?" Lara queried him.

"She is part of my own history. I knew Ethne as a little one," he told her.

"Why does Enda want a child of me when the Forest folk do not mix their blood with that of outsiders, Og? For that matter, why did he and Durga buy me?"

Og sighed. "It is a long and tragic tale I have to tell you, but you will understand when I have finished. Many years ago the Forest was ruled by the ancestors of these men who now people it, the giants who served them and the faeries of the Forest who were the Forest Lords' allies in everything they did. Durga's grandfather was Head Forester then. One day in the autumn a group of his men were out hunting. They had spent the day chasing the most beautiful roe deer any had ever seen. They should have known better, for the deer wore a jeweled collar about its neck. It was obviously magic. The day was coming to an end when the beast was finally cornered in a clearing.

"As they prepared to shoot it with their arrows it turned from a roe deer into a beautiful faerie woman. Seeing her, their lust for the hunt became a lust for the faerie woman. She laughed at them, mocking them for being so foolish as to follow her the day long.

Now, she said, they would go home to their halls empty-handed. Madness ruled what happened next. The hunting party attacked the faerie woman, who was weak from having sustained another's shape all day. She could not fight back. Each of the men had his way with her, and when they had finished they killed her, taking the beautiful jeweled collar she had worn about her neck back to their Head Forester. The faerie woman's body they left lying where they had violated and murdered her.

"That same night as they sat in the hall of the Head Forester bragging on their day, Maeve, the faerie queen appeared. She demanded justice for the slain faerie from the Head Forester, but he refused. The faerie woman had taunted his men all day through the deep Forest in her guise as a roe deer. It was one thing, he said, for the faerie to amuse herself for a short while with the hunting party, but she teased them the day long, only revealing herself when she was finally cornered. And then she did not offer an apology, or give them another deer in exchange to take home for their trouble.

"Instead she mocked them and called them foolish. She flaunted her beauty before them. The faerie woman had gotten what she deserved, the Head Forester told Maeve, and it should be a lesson to all of Maeve's people to cease their torment of the Forest Lords with what they called playfulness. There was no justice to be rendered.

"The faerie queen was very angry, but the faeries of the Forest had been such longtime allies of the Forest Lords she hesitated at first to destroy that alliance. 'At least return the bejeweled collar,' Maeve asked the Head Forester, but before she might even finish her thought the Head Forester cried out that he would not. He had given the collar to his wife. It would serve as a forfeit for his hunters' wasted day. 'Then give me the lives of five of your hunters in exchange for the faerie woman's death,' Maeve said to him, blood for blood. The faerie woman was young. She was foolish, but she has paid a terrible price for that foolishness, Queen Maeve reasoned, attempting to hide her anger, trying to retain the alliance between the faeries and the Forest Lords.

"But the Head Forester remained adamant, his wife by his side smirking, fingering the collar about her neck. Maeve offered the Head Forester a month's time in which to rethink their difficulties, but he told her no amount of time would ever make him reconsider. What was done was done. The faerie queen could restrain her anger and her outrage no longer. She pronounced a curse upon the Forest Lords that has been their secret shame ever since. No one on Hetar knows it, but me, and if they knew I knew it, I should be slain like all my kind who once lived in this Forest," Og said gravely.

"What was the curse, and why were the giants slain? I was told they died in a plague." Lara was fascinated, but Og's story still did not explain why Durga and Enda had paid such a high price for her, or why they even wanted her.

"You know how proud the Forest Lords are of their heritage. How they claim to be the oldest of the peoples on Hetar. How they do not mate with outsiders. Maeve's curse on them was one that can never be lifted. She raised her hand that night and said that never again would the women of the Forest clans bear children. Neither sons nor daughters. If they wished to continue to exist they would have to mate with outsiders in order to gain the sons, and those sons would be forced also to mate with outsiders in order to reproduce. The daughters they created would be either rendered infertile, or able only to birth females. Their proud and pure bloodlines would disappear in the next centuries until all trace of who they really were would be gone from Hetar.

"And then Maeve, the faerie queen, pointed a long finger at the wife of the Head Forester. Almost immediately the collar about her neck began to tighten until the woman was strangled, and died. Maeve then stretched out her hand, and the collar flew into it even as she disappeared in a clap of thunder from the hall," Og concluded.

"How terrible!" Lara said softly.

"It was but the beginning," Og continued on. "All the women who had been carrying children in their wombs at the time Maeve cursed the Forest clans either miscarried or bore dead infants. And no matter how vigorously the men of the Forest seeded their women, no children of pure lineage have been born to them since. After several years the Forest Lords were forced to admit the curse was real. At first they sought for the faeries themselves in an effort to have the curse lifted, but they could not find them. The men of the Forest began to mate with outsiders, and suddenly their halls were filled with children once more.

"The mothers of these children were kept alive only until the children were weaned from their breasts. Then they were slaughtered, and buried deep in the Forest. The children were raised by the wives of their fathers, and only learned the truth when they came to manhood and needed to reproduce themselves. It has been a fearsome secret to keep, but kept it they have. No one knows. They import women as household slaves, but they are actually used for breeding purposes."

"That is why Durga didn't want little Noss!" Lara exclaimed. "He asked her if she had linked with the moon yet, and she said no. It was then he refused to have her, making such a great fuss, and Truda in her effort to please him exposed my existence to the Forest Lords."

Og nodded. "Truda is growing a big belly," he told Lara. "I overhear much, for few pay a great deal of attention to me," he chuckled. "Now I shall tell you something else I overheard. I know the reason they insisted on purchasing you, Lara. They believe if they can get children on a faerie, they can expunge the curse Maeve put on them."

"But I am only a halfling, and besides, there is no way I could ameliorate a curse placed on them by a faerie queen. I know nothing of magic. My faerie mother deserted my father and me when I was only a few months old. I am said to look just like her, but I know nothing of her world, Og."

"She thought enough of you to give you a crystal guardian," the giant noted, looking down at his young companion. "Let me tell you something of her world. As the daughter of a faerie woman, you have all her powers, although you have not known it. You are not with child yet, are you? Yet it is said that Enda comes to your bed almost every night. I know why you are not with child—you do not want his child, and a faerie woman never gives children to those she does not love."

"They do not know this, do they?" Lara said.

"Nay, they don't. There is much they do not know. My kind served the Forest Lords for as long as memory allows, yet they slew my people. When they could not find the faeries of the Forest they sent the giants to look for them. When we could not find them, they set about killing us, for we knew their secret and they would not have it revealed.

"I was in my mother's belly at that time. Her name was Oona, and she managed to flee into the deepest part of the Forest where she bore me. We lived in a cave and saw no one but the beasts. It was there I met Ethne. She is not a faerie, but a faerie spirit. It was she who told me what my mother did not—that all giant memory is passed on to their unborn children in the womb. That should I ever fall into the hands of the Forest Lords I was to pretend to be innocent of all that had passed before my birth. And when I was four years of age they found us. They killed her, but me they spared for before she died she told them I had been born but four years prior.

"I was brought back here and raised in Durga's hall, although in those days it was his grandfather's hall. When I became too large to live in the hall I was given the bathhouse to attend, and to live in. I am small for my kind, they have told me."

"Poor Og," Lara said, taking his huge hand in her own two, and giving it a little squeeze. "What a terrible life it has been for you, having to pretend ignorance, and yet knowing so much. I wish there were a way in which I could help you."

"It is I who must help you," the giant replied. "Winter is coming, and if you are not with child by winter's end, Durga will wonder why."

"Perhaps he will sell me into another province? They do not know I am privy to their secret. Certainly they will want to recoup their losses as best they can," Lara said.

"Durga, but that he is considered the eldest of his clan, would be sweeping out horse stalls," Og said. "His family has always ruled the Forest. It is his right, but he is a stupid man. If you fail him he will be angry, and if he becomes angry he is just as apt to slay you as his grandfather's men did that poor faerie woman seventy-five years ago."

"But not yet," Lara said.

"No, not yet," Og agreed.

"I must bathe quickly now," Lara told him. "They will wonder why I have been gone so long. Go now, and we will speak again."

The giant nodded, and left her.

She washed herself quickly, then hurried back to the hall. Truda was seated by the fire, and seeing Lara beckoned her over. There was no way to avoid the woman and so Lara joined her, holding out her hands to warm them. Truda's belly was very obvious, and her pride in her condition was irritating.

"Where have you been?" she demanded of Lara.

"It is not your place to question me," Lara told her, "but you surely know I go to bathe each day at this time."

"You were gone longer than you have been in the past," Truda said.

"The water was very hot, and I am chilled to the bone these days. I remained to soak, and it felt wonderful. It is almost time for the Winterfest," Lara replied. "The City was not as cold as it is here. Do you not feel it?"

"I feel nothing but the kicking of my son in my belly," Truda responded proudly. "My lord Durga is a vigorous lover, and I am a fertile field for his potent seed. You will see soon enough, as his brother does not seem to plow as fine a furrow with you. My lord Durga says he will be visiting you soon for shortly I shall be unable to accommodate his lusty nature." She smirked at Lara.

"It shall be as the Celestial Actuary ordains," Lara said sweetly. "If I am meant to give one of these Forest Lords a child, I will. But will they not favor my offspring, with its faerie blood, to that of a slave woman?"

"You are a slave, too!" Truda said angrily, her hands going to her belly.

"But I am special, being half faerie," Lara taunted her wickedly. And then she turned, and went down the dim corridor to the sanctuary of her rooms. Stepping inside, she was shocked to find Durga there awaiting her. Her heart began to beat nervously. "My lord," she greeted him.

He arose from the chair by the hearth where he had been sitting. "You smell sweet," he said. "Are you just come from your bath, Lara?"

"Yes, my lord," she replied. Her hands by her side were balled into fists, her fingernails digging into her palms.

He took a step toward her, and Lara instinctively backed away. He smiled wolfishly, and reached out for her before she might evade him again. Drawing her against his chest he said, "I desire you, faerie girl. I am a man of vast appetites, and the big-bellied bitch in the hall can no longer be mounted lest I endanger my son. You belong to me as well as to Enda, and he is gone for the next few days on a hunting trip. While he is gone you will open your legs for me."

"Does my lord Enda know you do this?" Lara asked him.

Durga smiled, but it was a cold smile. The fingers of one large hand dug into her scalp, and he yanked her head back. "Yes!" he said. "And do not ever dare to question my actions, faerie girl. I am master in this hall, and you are my slave." He pushed her against the door to her bedchamber. His hands reached down, sliding beneath her gown to cup her bottom. He lifted her up, commanding her, "Put your arms about my neck, and your legs about my waist, Lara," and when she obeyed, afraid to do otherwise, he released his grip on her a moment, lifting his tunic up to release his manroot, which he then pushed into her with a smooth, hard thrust. "Now, faerie girl," he said, his hands cupping her buttocks once more, "you are going to be well used, and thoroughly seeded by the hour of the evening meal."

Lara was in shock. Enda had always been gentle and thoughtful with her. She was even learning to gain great pleasure in their passion. Durga, however, was a hard man, and a cruel lover. He ground into her brutally, making her whimper with each thrust of his loins. She thought of the faerie woman Og had told her about today, and realized that this is how the poor creature must have felt as she was violated. Her head slammed against the bedchamber door as he pushed into her again and again. And then it was over. With a roar he released his seed into her and lowered her to the floor. Lara's legs buckled, and she would have fallen but Durga caught her up in his arms and, kicking the door open, brought her into her chamber, and laid her on the bed.

"I'll get you some wine, faerie girl, and then we will begin again," he told her, going back out into the day room. When he returned, Lara had managed to seat herself on the edge of the bed. He handed her the wine. "Drink it all down, and then get out of your gown, Lara. I don't want you damaging your clothing for you have little enough."

She swallowed the wine almost eagerly, relishing the fact that it burned her throat as it meant she could still feel something. He took the goblet from her when it was gone, and she stood up, disrobing slowly, her fingers all thumbs as she undid her laces. She laid her gown aside, and pulled off her chemise.

"On your back now, faerie girl," he ordered her, and as she lay upon her bed she saw that Durga had also disrobed, and was now quite naked. She trembled, to her surprise. It was unlike her to be fearful of these men, but the tale Og had imparted to her earlier made her realize how dangerous the Forest Lords really were.

He was a big man, his hairy arms and legs like the thick tree trunks in his Forest. His chest was massive and broad and covered in wiry dark curls as was the area surrounding his manroot. He climbed into the bed and pulled her up into his arms. His fingers tugged the pins from her long gilt-colored hair. "It's like thistle-down, faerie girl," he complimented her. Then his hand patted her mons. "It matches the pretty curls you have grown back since you came to us." A finger pushed between her nether lips to find her jewel. He began to play with it gently. "You should have begun a child with my brother by now, Lara. Perhaps his seed is not as po-tent as mine. Perhaps he weakens it going between two women at night. My seed is fertile. I will plant your hidden garden fully and well in the next few days. You will ripen with my child, faerie girl."

"I am not some animal to be bred!" Lara cried out, finally find-ing her voice.

"That's exactly what you are, my pretty faerie girl. You are a sweet beast to be bred." He pushed two fingers into her, moving them vig-orously, then withdrew them. "Almost ready," he noted. "Has Enda taught you to play with his manroot yet? I expect not. He gets lit-tle joy out of it, but I enjoy it. Take it in your hand, Lara. Fondle it gently. Tickle the seed sacs beneath it. They are filled with life!"

She took him in her hand, afraid to disobey him. He made a sound halfway between a growl and a purr, praising her skill and encouraging her onward. Her fingers moved beneath his manroot to tickle the seed sacs. They were almost icy to her touch. She fon-dled them in her palm, restraining her urge to squeeze them so hard they would pop.

"That's it, girl," he said approvingly. His hands fondled her young breasts, squeezing them tenderly, pinching the nipples sharply so that she squealed aloud. He laughed saying, "Such pretty little ap-ples, faerie girl. Now, on your back!" And he dumped her from his lap onto the mattress. "Put your hands above your head now." His dark head lowered, and he kissed her breasts and her belly, his bushy black beard scratching her delicate skin. Then without another word he was atop and into her, thrusting and withdrawing as he panted with his exertions.

Lara closed her eyes. *A sweet beast to be bred.* She would not be bred, for she wanted no child of this man, or his brother. But neither her beauty nor her faerie blood would save her from their revenge if they chose to kill her. She had to get away from the Forest Lords before they grew suspicious of her. But how? And where could she go that she would not be branded an escaped slave? She shuddered, and Durga took it for passion rising in her and redoubled his efforts on her body until finally he cried out loudly, satisfied for the interim.

"By the old Forest gods, faerie girl, you know how to give a man pleasure," he told her approvingly. Then he arose from the bed. "I'll send some supper for you, but rest, for tonight I will share your bed until the dawn. This brief interlude has but whetted my appetite for your sweet faerie flesh." He pulled on his clothing again, and left her.

For the first time since she had left her family, Lara cried. The human side of her was showing itself at last, after months in which her faerie blood had allowed her to be as hard as nails. It had aided in her survival, but with Og's tale today she was only too aware of her precarious position within the realm of the Forest Lords until she produced the desired child. She needed to speak with Og, but she dared not leave the hall again today. And the night loomed long and dark ahead. She rose from her bed and washed herself clean of his juices, but his scent still clung to her body. The tears kept coming until finally she fell into a fitful sleep.

It had been early afternoon when she dozed off, but the sun had been already setting, for winter was upon them. Lara awoke in darkness but for the scrap of flame in the bedchamber hearth. She scrambled up and fed the fire until it was blazing again, then dressed, went into the dayroom and repaired the fire there. A tray had been set on her table, and as the food was hot she guessed that the footstep of the servant delivering it had awakened her. Everything smelled delicious, and she found she was hungry. She ate everything on the tray, and then began to drink from the carafe of sweet wine. She was going to need it to sustain her courage in the hours ahead. When Durga finally entered the room, she was able to muster up a small smile, which pleased him greatly. But the night was a long one.

In midmorning when Lara was finally able to rouse herself from her bed, she dressed quickly and fled the hall for the bathhouse.

"What is the matter, Lara?" Og demanded, seeing her lovely face with its tearstains. "What has happened to make you weep? Faeries rarely weep."

She told him, the tears coming again, and to her surprise he lifted her up, and cradled her against his shoulder. It was an incredibly comforting gesture, and leaning her golden head against the giant's shoulder seemed to renew her strength. "You can put me down now," she said finally, and he gently set her on the floor.

"How typical of Enda," he said scornfully, "to go off without telling you his brother would come to your bed. He is the more beautiful of the two, but he has less character. They are unique, you know, for they share not only a father, but the same mother as well. Before Durga was weaned from her teat and given to the lady Ida, the slave who bore Durga managed to lure his father into her bed again, and conceived Enda. I think she had discovered what was happening, and tried to save herself that way. Of course, they killed her after Enda was weaned. Her master never visited her bed after Enda was born."

"Poor girl," Lara sympathized, "but for Enda to go off and not tell me what to expect was more than unkind. It was cruel!"

"It was," the giant agreed, "but typical. Enda is a beautiful weakling. Durga is a crude fellow, but he is proud of his family, and desperate to maintain the fiction of their heritage. For centuries, each of the clans in the Forest have only intermarried with one other family. The bloodlines have never varied. They were becoming very inbred, and in a way, Maeve actually did them a kindness. But Durga and his generation have only a quarter pure Forest blood in them. Their children will have less. They know it, and fear if their secret is revealed they will be considered weak enough to be attacked. Still they maintain the old ways, and keep to their traditions and customs. But times change, Lara, and nothing remains the same forever, even if we might wish it so," Og said. "I had thought you would be given more time, but Durga has always been an impatient man. You must escape the Forest, and very soon, I think."

"I will be considered a runaway slave," Lara said.

"Nay, for the law gives you some small protection. Once you have crossed the border into another province without being caught, and can live free for a year and a day, you are legally free, Lara. The only place to which you may not return in safety is the Forest or the City. But live free a year, and you can return to the City."

"But if I cannot return to the City now, where can I go?" she queried him.

"Ask Ethne," he told her with a smile. "She is your guardian and your guide. Now, you must bathe before they wonder why you are gone so long," the giant said with a smile. "Ethne will have some of the answers that you seek, Lara."

"Ethne once told me I should find a good friend here in the Forest. I believe that friend is you, Og. You must come with me. I cannot go without you."

"I have often thought of travel," Og said. "I am told there are other races of giants on Hetar, but I have always been afraid to probe my memory too deeply for fear of what I would find. Perhaps now I should. I owe the Forest Lords nothing."

"We must make a plan," Lara said.

"The best plans are those carefully considered," he advised her. "I know what you must bear now can only be difficult, but if we are hasty, we could fail, and that would be far worse."

Og was right, of course, and Lara knew it. And now that Durga was certain that he could satisfy himself on her body at will, Durga came only in the night to grunt and strain over Lara. But her life grew no easier. Enda's bride, Tira, was open in her hatred. Truda, her belly growing larger by the day, could scarce contain her jealousy. Even the soft-spoken Sita avoided her unless there was no other choice.

Enda returned from his hunt six days later. He brought a great deal of game with him, and was welcomed joyously. Now the hall's larder was full for the long winter ahead. Lara was mending a piece of clothing when he swaggered into her chamber and, sweeping her into his arms, kissed her heartily.

"Did you miss me?" he demanded with a boyish grin.

"I had no time with your brother between my legs every night," she returned angrily. "You could have told me, my lord!"

"But you knew he would come eventually," he attempted to excuse himself. "He owns you, too. I thought it a good opportunity as I had to be away, and his woman has a big belly now. Did you please him?"

"He thinks your seed too weak," Lara said cruelly. "He says you have rendered it impotent running between your wife and me, which is why I remain barren while Truda burgeons with his offspring." She smiled, but it was a cold smile.

He slapped her hard, and Lara's head snapped back. "Be careful, faerie girl," he warned her. "If you do not continue to please me you could become a Pleasure Woman in the hall, servicing any man who desires you."

"It would be a most generous gesture, my lord, considering the price you and your brother paid for me. More than generous," Lara said, ignoring the stinging in her cheek. "You would probably do better to sell me and recoup some of your loss."

"Never!" he snarled. "You will continue to be seeded by both my brother and me until you produce the child we desire of you, or I will kill you with my own two hands. I will share you with my brother, but no other, Lara."

Lara said nothing more on the subject, nor did she bait him again; but turning away from him, she concentrated on her sewing once more. Enda slammed from the room angrily, and she did not see him again until the evening meal. He came into the hall arguing with his wife, and Tira, spying her rival, gave a shriek of outrage.

"You went to her first! I am your wife, but you went to the Pleasure Woman first! I will not stand for it! I will not! How dare she come into the hall when I am here?"

"Be silent, Tira, you do not understand," Enda said.

"No, I do not! I want my own hall, and when I have it I will allow none of your Pleasure Women in it. My sister may put up with it from your brother, but I am not Sita!"

Lara gathered up her food and quickly exited the hall. Obviously Enda's wife was not aware of the situation regarding the Forest Lords. Until she understood, she would accept no child of another woman. Behind her, Lara heard Tira cry out in pain, and the slap of flesh against flesh. Tira was being beaten for her rebellion. Poor girl, Lara thought. But even she knew enough not to argue with a man in a public forum.

Each night from then on both Durga and Enda came to Lara's bed. The two men took turns using her until they all would finally fall asleep. At first she hated them, until the night she realized that they bored her in their competition to get her with child. After that she lay placidly thinking of her escape, moaning now and again, thrusting up to meet their downward rhythm, and they were content with her.

The Winterfest was coming, but there had been no snows yet. A Winterfest without snow was unusual, but they prepared for it anyway. Og had reasoned that the night of Winterfest would be a good time to make their escape. Durga and Enda would be celebrating with their wives, as Winterfest was considered a prime occasion for conjugal bliss. They had already told Lara she would be left alone, and should seize the opportunity for rest. She thanked them, and wished them good fortune with their wives that night.

"If one of your men should come to my chambers, shall I allow them in?" she asked innocently.

"No!" Both Durga and Enda spoke with one voice. It would be unthinkable if Lara was successfully seeded by one of their clansmen when she had not been seeded by one of them. "And all will be told you are off-limits to them. You are to rest. The winters in the Forest are long, and we will want you to ourselves," Durga said.

Lara gave them a smile. "I am grateful for your kindness, my lords."

"At least there is no snow on the ground now to show the direction in which we go," Og told Lara. "I will carry you so we may make better time. You are lighter than a feather, my faerie friend."

"Where will we go?" she asked him.

"I am not certain yet. There are faeries yet in the Forest, although I am not certain where. But perhaps it would not be wise to seek them out. We could flee to the Midlands, but then we are caught between there and the City, where you could be reclaimed by the Forest Lords. I think we have but two choices. We must either go into the Desert realm of the Shadow Princes, or into the Outlands. Perhaps Ethne will advise us if you ask her."

"My father used to tell me that the Outlands are a dangerous place, filled with war and tribal rivalries. The Outlanders are not civilized at all. I will ask Ethne, but I think we must go into the Desert. I am sure we can find shelter and work. You are strong, and I can earn my bread with my sewing. We will survive, Og."

"Lara, you are far too beautiful to go unnoticed. You will not have to survive as a seamstress. One of the princes is certain to favor you, and want you for his lover."

"I will never be a slave again!" Lara said fiercely.

"The women who give pleasure to the Shadow Princes are all free," he told her. "The Shadow Princes want no woman who does not come to their arms willingly."

"How do you know this?" she asked.

"My people have traveled Hetar for centuries, and learned many things. I have known them all since my first moments in my mother's womb," he explained. "We have nothing to fear from the Desert peoples, Lara."

"How do they live there?" she said.

"The common folk live in tents, and travel the surface of the Desert trading with the caravans that pass through. The Shadow Princes live in great palaces carved from the tall Desert rocks. They raise horses."

"How will we cross the border without being caught?" she wondered.

"The road is not the only place to cross the border," he told her with a wink.

THE HALL of the Head Forester was decorated for Winterfest with pine branches and holly. Outside in the clan villages, great piles of wood were raised for the bonfires that would be lit at the exact moment of sunset. The fires would burn high and strong until the dawn, when they would be extinguished with the sunrise. There would be feasting, dancing and drinking the night through. Songs of the old days would be sung, and scarce a girl of marriageable age would be left untouched. For a full week before, the women in the hall cooked and prepared for Winterfest.

Og revealed to Lara their method of escape on the day the Winterfest dawned. "You must not go through the hall tonight, for you must not be seen at all," he said. "You are slender enough to get through the window in your bedchamber. Climb onto the great tree branch outside of that window. I will guide you to the branch below from where I may pluck you down. I will put you into a pouch on my back, where you will be safe and hidden. No one will pay a great deal of attention to me, if indeed they even notice me in all the celebration. With my long stride we can be over the border before moonset. Dress warmly, and eat as much as you dare without attracting attention," he advised her.

Durga came to Lara's chamber in early afternoon, but he had not come to couple with her. Neither he nor Enda would touch her until Winterfest was over and done. By ancient tradition, husbands seeded only their wives during Winterfest, and among the

Forest clans tradition was always observed. The Head Forester had come to tell Lara to bar her door from her side of the chamber. "I will bar it from the outside as well. It will not be opened until tomorrow, when I come to tell you that I have unbarred my side," he said. "Go to the hall now before sunset, and fetch the food and drink you will need, faerie girl. I likely will not come until midday tomorrow, as I will eat and drink well tonight—and of course, seed my wife as much as I can, which I think you know will be many times." He leered at her wickedly. Then giving her a hearty kiss and smacking her bottom, he went off laughing.

She did not see Enda, to her relief, when she went out to fetch her food and drink for the next day. Lara filled her tray with as much as she dared, knowing she could claim Durga had told her to as she must remain in her chambers. Placing the food in her day room she returned to the hall, seeking out Sita to ask if there was any mending she might do while she remained locked away.

"You must not work during Winterfest," Sita said quietly. "Tradition dictates it is a time of celebration. You look tired, faerie girl. Eat and rest, for the winter will be particularly long for you until you bloom with a child." She appeared almost sympathetic, Lara thought.

"Thank you, lady, for your kindness," Lara told her. "And I wish you a joyous Winterfest." She gave Durga's wife a small smile and then returned to her own quarters.

Darkness fell quickly that day, and the moon would not rise until late. From her windows through the bare branches Lara watched the red-gold sunset, and then the fires began to spring up as if the light had been transferred. Soon Lara could hear the singing and carousing from both Durga's hall and the village below. She ate what she could, and wrapped bread, cheese, apples and pears in a napkin which she tied up carefully. Next she transferred the wine from her carafe into a water skin that Og had given her. She dressed herself in all three of her chemises and gowns, tucking her pearwood brush into the pocket of her cloak, which lay across the foot of the bed. As an afterthought she added her sewing implements. Then she lay down to rest, and slept for several hours until she was awakened by the sound of pebbles being thrown at her window. Rising, she went to the window and opened it.

"Og?" she called softly.

"It is time, Lara," his voice whispered back.

"A moment while I gather my things," she said to him.

"Hurry!" he returned.

She had barred her door earlier when she heard Durga outside fitting a great timber across the portal from his side. She had noisily turned the lock, and set the small iron bar into place, hearing his grunt of approval as she did so. Now she quickly donned her cloak, strapped the wineskin across her chest, and gathered up her packet of food. Opening the window she called down to Og to catch her pack so her hands would be free to climb. Then she dropped the shawl, hearing his grunt as he caught it.

Carefully, Lara climbed out onto the thick wide branch, her only light coming from the fireplace in her bedchamber. Turning slowly, she pulled the window shut behind her. Then following Og's whispered instructions, she inched out upon the branch, remembering not to look down. The giant instructed her to sit down upon the branch, and to her relief, she felt the tree limb below her feet, as sturdy as the one above. She stood upon it, and moved out upon the second branch. Her heart was hammering, for it suddenly occurred to her she could easily be killed if she fell. She stopped, frozen.

"Just a few feet more, Lara," Og encouraged her gently.

She forced herself forward again. Praise the Celestial Actuary that there was no wind. The night was very cold, however. Above her the black skies were filled with twinkling stars. She thought for a moment how very beautiful it all was, and then she heard Og instruct her to sit down carefully on the branch. Lara did, and immediately she felt him pick her up. She was set down in the pack on his back, and she smiled to discover he had lined it with furs, and there was a fur robe to keep her warm. Her pack had been set there, too. Lara undid the strap of the wineskin, and laid it aside. Her quarters were not commodious, but there was enough room to be comfortable.

"Are you settled?" he whispered to her.

"It's lovely!" she told him.

"Then we are off!" he said. "Remain quiet, Lara, particularly if we are stopped."

But they were not stopped. Og moved quickly and quietly from the vicinity of Durga's hall and its village into the deep Forest. He carried a small lantern with him to light his way, carefully avoiding the villages of other Forest Lords and the Winterfest fires that blazed in some of the more remote locations. Finally the full moon arose, and he put out the lantern, hanging it on the wide leather belt he wore around his tunic. His stride was great, and halfway between the darkness and the dawn he exited the deep woods, finally reaching the scrubland of the border. He had kept off the main track, and now the ground beneath him became more sandy. Around him, great dunes began to arise.

Deep within the pack, Lara lay sleeping. She was warm, and felt safe for the first time in months. The rhythm of the giant's steps lulled her, and although she had meant to stay awake she couldn't. When she finally did awaken she reached instinctively for the crystal about her neck. *Ethne?* she whispered softly.

I am here, the guardian of the crystal answered her.

What will happen now?

You will simply continue your journey, Ethne responded. *It is yet the beginning.*

When will my journey end? Lara asked.

When you have completed it, Ethne told her. *Do not ask foolish questions of me, child.*

How will I know when I have completed my journey? Lara persisted.

You will know, Ethne replied, and the flame flickered, and grew dim again.

"Og," Lara called. "Are we free of the Forest yet? It seems the air is growing warmer. I have thrown off the furs."

"We are already in the Desert, Lara, and it is almost dawn. I am seeking a place for us to shelter, for the day will be hot. I believe there is an oasis up ahead. Remain safe within my pack for a bit longer," he advised.

She took his advice because as long as she remained his passenger, he was able to travel faster. She had never seen a Desert, and did not know what to expect, but it was certainly getting hotter with each step he took. She had never before felt such heat, but after the damp winter's chill of the Forest she could not complain.

"Ah, there is the oasis up ahead. There will be shade and water for us," Og said. "Or so at least my memory recalls."

"Are there people there?" Lara asked him.

"I don't know," he answered her. He took several more steps, and then they were there. "I am going to lift you out now, Lara," he told her. "I shall set my pouch down so you may exit." Carefully he undid the buckles that had secured the pouch to his big body, and then he gently set it upon the ground.

Lara stepped forth, blinking in the startling daylight. She looked up. The sky above was a clear bright blue. There wasn't a cloud to be seen. The sun shone down upon them hot and fierce. The trees around them were tall with rough-barked trunks, and leafy green fronds; they were nothing like the trees she had seen before in either the Forest or the City. There was also a small pool with a waterfall, which she thought amazing in the midst of all this barrenness. Looking further, she espied a stone well at the oasis's center. And then turning, Lara gazed beyond the border of strange trees. An endless sea of sand stretched before her. There wasn't a living soul to be seen anywhere but for her, and Og.

Chapter 8

"IT IS BOTH BEAUTIFUL and frightening," Lara said softly. Above her, a hawk soared.

Og nodded slowly. "I have the knowledge of what the Desert is from my collective memory," he noted, "but like you I have never before seen it. It has great majesty, but I sense it can be dangerous. I think because of the sun and the heat we would do well to rest here during the day, and not travel until the night. Perhaps we should remain here until we can learn what phase the Desert moon is in, for it will not be full as the Forest moon is now. We have food, and if the well is not dry, we have water, too." He walked over to the stone edifice, and lowered the bucket.

Lara heard a splash as the bucket reached water and watched as Og tasted the liquid in the returned bucket. "Is it sweet?" she asked him.

"Aye, we are fortunate," he told her.

"Why is it no one lives here?" Lara wondered aloud.

The giant shrugged. "The Desert folk wander part of the year, and the other part of the year they live at the foot of their princes' castles. We must find a settlement in the next few days before we run out of food. I doubt there are many oases such as these. We will not be as fortunate when we leave here."

"Perhaps we'll find a village, Og. Or we could walk across the Desert into another realm," Lara suggested brightly.

"Beyond the Desert is the Outlands," he told her. "It is the most dangerous place on Hetar with no form of government, or laws. The people there have loyalty only to themselves, or perhaps their clans or tribes. You have said yourself that it is very uncivilized. I don't want to go there, nor should you."

"What if we have no choice?" Lara asked him.

"Pray the Celestial Actuary that we do," the giant told her.

"Search your memories, Og. If there are giants in other provinces of Hetar, perhaps there are giant clans in the Outlands as well."

"Aye, there are giants there, too, but I will not speak of them," he replied. "Are you hungry, Lara? You have not eaten since last night."

"Are we far enough into this Desert not to be caught?" she asked him.

"We are many leagues from the hall of the Head Forester," he reassured her. "Even if they rode out at sunrise today, they could not catch us for several days, and we are well into this kingdom."

"We have no papers," she said. "What if we meet a caravan?"

"We are a giant and his mistress traveling through the Desert," Og said. "And there is no caravan. This oasis is off the main track. Now I shall set up my pack as a tent for you to shelter from the sun, lest your fair skin be burned. We will eat and rest. Perhaps you would like to cool yourself in the pool by the waterfall." As he spoke he emptied out the knapsack in which Lara had traveled the previous night. Several wooden poles had been used to give the pack its shape. Og removed them, and used them to make a shelter. He hung Lara's wineskin, and spread the furs tanned side up for a bed.

"I am going to seek what wood I can find, and any dried fronds from the trees. We will burn them tonight in a fire to keep any beasts away," Og told his young companion. "See the ring of stones there? Others have made fires here."

The sun was growing hotter. Lara coaxed Og to cease his work, and come into the tent. He could not stand in it as she could, but he was able to crawl in and sit, provided he kept his head low.

Lara fed them from her small stash of food, and Og surprised her with several loaves of bread he had managed to secrete for himself. They drank a little of the wine to assuage their thirst in the heat of the day, and then lay down to sleep. When they awoke, it was early evening. They were hot, and Lara felt a headache coming on.

"I can't swim," she told Og, "but I can cool myself in that pool. Come with me, and enjoy the water, too."

"If I went into that pool," he chuckled, "I fear I would cause all the water in it to flow out. But I will certainly soak my feet."

Together they walked to the little pool, and Lara waded in up to her neck, sighing with delight, for the water was indeed cold. She had earlier removed the extra garments she had worn on their escape, and now wore just a fine cotton chemise, which would dry quickly enough in the hot Desert air. The bottom of the pool was soft yellow sand, and she scrunched her toes in it happily. In her entire life she did not think she had felt so free, and she smiled at Og, who sat on the edge of the pool, a look of bliss upon his face as he soaked his feet in the cold water, lifting a hairy leg now and again to let the waterfall splash over his feet, ankles and shins.

The hot air dried them swiftly, and as night began to fall the air grew first cool and then almost cold. They were glad of the furs in the tent. They ate the remainder of Lara's bread and cheese, and finished her wine. Og lit the fire by simply pointing a finger at the kindling and saying, "Fire light!"

"How on earth did you do that?" Lara wanted to know.

"All giants have certain abilities," he remarked. "The Forest giants can light fires by just pointing and commanding. How do you think I heated the water for your daily visits to the bathhouse? We must take turns keeping watch, Lara. I will take the first shift, and awaken you in several hours."

"Why do you need to watch?" she asked him. "Do you think Durga and Enda will come after us?"

"Nay, but there are wild animals here in the Desert. Now get some rest, Lara. Soon it will be your turn to watch."

She lay down in the makeshift tent to sleep. She had never known such quiet and such peace. Not even the Forest had been so silent. She was safe, she knew, as Og sat cross-legged before the fire singing softly to himself. Lara's eyes closed, and she slept a dreamless sleep until Og gently shook her shoulder to awaken her for the watch. Drowsily, she arose.

"I have built up the fire, and there is no wind tonight," Og said. "The Desert moon is high in the sky. Awaken me just before it sets," he instructed her.

Lara sat by the fire, and soon the air was rent by the sound of the giant's snores. She grinned and then grew serious, considering the day she had just lived through. At this time the previous night she had been in her chambers in Durga's hall. Now, if Og was correct in his estimation, they were many, many leagues away from that hall, and from the Forest. He had told her that each step he took was a full league, and he had traveled many hours once they left Durga's realm. When had they discovered her missing, she wondered, and what had they done? Had they discovered Og missing yet, or just dashed off seeking her? Knowing Durga and Enda, they had mounted up, and with their men, gone racing off to find her. It would not be until they discovered Og missing, too, that they might realize that Lara was with the giant. But Og had encountered no one since leaving Durga's village. It would not be known in which direction they fled.

Suddenly Lara heard the faintest of rustles in the growth by the pool. She stared hard into the darkness. "Is someone there?" she asked softly, but there was no answer, and she was surrounded by deep silence again. In the sky above her the copper moon was in its first quarter, and a shadow of cloud moved swiftly across it. She shivered briefly, hugging herself with her arms. Then laughing softly at herself for being foolish, she turned back to the warm fire. A rat, most likely, she decided, come to drink from the water of the pool.

In the darkness the man stared quietly at the beautiful maiden. She reminded him of a faerie, but she could be only part faerie, because there was also something very human about her. He had seen her but briefly from the air this morning, and wondered who was camping at the oasis of Zeroun. It was well off the beaten track, and her giant companion would have to travel almost an entire night to reach a settlement. Drawing his cloak about him the man became invisible and quickly slipped into the tent where the giant lay snoring. Bending down, he murmured into the large fleshy ear, "Go north tomorrow evening. By dawn you will reach safety. Remember, north. The great constellation, Belmair, will guide you." Then he departed the tent, and was gone. Og stirred restlessly, but did not awaken.

Lara nodded by the fire, half asleep now. The shadow gently placed more wood upon the blaze so it would not go out, and then disappeared into the darkness. Lara started awake. She had no idea what had roused her, but everything seemed to be fine. The fire was burning high, and she could hear Og's snores coming from their tent. She smiled, thinking how wonderful it was to be free of Enda and Durga. What foolishness to believe having children of her body could end a curse placed upon them by a faerie queen! She had no magic, although Og said she merely lacked the knowledge of how to use it. But if she were interested in this alleged magic, who would teach her how?

She was glad for the fire, and surprised that the night had grown very cool. After the heat of the day she would not have thought it. She watched the quarter moon make its journey across the skies. She had now seen three of Hetar's four moons; the pale blue moon of the City and the Midlands, the light green moon of the Forest and finally the copper-colored Desert moon. She had heard that the coastal moon was a warm butter-yellow. Of course, in the Outlands, one could see all four moons at once—but each shone a silvery white on that side of Hetar. The moon before her was now ready to set. Rising, Lara went into the tent and wakened Og.

He rose sleepily, giving her a warm smile. "You will sleep again," he said. "We will remain here today, and then tonight we will go north. I think we will find some sort of settlement to the north." Crouching, he shook out the furs for her.

"How can you travel so far with each step you take?" Lara asked him, laying down again. "Your legs are long, but certainly not long enough to go a full league with each step that you take, Og."

"It's my magical boots," he said. "I asked Durga's grandfather, who found me in the Forest, if I might make myself some boots. I was only eight at the time, and had been barefoot all of my life. I told him my feet grew cold in the winter months, and if I lost my feet I should be of no use to him. He liked having the only surviving Forest giant for his own slave, and so he said he would have boots made for me, for what would a boy know of making boots? I was grown when he finally died, and without anyone else's knowledge I then made my own boots according to the knowledge I inherited from my people. No one noticed that the boots I wore were different. I walk normally, except when I tell the boots they must walk a league. Then my stride lengthens, and I can cover great distances," he explained.

"Why didn't you run away before?" Lara wondered.

"There was no reason to," he told her.

"But the Forest folk were not kind to you, Og," Lara protested.

"Nay, they were not, but they were all I had, faerie girl. For better or for worse they were the only family I possessed," he told her. "But now you need me. You are young, Lara, and you have no idea of the powers within you. Until you learn how to access those powers, and use them wisely, I must be there to protect you. In my mind's eye I remember the faeries of the Forest. Your mother was surely one of them. The Forest giants were the faeries' allies. It is my duty to keep you safe for this part of your journey. Eventually you will not need me, but now you do."

She smiled up at him. "I want you with me forever, Og," she told him, and then closing her eyes, she fell asleep. She did not see the love he had for her in his pale eyes.

Lara slept until the afternoon. Og had slept beneath the shade of the palm trees near the pool. He woke to see Lara entering the water. She splashed about, calling to him to put his big feet into the water again and cool them. He did, smiling down at her. They ate a loaf of the bread he had taken, and an apple each. They filled the empty wineskin with cold water from the well. Og took down the makeshift tent, reconstructing the knapsack once again. He replaced the furs, but this time with the tanned sides up. Lara had repacked her few possessions in her shawl. She would use her cloak tonight if she felt cold. Og's remaining loaves and Lara's apples went into the knapsack along with the skin of water.

"Ready?" Og asked her, and when she nodded he picked her up and set her back into the knapsack before strapping it on his shoulders once more.

"Which way did you say we would go?" Lara called to him.

"North," he answered. "I just have the feeling that we will reach a village of some sort if we travel north tonight."

"By the morrow?" she wondered aloud.

"Mayhap, but if not, the next day. If we have not found a settlement by the time the sun is high," he told her, "I will set up the tent, and we will just sleep the day away. We have enough water for several days if we are careful."

Og walked across the Desert all the long night. He used the great star, Belmair, which was always in the northern skies, as his guide. Within the safety of her transport, Lara did not sleep for she was more than well rested. She lay on her back looking up at the black skies with its twinkling stars, and then as the stars faded, the copper-colored moon. As the night began to wane Og saw great cliffs rising up from the Desert floor ahead of him, and at the bottom of the cliffs, a settlement of black tents. He was vastly relieved.

"Lara," he called to her, "we have found some sort of civilization, but I would have you remain hidden until I am certain these people are friendly. It is not quite dawn yet, and I see no one stirring. I will sit down and wait." He sat down atop a sand dune.

"Very well," she answered, "but please don't be long. I want to get out of this sack and stretch my legs."

"There seem to be some shepherds stirring," he told her. "I will ask them who is their leader," Og said.

The shepherds gazed openmouthed at the giant, but they were not afraid. It was rare that strangers came into the Desert, for there was nothing in the Desert of any worth. No valuable ores, or gemstones. No fertile fields. It was a barren place where to the amazement of the traders and the Midland Merchants, beautiful horses were raised. How they did not know, nor did they care as long as they might purchase and resell the beasts at a great profit.

"I am Og," the giant said. "I am peaceful. Can you take me to your headman? I would ask his permission to pitch my tent among yours."

"I am Umar," a young man said, coming forward. "My father is headman here. I will take you to him."

Og followed Umar, who introduced him to his father, Zaki. Og made his simple request of the headman who asked, "How will you earn your bread, Og? We are simple folk, and have naught to spare for the idle."

"I carry my mistress in the sack on my back," Og said. "She is a fine seamstress, and I can bear heavy loads for you. We ask no charity."

"Then pitch your tent on the edge of the settlement," Zaki told Og. "We can use your strong back."

"Do you have a prince?" Og inquired.

"Of course," Zaki said. "He is called Kaliq, and his palace is in the cliffs above our settlement. He will not mind you joining us.

He is a good man. You are a Forest giant. I had heard all your kind were dead."

"They are. I alone represent my race," Og said.

"What happened?" Zaki asked curiously.

Og shrugged. "It was before I was born. My mother survived into my childhood, but she never spoke on it. It made her too sad."

"Well, and I should think so," Zaki replied. "Go on then, and welcome," he said.

Og found a sheltered spot on the edge of the tent village and, lifting Lara from her place, he tipped the pouch out, and set up the tent once more. The settlement was beginning to stir now. Og examined the furs, and then took one of the fine robes.

"I'll trade this for some things we will need," he said, and hurried off. When he returned he had an iron cooking pot, several implements for setting the pot up over the fire, a large spoon, a knife, five cushions, a piece of cloth and a basket of food and spices for cooking. He was very pleased with himself.

While he had been gone Lara had made beds for them with the remaining furs, and set their belongings next to each mattress. She took the cloth he brought and strung it across the little tent to give the illusion of privacy. Settled, they sat down to dine on bread, new cheese and water from the oasis.

"I will now go out, and seek work for us," Og said. He returned with mending that the village women didn't wish to do, but that needed to be done. In just a few days Lara's reputation as a fine sewer spread. She did not venture much from the tent for fear that her beauty would be discovered. When she did go out she covered her gilt hair, and her face as well. The villagers considered the seamstress modest and respectful, and fully approved. But they were curious as to whether she was young or old, and where she had come from. Since she spoke to no one but her giant servant they could not ask. It was very intriguing.

Then one day, one of Prince Kaliq's servants came to Lara's dwelling, bringing with him a pale gray silk robe and a basket of fine threads. "My master wants to know if you could embroider this garment for him?" the servant said.

"I can," Lara replied, "but it will take time, for it is fine work. Is it for a special occasion? Is there anything he particularly wants in the design?"

"It is for the horse breeding festival in six weeks," the servant replied.

"Come back in a moonspan," Lara told the servant.

Og was delighted. "Your reputation for fine work is spreading. What will you design on the robe? Zaki says this festival is a very important one."

"I wish I knew what this prince looks like," Lara said.

"He will be blue-eyed and dark-haired like all the Desert people," Og responded.

Lara laughed. "I suppose it really doesn't matter," she said. "He will pay well if my work pleases him, and we will be comfortable for months. We might even purchase a real tent from the tent maker. His wife told me he has one that would allow you to stand up instead of always crouching."

Og chuckled. "Yet this old pack of mine has served us well, Lara."

"It has indeed," she agreed.

Lara thought for several days about the embroidery she would do on the prince's robe. To embroider horses on the garment in so short a time was an impossibility, she decided. So she embroidered a design on the back of the robe showing the black Desert cliffs beneath the copper moon, and on the front of the garment she embroidered delicate silver and blue stars in twin bands that ran from neck to hem. Around the wide cuffs of the robe she stitched a geometric design of black and copper. It was elegant, and most effective. Lara was pleased with herself.

When the servant returned after several weeks for the robe, he brought with him an invitation from Prince Kaliq. "You are invited to join the festivities, lady. A litter will come for you tomorrow," he said.

"I am a poor woman," Lara murmured. "I have no garment that would be suitable, and I would not have the prince think I do not honor him. But please thank your master for me."

The servant bowed, and departed with the embroidered robe. The following morning he reappeared with a packet which he gave to Lara. "My master sends you this." He bowed to her. "The litter will come for you in the midafternoon hour."

She unwrapped the packet. Inside was a simple sleeveless, round-necked garment made from an iridescent silk. Lara held it up, stunned.

"You will have to go now," Og told her. "They say these Shadow Princes are magic."

"Why are they called Shadow Princes?" Lara asked him.

"They are rarely seen, and are said to have the power of invisibility. They slip in and out of the mind easily, I am told."

"I need a bath," Lara said. "And my hair is filthy."

"I'll speak with Zaki," Og said hurrying out.

Why did Prince Kaliq want to see her, Lara wondered? It could not have been because he liked her embroidery, for he had not seen it when the invitation was issued. Nor had he seen her. Or had he? She recalled the noise that night at the oasis as she sat watch. Could he have been watching her from the shadows? Ridiculous! She had heard no horses, nor were there any footprints in the sand of the oasis other than hers and Og's. Besides, that oasis was leagues away from the settlement. He was probably curious because of Lara's caution in shielding her beauty from the people of the settlement.

Og returned. "Zaki says there is a pool of flowing water within a small cave at the foot of the cliff. You are welcome to bathe there, and his wife sends you this." Og handed her a small cake of soap. "I will stand guard, Lara, that you not be disturbed. You had best hurry if your hair is to be dry in time." He led her to the cave Zaki had showed him.

The cave was empty, but it was filled with a lovely blue light. Lara slipped into the water, expecting it to be cold, and gasped with surprise to discover it was quite warm. Delighted, she washed first her long hair, and then herself. Climbing out of the pool, she sat naked upon a flat rock, and dried her hair and body with a clean piece of cloth. She slipped back into her clean chemise, and wrapped her hair in the damp drying cloth. Then she covered her face, and hurried from the cave. "It was wonderful!" she told Og as they moved quickly back to their own tent. "The water was hot, not cold! And the light inside is clear and blue."

"You will just have time to dress," Og told her. "Remember that if you refuse his advances he will allow you to return here, and you will not be punished. The Shadow Princes do not force women into their beds. It is said they prefer mutual passion. Their women are all free to come and go as they please," the giant reminded her.

"What makes you think he desires me?" Lara said. "Perhaps the invitation is merely a polite one because I embroidered his robe. He can know nothing of me, or my beauty. He is simply curious to see the seamstress."

Og chortled. "He sent you a gown. It's just the right size, and it's lovely."

"It's obvious that I am a slender woman, even wrapped in my cloak," Lara said.

"No, he knows what you look like, I am sure," the giant said.

Lara slipped behind the curtain that divided her sleeping space from the rest of their little tent. She pulled off the chemise, and slipped the iridescent gown on over her head. It fit as if it had been made for her. Her young body glowed through the fabric. She could not wear a chemise beneath this garment, for the chemise was not cut in the same fashion—she was meant to wear nothing beneath the gown. To her surprise, a pair of simple sandals had been left next to the gown while she was bathing. Reaching for her pearwood brush she brushed the tangles from her long hair, and then plaited it into a single thick braid.

"The prince's litter is here," Og called to her.

Lara stepped from her private space. "I suppose I am ready," she said.

"You are beautiful!" he exclaimed. "This prince will fall in love with you without a doubt. He is a fortunate man." There was a wistful tone to his voice, but she didn't hear it, or see the sadness in his mild blue eyes.

"Love is an illusion. There is nothing more to it than lust or mutual convenience," Lara said quietly. "If he desires me, and I him, we will couple, but that is all."

"You have a faerie's cold heart," Og said. "But one day you will fall in love, Lara, and that heart will grow hot as your human blood warms it. You will see."

"I shall try to bring you an especial treat from the prince's castle. I know how you love sweets, dearest Og." Then Lara walked outside to the litter chair awaiting her. It was not like the grand litter Gaius Prospero had sent for her. It was a simple conveyance of fragrant cypress wood, hung with diaphanous pale gold curtains. Two Desert men were its bearers.

Immediately the litter was lifted up, and the two bearers seemed to virtually fly over the ground until they reached the foot of the great cliffs. An entrance magically appeared, opening to allow them through. Lara was fascinated. Were the Shadow Princes faerie folk? She hoped she would soon learn the answer. Inside the cliffs, a road led upwards, lighted by crystal lamps filled with bright dancing creatures. What were they? She was going to ask. She had to ask. And then another door was appearing and opening before them.

The bearers never broke stride. It was as if they knew the way would be made smooth. They entered into a tall, wide corridor with walls of white marble streaked with gold, and lit by similar crystal lamps, but that these hung from a high vaulted ceiling. The floor beneath their bare feet was great squares of black-and-white marble. At intervals along their route were striped marble columns atop which were great onyx vases filled with a colorful array of bright flowers, some of which were unfamiliar to her.

Now on her left an open colonnade appeared, and the bearers set the litter down.

A tanned hand drew the curtains aside and helped her out. She hadn't seen him there when the litter had come to a halt, but he was certainly there now. He was tall, and ageless, but obviously no boy. His eyes were a startling bright blue, his short-cropped wavy hair, as black as night. He was the handsomest man she had ever seen, with sharp aquiline features and high cheekbones. Warm lips touched the back of her small hand. "You are half faerie," he said. "How charming! Welcome to Shunnar, Lara."

"Thank you, my lord. Are you Prince Kaliq?" she asked, feeling suddenly shy.

"I am," he told her, and tucked her hand in his silk-covered arm.

"You are wearing the robe I embroidered!" Lara cried, delighted.

"You have great talent with a needle," he told her. "Who taught you? Your mother?"

"Nay, my faerie mother deserted us when I was an infant. My grandmother taught me. She raised me until I was ten, but then the Celestial Actuary called her home," Lara said.

"Come, let me show you Shunnar," he said. He led her over to a balcony between the columns. "There are the horses we raise below. Beautiful, are they not?"

Lara was astounded by the sight. Within the great Desert cliffs was a greater valley, and an incredible greensward filled with herds of beautiful horses. She looked up at him. "How is this possible? Is it magic?"

He laughed. "Must it be magic? Could it not simply be an aberration of nature?"

"Is it?"

He shrugged. "Perhaps. It has been here as long as we have."

"And how long is that?" Lara asked him.

"Since the beginning, at least according to the chronological records of our kind," Prince Kaliq told her.

"The Forest Lords claim to be the oldest clans on Hetar," she answered him.

He laughed scornfully. "How would they know? They never venture beyond the boundaries of their trees. Their pride in their heritage is both overweening and foolish. The Desert clans have been here as long, if not longer." He looked down at Lara. "Is that where you come from? The Forest? The giant who guards you is a Forest creature. We had heard they no longer existed."

"They do not, but for Og," Lara said.

"Your mother was surely a Forest Faerie," Prince Kaliq said. "You have the coloring so typical of that race, with your golden gilt hair and green eyes."

"Are there faeries in the Desert?" Lara asked him.

"We call them Peries, and yes, they exist here. They are rarely seen, however, as they prefer their own company to that of other races. But we have no giants. They always seemed to prefer the Forest and the mountains. What happened to the Forest giants. Do you know?"

"Aye. The Forest folk wiped them out. Og was in his mother's womb. She escaped the slaughter, and fled into deep Forest where she had her child alone, and survived with him for several years. Then she was caught, and killed. Og was just four. They let him live, and taught him to serve them as his predecessors had done."

"Why did this happen?" Prince Kaliq queried Lara.

"The giants knew a great secret affecting the Forest clans. But the Forest Lords did not want that secret known. They slaughtered the giants to protect themselves. They allowed Og to live because they thought he would not know their secret, but he did. The giants pass along their entire history and memories to the next generation in the womb. Og knew it all. But he kept his own counsel in order to survive. Only when he thought me in danger did he consider escaping his cruel masters."

"What is this terrible secret of the Forest Lords?" he asked her.

"That will be for Og to tell you if he chooses to do so," Lara answered.

"You do not seem inbred enough to be even part Forester," the prince remarked. "Where are you from?"

"I come from the City, and that is all you need know," Lara said. She had so far avoided telling him much of her own history, but Kaliq was not a man to be denied when his curiosity was aroused.

"Tell me!" he commanded her.

Now it was Lara who laughed. "Why is it important to you?" she countered, looking up into his handsome face. "Has your curiosity not already been assuaged by seeing what none in the village have seen? That I am young, and half faerie, and some would call me beautiful."

He took her face between his two big hands. "I had seen you before today," he told her. His lips were dangerously near hers.

"At the oasis as I kept watch in the night," she said, "I thought the rustling in the bushes was a rat come to drink at the pool, and yet I felt something more. Was it you?"

He nodded, and gently brushed her lips with his.

"But there were no footprints in the sand; and I heard no horse," Lara told him. "How did you reach the oasis? And for that matter, how did you get back here without our seeing you?"

"Did you hear the scream of a hawk above you that day?" he asked her. He spoke against her mouth, his blue eyes engaging her green ones, her head still between his hands as he refused to allow her to look away.

"Aye." She was almost breathless with his touch. His jeweled eyes.

"That was I," he told her.

"You are a shape-shifter!" She drew away, a little afraid now.

His hands released her heart-shaped face. "When it pleases me," he admitted, "and that day it pleased me greatly to watch you as you swam in the crystal waters of the oasis of Zeroun. You have a beautiful body that matches your face. Are the bruises on your inner thighs gone yet? Who dared to mark you so cruelly?"

Lara turned away from him, looking down into the beautiful fertile valley below, her hands spread out flat upon the balustrade. "My father was a mercenary," she began. "A great swords-man who was meant to rise in the world, not remain among the lower orders. But we were poor. And the rules of the Crusader Knights are quite firm."

"And foolish," Prince Kaliq said quietly. "What does a man's appearance matter if his talents are legend? So your beauty was bartered in exchange for the gold to make your father's application a reality. What happened then?"

"I was willing," Lara told him. "There was no coin for my dowry, and therefore no hope of a marriage for me. I was to be sold by the Master of the Merchants Guild into a Pleasure House. But the Headmistress of the Pleasure Guild would not permit it. She said there was already infighting going on as to who would purchase me. That patrons had begun arguing over my first-night rights. She said I would cause naught but trouble, and she forbade my sale.

"So I was consigned to a Taubyl Trader, Rolf Fairplay. He meant me for a Coastal King. There were other women with the trader's caravan meant for the Forest Lords. One, however, did not suit them, and the Head Forester was angry. Then a mean-spirited woman in the special consignment told the Head Forester that there was another slave carried by the trader. They demanded to see me, and nothing would do but that they purchased me."

"You are not an ordinary slave," the prince said. "You must have cost them a fortune. I am surprised they paid it."

"It was my heritage that fascinated them," Lara murmured, "and part of my story is wrapped up in Og's tale. You know all you need know of me now. I am an escaped slave, but I am told I cannot be retaken in the Desert. I am told if I can live free for a year then I am legally free, and can return to the City without fear."

"Do you want to return?" he asked her.

"I don't know. Somehow I think my journey is just beginning, my lord." Lara told him, and she turned to face him once again. "Is your curiosity satisfied now, Prince Kaliq? May I return to the village?"

"Of course you may return, but I had hoped you would remain to see the breeding of the mares. My fellow princes and I have several stallions. Each is let loose, one at a time, to choose the mares he will have. The stallion drives them off from the main herd, and mates with those mares who particularly please him. The mares are owned in common by all. The mares that are mated are then taken to the stables of their stallion. We wait to see if the individual stallion's seed has taken. If not, the mares are released back into the common herd. That is how we keep the bloodlines pure."

Lara looked back at the valley below, and it was then she saw open balconies similar to the one where she now stood. "All the palaces are clustered about this valley?" she asked him.

"Yes," he replied.

"Is there to be a feast?" she said.

"Aye."

"Then I will stay. I am tired of bread and cheese, goat's meat and water," Lara said. "And may I bring some of your feast back to Og?"

She charmed him. Part of her was so sure, and another part of her was so girlish, and a third part of her was so mysterious. He wanted to know, and to examine each bit of her, but the prince also knew he would have to have great patience. "Of course. There will be more feast than appetites, as always. Your giant may have whatever is left over for himself, and I am glad to give it to him. What does he like to eat best?"

"Everything." Lara laughed. "The Forest folk did not treat him well, and fed him badly. He will welcome new foods, particularly the sweets. He, too, is tired of bread, cheese, goat meat and water. We haven't had any wine since we drank the last at the oasis. What did you call it?"

"The oasis of Zeroun. Once a very learned man made his home there, Zeroun the Wise," the prince explained.

"I liked it there," Lara said. "I liked the peace, and the pool with its waterfall. I liked the sun, and the trees that did not hide everything, but just sheltered us from the sun. I think I could live there and be content."

He smiled at her. "The Desert can be cruel," he told her.

"As cruel as men?" she asked softly.

He was surprised by her astuteness. "Sometimes," he answered. His knuckles grazed her cheekbone. "What a pleasure it is to look at you, Lara. You are so fair. You know that I would make love to you," Kaliq said, "but I will not unless you wish it as well."

"Love is a girlish dream," Lara told him. "You wish to copulate with me, and satisfy your desires on my body. Do not hide behind the nebulous word 'love,' my lord prince. I do not need to be cajoled. You are attractive, and eventually, if it is indeed my choice, I may enjoy your passion. But not today."

The Shadow Prince looked horrified by her blunt words. He stepped away from her, saying, "I will have you escorted back to the village, Lara." And then he disappeared into a haze that had suddenly formed around him.

Lara shrugged. She had obviously offended him, and she was sorry. She had enjoyed his company. But like all the men she had known since leaving her father's house, the prince was only interested in pleasuring himself with her. At least he had not forced her as her Forest masters had. If he summoned her again she would yield herself to him as a gesture of apology.

"Lady, your litter awaits," a servant at her elbow said.

Lara turned and followed the man to her transport. The return trip seemed far quicker than her coming had been. She was in front of her small tent again, feeling the heat of the sand beneath her sandals. She entered the dwelling.

Og turned, surprised to see her. "What has happened?" he asked.

"I said no, and he sent me back," Lara replied.

Og shook his head. "Was he offended? They are not used to being refused, these Shadow Princes. It is rumored they are the finest lovers on Hetar."

"I wonder who began such a rumor," Lara said dryly. "They are the greatest lovers, and the Forest Lords are the oldest and purest clan. I am fast learning to believe only that which can be proven." She laughed lightly. "You said they leave the option to their partner, Og. I chose not to lie upon my back and spread my legs for this prince. Now I would get out of this gown and into something more practical. I have a pile of mending to do, and we will not be paid unless I sew."

The giant shook his head. Lara was behaving in a foolish manner. Gaining favor with this prince could certainly improve their living conditions. Her needle and his strong back could not earn them enough to purchase a real tent. The villagers were not rich. He and Lara were just managing to feed themselves with their labor, and a system of barter. But then he considered that the prince had seen what no one else in the Desert had seen— he had seen Lara in all her beauty. One small rebuff would surely not discourage Prince Kaliq. Lara's resistance was but a minor setback.

Later, as the evening came on, a group of the prince's servants arrived bearing dishes and platters of the finest foods. There was roasted gazelle, grape leaves stuffed with meat and rice, small flat breads still warm, a bowl of thinly sliced cucumbers in yogurt, a stone jar of honey, a platter of fresh fruits of every kind—even some Og's memory could not identify—along with a basket of honey cakes and a bowl of sugared almonds. And there was wine! The feast was set without a word on the floor of the tent and the servants quickly departed.

"Come quickly!" Og called to Lara.

She came from her place behind the curtain where she had been sewing in the fading light of the day. Her mouth opened in surprise as she gazed upon the feast before her. "Where has this come from?" she asked him.

"It has surely come from the prince," Og told her. "There is even wine!"

"I had agreed to remain for the feast if I might take home the leftovers for you," Lara murmured. "Then he became offended at something I said, and sent me home."

"What did you say to him?" Og demanded to know. His mouth was watering at the smells of the food. "Sit down——" he gestured at her impatiently "——we can talk while we eat. I did not realize how hungry I was until this all arrived." He cut several slices of the roasted gazelle, putting it on one of their two wooden plates for her. Then taking up the haunch of the gazelle he began to eat with gusto.

Lara helped herself to two of the stuffed grape leaves, some bread, yogurt and fruit. Then she began to eat, surprised at how hungry she was. They had been starving, especially Og, and she hadn't even realized it. Lara chewed slowly, lest she get sick with this rich meal Prince Kaliq had sent them.

They ate, and Og listened as Lara recounted every moment of her visit to Prince Kaliq. Finally when she had finished he said to her, "Of course you offended him. The Shadow Princes believe deeply in love, and its many powers. By rejecting love and all it stands for you insulted him."

"How can I know of this elusive thing you call love?" Lara demanded of him. "My innocence was cruelly taken, and then my body used over and over again by two brutal men who only sought to plant their seed in me in hopes a child of mine might lift a curse placed upon them. A well-deserved curse, I might add. The Forest Lords are proud and stupid and cruel. Do you think they believe in this love? I certainly do not."

"Love exists," Og insisted.

"If you know that it is only from your shared memories, not from personal experience," Lara replied cruelly. "The Forest Lords and their women were hardly kind to you, Og."

"But I remember my mother, and how she loved me. Loved me enough to escape the carnage that terrible day that I might be born. Loved me enough to protect me as long as she might," he responded.

"A parent's love I understand," Lara agreed, "for my father loved me. But do not tell me there is a different kind of love between a man and a woman. There is only lust, Og. This love the prince believes in does not exist. It never has. It is an illusion." She reached for a honey cake, and bit into it with relish.

"Some day you will learn differently," Og told her quietly. He put down the gazelle haunch that he had stripped of its meat to the bone, and picked a small bunch of grapes from the platter for himself.

"I am grateful for Prince Kaliq's kindness in sending us this fine meal. We must share the honey cakes with Zaki and his family. Some of the fruit, too. Nothing will keep in this heat," Lara said practically.

Og nodded. "It cannot hurt us to curry favor with the village headman," he agreed. "But let us eat our fill first, please," he pleaded.

Lara nodded. "My sweet tooth is not yet satisfied," she told him, taking a peach.

When they had finished, however, they gathered up the remaining flat bread, the bowl with the cucumbers and yogurt, the dish with the grape leaves, and the one with the honey cakes, along with some of the fruit. They carried it to Zaki's tent. His family had just sat down to their meal. Zaki was effusive in his thanks even as his younger children eyed the bounty.

"It is most kind, most kind!" he told them.

"The prince sent the food," Lara said. "We could not eat it all, and are happy to share it with you who have been so kind to us, Zaki." She bowed to him, and then turning, departed his dwelling.

"Why is she always veiled and muffled in shapeless robes?" Zaki asked Og.

"Because she is so beautiful that the mere sight of her causes conflict and strife," he told the headman. "She does not wish to be surrounded by contention, and so she covers herself to protect those around her," Og explained.

"Will she become the prince's woman?" Zaki asked.

"I do not know," Og replied. "She does not understand love."

"If she will let him, he will teach her," Zaki responded.

"Perhaps," Og said, and then bowing he departed the headman's tent to return to his own. He called out to Lara behind her curtain as he entered. "Zaki is delighted with the food. I believe we may have a place here as long as we desire it. But shall we remain forever, Lara?"

"I don't know," she replied. "For now, I am content with no demands made upon me but to sew. We will get a better tent soon. The tent maker's daughter is to be married soon, and will need a proper gown for the occasion. The gown is simple enough, but no one can embroider like I can. These Desert people know nothing of that art."

"You are clever, and meant for more than you now have," Og said. "Good night, dearest Lara. May your dreams be happy ones."

"Good night, my dear Og, protector and best friend," Lara said. She curled onto the furs, drawing a light coverlet over her. It had been an interesting day. She wondered if Prince Kaliq would call her to his presence again. He was such a beautiful man with his blue eyes and wavy black hair. When he had looked at her she had actually felt a small measure of curiosity; might he possess some magic that would put the warmth back into her soul?

Despite Og's blessing, her dreams that night were not happy. She dreamed of Enda and Durga ravaging her body, and awakened with a gasp, trembling so violently that it was some time before she was able to regain her composure. Were they looking for her? Would they find her?

Lara reached down for the crystal and saw the flame burning steadily. *I can't go back,* she said within her mind.

Do not fear, Ethne's voice reassured her.

Then why do I dream?

At the moment men are your greatest fear, Lara, but the Forest Lords will not venture far from their trees. You are safe here.

Why do men always want to possess my body, Ethne?

Because it is a beautiful body, and most men believe in love. To love a woman is to possess her body, among other things, Ethne told her.

What other things?

That is for you to learn. Ethne's laughter tinkled knowingly.

I hate it when you say things like that to me, Lara grumbled. *It is all so mysterious, and how am I to learn if you will not teach me?*

You must learn from others of your kind, both human and faerie, Ethne told her. *It is my task only to guide and protect you.*

A Shadow Prince would be my lover, Lara told her guardian.

Ahhh. Ethne's voice grew soft as if she were remembering something wonderful. *He will give you such pleasure, Lara. The Shadow Princes are truly the masters of tender passion and love. There are none like them anywhere but here. How I envy you!*

I said no.

Ethne sighed almost irritably. *Your experience with passion to date has not been pleasant, I am the first to admit,* she said, *but you must put it behind you.*

I dream of Enda and Durga, of their cruelty and brutality, Lara said.

Foolish girl! Why did you not tell me? Ethne demanded. *I can rid you of those dreams. You must think only of this prince who would love you. He will teach you the lessons you must learn in order to move on with your life. Do you think fate has planned for you to sit sewing in a Desert encampment for the rest of your life?*

No, Lara said, chastened.

You have a great future, Lara.

What is it? Lara asked her excitedly.

You are not ready yet to know, but you will when the time is right, Ethne replied.

More of your cryptic enigmas, Lara muttered.

Ethne chuckled. *You are forever wanting to run before you have learned how to walk,* she said. *Enjoy the journey,* Ethne advised the girl. *Learn as much as you can before you reach your destination, my child. Do not waste the opportunities that are being put before you.*

If my fate is already planned, I suppose I have no other choice but to go along with it, Lara murmured.

There are always choices. The stratagem is to choose wisely.

I would not have chosen Durga and Enda, Lara replied.

Again Ethne laughed. *Yet you have learned from them, my child.*

What have I learned from those two? Brutality? Stupidity? Cruelty?

You have learned what love is not, the guardian of the crystal said softly. *Now go and learn what it can be.*

Chapter 9

PRINCE KALIQ rode into the village the next afternoon and he directed his horse to the tiny tent shared by Lara and Og. Lara sat outside beneath an awning, sewing. The giant was nowhere to be seen. The girl looked up at him. He held out his hand. "Come!" he said imperiously reaching down for her.

Lara stood and let herself be swept up onto the prince's horse. "How masterful you are," she teased him mischievously.

"I do not know why I want you," he said. "You look like an old crow in your enveloping black garments. And you are ignorant beyond any I have ever known." He moved his horse away from the tent and toward the entrance to his palace at the bottom of the cliff.

"You want me because you have seen me without my enveloping garments," she told him. "And you want me because you desire to teach me your ways," Lara said. "I am a mystery to you, my lord, am I not?"

"You are not stupid," he admitted.

"Nay, not stupid, just ignorant," she mocked him, and he laughed.

"I will probably fall in love with you," he grumbled, "and you will break my heart, Lara, won't you?" He guided his mount past the cliff's entry, and onto the inner road.

"I told you yesterday, my lord, that I do not believe in love. It does not exist. But I am also now informed that for the Shadow Princes love is paramount. If you know that I will break your heart, then it is best you not fall in love with me," Lara advised him.

"Love is not a logical emotion. It will not obey the science of reason," Kaliq told her. "That is the first thing you must learn, Lara. Love happens. There is no rationale for it. You cannot control it, or the passions it arouses."

She was seated before him on his stallion. One arm held her gently but firmly against him. He wore white silk trousers, and an open-necked white silk shirt. About his waist a black sash was wrapped, and his boots were black leather. She found her cheek resting against his bare chest. His skin was smooth, warm, fragrant. "I don't understand," Lara told him. "You speak in riddles."

"It is because you don't understand that I have come for you today," he said. "Someone as beautiful as you are, Lara, should not be ignorant of the pleasures of love. What happened to you in the Forest that you encased your heart in ice?"

"I am told daughters born of faerie women have the same cold hearts as their mothers," Lara said.

"Only if they choose to," he responded.

"What can you know of faeries, my lord? You are not one, are you?"

"Nay, I am a Shadow Prince, but I had an ancestress who was a Peri. Faerie blood runs in my veins, thought not to the extent that it does in yours, Lara. Now tell me of the Forest, and why you enclosed your heart in an icy cold. We shall not cease riding until I have learned all."

"Surely we are almost there," Lara said.

"We will not be there until I have learned what I need to know of you," the prince said in a stern voice. "Tell me."

Lara looked up into the handsome face, and began to speak. "The trader swore I was meant for a Coastal King in order to protect me from the Forest Lords. But they offered him far more than he had hoped to obtain for me. He was afraid it was a ruse, and so I advised him to accept their offer but refuse to make the trade until we were at the borders separating the Desert and the Forest. They were not pleased, but they agreed. And so it was done. I later learned it was my faerie heritage that fascinated them. They wanted to get a child on me to ease or even erase a curse placed on them by Maeve, the queen of the Forest Faeries. They thought a faerie child born of my loins and their seed would soften her heart against them. Of course it was madness on their part."

"Why did they want a child with faerie blood? The Forest Lords do not mix their blood with that of outsiders," Kaliq said.

"Yesterday I said it was Og's tale to tell, but I realize now it is mine, too," Lara told him, and so she did, beginning with the murder of Maeve's faerie kinswoman and ending with the slaughter of all the Forest giants, but for Og. "The giants knew the Foresters' shameful secret," Lara continued. "Maeve's curse had made it impossible for them to breed children upon their own women. Stealthily they mated with outsiders, giving those children to their wives, who claimed them as their own. And with each new generation born, the blood of the Forest Lords grew thinner and thinner.

"The Foresters allowed Og to live because they believed he didn't know their secret," she said, "but he did, for giant memory is passed on in the womb. He was trained to serve as his people had served."

"The Forest giants were known for their gentle natures, and kind hearts," Kaliq said softly. "They would not have known how to fight back against the Foresters."

"If not for Og I should not have escaped, and would soon be dead," Lara replied. "He knew what I did not. That no woman with faerie blood will give a child to a man she does not love, or at least desires, and when he told me I was terrified. Both the Head Forester and his younger brother were pumping their seed into me several times daily. They were beginning to become suspicious as to why my belly was not growing with a child of theirs. They didn't

care which one of them fathered the child on me, but they wanted
that child, whom they believed would be their salvation."

"Were you a virgin when you came to them?" he asked her.

Lara nodded. "That was the other reason I was so expensive."

"And when their bodies joined with yours what did you feel?"
he asked her.

"My body had begun to respond to the younger brother, Enda,
but I hated them both," Lara told him. "When the Head Forester
would lie with me, I would slip away into the deep recesses of my
mind. It was easier then to bear him."

Prince Kaliq's eyes filled with tears at her recitation. "That you
should have suffered so, my beautiful Lara," he said, his voice
choking. "Please, I beg of you, let me show you what true passion
between two friends can be like. I will not lie to you. I do desire
your body, but only because it is such a beautiful body, and should
be loved as only I can love it." He bent and brushed his lips against
her mouth.

"You seek me for your pleasure," Lara said low.

"I seek to give you pleasure!" he corrected her. "Those cloddish
Forest creatures know naught of pleasuring a woman of any ilk.
They know only how to grunt and sweat over a woman's body. They
think nothing of the woman. She is a vessel to them in which they
hope to grow their seed." His blue eyes were stormy with his angry
words. "You are meant to love and be loved."

"And what am I to you, my lord prince?" Lara asked quietly.

"A comely woman to be admired, caressed and utterly adored,"
he told her. "I would worship at the shrine of your beauty, Lara,"
the prince said fervently.

"You want no child of mine then?" she asked him.

"No," he told her quietly. "I want only you, and the pleasure we
can give each other, Lara. Nothing else, I swear!"

They were suddenly at the entrance to the hallway of the palace. The stallion stopped, and a servant lifted Lara down from the
saddle as the prince leapt down behind her. Taking her hand in his,

he led her into the beautiful corridor she had previously been in the day before.

"Will you trust me to teach you the joys of passion?" he asked her.

"Yes," she said simply. His words had intrigued her. Was there more to two bodies uniting than just grunting and straining? "I am curious as to whether what you hint at is real, or merely a belief you refuse to give up."

He laughed. "You will soon see, Lara. You will soon see, but first we shall watch my favorite stallion choose his mares and mate with them."

"Did that not happen yesterday?" she asked him.

"I would not allow it without you," he told her.

"I am not suitably garbed to be seen publicly on your balustrade, my lord," she told him.

"There is time to prepare you," he told her. "Come! You must be bathed. You have, I fear, the scent of the village goats on your skin, and in your hair. Hair like yours should not even hint of goat." He led her quickly from the main corridor down a narrow hallway at the end of which was a great wooden door.

Outside the door a guard stood. Seeing the prince and Lara he turned sharply and flung open the portal so that at no time did they slow their pace. A serving woman hurried forward to greet them, bowing obsequiously to the prince. Without even being told she took Lara's all-enveloping garments from her. Beneath, Lara was wearing a sleeveless round necked gown of a natural colored linen she had recently made for herself. She slipped from her sandals.

The serving woman next undid the ribbons at Lara's shoulders, and her gown fell to the floor. She stepped from it not in the least embarrassed by her nudity.

"You are even lovelier than I had anticipated," Kaliq told her, shedding his own clothing. While every bit as tall as the Foresters she had known, he was far more slender, Lara saw. His skin where the sun touched it was like bronze-colored satin, but where the sun could not reach it was like golden cream. She thought him beautiful, and smiling, told him so.

"Then we are well matched," he replied, "but I knew it the moment I saw you at the oasis. Come now, and let me wash you." He led her into the bath where there were several smooth depressions in the marble floor against a wall. Water fell from curved spouts in that wall. Placing her in one of the hollows the prince took up a sponge laden with soft soap, and began to wash Lara.

"I can wash myself," she protested softly.

"But is this not much nicer?" he said. The sponge moved over her chest, neck and shoulders. Then it was swept over her breasts with great care, and down her torso. Kneeling, he washed her thighs, legs and feet then, turning her about, sponged her buttocks, stood up and did all of her back. He set her firmly beneath the curved spout and rinsed the foamy soap from her skin. Finally drawing her from beneath the water, he announced, "I will now wash your lovely hair." And to her surprise he did. When he had finished, he wrung out the long tresses and pinned them wet atop her head, giving her a hard kiss as he did so. His hand went to her pubic mound, fingering the golden curls.

"I have been denuded there before, but in the Forest there were no such niceties. How would you have me, my lord prince?" Lara asked him.

"Your curls are charming, but I prefer a woman's body to be smooth and free of hair but for her head," he told her. "I will go and wash myself. The alabaster jar has what you will need, and the bath attendant will help you. When you are finished we will dress. There is no time for massage now, but later I will caress your body with scented cream."

The bath attendant came, and there was nothing for Lara to do but stand patiently as the woman smoothed the thick paste over her legs, mons and beneath her arms. Within minutes she was being rinsed free of her superfluous hair. She stepped from the basin, and Kaliq was there, wrapping her in a towel.

"Come, we must dry your hair," he said, and seated her upon a marble bench. With another towel he rubbed all the water from her hair, and then began to brush it with expert strokes. "I love your hair!" he said. "It is like the finest thistledown. Only Forest Faeries have such hair. What was your mother's name?"

"Ilona," Lara answered. She could get used to being bathed and brushed by this handsome man. And to her surprise, at no time had he made suggestive remarks, or touched her in a sensual manner. Nor had the sight of her even aroused his manhood, a slender length of flesh she had discreetly noted.

"Then you are, I believe, Maeve's granddaughter, for Maeve had a daughter named Ilona. She was a rebellious girl for a time, but now I understand she remains by her mother's side, for Maeve is very old and reaching the point where she will fade away into the next world," Prince Kaliq said. "Ilona will be the next queen of the faeries, my beauty."

"Did you know my mother?" Lara asked him.

"Only by reputation," he answered her.

"How old are you?" she queried, suddenly curious.

He laughed. "I am older than you, of course, but I am yet young enough to be your lover, and teach you of passion, delight and desire," Kaliq responded. He began to plait several strands of her long gilt hair, but left most of it hanging free. When he had finished he stood up. "Come, it is time for us to dress so we may view the matings between my stallion and the mares."

Silent servants brought them comfortable white silk kaftans with the necklines embroidered in gold threads. Golden sandals were provided for their feet. When they were garbed he took her hand, leading her from the baths down the narrow hallway again and back into the wide open corridor overlooking the green valley where the large herd of mares grazed peacefully in the sunlight. There were horses of every color—black, white, gray, chestnut, bay, dun, sorrel and roan.

Prince Kaliq lifted a hand, and almost immediately a great white stallion was released into the valley. Snorting proudly, his coal-black mane and tail flying, he dashed among the mares who scattered, panic-stricken. The first mare he separated from the herd was a dainty black. She stood trembling as the stallion covered her with his large body, nuzzling at her neck and breathing heavily. When he had finished with her, servants raced out to capture the mare and lead her away.

The stallion seemed tireless. He cut one gray, two white and three chestnut mares from the herd, mounting each as he had the black mare, filling them with his foaming seed. But he was not yet satisfied. He circled the herd again and again, looking, seeking, and then Lara saw the delicately built golden mare. The stallion saw her, too. He stopped, rearing up on his hind legs as he made quick eye contact with the mare. He began to move toward her, ignoring the other mares in his desire to reach her.

The golden mare saw him coming and, turning, fled the white stallion, but he quickly caught up with her, pushing her with his velvety muzzle into a corner of the greensward, screaming with triumph as he mounted her. They could see the stallion's great penis as he slowly pushed it into the mare. Lara was not even certain if she was breathing at that point. Then the prince's arm slipped about her waist, his breath soft on her skin. She could feel the slim length of his body pressing against her slender frame. He nuzzled at her pale hair, and to her surprise Lara felt a stab of pure desire in her vitals.

"It is exciting to watch, isn't it?" His breath was hot in her ear.

"Yes," she murmured, surprised that she could talk at all. She was trembling. "I could never have imagined anything like it." Her legs felt weak, and instinctively she leaned back against him, concentrating on the golden mare now being led away as, bored, the stallion began to graze in the green grass.

He kissed the soft nape of her neck. He could sense her confusion, yet he could also feel her resistance beginning to ease. He pressed his advantage, for this first time their mating must be swift lest she grow wary again. There would be time for the slow, drawn-out pleasure of passion that he well knew how to give. But this first time he must show her that the coming together of a man and a woman was sweet and tender, not hard and cruel. "I shall be the white stallion to your golden mare, Lara," he told her. "Did you not find the mating between those two symbolic?" His hand undid the neckline of her kaftan, baring her two breasts, and he began to fondle them gently. "A woman's body is to be treated with tenderness, and worshipped," he told her low.

"The Forest Lords thought of a woman's body only as a vessel," she replied.

"I saw the bruises on you, Lara. Tell me they did not beat you," he said.

"Nay, they treated me as well as they knew how to treat a woman, for they sought a faerie child of me. But their manner was rough, as I have said." His hands on her were unlike anything she had ever known. She sighed, realizing that she was actually enjoying his touch, watching as her nipples hardened when he teased them.

He smiled as he sensed her reaction to his hands. She had the loveliest breasts. They were like small summer fruits, round and perfect, but not yet quite ripe. He caressed them, one in each hand now. His lips brushed the graceful curve of her neck, nuzzling her long hair aside, moving down to the soft curve of her shoulder. Her head fell back against him, and her green eyes were closed. She sighed again, this time more deeply.

"You are not sickened then?" he asked her.

She shook her head in the negative. "I like it," Lara told him. "Is it always like this, my lord prince?"

"I will try to make it so, especially as you have had such a bad experience with the Foresters," he told her. Then his hands fell away from her breasts, and he turned her about to face him. His lips began to kiss her—first her mouth, which he explored tenderly with his tongue, then her face and her eyelids.

Their bodies were touching. Her breasts against his smooth chest, her belly and legs pressed to his warm flesh. His arms wrapped about her, holding her as close as he could. She could feel his manroot stirring and swelling as his desire increased, but instead of being repelled, more than anything Lara wanted her body joined to this man's. And she knew he waited for her to tell him so. "Yes!" she whispered against his mouth.

He drew her down to the floor, and to her surprise there was a soft silken mattress beneath them. He turned her onto her stomach. "I want to mount you like my stallion did," he groaned. "Raise your buttocks up for me, Lara, my love." And when she did he covered her as his stallion had covered the little golden mare, his manroot finding her silken passage and sliding into it. "Remember the beast," he murmured in her ear. "Remember his size, and feel me growing within you. I am the white stallion, and you are the sweet golden mare he desires." He thrust hard.

Lara cried out, but it was not with fear. His words excited her. She actually could feel him swelling within her, and imagined the stallion's length and power as he had taken the mare. She was the mare, and the stallion was driving himself within her body with a fierce rhythm. She could feel her own heart beating wildly as she realized that she wanted this man. Truly wanted him. She could hardly breathe with her own excitement. She wanted him to go on forever. "Oh, my lord!" she finally managed to cry out.

His teeth sunk into her neck. His haunches contracted and expanded with his efforts. He allowed the magic in his veins to guide his manroot as he pleasured the girl beneath him, and gained from her the most incredible pleasure he had ever known. He groaned, knowing it must end soon, but not wanting it to, until Lara cried out again, and he recognized the sound as a woman about to reach the apex of her pleasure.

Her head was swirling. There were bursts of color behind her closed eyelids. Within her she felt what she had never experienced before. A tightening, a quickening, a wild burst of tremors that shook her to her very core. She sobbed his name once. "Kaliq!" She felt his juices flooding her, and then Lara fainted with the emotions he had aroused within her.

When she finally opened her eyes several minutes later, she was lying on her back. She raised herself on one elbow. He lay next to her, his eyes closed. They were in the middle of the wide corridor on the mattress that had so mysteriously been there for them. "What will your servants think?" Lara said softly.

His blue eyes opened. "My servants are wise enough to keep their thoughts to themselves," he told her. "You are an incredible creature, Lara. You felt pleasure, didn't you? It was not like that for you before, even when your body responded to the Forest Lord. Today you responded body and soul."

"Yes," she told him. "It was an amazing experience. Can it be that way all the time? Should it be?" Lara wondered.

Reaching up, he pulled her down, and kissed her mouth a long slow kiss. "It will always be that way when you and I make love, my faerie girl."

"Do not call me that!" Lara cried. "The Foresters called me that."

"Then I shall never call you that again," he promised.

"The mattress?" She quickly changed the subject.

He laughed. "I have some magic, although I do not practice my skills as much as I should. When I knew we would make love I quickly conjured us a soft place to lie."

"In a most public place," she murmured. "What if someone had come upon us? Comes upon us?" She looked anxiously for her kaftan.

He laughed softly. "They will not," he told her. "My servants know me well, and knew what watching my stallion with the mares in the company of a beautiful girl would lead to this afternoon. No one will disturb us."

"I should get back to the village," Lara said.

"Stay with me," he said to her.

"I am not ready to give you that much of myself quite yet," Lara told him honestly. "I am only beginning to get used to the idea that I am a free woman. Og says that the Foresters can not reclaim me here, or ever again if I can manage to keep out of their sight for a full year. Is that true?"

"Yes," he replied. "Remain with me for a year, and I will protect you from them, Lara. You will never give them what they want, but I think they would not believe you even if you told them so. They are brutish men with little intellect."

"Swear you will not fall in love with me," she said to him.

"Why?" he demanded, smiling at her, his hand caressing her face.

"I have told you. I do not believe in love. But you do, and you are a kind man. I would not hurt you, my lord Kaliq," Lara said quietly.

"The decision is mine to make," he told her, "and who knows? I may teach you to love. But whether I can or not, say you will remain at least a year with me that you may be truly free, Lara. I can teach you many things other than love."

"You would share your magic with me?" she asked him.

"You should have magic at your disposal, Lara, for you are half faerie," he said.

"I think Ethne would approve," Lara replied. She held up the thin gold chain, and dangled the star crystal before his eyes. "Do you see the flame within it? That is Ethne, my guardian. My mother put this chain about my neck, my father once told me."

"Ask Ethne then if Maeve is your grandmother," the prince advised her. "If it is so you should meet her before she fades away entirely."

"She has other grandchildren, I am sure," Lara said almost bitterly.

"But no child of Ilona's," he told her. "If that Ilona is indeed your mother she never bore another child for human or faerie man."

"I will ask Ethne," Lara responded. Then she arose from the mattress, and picked up her kaftan from the floor of the wide corridor. "If I do not return Og will worry," she said. "Where are my clothes?"

"You are not to wear those ugly garments again," he told her.

"I do not want the villagers seeing me as I truly am, nor do I wish to be the cause of undue notice," Lara told him. "You know that gossip travels on the wind, and the north wind will enter the Forest now that winter is there. If I am seen, word might reach Enda and Durga. Despite their misgivings they will come into the Desert seeking me. And if they find me, Hetarian law or no, they will take me back with them. I must remain covered and veiled at all times."

"Then remain with me, and be safe," he said.

"What of Og? I cannot leave him, for without him I would have never escaped the Forest," Lara replied. "He is my friend. I will not desert him."

"He may come into the palace and be with you," the prince suggested. "He is not the largest giant I have ever seen. I suppose it comes from his mother's time in hiding, and a lack of food in his early years."

"He is six cubits tall," Lara defended Og. "And he has his own magic. His boots can go a league with each step he takes!"

"Nonetheless he is a small giant," Kaliq said, and standing, he drew on his own kaftan. "My palace ceilings will be high enough to sustain him. I will send a servant to the village to fetch him."

"What of my sewing?" Lara said. "The villagers have come to depend upon me."

"Yes, you have made yourself quite useful to them," the prince noted. "The women will have to do their own mending again, I fear. There are other things you must learn, Lara. You are intelligent, and have a certain wisdom. You need to know more about Hetar and its peoples if you are to eventually continue on your journey."

"What do you know of my journey?" Lara asked him, curious about his words.

"I know nothing of it but that you will remain with me no longer than a year," he told her. "Once you can be assured of your safety you will go. I see it when I look at you." He caressed her cheek again. "Do not look sad, Lara. I am but a stop on your journey. We will not waste our time together, however. There is much I can teach you. You asked me how old I was before, and I said I was older than you. I am much older. I have been here since the beginning of time, as have all my kind. You see no society of women and children among us, for there are none. There never have been. Our kind came from the purple shadows, and one day we will return into those shadows. We share our pleasure with the women to whom we are attracted, and who find us congenial. We raise and sell our horses, keeping to ourselves as much as we can. Hetar is changing more each day. Soon the time will come when the people have to choose between the light and the darkness. It will not be an easy choice to make, but make it they must."

"What has this all to do with me?" Lara queried him.

"I do not know, but it does," he told her. Then he clapped his hands together, and at once a servant appeared. "Send servants into the village to escort the giant, Og, to the palace. See they pack up all his and the lady Lara's possessions."

"At once, my lord," the servant said, bowing, and he hurried off.

"How do you know?" she demanded.

He laughed. "I just do. Now come, I will show you where you will live." He brought her to a suite of beautiful rooms that all opened out into a cool, green garden. "My apartment is across the garden," he told her. "We will always be near one another, Lara. How many servants would you like?"

"I am capable of taking care of myself," she told him.

"You are my chosen," he replied. "You must be served."

"Og will serve me," Lara said.

"No. I want Og to work with my horses. Forest giants are extraordinarily good with animals. You must have a serving girl, and I think I have someone who would do well. I bought her off the last Taubyl Trader who came through several months back. She is young, and was very frightened, but she has learned well, my head serving man tells me. She will be as much a companion to you as a servant. Her name is Noss."

"Noss!" Lara cried. "That is the girl the Foresters would not have! Yes, she will suit me admirably, my lord Kaliq."

"Then I will send her to you," he said. "For now, explore your quarters. They were conceived with you in mind." He turned, and was quickly gone in a swirl of his white robes.

Alone, Lara reached down and raised the crystal to her gaze. *Am I safe with him?*

The flame flickered. *That is a question to which you already know the answer,* Ethne said. *Ask what it is that you really desire to know from me.*

Is Maeve, queen of the Forest Faeries, my grandmother?

Yes.

And her daughter, Ilona, the faerie woman who bore me?

Yes.

Why did you not tell me before, Lara demanded?

You did not ask, and it was not time for you to know until you did, Ethne replied.

Why?

Ethne gave a watery chuckle. *Because it is,* she responded.

Do not be smug, Lara said, irritated. *It ill becomes you. I do not know if I like all this mystery and magic that seems to surround me these days. Why did my life have to become so damned complicated? I liked living in the City. I liked being nothing more than my father's daughter. Now I am not certain what or who I am.*

Be patient, Lara, Ethne's gentle voice soothed. *You have a destiny, and it must played out. But for now you are safe with the Shadow Prince. He is one of the wisest of them, and will impart much knowledge to you. Learn from him.*

"Lara!"

She turned, and then held out her arms to Noss. "Noss! How glad I am that you are now safe. Rolf Fairplay kept his promise to me." She hugged the young girl.

"I am to be your servant and companion, the prince has told me," Noss said. "How did you get here, Lara? I cried so hard when I saw you being taken away by the Forest Lords. My eyes got all swollen with the salt of my tears."

"I escaped the Forest at Winterfest," Lara said, and then she explained all to Noss. "Og will be here shortly. You will like him. I could have never done it without him. He is the kindest and gentlest fellow I have ever known. Now, tell me how you have fared since we were last together."

"There is little to tell," Noss replied. "We crossed the Desert for several days, and when we reached this palace the trader brought forth all manner of goods. The headman here told Rolf Fairplay that he need a young serving woman. Rolf explained he had but one slave, very young, and inexperienced. The headman said he wished to see me, and when he had he asked me if I could be content as a servant to his prince. He said I would be taught what I needed to know—that the prince did not beat his servants, and I should not be a slave, but free. Rolf protested that I was a slave, but the headman smiled, and said while he would buy a slave, he would free the slave once it became the prince's property. It was their custom. Shunnar is a pleasant place, Lara. I have been treated well. But until today I have done little. When I have spoken to the headman he has simply said that my time had not arrived. Now I know why. It is as if they were waiting for you to come here," Noss finished.

"Perhaps they were," Lara agreed.

"Are you the prince's lover?" Noss asked ingenuously.

"Yes, it would seem I am now," Lara admitted aloud.

"He is so handsome," Noss sighed. Then she grew serious. "What of the others? What happened to them? Were the Forest Lords cruel?"

"The other five are all with child by their masters," Lara said. "Truda by the Head Forester himself. His name is Durga. He and his younger brother, Enda, were my masters. They sought to get me with child, but faerie women, even half faerie women as myself, will not give children to men they do not love. I did not know that, but when Og told me I knew I must flee or be slain for my failures."

"How horrible!" Noss exclaimed.

"If I can remain free for a year and a day the Forest Lords will have no claim on me. Prince Kaliq wishes me to stay with him. He says he will keep me safe."

Noss sighed. "He is so romantic," she said. "Sometimes I wish I were old enough and beautiful enough to attract the attention of a man like that."

"You are a very pretty girl, Noss," Lara told her. "But I think if you believe in love you must let it come to you. One day it will."

"If I believe in love?" Noss cried. "Everyone believes in love, Lara."

"I don't," was the answer, "but we must not get into a discussion over it. Come and help me explore these beautiful rooms that the prince has said are mine. They seem even finer than my father's new house in the Garden District."

Together mistress and servant walked throughout the magnificent apartment. There was the antechamber where they had greeted one another and a small dining room that opened out on the garden and was off a dayroom. There was a little bedchamber, and a large bedchamber. There was even a private tiled bath with its own small bathing pool. The marble floors were covered with beautiful woolen rugs in jeweled tones of ruby, sapphire, amethyst and emerald. Sheer pale gold draperies blew in the soft Desert air from the windows. The furniture was of ebony accented with gold, some of a design Lara had never seen. It was some type of seating, and was plush with cushions and pillows. The bed in her bedroom was set upon a dais, and hanging from a large brass ring in the ceiling were the same pale gold gossamer silks as at the windows. The room itself had walls of pale wood painted with flowers and Desert animals.

"I have never seen anything so beautiful," Noss breathed slowly.

"Neither have I," Lara agreed.

"There is a door on my room," the younger girl told Lara excitedly. "Will you permit me to close it?"

"Of course," Lara said. "Remember that you are a free servant."

"And I have a real bed, not a pallet! I have never had a real bed," Noss told Lara. Then she walked over to a tall wardrobe, and opened its doors. Inside were all manner of gowns and sandals. "Look!" Noss said to Lara excitedly. "Have you ever seen such lovely things? It is as if he were expecting you, Lara."

"He was," Lara answered her. But how had he known unless he knew what her destiny was to be? "Who else lives in this palace, Noss?" Lara asked the girl.

"Only the prince and his servants. I have seen others like him, though. They come in the evening, and sometimes dine with him," Noss said.

"No other women?" She was curious. How could she not be curious?

"Sometimes. They come and they go, but usually when the others are here. In the time I have been here there has been no woman living in this palace, unless she was a servant as I am."

"How many servants?" Lara probed.

"There is the headman, some who cook, some who clean, some who do the laundry. Most are older women. They have all been kind to me, more so than my own family," Noss revealed.

"Then the prince is a solitary man," Lara noted.

"But for his brother princes, yes," Noss said.

"La-a-a-ra!"

"Gracious, what is that noise?" Noss cried.

"'Tis Og, my giant companion," Lara replied. "Come quickly before he shouts the palace down." She hurried through the apartment and out into the public corridor where she found Og standing.

"This is a fine palace, and the prince has asked me to help with his mares," Og said. He bent down, looking at Noss. "And who is this wee creature?"

"This is Noss," Lara answered him.

"The one Durga would not have, eh?" Og remarked.

"The very same. Please do not frighten her, Og. She is not used to you as I am," Lara said. "The prince has set her to wait upon me."

"Aye, you need another female to be with," Og agreed. "Now, is it all right with you if I help tend to the prince's horses? When I was not in the bathhouse at Durga's village I kept his horses for him. I am good with animals."

"You are not my slave, Og, you are my friend. You are free to do what you choose, and if the horses please you, then yes, look after them."

Noss had finally found her voice again. "I never saw anyone as big as you before," she said.

"I am told I am small for a giant, but six cubits high. There are others far larger than I, little girl," Og responded with a grin. "Well, I'll tell the prince we are agreed, Lara. When you decide to leave this place, if you do, I will come with you. We are companions, eh?" He chuckled, and then turning was gone.

"How did you ever meet him?" Noss wanted to know. "I have heard little good about giants, Lara."

"He was held prisoner in Durga's village," Lara said. Og's history was too complicated a story for the simple Noss. "We decided to escape together, and I could not have done it without him. He is a kind and gentle fellow, Noss. And a good friend to me in my time of trial. One day I will tell you why the Forest Lords wanted me, and it is not a happy story. You have no idea the trap you escaped, little one. One day I shall tell all of Hetar the story of the Forest Lords and their duplicity. But for now, I need to bathe and to rest." She reentered her apartments.

The little bath was wonderful. Pinning up her long hair, she washed herself standing in a marble hollow, rinsed, and then went to soak in the warm scented water. She invited Noss to share her bath, but the girl was still too shy, and Lara thought how fortunate

Noss had been to avoid the brief life of a concubine in the Forest. Coming from the pool, she wrapped herself in a large drying cloth and went into her bedroom, where she found the prince sprawled upon her bed awaiting her.

"You look delicious," he told her, his blue eyes dancing.

"I have only just washed your wicked lust from my body, my lord," she said.

"As tempting as I find you, Lara, I but came to ask you to join me at supper. Noss knows where, and she knows the time." He arose from the bed, and drew her slowly into his strong arms looking down into her face. "Og found you?"

"Yes." Did she sound breathless?

"You are content with his arrangements?" His lips were practically touching hers.

"He will be treated well? And housed comfortably? And fed enough? His appetite is very large, for he is a big man," Lara said, her voice now a whisper.

"You have my word on it, Lara." His mouth closed over hers, and as she kissed him back she realized that were he not holding her in his arms she could not stand, for her legs felt very weak. "You taste delicious too, my love," he said softly, raising his head to look into her green eyes.

"Ethne says you were right," Lara murmured. "Maeve is my grandmother, and her daughter, Ilona, my mother."

"I will arrange for you to meet your grandmother, for as I have said she is very, very old, and will soon fade away entirely," the prince said. Then he kissed her lips lightly one more time, and released his hold on her. "I will see you at the twilight, Lara."

Fortunately the bed was behind her, and as her legs gave way she felt the mattress beneath her buttocks. Kaliq had the most amazing effect upon her. Pulling herself all the way onto the bed she fell asleep. It had been a day like no other she had ever experienced, and there was more to come.

The prince found Noss in the dayroom. "You will take good care of her," he said. It was neither a question, nor a request.

"Yes, my lord," Noss answered him. "She is my friend."

"More than you realize, Noss. Do you know what your fate would have been had you remained in the Forest?"

Noss shook her head. Her innocent eyes were wide with her curiosity.

He had been going to tell her the truth, but instead he said, "They would have worked you until you dropped. You would have been cold and hungry most of the time. You would have remained a slave, and not been made a free girl." He patted her cheek. "You are much better off in my household, Noss, than in the Forest."

"Oh, yes, my lord!" Noss said blushing .

"Bring Lara to the dining hall at the twilight. See she is garbed beautifully, and her hair dressed to show it to its best advantage. My brothers will be dining with us tonight. We are celebrating my stallion's success today in the mating." Then the prince swept from the chamber as Noss stared admiringly after him.

Lara slept for several hours, wrapped in her drying cloth. When she awoke to the sound of young Noss singing happily she realized it must be near sunset. She called out, and Noss immediately came into the bedchamber smiling, and bearing a goblet that she handed to Lara. She drank, and it was delicious. "What is it?"

"It is called Frine," Noss said. "It is a mixture of wine and fruit juice or juices. The headman explained it to me when I first tasted it. It tastes different to everyone who drinks it. I thought you might be thirsty, and there is a jug of it on the table in the dayroom," Noss said. "We have not much time. You are expected in the dining hall for the banquet at the twilight. Some of the prince's brothers will be there. I'm sure they will bring their women. The prince says you will be celebrating the success of his stallion today with the mares."

Lara felt her cheeks grow warm with her hidden thoughts. The stallion had indeed had his success. "I must choose a gown then," she said.

"I chose one for you," Noss said shyly. "You don't have to wear it, of course, but I thought it would look beautiful on you."

"Let me see?" Lara said.

Noss hurried off to return a moment later with the gown. It was the pale pink of a rose, and the gossamer fabric, which was shot through with silver threads, looked as if it had been woven by spiders. It was sleeveless, and the neckline fell in a graceful drape just beneath her collarbone. Dropping her drying cloth she let Noss slip the gown on over her head. It fell in simple, elegant folds.

Noss led her over to the wardrobe, and tapping one of the doors with a finger said, "Illuminate!"

Lara gasped as her reflection appeared in the door. "What magic is this?" she asked Noss.

Noss shrugged. "I don't know," she admitted, "but all the wardrobes do it if you tap their doors, and say 'illuminate.' Do you like the gown?"

"Yes," Lara admitted. "Are they all like this?" Her body was quite visible through the silky fabric.

Noss nodded. "Some even have cut-outs, but I thought you would prefer something more modest tonight."

Lara laughed. She would have hardly used the word modest in relation to this gown, she thought.

"I must do your hair now," Noss said. She sat Lara down upon a bench, and taking down her hair, she began to brush it out. Then she braided several strands with delicate jeweled chains and looped them up around Lara's face. She brushed the remaining long swath of gilt hair very lightly with oil of night lilies, and dusted with gold. Then she looked with a critical eye at her handiwork. She held up a round mirror in a polished silver-and-gold frame to Lara. "What do you think?" she asked anxiously. "Do you like it?"

"It's wonderful!" Lara told her. "How did you ever learn to do this?"

Noss shrugged. "My mother had beautiful hair. I used to play with it, and learned that way, I guess." She grew sad a moment. "I hope she and my father were able to buy their farm. I hope they are happy now."

"So do I," Lara said softly. "I am certain they are as happy as my father and Susanna are now. And look at us. Two mercenaries' daughters. What adventures we have had so far, eh?" She laughed.

"But your father is now a Crusader Knight," Noss said. "You did that for him, Lara. You know what happened. That is the hard part for me. Not knowing if it was worth it for my parents."

"I will ask the prince if he can find out for you, Noss," Lara said. "I know you will rest easier if you learn your parents' fate. Then you may follow your own fate without fear."

"My fate is with you," Noss said. Then she opened the wardrobe, and drew out a box made from mother-of-pearl that opened to reveal jewelry of all kinds. Noss selected a pair of thin silver hoops from which hung tiny pink gemstones that sparkled as they moved. She affixed them in Lara's ears. "There! You are ready. I will take you to the banqueting hall now. It is the twilight, and they will all be gathering now. You look beautiful, Lara."

"Thanks to you," Lara responded generously.

"No. You are what you are. You would be beautiful in a sack, and you know it, but you are too modest to say so."

"Aye," Lara said, "But it seems sometimes beauty such as mine is more a curse than a blessing."

"For now it is a blessing," Noss told her. "Come, we must go."

Chapter 10

NOSS LED LARA from her apartments down a hallway and out into the grand corridor. As they walked along it, Lara could see the sky above splashed with fading color, the blue of night hurrying forth, and the three large bright stars known as the Triad blazing directly over the valley. The corridor finally opened into a great banqueting hall, and it was there Noss brought her mistress.

"The prince awaits you," she said, and departed.

The hall was filled with dining couches upon which lounged handsome men and beautiful women. On a dais at the opposite end of the room, Prince Kaliq awaited her. She moved gracefully through the maze of seating, smiling back at the men and women who nodded in greeting. She was more than aware of the admiration of all. She almost sighed with relief upon reaching the prince who, holding out his hand, brought her up onto the dais and introduced her to the others.

"My brothers, this is Lara, daughter of John Swiftsword," he said.

"Hail, Lara!" The banqueting hall erupted with the greeting.

"Thank you, my lords," she replied.

"Come," he said, drawing her down onto the dining couch with him.

A servant handed her a goblet. She tasted it. Just wine.

"You are more beautiful each time I see you," he declared softly, kissing her ear. "I can barely restrain my desire for you." A single finger ran down her bare arm.

"Have you bewitched me?" Lara asked him. "You arouse in me feelings I do not understand."

"Tell me," he murmured against the ear he had just kissed.

"You touch me, a simple touch, and I want to make love with you again," Lara heard herself saying to him.

He smiled. "You do not know it yet, Lara, but you have a great capacity in you for passion. I have only just begun to tap the well of your desire. You must face your passion, and learn how to control it. This I will teach you, and I will tell you things that no others will tell you."

"What things, my lord?" Lara asked him.

"That men are weak, and women stronger. Understand this, and no one but you will control your destiny, my love," he said to her.

"Why would you tell me such things?" she said.

"To prepare you for that destiny, Lara. You will be with me but a short time. Then you will move on. It is written in the stars that shine above Hetar."

"What is my destiny?" She was curious. How could she not be?

He shook his head. "That is something that has not been revealed to me, nor would it. I am but a stop on your road. Nor will you understand until the day comes that you meet your destiny head-on. It is difficult for me to accept such a thing, but to do otherwise would be to betray my own people, and bring destruction upon them."

"You speak in riddles," Lara told him, "but you are very wise and so I must accept your words, my lord Kaliq. And I must believe I have come to you so that I may learn about love in its many incarnations—how to use it to my advantage, how to avoid the pitfalls it can present. Would you say that is correct?"

He nodded, smiling tenderly at her. "Aye, and I am glad that you understand, my love. Unfortunately I will fall in love with you, which is a luxury I have never allowed myself, Lara. I cannot help it. It is unwise, of course, but now and again one of my brothers does. We survive, of course, but we are never again the same."

"Then why do you do it?" she inquired curious.

"We do not do it deliberately. True love just happens. Sometimes fortune smiles, and both people fall in love with each other. That is a sweet miracle. But mostly it is just a feeling of desire and delightful lust," he explained. "Lust and desire can melt quickly away, however. True love does not."

She nodded. "Then what I am feeling for you is lust and desire?"

"Aye, but sometimes it is more, and you believe you are in love, but it is not so," he told her. "It is but a momentary passion that quickly fades."

"This is all very confusing," Lara said.

He laughed. "It is, isn't it? But trust me to lead you through the maze of emotions that will overcome you while you are mine."

"Stop!" Lara answered him. "With every word you utter I become more befuddled. I think I shall just enjoy the moments as I live them."

"A wise decision," he answered with a smile.

The servants now began serving the meal. They came to each dining couch, beginning with the prince's, offering platters, trays and bowls of food. To Lara's surprise there was fresh fish from the sea, and shellfish. The prince explained that it was transported by magic each morning to his palace. There were roasted meats and poultry, bread, several cheeses and a bowl of mixed lettuces. A large platter of fruits was brought around, and another platter of honey cakes. Their cups were never empty of the potent sweet rich wine.

The entertainment began with the fruit and cakes. To Lara's surprise Og appeared to wrestle with several beefy young men, but he won each match to the delight of the onlookers. Acrobats came to tumble and clown with one another. In one corner sat musicians playing upon pipes, drums, reed instruments, bells and cymbals. Finally came a troupe of lithe dancers in their silks moving rhythmically about the hall to the music.

Lara noticed that as the night wore on the guests were less and less interested in the entertainment. Several of the women now lay naked or half-naked while their princes kissed and caressed them. Then the dancers were gone, and only the musicians remained, their tunes becoming more and more sensual and urgent. She watched wide-eyed as one of the princes mounted his woman and began to pleasure her. The woman wore a look of utter bliss upon her face. Then two more princes began to make love to their partners, one sitting his companion upon his lap so they faced one another, the other entering his lover as she knelt before him, her buttocks raised.

Kaliq watched the play of emotions across Lara's face. "The banquets always seem to end like this," he said in a low voice. "Sometimes my brothers share their women. Look there." He pointed across the room to a dining bench where one woman was receiving her lover between her legs while a second prince pushed his manroot between her lips. "There are many ways of pleasuring," Kaliq said to Lara. He reached up and slid her gown from her shoulders, baring her breasts. Her nipples immediately grew tight as they were revealed.

Their eyes met briefly, and Lara watched, fascinated, as he fondled her breasts. His dark head bent, and he licked at her nipples. She felt a shiver of delight ripple down her spine. Then to her surprise, another prince joined them. Sitting behind her he put an arm around her waist, pushed her hair aside with his other hand, and began kissing the back of her neck. Two lovers? At the same time? In the Forest Durga and Enda had taken turns with her, but they had never loved her together at the same time.

"This is my brother, Lothair," Kaliq said. "He has been admiring you all evening, Lara, my love. I realize you had not considered such a thing, but I would like to share you with him for a short while."

"I long to sheath myself in your lovely body," Prince Lothair murmured in Lara's ear. His two hands were suddenly clasping her breasts as Kaliq knelt and, pushing Lara's thighs apart, lowered his dark head to lick at the soft insides of her thighs. The hands on her breasts were gentle, stroking and caressing her until she was weak with enjoyment. She felt Kaliq opening her up, spreading her nether lips, his tongue beginning to lick at the sensitive flesh hidden within. She whimpered, and moved restlessly beneath his touch as Lothair's big hands moved over her body tenderly setting it afire.

"Is she ready yet, brother?" Lothair said.

"Not yet," Kaliq replied. "Remember this is all new to her. She needs time to be truly free of her inhibitions." His tongue sought the sensitive little nub of flesh that was the core of her womanhood. He played with it, slowly touching, licking, coaxing her to release her fears, and Lara did.

It was simply too delicious. She had never considered two men pleasuring her at the same time, but after her initial astonishment she had come to realize she was enjoying their attentions. Enda and Durga had wanted only to satisfy themselves and get a child on her. These two princes wanted nothing more than to give her enjoyment. She sighed gustily, and then moaned as his tongue pushed itself into her sheath. "Oh! Oh!" she cried, and then the wicked tongue moved itself back to that sensitive bit of flesh, teasing it until her juices began to flow. "Oh, please!" Lara begged them. "Please!" She had never before felt such white-hot desire as was now coursing through her veins.

Kaliq raised his dark head from between her milky thighs. "She is ready," he said.

Prince Lothair lay Lara back upon the dining couch. He mounted her, his dark eyes burning with undisguised lust. He pushed slowly, filling her with his manroot. Kaliq had seated himself behind Lara, and now held her in a tender embrace as his brother worked the girl to a fever pitch that left Lara gasping for breath, and so pleasured that she screamed with her complete satisfaction. Lothair smiled down at her, giving her a passionate kiss that left Lara's head whirling dizzily as he withdrew from her. He kissed her hands, still smiling, and then left them.

"I want more," Lara begged, and Kaliq complied, covering her body with his, entering her, moving upon her while she clung to him, her nails raking down his long back. Harder and harder he thrust. Her legs wrapped about his torso. Deeper and deeper he pressed his manroot into her burning flesh until she was sobbing with a desire that threatened to overwhelm her. And then as suddenly as the storm began, it crested and subsided, leaving Lara weak, her beautiful face tearstained, her body at last satisfied. Turning her head she saw that the other princes and their women were now as fully engaged as they had but recently been. Lothair lay near them on his back, a darkhaired girl with strong thighs riding him vigorously, her eyes closed with her bliss.

"Now," Kaliq said softly, "you are beginning to learn and understand passion, and there is much more, my love. Much, much more."

"But can I survive it?" she teased him.

"You are half faerie, Lara, and none have a greater capacity for passion than those with faerie blood," he told her.

"I am exhausted," she said to him.

"Then sleep, my love," he told her.

"Here?"

"Everyone will," he told her. "And come the morning we will all go to the baths and refresh each other." He held the cup of wine to her lips. "Drink, and you will rest."

"What is in the cup?" she demanded of him.

"Sleep," he said with a smile, and she drank, finding he had spoken the truth.

When she awoke the golden light of day was filling the skies outside of the banqueting hall, and the others about her were beginning to stir. Kaliq was already awake, and rising, he led them all to the baths as he had said. Everyone was naked, and Lara thought how beautiful the bodies around her were. They washed each other in the floor basins, each prince with his partner. Then they entered the bathing pool, lounging and chattering about the fine feast of the previous evening, and Kaliq's hospitality.

"I hope," Lothair said to Lara, "that your enjoyment was as complete as mine. I can see you are young, and have little experience, but your faerie blood rose to the occasion. Thank you for sharing yourself with me, Lara."

She smiled at him and kissed his cheek, not knowing what else to say. As each couple departed the bathing pool and left the bath, they found servants with their garments awaiting them.

"I must see my guests off," Kaliq told her. "Go back to your apartments, and I will join you for the morning meal. Ah, here is Noss to escort you."

"Was it a wonderful feast?" Noss asked as they walked along together.

"I have never attended one like it," Lara admitted.

"What is it like?" Noss wanted to know.

"What is what like?"

"Not being a virgin," Noss said.

"How old are you?" Lara demanded.

"Twelve, almost thirteen."

"There is time enough for you to know such things, but now is not that time, Noss," Lara told her. "I will tell you when the time is right, I promise."

True to his word, Kaliq joined Lara for the first meal of the day.

When they had finished eating, Noss cleared the remnants away, and left them together. With a smile, Kaliq disrobed again, inviting Lara to do the same. They lay together naked on her bed, caressing each other and kissing. Neither of them, it seemed, could get enough of the other. He drank from her lips like a bee gathering honey. Her fingers brushed over his lean, hard body, exploring it in a leisurely fashion.

"I have never before," she said softly, "enjoyed learning a man's body."

He smiled at her. "I am flattered then to be the recipient of your curiosity."

"You tease me," she cried. "Do not! You know not what I suffered at the hands of the Foresters. To be used as a vessel by them, to feel desire but at the same time revulsion for them both was horrific."

"Ah, Lara," he reassured her, "if I tease you it is because I care for you. Put away all thoughts of the Foresters, and let me love you. Know that you are safe in my care. I will let nothing happen to you, my beautiful one." He kissed her gently. "Come now and let us take pleasure in one another, for we are both ready." He lifted her up, and sheathed himself in her lovely body, groaning as he felt the walls of her passage enclosing him with heated desire.

"Ahh," she sighed, taking him into herself as deeply as he could go. "Shall the mare ride the stallion?" she taunted.

"If it pleases her," he said, smiling into her green eyes.

"Nay," she surprised him by answering. "This time I would be mastered by you, my lord Kaliq. Make me forget! Make me feel safe in your arms!"

Rolling them over so she now lay beneath him, he began to thrust himself within her excited body. Slowly, slowly at first, making her whimper, making her want more. Then his tempo began to increase, and his manroot flashed swiftly back and forth, back and forth until Lara was sobbing with her pleasure, crying out with the satisfaction he could give her. She clung to him, her body weak and replete with the gratification he had so sweetly given her. Lara opened her eyes. "I wanted you to have pleasure, too," she said.

"I did," he assured her. "The look on your face alone almost brought me to a crisis before my time, but my will is strong. We finished together, I swear it," he promised, smiling down into her face. "But now, my love, the day is well begun, and there is much to do. Come, and we will bathe again in your own little bath." He arose from the bed, drawing her up with him, and together they did as he suggested. Then he left her, saying, "Today you begin your education, for that is the other part of my task with you. Master Bashkar will come shortly to begin your lessons."

"What have I to learn that you cannot teach me?" she asked him.

"You must learn about Hetar and its history. Not gossip and old wives' tales, but the truth. What do you know of the Outlands, for instance?"

"That it is a wild place of uncivilized men," she answered him.

"And how did it get that way when the rest of Hetar is so urbane and right?"

"I don't know," Lara admitted.

"Master Bashkar will teach you. Can you read and write at all?"

Lara nodded. "Some, and I know enough about numbers not to be cheated by the butcher or the baker."

"It's a start then," he said, "but there is much more for you, Lara. I can teach you passion, and about those who inhabit Hetar, but Master Bashkar will teach you everything else. Trust me. You must know as much as you can before you leave me."

"You said you would see that I met my grandmother," Lara reminded him.

"I always keep my promises," he told her.

Master Bashkar came. He was an old man with a long white beard and long white hair. He wore a broad brimmed hat of dark felt with a point, and walked with a tall staff that had a face carved into it. "This is Llyr," he said to Lara.

To Lara's surprise the eyes in the face opened, and Llyr observed her closely. "She is very beautiful, but astoundingly ignorant," Llyr pronounced.

"Your staff talks!" Lara exclaimed.

"You state the obvious," Llyr replied. "Why would I not speak? I have eyes to observe, and a mouth, not to mention a lean half body. I need no more than that."

"I beg your pardon," Lara said. "I have never seen anyone like you."

"She has manners, and that will count for something," Llyr murmured to Master Bashkar. "Now, let us see how much she knows. Precious little, I can tell already."

"Please sit down," Lara invited the old man.

"Do not mind Llyr, my child," Master Bashkar said. "He does have a tendency to speak his mind. He comes from an ash tree, and they are very frank, unlike the oaks and the maples. As for the aspen and birch, they hardly speak above a whisper."

"Oaks are dour, and maples chatter too much," Llyr observed.

"And the palms like those at the village oasis?" Lara asked.

"Palms are incredibly flighty creatures," Llyr said disapprovingly.

"Enough talk about your relations," Master Bashkar said sternly.

"I am certainly not related to a palm," Llyr snapped, and then his eyes closed.

Lara could not help but giggle.

The old man smiled and said, "Now, child, I must find out what you know."

For the rest of the day he sat with her, asking questions, nodding and tching. Noss brought them food at one point, gasping in surprise when Llyr demanded cheese and a mug of ale. His carved arms reached out from the staff to take the mug Noss brought. As the shadows began to lengthen over the valley, Master Bashkar finally arose.

"We have much work ahead of us, my child, and I do not know yet how much time we will have together, but never fear. We will manage. I will be back tomorrow morning at the ninth hour." He bowed to her, and departed.

"He seems a kind old man," Noss noted after Master Bashkar had gone.

"And wise. You must sit with me and listen so you may learn, too, Noss. Can you read or write at all?" Lara asked her.

"What use would I have for reading or writing?" Noss replied.

"Each skill you acquire makes you more valuable to your mistress," Lara told her.

"Will you teach me?" Noss said.

"I will. We'll start tomorrow before Master Bashkar comes," Lara promised.

The prince came to join her, and they ate their supper in the garden. Afterwards, he made love to her, laying her upon her bed naked, and spending almost an hour just stroking and kissing her body. He rubbed her with sweet oils until her skin tingled. Then he gave her the flask of oil, and told her to rub him. Her blood grew hotter with each stroke of her palms upon his bronzed flesh, but she suddenly realized that she appreciated the subtlety of the fragrant caresses. Their joining would be thunderous, and it was. She shuddered with pure desire as he slowly slipped his manroot into her body, sighing as Kaliq pushed deep. His mouth found hers, one kiss following another until it seemed as if their kisses had neither beginning nor end. She trembled, and he withdrew slightly, to her protest.

"Nay, my love," he told her. "You must learn to control your hunger, for only then can you control your lover."

"I don't want to control you," she gasped. "I just want pleasure!"

His laughter was soft. He kissed her lips again in a tender embrace. "One day there will be a man you need to control, must control, else he destroy you. So now you practice on me, and on the other lovers you will have in your travels, Lara. You must grow stronger with the pleasure, not weaker."

"Just this once!" she pleaded.

"No," he said. "Now make me desire you more than you desire me, my love. Tighten the muscles of your sheath to embrace my manroot, and hold it captive so it cannot release its juices until you are ready for them. Ahhh! That's it!"

She followed his instructions, and squeezed him hard. He groaned aloud, praising her. Lara was very surprised for she had never considered that a woman could dominate a man in such a fashion. Fascinated, she played with him for some time until he was begging her for the pleasure that fulfillment gave their bodies.

"Now!" she ground out into his ear, her nails digging into his shoulders. "Now, my lord!" And she wrapped her legs about him, closed her eyes, and let the pleasure overtake their bodies.

"You are incredible, and a wonderful student," he told her afterwards, and when he had recovered himself he arose from her bed. "Sleep now, my love. I will see you on the morrow."

"Wait!" Lara cried, raising herself on an elbow. "What of Maeve?"

"I have sent the message. Now we must wait, and see if she will come," he said.

"What if she does not, my lord Kaliq?" Lara asked.

"Then she does not," he answered, "but she will. You are her only grandchild. Your mother must have loved your father very much to refuse to spawn other offspring."

"Then why did she leave us?" Lara demanded.

"You must ask her," Kaliq said, and then he left her.

In the weeks that followed Lara never left the palace. The village in the Desert below was almost forgotten. She studied each day with Master Bashkar, Noss by her side learning at her own pace. Each morning before the old man came she instructed Noss in her letters, and then her writing, and finally she taught her how to read. Noss was surprisingly quick. For Lara, however, learning the history of Hetar was fascinating.

She learned that there was a High Council of eight that met in the City most of the year. Two members came from the Forest, two from the Coastal Region, two from the Desert and two from the Midlands, of which the City was considered a part. The council had a single overlord. The ruler of each of the provinces would take a turn as council head, rotating every three moon cycles, and only voting to break a tied vote. It was the High Council's duty to govern Hetar, to see that its laws were upheld, to make new laws, and to keep the Outlanders at bay and contained within their borders. The council worked with the guild heads to see that their civilization continued to run smoothly. She had lived in the City most of her life, yet she had never known of the High Council. "Why?" she asked Master Bashkar.

"Are there places of learning in the City or throughout the provinces, my child?" he asked her.

"For the wealthy, aye, but not for the ordinary people," Lara said. "What little I learned, I learned from my grandmother, who learned it from I know not where."

"It is not necessary to educate a people if you keep them content," Master Bashkar said quietly. "Give them a roof over their heads, enough sustenance to keep them from starving, free public entertainments, perhaps a small reason for living and you do not have to educate them. It was not always so on Hetar.

"Once all children were educated to their full potential in order that they might advance themselves if they chose, and be of use to our society. But that led to dissension as people began to think for themselves, and question their leaders. Those in power do not like being questioned. As those wise ones who instructed the young grew old and unable to teach, others took their places. But they did not teach as well, nor did they teach our history, or our great books and poetry. Mathematics became complex and convoluted. The ordinary folk could not understand it, but no one taught them the simplicities of mathematical skills, or logic. But they were kept fed, housed and entertained, and were encouraged to use their skills at whatever could bring them in a few coins. Education was no longer encouraged, and so finally it was no longer offered to the people."

"What is poetry?" Lara asked him.

"A story in rhyme," he told her. "I am sure you have heard street poetry, Lara, but it is unlikely you have ever heard the great sagas and songs of old that were once taught, and recited about the halls at night."

"No," she said. "I have never heard anything like that."

"Nor I," Noss chimed into the conversation.

"There is a great saga that was once told of how the Shadow Princes of the Desert came into being eons ago," Master Bashkar said.

"Prince Kaliq once told me he had a Peri ancestor, but he also said his kind had come from the shadows at the beginning of time," Lara said. "How can that be?"

"Before time as we now know it began," Master Bashkar said, "Hetar was a world of clouds and fog. The Shadow Princes came first from those mists. They were male spirits, and for several generations they mated with the faerie races they found here. Then the clouds cleared away, and the beauty of the planet was visible to all. At that time it was discovered there were others on Hetar as well. The Forest Lords descended from tree spirits and banded with the Midland folk who came from the earth spirits. The people from the Coastal Region had their origins in the sea. They built the City at the center of it all, and became civilized."

"But what of the Shadow Princes?" Lara asked.

"The faerie women they had mated with bore only sons. Discovering this hidden valley, they chose the Desert as their realm," Master Bashkar continued. "But soon it was feared there would not be room for all the offspring they were producing, for they were a fertile race. It was then the princes decided if the faeries would grant them long life and the same ability to reproduce only when they chose, they would remain in the Desert, joining the High Council as a part of Hetar, keeping clear of all dissension, yet trading with the others and welcoming them when they came. Women were no longer necessary to their society, nor were children. The Shadow Princes are a selfish race. Kind, but selfish. And so it has been for many centuries. Now and again new members are chosen for the council that the others are not made uncomfortable by their longevity and never-changing appearance. They take women they admire for their pleasure, but they always return them to their families with enough wealth to satisfy those families."

"But what if the women fall in love with their princes?" Lara asked.

"Then they are returned with broken hearts. It is not wise to love a Shadow Prince, Lara, and they try to be careful in their choices," he said.

"How came you here?" she wondered.

"I am an Outlander, a member of the Devyn clan," he explained. "Our society is very different from that of Hetar. The clan families keep mostly to themselves."

"I have never met an Outlander," Lara told him.

"You would not have," he told her with a smile. "We are despised by those who call themselves Hetarians. They are repulsed by our ways for we refused to allow ourselves to conform to their way of thinking, or their social order. They wear a cloak of civilization proudly, but beneath their veneer they are more savage than the Outlanders. Did the prince not tell me your father sold you into carnal bondage that he might advance himself and his new family? It is barbaric, and would not happen in the Outlands!"

"No!" Lara cried. "You do not understand! My father is a great swordsman, but without the means to advance himself into the Crusader Knights he was doomed to remain in the Quarter. My baby brother would have had no future at all. Nor would I, for there was no coin for my dowry. He had nothing of value but for me. The monies Gaius Prospero paid for me allowed my father to dress himself properly, to obtain new weapons, and fine armor. We knew he would win his tournament matches if his application could just be accepted, but it would not have been unless he appeared worthy. My father is a good man, Master Bashkar, and I was proud to be able to aid him."

"His great skills with his weapon should have made him more than worthy, Lara. Men should be judged by what they can do, and for no other reason," Master Bashkar said. "A fine appearance will not aid him on the battlefield, my child. You were the treasure your faerie mother gave him in return for his love. Yet he used you badly."

"My father did not desert me, Master Bashkar. If my mother had remained with us, could not her faerie magic have aided my father to gain his goal sooner? But she did not. I was but a few months old when she left us for another lover."

"She loved you, my child. Did she not put that chain and star crystal about your neck to keep you safe from harm? A faerie woman who gives a mortal man a child does not leave them without great cause."

Lara was more confused than she had ever been as she listened to Master Bashkar's words. Her whole life she had been told of how thoughtless and cruel Ilona had been. How she had ensorcelled her father as a youth, given the love-struck boy a half faerie child, and then recklessly left him to satisfy her carnal faerie nature, thereby breaking his heart. Had not her grandmother, Ina, said it often enough? And her father had never disagreed. Indeed, he spoke of Ilona as little as possible, and when he did the look in his eyes was painful to see. When she had been naughty as a child, Ina had often warned her she must not allow her mother's wicked faerie nature to overcome her. Now, however, she was being asked to embrace that nature, and unable to help herself, she was. And what's more, she found she liked that part of her that was faerie. But still she could not reconcile herself to a faerie mother who cared so little for her that she deserted her. She would never forgive Ilona. And her father was a good man, no matter what Master Bashkar said. The Master was an old man, and he did not understand the complexities of life in the City.

The winter passed, and spring came to the Desert. For the first time Kaliq took Lara from the palace. The rains had come for a brief time to the sands, and the Desert was abloom with a carpet of flowers. Lara was amazed by them as they rode forth.

"How can this be?" she asked him.

He shrugged. "It is an aberration of nature," he told her. "They will be gone in a few days, and then the sands will stretch golden again for as far as the eye can see. Each year at this time the flowers come into bloom. When they begin to die we will gather the fading blossoms to make potions and medicines from their seeds and petals."

When they returned to the palace within the cliffs, Lara was suddenly aware of how stifling it was in comparison to the great Desert. The urge to leave the Shadow Princes was suddenly tugging at her. She forced it back. She must remain the year and a day to be truly free. And where else would she go that she could be as safe? Og was more than content working with the prince's horses. He had friends among the other servants who were not intimidated by his size. She rarely saw him now but in passing. But she had her lessons with Master Bashkar, and she had Noss. And Kaliq instructed her each night in the arts of passion. Lara enjoyed his lessons best of all.

The months passed, and then one day when she had been within the Shadow realm for almost a year, the grandmother she had never known, Maeve, queen of the Forest Faeries arrived in Kaliq's dining hall one evening in her usual puff of lavender mist. She was barely visible, yet seeing her, the Shadow Princes came to their feet and bowed low. Kaliq came forward to lead her to a seat. He put a goblet of wine in her hand.

She drank from it, and her image strengthened. She was a beautiful creature even in her decline. Lara could but imagine what she had been like in her prime. Maeve was tall, and gracefully slender. She had silver hair like spun sugar that billowed gently about her now-thin face. Her pale green eyes were alert and sharp, sweeping about the room and taking in all. A once-full mouth was now thin with age, but there was a sweetness to it; her nose was straight and in perfect proportion to the rest of her face. She gave the impression of great fragility, but Lara sensed it was actually great strength. Maeve was garbed in elegant garments of forest-green and gold brocade, a golden torque about her slim neck. As Lara stared at her grandmother, her features faded slightly, but when the faerie queen drank again from the goblet in her beringed hand, the image was restored. It grew even stronger when she spoke to him. "Why have you summoned me, Kaliq of the Shadow realm?"

"I have that which you have longed for most, great Maeve," he said. "I have your granddaughter, Lara, only child of your daughter, Ilona."

Maeve's glance swept the hall at his words, and when they reached Lara a strangely sweet smile lit her aristocratic features. "Lara!" She breathed the word, and stood. Then unable to remain upon her feet she sat down heavily upon the bench, holding out her hand to the girl.

Unable to resist the soft call, Lara arose and came to kneel by the faerie queen's side. "I am here, grandmother," she said. A wave of tenderness swept over her.

Maeve reached out, and caressed Lara's face. Her touch was like being brushed by butterfly wings, the girl thought. The delicate hand fingered Lara's gilt hair. Then her fingers tilted the girl's face upward, and Maeve stared into Lara's green eyes. Lara felt as if a bolt of lightning had struck her. She immediately felt the bond of kinship with the faerie. "Ilona's child," Maeve said. Then looking away from her granddaughter, she turned her gaze again on Kaliq. "How?" she demanded.

The Shadow Prince recited Lara's tale, and Maeve nodded again and again as he spoke. He concluded by saying, "I have sheltered her, and taught her since she came, great Maeve. I know she will not remain with me for much longer, but I know how much you have longed to know her. I am glad you have come."

"I must summon my daughter," Maeve responded. "She must see her child."

"No!" Lara cried. "I do not want to see her! How can I ever forgive her for leaving us, grandmother? Forgive me if I hurt you, for I hold no ill will toward you, but I cannot see she who broke my father's heart when she deserted him for another lover."

The faerie queen's image flickered, and dimmed slightly. She quickly downed the contents of her cup, and was restored to their sight. "Your mother did not leave your father for another man, Lara. That is but what she told him so he should not attempt to dissuade her from her fate again. Your mother has always been my chosen. She will become queen of the Forest Faeries when I am finally faded away. My time grows short now. I needed her back in my own kingdom that she might learn her duties. She could no longer live in both your father's world and ours. It was her duty to return, and your mother has always known how to do her duty, no matter how painful. Several times she came to see you, but neither your father, nor your father's mother would permit her access to you. They said it was better for you. That seeing you, and then departing again would but confuse a child. Ilona finally accepted their wishes, though it pained her greatly. Were you not told this when you were grown, Lara?"

The girl shook her head slowly. "My father rarely spoke of my mother," she said. "It was my grandmother, Ina, who told me of my heritage."

"And slandered your mother in the process, I have not a doubt," Maeve said in dark tones.

"I'm sure she never meant to," Lara attempted to protect her father's dead mother, who had raised her so lovingly.

Maeve sniffed in disbelief, but said nothing further. Her grand-daughter had been deliberately misled into believing that her faerie kin did not love her. It was intolerable! And so very human. "You look exactly like your mother," she remarked. "And your mother must see you. I shall summon her now. You will treat her with kindness, Lara, for she has suffered, too. She loved your father. Still loves him, if the truth be known."

"He took another wife two years ago," Lara said. "I have a half brother."

"His love of her then was not as constant as hers for him," Maeve murmured scornfully. "But then I warned her that humans are a feckless lot."

"If you dislike humans so then why bother to remain here, or summon my mother? If she is used to the idea that I am gone from her life, why wound her if you love her?" Lara said angrily. She stared defiantly at the beautiful old faerie queen.

Maeve laughed. "That temper you possess, girl, is both human and faerie. I do not dislike humans, Lara. Indeed, some of my favorite lovers were humans, and I spawned seven half faerie children in my day. Your mother, however, was born of my union with a faerie lord called Tiburon, who was my chosen mate. He has long faded away into the next life, but you should know who your grandfather was." She turned to Kaliq. "I am not strong enough to reach out to Ilona. Will you do it for me?"

He nodded, and then he poured more wine into her goblet. "Drink, Queen Maeve, and I will bring your daughter to you. I suspect you will need a certain amount of strength for the meeting shortly to take place between Ilona and your granddaughter. Listen, but do not involve yourself in their affairs lest you shorten what time you have remaining here."

Maeve reached out again to Lara, taking the girl's face between her hands. "I have not lied to you, Lara. What I have said is the truth. Be kind to your mother. If you have any care for your faerie heritage, remember that Ilona gave you life, and while she could not be with you she gave you Ethne to watch over you. I am sorry the crystal guardian could not prevent your time with the Forest Lords, my granddaughter."

"I had heard you had no other grandchildren but me," Lara responded. "Yet you have had other children. Have they not wed, and taken mates?"

"My other children, five sons and two daughters, were killed in the war that ensued between the Forest Faeries and the Forest Lords following the murder of the unfortunate Nixa. They fired the portion of the woodland where we had our halls because they were angry at the curse I placed upon them. Your mother was born in the time after we had retreated deep into the Forest, where we could not be found by those violent men."

"If I had given them a child," Lara said, "could it have reversed the curse?"

Maeve laughed scornfully. "Not even I could reverse that curse. I was very angry. The curse was strong and irrevocable. What madness possessed them to believe that they might reverse it by getting offspring on half faerie girls I do not know. Yet you had to pass through their world, and treat with them for it is your fate."

"Everyone keeps saying it is my fate to do this, and to do that, but I do not understand at all," Lara grumbled. "What is this fate you all prate about?"

"I cannot tell you, Lara, for your fate is yours to unravel as you go through life," Maeve said. "You may change that fate, or not, but it must proceed in an orderly manner. That is the will of the Celestial Actuary."

Lara shook her head. "I do not understand at all," she replied.

"It is not the hour for you to understand," Maeve answered her, "but in time you will. I charted your stars the night you were born, for I was present at your birth, and even then much was hidden from me. You have a destiny, Lara, and it is for greatness. That much I know. That much I can share with you."

Another clap of thunder sounded in the banqueting hall, and Ilona appeared in a mist of royal purple. Not looking at anyone else, she hurried to her mother's side. Everyone was astounded at how much she resembled her daughter. "What is it, Mother, that you have had me summoned?" she asked.

Maeve raised a slender hand, and pointed at Lara with a thin finger.

Ilona turned and stared. Surprise and shock suffused her features. She could not speak at first. She was hard-pressed to even believe the evidence of her own eyes. This was her daughter! This was Lara! But how?

"Greetings, Mother." Lara finally broke the spell. "It has been some time since we last met." There was an edge of irony in the girl's voice.

Ilona heard it, and bit her lip. What could she possibly say to the daughter she had left behind sixteen years ago? "You are beautiful."

"They claim I am your image, and I will admit that seeing you is like peering into a looking glass," Lara replied. "It has been both a blessing and a curse to bear this beauty, and yet be half human, Mother. It would have been easier had you been there."

"I could not be!" Ilona cried. Then, reaching out for Lara's hand, she transported them into a private place away from the hall. "I will not speak with you of these things amid a crowd of strangers, Lara. I did not leave you willingly."

"Grandmother says it was because you could not live in both worlds any longer," Lara replied. "Then why did you not take me with you?"

"Your father begged me to leave you with him, Lara. I could not refuse him. I loved John. I always have loved him," Ilona said. "And I came back several times to see how you grew, but Ina would not allow it. She said you must be raised to live in the world in which they inhabited and not dwell upon things faerie. Finally she asked me not to return at all, and your father agreed. I was defeated."

"He has a wife and son now," Lara said cruelly.

"Does he?" Ilona murmured.

"And he is a Crusader Knight," she continued.

"Then his wife brought him the riches he needed to gain that goal. Oh, I am glad!" Ilona cried. "I offered him faerie gold, but he would not take it. Your father is a very proud man, but you know that."

"My father sold me into slavery to gain his goal, but do not be angered. I agreed to it, Mother. There was nothing else for me, as we were always poor. No man would have me without a dowry portion despite my beauty. In fact, my faerie beauty frightened many. The Master of the Merchants purchased me, and meant to resell me into one of the City's Pleasure Houses, but my beauty caused dissension among the Pleasure Mistresses. So I was consigned to a Taubyl Trader, and the Head Forester and his brother paid a small fortune for me because they believed the child of a half faerie girl would free them from Maeve's curse, poor fools. Knowing naught of my faerie heritage, I did not realize that because I hated them, their seed would not flourish in my womb."

"How did you learn of it?" Ilona asked quietly. Her daughter's recitation was so bitter, and she could see Lara was angry.

"Og, the Forest giant, told me. It was he who aided me to escape. He now takes care of the prince's horses," Lara said.

"I had thought the Forest giants were extinct," Ilona said softly. "We did not learn of their massacre until after it had happened."

"He was in his mother's womb. She fled only to be caught several years later when they slew her," Lara replied. "The Foresters do not know that giant memory is passed on in the womb. They did not want the shame of Maeve's curse made public."

"No, they would not," Ilona said. "The Foresters know nothing outside of their own world, nor do they want to know. I am sorry for what has happened."

"According to my grandmother it is my fate, my destiny," Lara responded sharply. "She blames my father, but I do not."

"Nay, you shouldn't. I know that your father loves you, and did what he believed was best for you. He might, however, have called upon me, and I would have aided him. He might have asked for my help. I would have given it, and surely he knew that. But your father was ever stubborn, yet had he really considered you at all, he could have called upon me. After all, you are my child, too. I am the one who carried you beneath my heart until your birth, and it was he who drove me away. If he had but asked, it could have been easier." Then catching herself she said, "But John was always an over-proud man. Tell me of his wife?"

"Susanna is a good woman. She was kind to me, and we were friends. But I think she was jealous that you had first captured my father's heart," Lara said. "And I was a reminder of you. At least my grandmother was not there to remind her constantly of how I resemble you."

"Ina is dead then?" Ilona did not sound grief-stricken.

"Several years now, yes."

"Your father's sword skills, of course, helped him win his matches at tournament time," Ilona said. "So now he lives well with a new wife and a son. His daughter, his old life in the Quarter, is behind him. And you have begun your journey, Lara. It will not be an easy one, I fear." She reached out, and touched the girl's face. "Do not be angry with me, my daughter. I have never stopped loving you, and I left Ethne to protect you as best she might. Her powers are very limited, however, as you have learned."

"What of my powers?" Lara wanted to know. "Do I have any?"

"Do you want them?" Ilona said.

"Yes! I want them because I never again want to be at any man's mercy, Mother! I am not afraid of this journey, this destiny you all prattle about, but I must be as well-equipped as any soldier if I am to survive and triumph."

Ilona waved her hand, and two goblets appeared, floating in the air before the women. The faerie reached out and, taking a goblet, offered it to Lara. "Let us sit and talk more," Ilona said, and there was a bench in the mist where they had stood speaking. She drew her daughter down to sit beside her. "Tell me which of the Shadow Princes is your host?"

"Prince Kaliq," Lara said.

"What has he taught you so far?"

"To enjoy passion. To control it so I remain the dominant," Lara said. "I lost my virginity to Enda, brother of the Head Forester. While easier than Durga, he was still a beast. I despised them both. But with Kaliq it is different. I think I may even love him a little," she admitted.

"Do not love him more than a little," Ilona warned, but she smiled at her daughter.

Unable to help herself, Lara smiled back, feeling a sudden rush of warmth for this beautiful faerie who had given her life. "And Kaliq has brought me Master Bashkar, from whom I have learned the history of Hetar as well as its great literature and poetry."

"Excellent," Ilona said. "Now there remains but one thing for you to learn."

"What is that, Mother?" Lara was curious.

"You must be taught how to fight, to protect yourself. When you have learned to defend yourself you will be ready to move on, and you must," Ilona said. "You have a..."

"A destiny. A fate. I know! I know! But what is it?" Lara asked.

Ilona sighed. "What little I know I cannot tell you, my daughter. You may change your fate slightly now and again as you move along life's path. If I speak on it I could spoil it. Have I not already done you enough harm?"

It was then Lara began to weep softly. "I missed you," she sobbed. "I needed you! Why did you go?"

"I was torn between two worlds, Lara. As my mother's only surviving child, I was chosen to follow after her as queen. Your father could not understand that a woman's duty is every bit as important as a man's. It was the only time he and I ever fought with one another. I offered to take him with me into my mother's kingdom, but he would not go. As proud as he was, as duty-bound, he had his own fate to follow, too, and he would not change it to permit me to follow mine. There was no choice but to separate, and so we did. I wanted you with me. He begged I leave you. In the end I realized it was better for both you and John that you stay. Perhaps I should not have listened to his pleas. Perhaps I should have taken you with me. But I did not. Even faeries make mistakes, Lara. Will you forgive me?" Her lovely green eyes scanned her daughter's face.

"Yes," Lara said simply. Her whole life she had wanted her mother. What a fool she would be to turn her away now. She embraced Ilona, and kissed her cheek. Then she sighed. "We will begin anew, Mother. Now you have cleverly avoided telling me of any powers I might have. But you must, I beg you."

Ilona laughed. "Very well," she agreed. "I can teach you how to draw people and objects to you. I can teach you to shift your shape as does your prince. I can show you potions and lotions of interest to the human world. I know now how to be queen. I shall remain with you for a short time. It cannot make up for the years we were separated, but it will give us an opportunity to know one another better. Will that suit you, daughter?"

"Yes!" Lara responded enthusiastically. "Yes, it will!" And she laughed happily.

Ilona laughed, too, and then she said, "We must return to Prince Kaliq's banqueting hall. His heart would be quite broken if he thought I had taken you off forever. Besides, I must return my mother to her own home shortly. She is so weak, and soon she will be faded away entirely. She can barely transport herself any longer, and coming here tonight took a great deal out of her."

"I am so glad that I had the opportunity to meet her," Lara said. "Will I see her again, Mother?"

"If you wish. I know it would please her greatly," Ilona said. She waved a graceful hand, and they were returned to the prince's banqueting hall where Maeve eagerly awaited them, smiling happily to see her daughter and her granddaughter reconciled and reunited at long last. Now she could fade away in peace.

Chapter 11

LARA BID HER GRANDMOTHER, the great Maeve, farewell. "I will see you again," she promised the old faerie.

Maeve shook her head. "Nay, my sweet child, you will not. I came tonight because Kaliq said you were with him, and out of the great friendship I have always had for the Shadow Princes, but I am too weak to come again."

"Then I will come to you," Lara said.

"Nay! I will not allow you in the Forest, Lara. The Foresters have sought for a hundred years in their feeble attempts to find me. We have eluded them for all that time, but I know there could come a time when they might discover us. I would not want you there to be retaken into bondage. I will never revoke the curse I placed upon them. They were ever an arrogant people, and for centuries we overlooked their bad behavior in order to keep the peace between us. Until Nixa was murdered. A foolish faerie woman, to be sure, but she did not deserve to die the way she did."

"I will be free soon of the Foresters' claim," Lara said.

"Do you think, my child, that they will heed the law? They will not, especially if they find you in their realm. I have seen you now, and you have been reunited with your mother, which was my desire. I shall fade away happily, Lara."

"But to lose you when I have only just found you?" she protested.

Maeve smiled. "It was never meant that I be a part of your destiny, Lara. Now give me a kiss, dear girl. It is time for me to go."

Lara put her arms about the old faerie woman and hugged her, noticing that it was almost like hugging the air. She kissed Maeve's cheeks several times. "Goodbye, grandmother, and thank you." She felt the tears beginning to roll down her cheeks.

Reaching out, Maeve brushed the tears away, and then before Lara's eyes she disappeared in a cloud of pale smoke. "Goodbye, Lara." Her reedy voice echoed softly.

"You have made her very happy," Ilona said to her daughter. "In a few weeks she will fade away completely, and I will be the new queen of the Forest Faeries. I will have to return then, and so we have little time together."

"I know that faeries live for several centuries, but if I am your only child, Mother, who will follow you?" Lara asked Ilona.

Ilona sighed. "Once my mother has faded and I am crowned, I must take a mate who will sire a child on me. Son or daughter, it does not matter as long as I have an heir to follow. The Forest Faeries have been ruled since the beginning of time by our family. Because you are half-human you are not eligible to follow me, Lara. Our line must remain only faerie," she explained.

"You preserve your purity as the Forest Lords once did, and continue to pretend they are doing," Lara remarked with a small smile.

"I suppose we do," Ilona replied. "I never thought of it that way. But if faerie blood becomes too thin the magic disappears as well. We are pleased to mate with humans, but my heir must be all faerie."

"Do you have someone in mind?" Lara asked her mother, curious.

Ilona nodded. "His name is Thanos. He has been my faithful suitor for many years. Since before I knew your father. He has been patient in his waiting." She smiled. "We are friends as well as lovers now. I will make him my consort."

"Not your king?" Lara was surprised.

"If he were king, he would take precedence over me," Ilona said. "Nay, he will not be king. Learn from me, my daughter. You were taught by your grandmother, Ina, a good but foolish woman, to be subservient to menfolk. That is the way of it in the world of Hetar. In the faerie world, women are the equals of their men, and oft-times their superior. Let no man tell you that you must give way to him. If you choose not to, you do not have to give way in love, or war, or anything else, Lara. This is your first lesson."

"Will you teach your daughter faerie ways then, Ilona?" Kaliq asked, hearing her words. He smiled to see them together, so beautiful, so alike.

"Yes, prince, I will. And I will beg hospitality from you for a short time as well," Ilona replied. "Who is your best warrior?"

"Lothair," Kaliq said.

"I want him to begin teaching Lara how to use a bow, a sword and a staff," Ilona told him. "She must have the ability to defend herself in this world. Her path will take her to dangerous places. I will provide her with the staff myself."

"I hope it is like Master Bashkar's staff, Llyr," Lara said with a smile. "It is always scolding, and complaining, but when Llyr praises you, you know you have done not just well, but very well."

"Aye, it is a staff with a spirit. It is called Verica, and when it speaks it gives you the advantage of surprise against your enemies," Ilona told her daughter. "But first you will learn to fight with just a plain pole so that you come to depend on yourself alone, and not another. Prince Kaliq can tell you that warring is a hard business, whether you war for a cause within a great army, or simply for yourself against the world."

"I will inform Lothair of your wishes, my lady Ilona, and it will be done," the prince told her.

In the weeks that followed Lara had scarcely any time at all to herself. The days were taken up with lessons from Master Bashkar in the mornings, and from Lothair in the afternoons. Lara invited Noss to join her in learning the martial arts as well as her other studies, and Noss, to everyone's surprise, turned out to be an archer of the first rank.

"Usually such skills are faerie," Ilona noted.

Lara preferred the broadsword and the staff, and soon excelled with both. Each evening mother and daughter would forswear the hall, and Ilona would teach Lara how to make certain potions, how to bring objects to her when she extended her hand, and most important of all, how to change her shape. This was the faerie skill that most fascinated Lara, and the first time she was successful at it she was astounded to find herself in the shape of a cat.

Ilona laughed as the small yellow feline jumped nervously. "Is that what you meant to be, daughter?" she asked.

"Yes," the cat replied. "I just didn't think I could really do it."

"Change back," Ilona said, and Lara stood once again before her mother. "Excellent! You have a good strong mind, daughter. Now, become a bird."

"What kind?" Lara asked.

"A songbird?" Ilona suggested.

Lara contemplated a nightingale. "Aral go!" she said, and becoming the bird she flew about the garden before lighting again upon a marble bench and saying, "Lara return! Mother, this is amazing! Can anyone do it?"

"Nay," Ilona told her. "This is your faerie blood that now sings in your veins."

"How long can I remain in a different shape?" Lara asked her.

"As long as you choose," Ilona said. "But allow few to know you are capable of this magic, Lara. And only those you completely trust."

"Just Kaliq for now," Lara replied.

Ilona laughed. "I will not ask why," she said, "but your secret is safe with the prince."

That same night a faerie man appeared suddenly in Prince Kaliq's hall as they dined.

"Thanos!" Ilona was immediately on her feet.

The faerie man, tall and handsome with golden hair and bright blue eyes, bowed to her, and then knelt. "Greetings, Queen Ilona," he said. "I have come to bring you home, for Queen Maeve is near gone and will not last the night. You must be there to claim your heritage as all queens and kings before you have been." His gaze went to Lara, and his lips twitched in a small smile.

Ilona nodded. Then she turned, embracing her daughter. "I must go now, Lara. The Celestial Actuary keep you safe in your journey. When you need me, you have but to ask Ethne. She will find me."

"Mother, I beg one final boon of you," Lara said. "Let me be there when you take Thanos for your consort."

Ilona shook her head. "Nay, your grandmother is right. We must keep you safe from the Foresters. You cannot come into the woodlands again while they seek you."

"Seek me? They are seeking me?" Lara was astounded. Almost a year had passed since her escape. "Why would they bother after all this time?"

"Because they still believe a faerie's child can help them break Maeve's curse on them, and they have not found another to take your place," Ilona told Lara. "You must soon leave Shunnar, my daughter."

Lara turned to Kaliq. "You knew?"

"Only recently," he replied. "I will explain later, my love."

Thanos had now risen to his feet. He put a proprietary arm about Ilona. "We must go," he said in a low, urgent voice.

Ilona pushed his arm away, giving him a sharp look. Then she embraced her daughter a final time. "I will give Thanos a son," she whispered to Lara. "I want no other daughter, for you are everything I could ever have desired in a female child. I ask your forgiveness for the years we have been apart."

"You have it, Mother!" Lara said generously, and kissed Ilona's cheek.

The faerie woman reached out and touched the girl's face in a tender gesture. Then she was gone in a puff of deep purple smoke, and the faerie man, a surprised look upon his handsome face, quickly followed her in a deep lavender essence of his own.

Lara laughed softly. "She will be a grand queen," she remarked.

"And he her king?" Kaliq asked curious.

"She will not make him king, but merely her consort," Lara answered.

"The women of your family seem to be independent creatures," Kaliq said. "Do you desire to be an independent woman also, my love?"

"I must be," Lara told him, "for if I am not I shall be conquered by those who seek to break my spirit. I shall never allow that to happen, Kaliq. And you would not want it either, my lord, would you?"

"Nay, I would not," he said. Then he led her back to the dining couch, and they returned to their meal. "You have become a stronger woman in your months here at Shunnar, Lara, but you will soon have to leave me. Your fate lies beyond our Desert kingdom, but the skills we have taught you, and those your mother has taught you, will serve you well, and help you to survive."

"I must ask Og if he will travel with me," Lara said.

"You may take Noss as well. She would be heartbroken if you left her behind," Kaliq told her.

"I will give her the choice, my lord, for Noss is yet a fearful creature. Here at Shunnar she would be safe and cared for, but with me, who knows the adventures I will encounter? Og is of more value to me."

"Noss has gained confidence with her abilities as an archer," the prince noted. "She could be a valuable traveling companion." He reached out, and ran a finger from her shoulder down her arm.

She smiled seductively at him. "The meal is not yet over, my lord."

"It will be soon, and you are the sweet I desire above all. The nights when you have remained closeted with your mother have been difficult for me," he told her. "And soon you will be gone from me, Lara. Few women have I truly cared for in my long lifetime, but when you leave me, my love, my heart will be most sore." He leaned forward and brushed her lips with his.

"Ah, Kaliq, my prince," she replied, "were it not for you, I should not know how sweet the loving between a man and a woman can be. For that I shall always be grateful."

And she kissed him back gently. "You will always have a part of my heart, and you will remain in my memory until my spirit fades away entirely like my faerie relatives," Lara told him with a sweet smile. "Let us make love here and now among the others, as we have previously done, my lord."

Her words seemed to echo throughout the banqueting hall. She was suddenly surrounded by the other princely guests. Kaliq held her out to them, and they drew her gown away from her. Her long lovely gilt hair was unbound, to be admired by them all. The princes caressed her with soft hands, and admiring glances. They covered her body with gentle kisses until she grew weak, and her legs gave way beneath her. But Kaliq held her in a firm grip as their tongues bathed her body, touching her intimately, and mouths suckled upon her breasts. She was enveloped in the most incredible cloud of sensation when they finally lay her back upon the dining couch, and Kaliq covered her body with his own, entering her in a single smooth action. Two of the princes pulled her legs up, and over her shoulders to allow her lover the deepest penetration of her body. They murmured encouragement, and when her eyes began to glaze with her rising passion, the last thing Lara saw clearly was their smiling faces. She had never felt more loved or cherished in all her life. And then she cried out with her fulfillment as Kaliq groaned with satisfaction, and she remembered nothing more except the thundering of her heart and the feeling of total and utter bliss that seemed to go on and on and on.

When she finally awoke she was in her own bed, Kaliq sleeping by her side. She wondered how long they had been there. Turning her head, she saw that it was still night outside, and suddenly she remembered the words that had chilled her bones earlier. Durga and Enda were looking for her. Would she ever be free of them? She would die before she let them take her again! But at least now she was no longer a helpless girl. She could fight them with sword and staff. She could fly away from them as a bird if she had to, or better yet she could take a cat's form, and claw their eyes out of their big heads. She actually shuddered with the pleasure her thoughts gave her.

"You are awake." Kaliq's voice broke into her musings. "Did you enjoy the evening? I know my brothers have said your pleasure in your own passion gave them great joy."

"What happened after I fainted away?" she asked him.

"You didn't faint, my love. You simply moved onto another plane of existence. Each of my brothers had his delight of you in one way or another when we had finished. You pleasured them between your legs, with your mouth, with your delicate little hands. They said no woman, human or faerie, had ever given them such enjoyment," he told her.

"Why can I not remember it?" she wondered aloud.

"You may one day," he said. "Your senses were very heightened, and I suspect they overwhelmed part of you although you were very vocal in your appreciation of their talents, and they were most flattered," he chuckled. "You have a great capacity for passion, Lara. As much as any full-blooded faerie woman. I brought you from the banqueting hall and bathed you myself so you would not awaken with the scent of desire fulfilled in your nostrils," he explained.

"It was as if I were saying goodbye to them all," she said.

"You were," he replied. "In your time remaining here at Shunnar you will see only me, and of course you will see Lothair for your lessons. Your mother left you a gift he will present you with today, for he says you are more than ready. Now it is still the middle of the night. Go back to sleep." He kissed the top of her head.

"No. I want to know how you know that Durga and Enda are still seeking me," Lara said to him.

"They entered the Desert two days ago, Lara. I received word yesterday. It will take them at least another week to reach Shunnar. They have not the advantage of Og's magical boots. And creatures of habit that these Foresters are, they did not leave their home to come this way until after their Winterfest. You have now been gone from them for more than the required time the law allows an escaped slave. You are free. Now go to sleep."

"Then why do they insist on pursuing me?" she demanded.

"Your mother told you the answer to that question," he replied.

"I must remain to face them," Lara said. "I cannot continue to have them racing behind me like hunting dogs on the scent of the prey. And this is the best and safest place for me to face them down, my lord."

"It is," he agreed. "Now go to sleep, Lara. You may not recall all of your vigorous activity this evening, but you body does, and it needs to rest if you are to be strong, and face your enemies."

"Aye, my lord," she agreed with a small chuckle, and she snuggled against his shoulder. "You have taken good care of me, Kaliq, my prince. I am grateful."

"You should be," he teased her. "Who else could have opened your world for you, and taught you how to love so well, you deliciously naughty creature?"

"Only you, my lord prince. Only you," Lara replied, and she kissed his lips.

"To sleep, you bold wench!"

"I hear and obey," she said, and effortlessly fell back into an easy slumber.

The following morning Kaliq decided he would take the shape of a Desert hawk in order to see the progress the Foresters were making as they crossed the Desert toward Shunnar. Lara wanted to join him, but he refused to allow it. "You have not yet held a different shape for a long period of time. I shall be gone the whole day."

"How can I learn if you will not allow me to accompany you?" she demanded.

"You could fall from the sky, and be injured or killed. No! If you wish to practice shifting you will do it here where you are safe, Lara. Trust me in this decision. Have you spoken with Og yet?"

"No," she said, disappointed. Then a quick smile lit her face. "I could be a mare amongst the other mares, couldn't I?"

"Aye, the valley is a good place to practice your shape-shifting. You don't have to be an animal or a bird, Lara. You might be a piece of the rock walls enclosing the valley. It would certainly be a safe choice," he suggested. Then he took her in his arms. "I would let you come with me if I thought it safe for you, my love. Your time with me is almost at an end, and I want to spend it all with you. But today I cannot."

She nodded, but Lara did understand his decision was really in her best interest. "I shall study my lessons, speak with Og and practice being a rock," she told him with a wry smile.

He laughed and, giving her a kiss, was quickly gone.

Noss brought her the morning meal, and then together the two young women went to await Master Bashkar's arrival. Then Lara told Noss of the impending arrival of the Forest Lords. Noss grew pale, but said nothing at first.

"I must soon leave Shunnar," Lara went on. "Will you come with me? You do not have to if you feel safer here among the Shadow Princes, but I should like your company."

"Will the giant come?" Noss asked.

"I hope so, but like you, the choice will be his," Lara responded.

"Will it be dangerous?" Noss wanted to know.

"Probably," Lara answered her.

"Where are you going?" Noss queried.

"I don't know," Lara replied. "I just know it is time for me to leave Shunnar, and both my mother and the prince were in agreement."

"But he loves you!" Noss cried.

"Aye, he does, but he also knows my destiny is not here. In fact, he knows it far more than I certainly do. They all tell me that when I reach my destination I will know it. It's a bit exasperating to have people speaking in such deep riddles, and hardly reassuring to those I would choose as companions," Lara concluded.

Noss laughed, to her surprise. "I will gladly come with you. Shunnar is a place of refuge as the Shadow Princes meant it to be, but I would go mad if I had to spend the rest of my life here without you. Surely I must have a destiny, too. And now that I am capable of defending myself, I am not so afraid, dear Lara."

"First, however, I must face Durga and Enda. They must understand that the curse cannot be lifted as my grandmother is now dead. They must know that a faerie woman will not give a child to a man she doesn't love. They must be made to face the reality of their situation, and cease the pretense of their blood purity."

"I'll just wait in the next chamber while you have that conversation," Noss said.

"Good day, my young ladies." Master Bashkar entered the chamber where they studied each day. He set several scrolls down on the table he used. "Today, we shall learn about the Coastal Kings. They are the true aristocrats of Hetar. They are richer than the Midland Merchants, for they sail our Hetarian seas in search of adventure and wealth. They are a great tall people with blond or red hair in various shades. Their eyes are all light colored. They keep much to themselves, but it is said they are well-spoken, well-educated and clever. A most unique society indeed."

"Have you been to the sea?" Lara asked him.

"Never!" the old man said. "But I have heard that the waters of it spread farther than the eye can see, which I find amazing."

"With whom do they trade?" she asked him.

"Everyone! The Taubyls who carry their luxury goods across our world, the Midland Merchants, the Outlanders whom they even welcome into their palaces and villages," Master Bashkar said. "They are certainly brave men."

"Perhaps the Outlanders are not as bad as we have been told," Lara suggested.

Master Bashkar looked at her strangely, then said, "They can be fierce. I hope that you never have to meet up with them but if you do, you will be prepared." He unrolled one of the scrolls. "Now this is the land of the Coastal Kings, the only one of the four provinces of Hetar to even have a coastline. Outlanders possess the remainder of it, alas."

"Why is the coastland so valuable?" Lara asked him.

"Because it offers an outlet to the rest of our world. Hetar is growing, my child. The population increases daily. They need new lands to house the people. New natural resources that can surely be found in the Outlands. Gold! Precious gemstones! Some in Hetar have traveled the Outlands. It is a place of great beauty, with wide grasslands and great mountains. But alas! It is controlled by the clan families of Outlanders, and the Coastal Kings protect them, refusing access by either land or sea. But the Coastal Province is the smallest of our states. One day Hetar shall have to force the Kings aside and invade the Outlands if they are to gain its land and its resources," Master Bashkar said.

"But you are an Outlander," Lara noted. "You would advocate this against your own people? I do not think that is right, and I am surprised, for I have thought you a most wise man, Master Bashkar."

"No Outlander believes in loyalty except perhaps to his own clan, Lara," he explained. "Because I wished to travel I was driven from the Devyn by my own father, who had expected me to become a great bard as he was. It was many years ago, but had not one of the Coastal Kings taken me into his care and educated me, I do not know what would have happened to me. My only loyalty is to myself, and so should your loyalty be to yourself, first and always. Now, we have strayed from our subject. The coast is responsible for most of the luxury goods made available to Hetar. While they trade with the Outlands for some of it, they do harvest the sea around them for fish and pearls. And they mine salt from the sea for all of Hetar."

Lara half listened as the old man droned on. She did not agree with him about loyalties. Yes, she must be loyal to herself, but what of those around her whom she loved? What of Noss and Og? Poor old fellow, Lara thought. He has probably never had a peaceful moment in all his life for fear of letting his guard down. Then suddenly she felt a hand slip into hers and, looking up, her eyes met Noss's in total understanding.

That afternoon they attended their class with Lothair. They worked with him in a large open chamber just off the valley floor. Noss practiced with her bow on an open terrace just beyond the columns, for since she was so good at it, it had been decided that it would be her only weapon except the dagger. But Noss had proved herself with the small blade, too, being agile and quick. She ceased her practice briefly to watch Lara and Lothair as they fought with blunted broadswords. Lothair was a good swordsman, but Lara had obviously inherited her father's knack with the weapon. She blocked her opponent's moves swiftly and easily, anticipating his every move. Lothair was grinning, obviously well pleased.

"Why do you grin like some loon?" Lara demanded, her blade slamming against his to prevent him bruising her.

"Because you have become so good at this," he chuckled.

"I am my father's daughter," Lara said.

"I agree. John Swiftsword would be proud of you," Lothair said, attempting to block, but being hindered by her faster blade. "You are, it seems, good at everything." And he leered wickedly at her. "How sweet you were in my arms last night."

"How could you notice? Was it not for a brief time?" she teased him.

He laughed aloud. "Aye," he admitted. "I cannot, I fear, resist your charms." Then he put down his sword. "It is enough for today, Lara. Practice is all I can do for you now. I have nothing more to teach you."

"Nothing at all?" she grinned. "I am disappointed, my lord."

He laughed again. "Put your sword down, wench, and come see what your mother has left you." He set his own weapon aside now, and walked across the large chamber.

Curious, Lara lay her own weapon down, and joined him. The Shadow Prince reached into the corner and drew forth a beautifully carved staff of ashwood. He handed it to Lara.

"Your mother promised you this, I believe," he said.

Lara took the staff in her two hands. She ran her hand down the smooth polished wood. She turned the rod in her hands until she was looking into the carved face on the staff. It was a long face with a long nose, a narrow mouth, and beneath that mouth a long curl of beard. The eyes in the face were closed. "Greetings, Verica," Lara said softly.

The eyes opened, changing the face from peaceful to fierce. "Greetings, Lara!" Verica answered her back. "Your mother, Queen Ilona, has asked me to serve you. She says you now have the proper skills to use me. Therefore, I pledge you my loyalty."

"I am grateful for it, and I thank you," Lara replied.

Verica closed his eyes again. Lara knew the staff spirits usually slept, or at least pretended to sleep when they were not needed. She was dying to try her new staff, but she realized now was not the time.

"I have a gift for you, too," Lothair said. Then he brought forth a beautiful scabbard containing a broadsword. "This is now yours. I had it made for you when I saw how good you were becoming with the weapon." He handed Lara the scabbard.

Taking it from him, she slowly drew the sword from the scabbard, and almost immediately heard a beautiful female voice declare in song.

"I am Andraste, and I sing of victory!"

Lothair laughed at the startled look on Lara's face, but to her credit she did not drop the sword. "I had a victory spirit forged into the weapon," he said. "Do you like her? She was made especially for you, to fit your hand, to be the correct weight."

Lara examined the blade. "It's a beautiful weapon, Lothair, but I would prefer to win based on my own skills, and not through magic."

"Andraste cannot be carried by someone lacking in the ability to be victorious," he explained. "Her desire for victory enhances your skills. In the hands of someone less talented she could not function, Lara."

"Thank you, my lord," Lara said softly. "Do all the Shadow Princes have such kind hearts?"

"It is our weakness, which is why we live as we do, isolated from the rest of Hetar," he replied. "You will keep our secret, Lara?"

"Always!" she responded with a small smile.

"Lara, come quick!" Noss called.

Putting the broadsword back in its scabbard, Lara laid it aside and, with Lothair, went out on the terrace. Noss was pointing upwards. Looking up they saw a Desert hawk, but the bird was flying erratically. Without even a single word between them both Lothair and Lara shifted their shapes before Noss's startled eyes. The two eagles, one slightly smaller than the other, rose up from the terrace, flying directly to the obviously injured hawk. Settling themselves on either side of the hawk, one wing each supporting the injured creature, their other wings catching the air currents in order to glide, they descended toward the terrace while Noss watched openmouthed. Touching down upon the warm tiles, the three birds immediately resumed their human shape. Prince Kaliq was bleeding from a wound to his left arm.

"What happened?" Lothair said.

"Damned Foresters!" Kaliq swore. "One of them could not resist shooting at me. They enter the Desert without our permission, and then they hunt when they know none but the Shadow Princes is allowed to hunt here. For men who adhere to their own customs so religiously, they have no difficulty in ignoring the customs of others."

"Noss, get a basin, and some rags," Lara said. Then she carefully examined Kaliq's wound, and pronounced, "It is not serious, my lord. Nor is it deep. You were but grazed as the arrow passed by you."

Noss came quickly with the water-filled basin, rags and the herbs needed to poultice the wound. She held the ewer as Lara quickly cleaned Kaliq's injured arm. The arrow had, as she had suspected, pierced the skin but slightly as it passed its target. The hawk had obviously swerved, avoiding serious damage or death. The wound was neither deep nor dangerous, but it would be painful for a few days. She bandaged him, enclosing a packet of herbs within the cloth, and then announced, "You will live."

"Small comfort," he grumbled. "I saw who did it, and when he stands before me he will suffer my wrath. Now do you understand why I did not allow you to accompany me, Lara? I have much practice as the Desert hawk. You do not."

"As I agreed with you this morning, my lord," Lara told him gently, and then took his other arm. "Come. You must rest. The day alone has surely been tiring. You will tell us about it when you have slept and allowed the healing to begin." She led him away.

"You and Lara turned into birds," Noss said to Prince Lothair.

He nodded, smiling faintly.

"I did not realize she possessed faerie magic. I would expect it of you princes, but not of Lara," Noss said.

"Did it frighten you?" he asked.

Noss thought a moment, and then she said, "Nay, but I was surprised."

He nodded. "Will you still accompany her knowing this?" he asked.

"Of course!" Noss never hesitated in her reply. "She is my friend."

Lothair nodded again, and then he said, "You should know that both the staff left for her by her mother and the sword I have had made for her possess spirits of great strength. The staff is Verica. The broadsword, Andraste. Will you be afraid?"

Noss thought again a long moment. "No," she told him. "But tell me, my lord, does my bow or my dagger have a spirit?"

Lothair laughed. "Nay, little one. They are but a bow and a dagger."

"Thank the Celestial Actuary!" Noss breathed. "Lara is used to such things, for she is partly faerie, but I am just an ordinary girl."

Lothair laughed again, and then he said. "Not really so ordinary any longer, Noss. Now run along, and see if Lara needs your help putting my brother to bed so he may heal. He will be very difficult, for he does not like to be sick."

"I will go at once, my lord," Noss replied, and she set her bow and quiver aside before hurrying off.

Kaliq was surprised to find himself in a weakened condition, but Lara and Noss remained with him for two days as he healed. He was both furious and vengeful by turns. Much of his anger stemmed from the treatment Lara had received at the hands of the Forest Lords, she knew. But the insolence exhibited by the Foresters in entering the Desert realm without permission, and then attacking a Desert creature knowing it was forbidden, burned deep within the Shadow Prince. But on the third day he seemed stronger, and more himself again.

"Did you speak with Og?" he asked her.

"There was no time," she answered him.

"Nor time to be a rock?" he said with a small smile.

"Only time to be an eagle," she told him.

"Thank you, Lara," he said. "Your instincts were perfect in the situation."

She shook her head. "Looking back I am astounded at what I did, my lord. As Lothair and I rose up to help you, I thought only of one thing—bringing you safe home. He did not speak a word to me. We just acted in concert. You were in danger, and needed our help. We gave it as best we could."

"You did well, my love," he praised her.

"My mother left me a staff. It is called Verica. And Lothair had a broadsword made for me with a strong spirit called Andraste," she told him. "Did you know he was making the weapon for me, Kaliq?"

"Aye, he asked my permission first, for you are my lover, Lara, and he would never offend either of us. I thought you would be pleased, and you are, I can see."

"Do the Forest Lords know how to enter Shunnar?" Lara asked him.

"No. They must wait below in the village until we acknowledge them and have them brought to us." And Prince Kaliq smiled a wicked smile. "How short are their tempers?"

"Very," Lara said smiling back.

"Two days?" he inquired of her.

"Three," she responded with a grin. "They will suffer with the heat as they wait. And if they are rude to the villagers they will suffer more. Zaki will allow no disrespect of his people, as you well know. How long before they are here?"

"Two days if they continue at the pace they were traveling. They were riding lemaxes, not horses, however. Lemaxes are used to the Desert, and travel it well, but they are not swift. Still, horses would not have survived," he said.

"Too bad they did not travel by horse, then," Lara muttered darkly.

"Go and find Og," Kaliq said. "You must settle your travel arrangements soon, Lara. You will leave when this matter with the Forest Lords is settled between you."

"So soon?" she said surprised.

He nodded. "Go, my love, and speak with the giant now."

She left him, and finding her way through the corridors and down the staircases of the palace, arrived at Kaliq's stables, which were located at the bottom of the cliffs opening out onto the green valley. She found Og, whom she had not seen but in passing since she had come to Shunnar over a year ago. There had never been any time, and now she felt guilty. He was brushing a small golden colt in a wide stall.

"Lara!" He smiled warmly at her. "You will be going soon, then. Come and sit with me here on the hay and we will visit for a while." He pushed the colt away.

"Does everyone know this but me?" she asked him, hugging him as he bent down to greet her. "Will you come with me?"

"No," Og said. "I am happy here at Shunnar. The prince has put me in charge of his stables now, and when I desire it, a wife will be found for me among the Desert peoples. Zaki has promised it. I am a small giant, and there are some large girls among Zaki's people. I am respected, and earn my own living now. He says I am quite a good catch," Og chuckled.

"I am so glad for you!" Lara told him honestly. "You go to the village then?"

"As often as I can," Og told her. "I enjoy the company of Zaki's people. The prince has promised when I take a wife I will have my own quarters within the palace, where I may bring a wife and raise children. For now I have been content to sleep in the loft above," he explained. "Where will you go?"

She shrugged. "I don't know yet. Where the wind takes me, I suppose."

"Alone?"

"Nay, Noss is coming with me. She has become quite a good archer. I seem to have my father's talents, and I have become fairly proficient with the staff. My mother gave me one called Verica. Prince Lothair has given me a sword, Andraste. I am not afraid as I was when we escaped the Forest, though Durga and Enda come this way even as I speak. They think to reclaim me, but we are free now, dear Og. A year and a day have passed. The law of Hetar is on our side now, not theirs," Lara said triumphantly.

"When they learn your bloodline they will want you even more, granddaughter of Maeve," Og answered her.

"Did you know?" Lara asked him.

"I suspected it when I learned your mother's name," he said, "but what good was the knowledge to either of us then? It could only have made your life worse. I learned long ago how to keep secrets, Lara. I will stand by your side when the Foresters arrive. They are dense men, but they have surely realized when I went missing, too, that we had effected our escape together. They will not want me back, for even if I do not tell them I know their secret, I know enough to shame them should I speak. They must say aloud before witnesses that I am now free, that I may live the rest of my life without fear for myself, my wife, or my children."

"I met Maeve," Lara told him.

"Did you?" He was impressed.

"She was fading, and has since disappeared entirely. Ilona is now queen of the Forest Faeries. Maeve told me she would never lift the curse, and no one else could. The Foresters are doomed. Whether they admit it or not, the purity of their blood is almost extinct," Lara said quietly.

"Durga will never accept it," Og said.

"He has no choice," Lara replied. "I will send for you when the Foresters arrive, Og. Be ready." Then taking up his big hand she kissed it, and wrapping her arms about his thick neck she kissed his rough cheek. "Be happy, dear Og. You deserve it." She stood up. "I must return now. Kaliq was slightly injured, and I am nursing him."

"What happened?" the giant asked, and Lara quickly explained.

"He taught you to shape-shift?"

"My mother taught me. She was here a few weeks, and passed on certain faerie magic to me so I will be safe in my travels," Lara explained. "I must go now." And with a wave of her hand she hurried from the stables, leaving the giant behind.

"WILL OG COME?" Kaliq asked her when she returned to him.

Lara shook her head. "You knew as much, didn't you?" she said.

"Yes, but it was not for me to tell you," he replied. "It is better this way, for wherever you go, Lara, you want to travel discreetly, and even a small giant six cubits high could attract unwanted attention to you. There are going to be times when you don't want attention."

"I feel the pull of something, Kaliq," she told him. "What is it?"

"Your destiny," he said.

"But I cannot go until you are healed," she said. "Nor until Durga and Enda understand I will not be returning to them. I cannot imagine how I am going to be able to convince them." She sighed. "And it is my problem, isn't it?"

"The law of Hetar is on your side, Lara. A slave who remains free for a year and a day is no longer a slave," he reminded her. "And any slave seeking refuge in the Desert cannot be taken back. They have no rights to you, my love."

"I suspect they will not see it that way," Lara remarked.

She was right, of course. Two days later, Durga, Enda and a party of six other Foresters arrived at the cliffs hiding the valley of the Shadow Princes. They were informed by Zaki that they would have to wait until Prince Kaliq and his brothers were willing to see them. Zaki had been warned that these men of the Forests had short tempers, and so were to be fed, watered and avoided until it was time to admit them to the presence of the princes. And at the end of three days, Durga and his companions were growing restless and angry. Not until the fourth morning did Zaki greet them.

"The princes have agreed to see you this afternoon, my lords," he said. "When it is time I will bring you to them." He bowed.

"You've known the way to them all along?" Durga exploded.

"Of course I know the way to my lord's palace," Zaki responded.

"And you have allowed us to remain here roasting in your wicked weather for three days?" Durga snarled. His face was burned with the sun, and he had grown angrier with each minute they had been forced to wait. "Do you know who I am?"

"You are the lord Durga, the Head Forester," Zaki said in irritated tones, "but it would not have mattered who you were. If my lord was not ready to see you then he was not ready to see you. Nor were the others. I will return at the appointed hour."

"Calm yourself, brother," Enda said softly. "This is not the Forest, nor are we the masters here. Remember why we are here. We are here for Lara, and we will regain her. Tonight each man of us here will mount and seed her. She will give us a faerie child, Durga. We will make her, and we will keep using her until she does. We are close to our goal now. Do not despair, brother."

"You think this Shadow Prince will release her to us willingly?" Durga snapped.

"That is why we went to the Magistrate's Court in the City, brother. How many have lost slaves to these Desert men over the years, and certainly none as expensive as Lara? The magistrate was yet angry that the Head Mistress of the Pleasure Guild had forbade her sale to any of the Pleasure Houses. He owns one himself, and had hoped to have her. She would have made him a fortune. He told me that when we were finished with her he would purchase her from us. Not for what we paid, but for at least half. By agreeing, we have managed to circumvent the law of the land, brother."

"We cannot sell her to anyone, for she will surely learn our secret if we allow her to live. And if she escaped once, she can again," Durga replied.

"Og helped her," Enda said. "Remember, brother, they both disappeared at Winterfest. They had to go together, and they must be here, for they are nowhere else we have searched over this year. The giant may remain here if he chooses, for he has been gone more than a year and a day. But Lara must be returned to us, and the law is on our side, Durga. Remember that."

Zaki came at the appointed hour, and telling the Head Forester's men they must remain behind, listened to Durga's long-winded protest, and then said, "I have my orders, my lord. You and your brother. No one else. Will you come, or shall I return to my prince and tell him you have refused his invitation?"

"Their hospitality is legend," Enda murmured. "I have never heard of them murdering a guest. Come, brother."

Grumbling, Durga followed Zaki. When they reached the cliff's entrance they were offered horses to ride. Mounting, they followed Zaki up the wide, winding path until they reached the entry to the colonnaded corridor. They dismounted, and now followed Zaki on foot, gaping at the tall marble columns, peering wide-eyed over the balustrade into the great green valley below. Here the breezes blew cooler than in the village. Then Zaki led them into a great room where Kaliq awaited them. By his side were both Lara and Og. Lara was clad in leather trousers and a silken shirt. A jeweled leather belt encompassed her narrow waist.

"I told you she was here!" Durga said triumphantly. "First I am going to beat her. We were too soft on her last time. She needs to know who her master is, Enda. Look at how proudly the bitch stands. Soon, very soon, she will beg for our mercy!"

"Greet the prince, brother!" Enda hissed. The sight of Lara, more beautiful than he recalled, set his pulses racing. He could scarcely wait to put his manroot into her again. He wanted to punish her, too, but in a far different fashion than his brother.

"Hail, Kaliq, Prince of the Shadows," Durga said.

Kaliq nodded in acknowledgement, but did not speak.

"You have my property, and I want it back," Durga spoke boldly.

Kaliq now stood up from his chair which had been set upon a raised dais. "Lara has been gone from your tender care more than a year and a day, Head Forester. She is free now under Hetarian law."

"I have gone to the courts," Durga responded angrily. "The magistrate has ordered that such a law cannot apply to a slave of such great value. The giant is free, but Lara belongs to us." He waved a parchment at the prince.

Kaliq laughed scornfully. "And how can I be certain the paper you waggle before me is genuine, Durga of the Forest?"

"Do you doubt my word?" The Head Forester's face grew florid.

"Why should I believe a man who would attempt to circumvent our Hetarian laws?" the prince demanded. "The law says a slave free for a year and a day remains free. Yet you come with your paper to tell me otherwise? Do you take me for a fool, Durga of the Forest? I know you paid a small fortune for Lara. I think you seek to regain her in a most unlawful manner."

Durga glanced at the Shadow Prince, his slow wits digesting his words. Finally he said, "Look at the paper yourself, my lord." He shoved the parchment toward Kaliq. "Look and see if I lie. I will restrain my outrage at your questions, for I can understand you but wish to retain this valuable slave for yourself, and I cannot blame you."

The prince's elegant hand reached out to take the proffered deed. He glanced at it in a bored, cursory fashion, and then let it drop from his fingers. "If there is an actual magistrate of this name, and he actually signed such a breach of our laws, I can but wonder how much you paid him, Durga of the Forest," Kaliq murmured insultingly.

"Do you…do you…dare to accuse us of bribery?" Durga spluttered, his face bright red now with his anger.

"Aye," the prince replied, "but mostly I accuse you of stupidity in believing that you could invade our kingdom, attempt to thwart our laws and believe we would let you do it."

Durga's hand went to his dagger. He was almost foaming at the mouth, and shook off Enda's restraining hand.

"I know your secret," Og's deep voice suddenly spoke.

Durga paled. Then he said, "I do not know to what you refer, Og."

"Aye, you do," Og said descending from the dais where he had been standing. "I know of the curse Maeve placed upon your people."

"You cannot!" Durga replied. "You were not even born then."

"Giant memory is exchanged in the womb, Durga of the Forest. Our memories were our history, and my mother passed them all on to me before my birth. I know!"

"It makes no difference," Durga cried. "Lara will change all that. That is why we must have her back. She will help us regain ourselves."

"Nay, I will not." Now it was Lara who spoke. "The daughters of faerie women inherit certain traits from their mothers. Like faeries, they give no children to those they do not love. Since I despise you both, I will never give either of you a child. Any of you, my lord Durga. And my grandmother swore on her fading that she would never remove the curse from you, nor could anyone else."

Durga looked stunned. It was his brother who now spoke.

"Your grandmother?"

"Maeve was my grandmother, although until recently I did not know it," Lara said.

Durga began to moan. "We had Maeve's own kin beneath us in our beds, and yet we could get no child on her, brother." Then his small eyes turned on Lara. "Come back with us, and we will make you a queen," he pleaded, all thoughts of violence against her gone from his head. "Give us sons to free us from your grandmother's curse, faerie girl!"

"Even if I were willing, and I am not, it could not be. Maeve said it before her fading. The curse can never be lifted. Your purity is gone, my lords. Your father was but half Forester, and your blood is thinned by a quarter more. You live a lie, and no faerie will ever help you, could not help you. And it is all your own fault. If your grandfather had but punished those who killed the faerie woman, Nixa, if he had returned her torque willingly thereby preventing his own pregnant wife's death, Maeve would have forgiven the sin, angry as she was. But your grandfather's pride was overwhelming. He is responsible for the destruction of your race."

Durga, whose head had fallen to his chest with her first words, now looked up. His eyes had become enflamed with his desperation and madness. "You will return with us, faerie girl. And you will give us the children we need to restore our race," he snarled, reaching out for her. "You will come back!"

A deep feral sound arose from Og's throat. He would have moved forward but that Lara stayed him with her hand.

"The girl is ours," Enda said, attempting to sound reasonable. "Surely you can understand that, my lord prince. We have the magistrate's order. And the Shadow Princes are men who respect the law, and keep order themselves among the Desert folk."

"You bribed the magistrate, I have not a doubt," Kaliq replied in amused tones. "What did you promise him in return? Lara, when you had finished with her? Your brother would not allow Lara to live, or do you not understand that, my lord Enda?"

At that Durga leapt forward, his big clumsy hands stretching out for Lara. The girl stepped back but a pace, her arm reaching up to draw her broadsword from the scabbard on her back. She found herself filled to bursting with a ferocious anger. This beast of a man would not have her. She would never again be victimized by the Head Forester Durga, or any of his clan. Then, to even her own surprise, she jumped forward and with a single stroke decapitated the Head Forester as the sword sang loudly.

I am Andraste. I sing of Victory and I drink the blood of the unjust!

Durga's head rolled across the marble floor, his eyes wide, his mouth open in complete and utter shock. Crimson blood spurted from his severed neck and flowed over the marble floors. The head settled at Enda's booted feet. He looked down, and then up again. His eyes were filled with fear as he stared at Lara. A hesitant hand went to his own weapon, but Kaliq quickly spoke.

"Lara tells me you paid thirty thousand pieces of gold for her. I will give it to you, and ten thousand more in blood money for your brother's death. Under the law Lara was legally free of you several days ago. You have attempted to regain her by fraudulent means. We both know it, my lord Enda. Take the gold, and leave Shunnar. If I must bring this unfortunate matter to the attention of the High Council, how do you think they would rule? Lara's destiny is not with you. Nor is it even with me, I regret to say. And it occurs to me that if your brother had no son, then it is you who are now the Head Forester. Did Durga have a son?" A small smile played about the prince's mouth.

"No. Just daughters." Enda had now found his voice again, and lied easily to the Shadow Prince. The bitch Truda had whelped a boy, but he was weak, and had been sickly since his birth. His brother had beaten Truda badly for it, as he blamed the woman. No one would consider it odd if the boy died suddenly. And no one would be sorry to have Truda gone from their midst. She had been a troublemaker from the very beginning. Durga was dead of his own stupidity. Enda would tell no one how his brother died. He would say Durga had a fit when he could not regain Lara. Of course there was the matter of his brother's head and body being separated.

"Then we shall consider this matter settled between us? And between Lara, and your family?" the prince purred. "If you would like we will bury your brother. His body would decay too badly if you attempted to take it with you back to your Forest realm."

Enda nodded. Had the prince read his mind, he wondered uncomfortably? "When I have the gold in my possession," he said, and then his eyes went to Lara. If only he could have gotten a son on her, he thought regretfully, but he had understood her words.

"Let me kill him, too, my lord Kaliq," Lara said, and was pleased to see the Forester grow pale beneath his sunburnt skin.

Kaliq laughed. "So, my love, the warrior's blood now sings in your veins. But nay. We will not start a war over you, as flattering as I am certain you would find it. Hetar must remain at peace for now. Soon enough the clouds will gather."

"Very well," Lara agreed. She smiled at Enda. "I will not kill you, though it is tempting, my lord Enda, and your neck is not quite as thick as your brother's was."

To her surprise he answered her, "I am sorry you could not love me, Lara. Even though I understand what you have said is the truth. The purity of the Forester's blood is a thing gone, yet I would have liked to have had a son by you."

"Go home, my lord," she told him. "Be thankful that my lord Kaliq has stayed my hand. Never again will anyone use me for their own advantage." She bent, picking up Durga's head by its hair. She stared into his face briefly, saying as she handed it to Enda, "And take this with you."

He recoiled, forcing back the bile that rose in his throat as he was forced to stare into his brother's dead face. His legs felt weak, and he slipped on the bloody floor.

"Lara, my love, do put the head down. We will dispose of it. You really are frightening the new Head Forester. My lord Enda—" he now directed his speech to the Forester "—Zaki will lead you back to the village where you will find the gold already waiting for you. Use the lemax your brother rode to carry it. You will depart this evening. Our moon is now full, and you will find traveling at night is more comfortable in the Desert. I bid you a safe journey."

Enda nodded, bowed, and turned about to follow the headman. His last glimpse of Lara caused an icy shiver to ripple down his spine. She was industriously cleaning his brother's blood from her sword. Once he wanted nothing more than to possess her totally. Now he prayed to the Celestial Actuary that he never had to see her again.

Chapter 12

"I CANNOT BELIEVE that I killed him," Lara said afterward as they ate their evening meal in the private garden that separated their individual quarters. "I don't know what happened, but I was suddenly filled with an anger such as I have never known, my lord."

"Blood lust," he said dryly. "And now perhaps you are beginning to understand, Lara. In your life you have been a good daughter. Then you were to be a Pleasure Woman, but that is not the destiny fate meant for you to follow. It is not written that your beauty be used just for the gratification of others. You are meant to be strong. To lead."

"But women are subservient, my lord. It has always been that way," she replied.

"Not everywhere," he told her. "Only in the provinces."

She looked puzzled, and he further explained.

"In the provinces, women have been kept obeisant for a reason. It is believed women cause disorder, for they are known to question, protest and dispute if permitted. Men, however, accept what is told them, if it is told to them by someone they respect and trust. The High Council wants no difficulties. They want peace. They want industry and trade to continue as they always have. They want profit, and profit does not necessarily come with social change. The

High Council wants everyone to keep their place, and those who are allowed up the social ladder come only in the prescribed way, as did your father. But change is coming, Lara. It must come if Hetar is to survive. The old ways are coming to an end, and you are to be part of that change."

"I hear your words, my lord, but they make no sense to me. I don't even know where I will go when I leave Shunnar, but I know I must go," Lara said. "I sense my time with you is coming to an end, Kaliq. Part of me is saddened by that knowledge, yet part of me looks forward to leaving this peaceful haven you have provided me these past months. I cannot hide away from the world forever. I find to my surprise that I am curious to see all the wonders in all the lands Master Bashkar has described. I feel I am changing once again. It is both a little frightening, and yet very exciting."

She was very confused by everything that had happened today. She had taken a life, and yet she felt absolutely no guilt over Durga's death. Indeed she felt a strange pride in her skills at removing his head in a single swift stroke. "I wish Lothair had been there," Lara said aloud.

Kaliq laughed, knowing what she had been thinking. "Yes," he acknowledged, "he would have been very proud of you, and of himself, too, I think. He has been your instructor, but your skills, he tells me, come to you naturally. He says he has but refined them. Durga's death was a far more merciful one than he deserved."

"You say change is coming to Hetar. Tell me, I beg of you!" Lara pleaded.

He shook his head. "You have a destiny to live out, my love. You must follow your own path, not one that is set out for you. You will make errors, Lara, for that is part of the learning process, but you will survive. That much I will tell you. And you will triumph."

"But where am I going?" Her look was distraught.

"Pick a direction, my love. You do not want to go back, for the Forest lies in that direction. So the Midlands and the City are forbidden to you for now. You can go toward the sea, or you can enter the Outlands. One way will serve to interrupt your journey. The other will bring you closer to your fate," he told her. "Think carefully before you choose." He took her small hand in his, comforting her confusion.

"Must I decide tonight?" she asked him.

"Yes," he said, "for tomorrow you will be gone."

Lara gasped. "So soon? Oh, please, my lord, a few more days with you!"

"No," he said. "Your time here with me is over, Lara, so think on it for a few more minutes, and then tell me. Would you like Noss to make the decision with you?"

She nodded. "It is her destiny, too," Lara said, and called for her friend to come and join them.

The prince explained the dilemma, then rising said, "I will leave you to discuss what you will do. Call me when you have decided, and I will return." He bent and kissed Lara's lips softly. "Choose carefully," he repeated. Then he was gone.

"We go tomorrow," Lara told Noss. "But where? To the sea, or to the Outlands? I do not know what to do."

"If we're free can't we go back to the City, and live with your father? I will be your servant, Lara. I loved the City, and to live in luxury in the Garden District would be wonderful," she sighed.

"We cannot go back, Noss. We need to go forward, but which direction shall we take? Did not Master Bashkar say that the Coastal Kings are the true aristocrats of Hetar? Yet Kaliq says one way will interrupt my journey while the other will move it forward. I think to go into another of Hetar's provinces might put a halt to this destiny they all seem to believe I have. While we have never been there, either of us, it is still a place of civilization and order. Everything they tell us the Outlands is not."

"But the Outlands are an unknown for us, Lara," Noss noted. "If we are to be safe should we not go to the sea?"

"Noss, both you and I can well defend ourselves," Lara replied.

"I heard what you did in the reception hall today," Noss half whispered. "I do not think I could kill anyone, Lara. I think you were very brave."

"I was never going to be free until Durga was dead," Lara said. "He would not or he could not understand that no woman with faerie blood can be made to give a child to a man she does not love. He was determined to have me back. He could not be reasoned with, and I had no other choice but to slay him. And when I did, Andraste sang that she drank the blood of the unjust."

"Did not Enda protest?" Noss asked.

Lara laughed. "I think he was too frightened to, and then the prince reminded him that if Durga had no male heirs, Enda was now the Head Forester. Kaliq gave him the thirty thousand pieces of gold the brothers had paid for me, and additional blood money for Durga."

Now Noss laughed. "Then you are truly free, Lara! I am so glad!"

"Tomorrow we will leave Shunnar for the Outlands," Lara said in sure tones. "To remain within our orderly civilization is not my way, Noss. The Outlands are where I need to be." She touched the crystal about her neck. "Ethne? Do I choose well?"

The flame within the crystal flickered, and she heard Ethne say but a single word to her. *Aye.*

Lara looked at Noss. "You can stay if you are afraid. I would understand."

"No," Noss said. "We have been bound together since we traveled in the caravan of Rolf Fairplay. I sense it. Aye, I am afraid, but where you go, Lara, I will follow. That, it would seem, is *my* destiny."

And so it was that they found themselves the following morning bidding the prince and Og a final farewell. Kaliq had not touched Lara as a lover that last night.

"I must learn to live without you," he said quietly, and she realized she understood.

In the morning he brought her a pair of soft medium-brown leather trousers lined in silk, a natural-colored silk shirt with wide sleeves and a V neckline as well as a pair of fine brown leather boots with a matching vest. He brushed her hair himself, braiding it into a single plait and covering her shining head with a dark green kerchief. Last, he strapped her sword and scabbard across her chest and back.

"Do not," he advised her seriously, "allow your beauty to detract from your journey. Dress plainly. Keep your hair hidden from strangers as much as you can, lest they realize you have faerie blood and be afraid unnecessarily. You are capable of defending yourself, and you must do so. If you are threatened, act immediately, as you did with Durga. You are not afraid, are you?"

"I am not," she said, "and yet I am. You have taught me the difference between passion and lust. You have taught me to enjoy and revel in my pleasure as well as that of my lover. Lothair has taught me weaponry. Master Bashkar has taught me about Hetar, so that I am no longer woefully ignorant of our land. Knowing that my mother did not leave me willingly, and that she loves me, has both strengthened and gladdened my heart, although I am saddened by my father's portion in the deception that kept us apart. Still, he did what he believed best. I thought I was ready before yesterday when Durga came. Yet at the moment I slew him, I realized that I had not really been free to move forward. I want no one protecting me, thinking for me. I want to live my own life, on my own terms." She put her arms about the prince's neck. "My time with you, Kaliq, has given me all of this, and for that I thank you." She kissed his cheek, and then drew away smiling at him. "Now I must go."

He nodded. "There is one thing I was not permitted to give you, Lara. That privilege belongs to another. I was not allowed to give you my love. But one day you will meet the man who will. I hope you are able to love him back." And having said those words, the Shadow Prince led Lara and Noss down to the stables. He had quietly secreted her pearwood brush in the pocket of his robes, but within her pack she would find a delicately made gold one to replace it.

In the stables, Og awaited them, holding two horses. Lara was mounted upon a small golden stallion with a creamy mane and tail, Noss upon a white mare with a black mane and tail. Each of the animals had full saddle and water bags. Then to Lara's surprise, Og took the reins of the two horses. She looked to the prince for an explanation.

"Your decision necessitates you depart a different way from that which you came," he said. "Og will set you on the right path. The horses are my gift to you and Noss. May the Celestial Actuary guide you well, and keep you both safe," Prince Kaliq said. Then he bowed to them, and Og led them from the stables.

Lara looked quickly back, but Kaliq had disappeared into the shadows, as was his custom. She turned to look ahead, and was surprised to see Og leading them out into the valley. The horses increased their speed, but he easily kept up. She looked up and was amazed by the height of the great gray stone cliffs surrounding the valley. From the balustrade of the palace they had not seemed so very tall. Before them the herds of mares, many now with their foals, scattered as Og shooed them out of the way. The valley was far wider than she had thought, Lara decided. Finally they reached the other side, and Og began to lead the horses parallel to the steep face of the rock. Then he stopped.

"We are here," he said.

"Where?" Lara asked, searching the cliff for an opening.

Og grinned. "Here!" he repeated, and with a wave of his hand an opening appeared in the dark rock.

"How on earth did you do that?" she demanded of him.

"The prince taught me. Not only am I in charge of his stables, I am his gatekeeper as well. Each of the Shadow Princes has a gate-keeper whose duty it is to offer admittance to the valley. It is a magic skill rarely used, however. Now listen to me, Lara. You will enter a tunnel through this opening. It is well-lit, and safe. Each torch you pass will dim itself as you and Noss go by, for the only way open to you is forward. When you exit the tunnel it will close behind you. You will be in the Outlands then. Your packs contain clothing, food and water. There are no valuables to be stolen. Your sword is on your back, and you know how to use it. Verica rides in his own leather holder by your right hand. Noss, you carry your bow and quiver on your person. Your dagger is at your waist. You, too, know how to use your weapons. Be always watchful, and trust no one but yourselves. The Outlands are not the provinces." He handed each of them a small leather bag that jingled. "Not enough to draw attention, but it will get you by. Lara, you will find a gold piece sewn into each of your vest pockets. May the Celestial Actuary keep you safe, my dear friend."

Lara leaned forward, and standing in her stirrups stood to kiss his cheek. "Be happy, dear Og. I owe you my life, and one day I hope to repay the debt," she said.

"Do not make me weep like a child," he groused at her. "You owe me naught. We saved each other. I am proud to have played a part in your life, Lara. Go now." And he slapped the rump of the golden horse who moved forward into the tunnel, the white horse behind him.

When Lara turned to look back, the cliff wall had already closed behind them. For a brief moment she felt the stirrings of panic. Then taking a deep breath, she turned her face forward. They rode for a time in silence, the only sound in their ears that of the horses' hooves on the smooth rock pathway they traveled. Behind them each torch they passed hissed out with a snap, as Og had said they would. It was eerie, and yet they both felt safe.

Finally Noss spoke. "How much farther do you think it is?" she wondered.

"I don't know," Lara replied. "But at least here I know we're safe. Who knows what will happen when we exit into the Outlands? Are you afraid, Noss?"

"A little," the girl admitted, "but I suppose I'd be a fool if I weren't," she concluded with a small chuckle. "I wonder what we'll find. And if we want to get back to the provinces, how will we ever find our way?"

Lara shrugged. "I don't know," she admitted, and they both grew silent again.

The passage went on and on for what seemed a very long time, but the horses plodded on, sure-footed and steady in their pace. Finally they saw the tiniest pinpoint of daylight up ahead. It grew larger and brighter as they moved toward it, revealing itself at last as an opening at the end of the tunnel. They stopped and stared as one, and then Lara drew a deep noisy breath and they forged forward into the daylight. Behind them the last torch dimmed, and the opening in the rock wall closed with a soft rumble. Lara didn't dare to turn about for she was afraid that she would cry if she did, and she suspected that Noss would, too. This was no time for histrionics.

They stared ahead. Before them a green plain stretched as far as the eye could see. In the distance they saw a range of hazy purple mountains lying on the horizon. But there was no sign of civilization. The land was more beautiful than anything else she had ever seen, Lara thought. Pristine. Untouched.

"Which way do we go?" Noss whispered, stunned by what her eyes beheld.

"Straight ahead," Lara answered, and her laughter echoed in the clear air. "There has to be someone, or something to be found eventually." She spurred the golden stallion into a gallop. They had been penned up in that tunnel forever, it seemed. She heard Noss's white mare coming behind her, and laughed again as the wind hit her face, and the tiny tendrils of hair escaping from her bandana blew about her face. It was wonderful! She had never felt so free in all of her days. Or more at home, she was startled to realize. At last, the horses slowed to a stop. Looking back Lara saw the cliffs had vanished, and realized the magic that had been involved in bringing her into the Outlands.

Noss was openmouthed. "The cliffs, Lara. Where did they go?" she managed to stammer. "We have not ridden that far, for the mountains are still a forever ways away."

"Prince Kaliq has performed a great magical feat for us," Lara said. "I do not know how, but we are obviously just where we are meant to be, Noss." She laughed again. "Isn't it wonderful?"

"It's big," Noss observed. "Very big. Where are the farms? A village or two? Where are the people and the herds? I can see naught but this plain all around us."

"And a stream of water," Lara said pointing to the animal's feet. She loosed the reins so her beast might drink. "I must name my horse, for Og did not tell me what to call him," said Lara.

The horse raised his head, and turning said to her, "I already have a name, mistress. I am Dasras. It means handsome, and as you will have noted I am very handsome. The mare is Sakari. She also has the ability to speak, but she is shy."

Lara was speechless for a moment but then she said, "Thank you, Dasras. Noss, did you hear? Your mare is Sakari. We thank you both for carrying us so safely. Refresh yourselves while you may, for we shall travel onward until dark."

The stallion turned back to his drinking, the mare joining him.

"A horse that talks? I never knew a horse that talked!" Noss exclaimed. "I rather like the idea. As long as Sakari and I are together I will have someone to chat with, Lara. Isn't that nice?" She looked quite pleased.

Lara refrained from giggling. "Are you ready to move on?" she asked. "We may have to camp in the open tonight."

But as they moved on, the plain that had seemed to go on forever began to roll gently, and they discovered it was not as flat as they had thought. As the day wore on, and the sun began slowly to sink, Lara searched for a place they might shelter for the night. Finally, ahead of them, she saw a pleasant grove of trees with another narrow stream flowing through it. She led them to it, and dismounting said, "I think we should be safe here."

"We have seen neither man nor beast all day," Noss said nervously. "What will the night bring? Should we light a fire to keep away savage beasts? Yet a fire could draw bandits to us."

"If we had a better shelter," Lara said, "we could avoid a fire, but Dasras and Sakari must be protected. We'll make a small fire. Others have camped here before us, Noss. See the little ring of blackened stones, and the bits of burned fuel? Let us look for some wood, but we will not start our fire until near dark."

"Do not unload us," Dasras said. "The weight we carry is not heavy, and if you must depart quickly you do not want to lose your few precious supplies. And set your staff in the ground with a view of the plain that he may watch for us. We will graze at our leisure just beyond the trees."

"You offer good advice for one so young," Lara replied.

"My father was a great campaigner with the Shadow Princes long ago. He has taught me all that I know," the stallion answered.

Lara pulled Verica from his place on her saddle. "Wake up!" she said to him, and his eyes flashed open. "You must keep watch for us this night, Verica." She drove the staff into the ground on the edge of the trees.

"Are we looking for anything in particular?" Verica asked dryly.

"Savage animals. Hostile riders," Lara replied, a small smile tugging at her lips.

"In other words it is up to me to save you from disaster," Verica said.

"Exactly!" Lara agreed, now grinning. "We have to light a fire which will serve to keep the four-footed beasts away, but not necessarily the two-footed ones."

Verica chuckled as Lara turned away to gather firewood. She and Noss set up a conical pile within the ring of stones. The sky was now aflame with the sunset, and the darkness came quickly afterward, surprising them. There had been virtually no twilight. Using the faerie magic her mother had taught her, Lara pointed to the stone enclosure and said, "Fire, light!" Immediately a flame sprang up within the cone. "Low," Lara commanded it, and the fire burned low.

"Well don't that beat flint, stone and dried grass," Noss said admiringly.

"I'll call the horses," Lara said. "We had best see what we have in those packs to feed us." She whistled for Dasras and Sakari, who trotted back into their encampment. Rifling through the saddle-bags she drew forth a carefully wrapped packet. Opening it, she exclaimed, "Faerie bread!"

"What's faerie bread?" Noss asked, taking the piece handed her and looking at it suspiciously. She sniffed at it.

"It will satisfy your hunger," Lara said. Ilona had introduced her to faerie bread. "Take a bite of it," Lara told her.

Noss bit into the chunk, and suddenly a beatific smile lit her face. "It's good!" she said.

"Have just a little bit of it. We have no way of knowing how long our stores must last."

When they had finished eating, Lara said, "I will keep watch for part of the night, and you will keep watch the rest of it." She walked over to Dasras, and pulled a heavy cloak from behind her saddle. "There's one for you with Sakari," she told Noss. "The early watch, or the late watch?" she asked her companion.

"The early," Noss said. "When shall I awaken you?"

Lara looked up into the sky above them to see the Triad, risen perhaps an hour now. She pointed it out to Noss. "When it reaches the midheavens wake me, unless of course you need me before then."

"I will," Noss replied, and watched as Lara lay down near their little fire and rolled herself in her cloak. Lara was soon asleep, and Noss sitting by the fire thought how peaceful the night was. Too peaceful. Not the sound of an insect, or a night bird. Getting up, she walked to where Verica stood guard. "It is so quiet," she said to him.

"Yes," he said, "nothing stirs, neither man nor beast. Do not fear, Noss, for my eyes can see through the darkness, and for now there is nothing dangerous to be seen."

Noss walked back to the fire. The horses were grazing peacefully within her sight. She sighed. Traveling with Rolf Fairplay had been very different than this. Then on the horizon a new moon rose, the pale blue of the Midlands. Shortly thereafter a second moon in its first quarter stage arose, and it was the light green Forest moon. It was followed by the full copper moon of the Desert, and lastly a butter-yellow waning moon. Noss was astounded. She considered waking Lara, but then she realized that Lara would see it when she awoke her shortly. With the light of all four moons most of the stars had disappeared, but the Triad still shone brightly, to Noss's relief. She could have never imagined the adventures she was going to have, and they had only just begun.

Noss roused Lara at the appointed time, now sleepy, but remembering to point out the four moons of Hetar. Lara was refreshed from the several hours of sleep she had had. She went into the shelter of the trees to relieve herself. Then she sought out Dasras, and took a water bag from her saddle. She drank, replaced the bag, gave the stallion a pat and went to sit by the fire. Master Bashkar had told her that in the Outlands the four moons of Hetar could all be seen. Three of them she knew, of course, but the butter-yellow quarter moon was new to her. This then would be the moon that shone over the Coastal Province. Once all four moons were risen completely, their colors faded gradually away, and they turned silvery white. The third moon was setting on its horizon as the skies brightened in shades of pink both deep and light, pale lavender, orange and gold. Above the vibrant colors the sky grew bright blue. The birds began to twitter, and then the blazing red sun burst over the horizon. Lara stood, stretched and then went to wake Noss.

They ate their faerie bread and drank from the clear stream, refilling the little they had taken from the water bags the day before. Lara drew Verica from the earth, thanking him for his night watch. She brushed the dirt from the bottom of the staff, replacing it in its holder on her saddle. Lara ordered the fire out, and they departed the grove that had served as their shelter.

The vast rolling plain stretched on ahead of them. They rode at a leisurely pace, not wanting to tire the horses when they had no idea where they were going. At midmorning they heard, first faintly, and then more distinctly, the sound of many horses behind them. Lara turned. She could see a group of riders in the distance behind them.

"What will we do?" Noss half sobbed. "We have no place to hide."

"Calm yourself," Lara chided the girl. "If we run, these riders will think we have something of value, or something to conceal. We will continue on as we have been. They will either pass us by, or inquire to our destination. I will speak for us. Do you understand?"

"You are so brave," Noss said. "I should be, but I am not."

Lara laughed to herself. *Right now I am terrified,* she thought, *yet I must appear calm and in control of myself and the situation. I must remember what Kaliq said. I have a destiny. If that destiny were to be killed easily and at a young age, the Forest Lords would have done it. I have not come into the Outlands to be murdered.*

They pressed onward, and eventually the riders behind them caught up to them, and they found themselves surrounded. Lara and Noss sat straight in their saddles, eyes ahead. They rode for a time within the group of horsemen. All were silent, and then the horse next to Lara's reached out to bite Dasras.

"Control your mount!" she snapped at the animal's rider.

"You ride a stallion as do I," was the reply.

"Yes," Lara said.

"It is unusual for a woman to ride a stallion," her companion remarked. "And particularly, so little a woman."

"Dasras and I suit each other," Lara answered him boldly. The man next to her laughed. "I am Vartan of Clan Fiacre," he said, "and you are very beautiful as well as very brave. You did not flee my riders, though you knew we were behind you."

"I am Lara, daughter of Swiftsword, and why would I run? This is Noss, my companion." She turned her head to look at him. He was a big man, and tall. His long black hair was pulled back and held by a leather thong. His face was oval in shape; his cheekbones high; his mouth long and narrow. His gaze engaged her most directly, clear and light blue, and filled with both amusement and frank curiosity.

"You are two little girls on rather good horses all alone on the plain," he said. "Should you not be afraid?"

Lara's green eyes never left his as she spoke. "The sword on my back is Andraste. It is not there for decoration. I know well how to use it, and we have killed before, Andraste and I. Noss and I are travelers from the City. We carry nothing of value in our packs. You are free to search them."

He laughed again. "Where are you bound for, Lara, daughter of Swiftsword?"

"I don't know," she told him. "We have never been in the Outlands before, and all we know of it is that it is uncivilized, or so we have been told."

"Hetar," he sneered, "so smug in the assurance of its civilized ways."

"It is all Hetar," she told him.

"The High Council doesn't consider it so," he said. "For them Hetar is the four neat and tidy provinces of the Midlands, the Forest, the Desert and the Coastal Regions. We are the Outlands, filled with ignorant savages, unable to live by the rule of law. I curse their law!"

"It has nothing to do with me," Lara replied. "I departed the City over two years ago. I cannot go back."

"Why?"

"Where are you going?" she asked him, ignoring his question.

"Our encampment," he answered her, "and then to the village of Camdene," he told her. "Would you like to travel with us? Not all those you meet out here on the plain will be friendly, Lara, daughter of Swiftsword."

"I should appreciate your company," Lara answered him, "but you need not be friendly, my lord Vartan. Just companionable."

He nodded. "And tonight you will tell me how you came to be in the Outlands."

"Around the fire," she agreed. "And perhaps you will tell me what you do out here on this lonely land. We rode all day yesterday without seeing man nor beast."

"You camped in the grove of Drem. We stopped to water our horses there earlier. You were fortunate to find it for there is not another like it for miles," he told her.

"I have never seen so much open land," Lara told him. "It is beautiful and frightening all at once."

"Aye," he agreed. "Your High Council would like to annex some of these lands if they dared. The Outlands are rich in land and other resources they are greedy to possess. The provinces grow more and more crowded."

"What do you do here?" she asked him.

"We live free," he said, and then he amended it. "Some farm. Many tend to their herds. Our villages are like villages everywhere. The Fiacre have more villages than any other clan in the Outlands. I rule the Fiacre."

"Will we reach your village today?" Lara asked him.

"Nay, not until tomorrow," he said. "We were told strangers had entered our lands, and came out several days ago to find them. You are the only ones we have found so far," he said.

"We cannot be those you seek," Lara said. "We only entered the Outlands yesterday from the Desert Kingdom."

"That cannot be," he said. "The border between us and the Shadow Princes is at least three days away."

"We came through a tunnel in the cliffs," Lara said.

"What cliffs?" he asked, puzzled.

She laughed softly. "They have made some magic, I suspect," she told him. "In the Desert where the great cliffs rise the Shadow Princes have their palaces. If you are a guest in these palaces you will discover a wonderful valley between the cliffs where the princes raise their horses. Yesterday Noss and I were led across that valley from Prince Kaliq's palace. We entered a tunnel and traveled for several hours before we reached its end, which opened out onto your plain.

After we had ridden for a time across your land I looked back, but the cliffs from which we had exited were gone."

"Why have you come here?" Vartan wondered.

"I don't know yet. I just know that given the choice of the Coastal Province or the Outlands, my instinct told me to come here," Lara explained.

"Have you magic?" he asked her.

"Some," she said lightly, "but nothing powerful of which I am aware. I can light a fire without flint and stone." She gave him a small smile.

"A very useful magic for a traveler," he told her, returning the smile.

"Have you magic?" she asked him.

"Some," he said, not elucidating further, and then Vartan chuckled at her delicately raised eyebrow. "I shape-shift," he said. "*Fiacre* is a word for eagle, and I take the form of my clan's badge sometimes. Each leader of the Fiacre is given this gift. It is generally useful."

"Indeed," she said dryly, but did not reveal her own proclivities to him. Not yet. "Why did you simply not seek for these intruders as the eagle?" Lara asked him.

"I had no chance. Most do not know of the ability I possess. They would be afraid," Vartan told her. "Shall we keep it our little secret, Lara, daughter of Swiftsword? You appear to be a girl who can keep secrets."

Now it was Lara who laughed. "I can, and I do," she agreed.

Noss pushed her mare closer to Lara's stallion. "There is a man who keeps looking at me as if I am his next meal," she murmured.

Vartan heard her, and looked quickly about him. "'Tis Liam, little girl, and I will tell him he is frightening you. He is a good fellow with a soft heart who would not harm a flea. But he is obviously taken with you." The lord of the Fiacre chuckled and dropped back a few paces to speak with the red-haired man who gazed so intently at Noss. When he rejoined Lara and her companion he said,

"Liam would like to know if you are married, young Noss? 'Tis not a question a man of the Fiacre asks casually."

"Noss is only thirteen and a half," Lara said quietly. "She is a virgin. She is too young for any man, and she must want the man who weds her one day."

Vartan nodded. "I will explain all of this to Liam. But Noss," he directed his question to her, "might you allow him to become a friend? He will not, I swear to you, harm a hair of your head."

Noss looked to Lara questioningly. "Should I?"

"If you wish it I see no reason to deny yourself the company of a fine young man," Lara replied. "But he must treat you with respect," she warned.

"I will see he does," Vartan replied, and then dropped back again to speak with the red-haired Liam, who listened, and then grinned happily.

Noss blushed when the young man looked to her again, lowering her head shyly as Liam moved his horse up next to Sakari.

Vartan rejoined Lara, and the two rode ahead a ways. "How old are you?" he demanded of her, "and are you a virgin, too?"

"I am sixteen, and I have experienced the giving and taking of pleasures," she told him. "How old are you, and are you experienced?" she countered.

"I have lived twenty-eight years, and I am considered experienced by those with whom I share a bed," he replied, and his blue eyes met her gaze.

"You should know I am half faerie," Lara told him. "If your people fear magic, then they fear my mother's people. You would not be wise to involve yourself with a woman like me. I have, I am told, a destiny to live out, my lord Vartan."

"Perhaps I am that destiny," he suggested.

Lara laughed. "An interesting excuse for attempted seduction," she remarked.

He grinned engagingly at her. "I think I am falling in love with you, Lara, daughter of Swiftsword," he told her.

"You are a fraud, my lord Vartan, for we have only just met," Lara reminded him.

"Have you never heard of love at first sight?" he asked her.

"I do not believe in love, my lord," Lara answered him. "You do not have to cajole me with sweet words, my lord Vartan. If I remain among the Fiacre long enough, and we become friends, then I will gladly share my body with you," Lara promised him. "But be warned that even half faerie women do not give children to those they do not love."

"Now," he said, "I am even more curious to learn your story, Lara, daughter of Swiftsword," he told her.

"Tonight," she promised. "We will speak together as the Triad blazes overhead."

They rode the day long, stopping only briefly to water their horses. Lara dug into her pouch, and pulled out a piece of faerie bread to share with Noss, who was all rosy with blushes from her ride with the Fiacre Liam.

"You are too young to be seduced," Lara warned Noss. "Do not let his sweet words or stolen kisses overcome your innate common sense."

"He is very polite," Noss half whispered.

"Then he is indeed a dangerous man," Lara cautioned. "Remember that unlike me you can conceive a child in your belly, Noss. Do you desire to be a mother at your young age? Think carefully before you let him insinuate himself between your legs. I should have to leave you behind, and we do not know these people. They are considered savages by those in the City."

"They do not seem very savage to me," Noss noted.

"Nay, and I do not believe they are. They simply wish to live their lives in a different manner than those who call themselves Hetarians," Lara said.

"I like this freedom that they have," Noss said softly.

"So do I," Lara agreed, "but I want to know more about the Outlanders, and sheltering with Lord Vartan for a short while is a good way to learn about them."

They reached the encampment, a small circle of tents. In the center of the circle a fire was prepared, and ready to light. When Vartan looked to Lara she shook her head in the negative. There was no reason to reveal her skills to others right now. She dismounted, noting that her buttocks felt sorer today than they had yesterday.

"How I would love a hot bath," she said to no one in particular.

"Tomorrow in my house we will bathe together," Vartan said, coming up next to her. "Come, and I will show you and Noss to my tent. You will sleep there tonight while I sleep outside keeping watch."

"You need not keep watch," Lara told him. "I will set Verica, my staff, at the entrance of your tent and he will watch over us."

"The sword has magic. The staff has magic," Vartan noted. "What else about you is magic, Lara, daughter of Swiftsword?"

"The horses talk," she told him, her green eyes dancing with mirth. "None of this is my doing, my lord Vartan, I swear it. These things were given to me by Prince Kaliq and his people to help keep me safe," Lara finished, almost laughing.

Vartan of the Fiacre did laugh at these admissions. He had not lied when he told her he was falling in love with her. He knew it in his heart from the moment he had laid eyes on her, but he also knew this was a strong woman. But could the lord of the Fiacre follow in the wake of a half faerie woman, even if he loved her? He did not know the answer to these questions. Yet.

They remained the night at the encampment. They did not eat faerie bread, but rather feasted on broiled rabbits the Fiacre clansmen had caught along the way. There was real bread, and cheese, and even wine. And after the others had all gone to bed, Lara and Vartan sat by the fire beneath the Triad and the four silvery moons of Hetar as she told him her tale. He was fascinated, repelled and angered by her recitation.

"How could your father…?" he began, but she hushed him.

"A man must be worthy to be a Crusader Knight," she said. "I was my father's only asset."

"His assets should have been his battle skills, his honesty and his loyalty," Vartan said.

"It is not the way of Hetar. A man's appearance is all-important, my lord," Lara replied. "If he could not look the part, what good his skills and ethics?"

Vartan shrugged. "Indeed," was all he could think of to reply. He listened again, scorning the foolish futility of the Forest Lords at paying thirty thousand pieces of gold for Lara in the belief she could remove the curse placed upon them by Maeve. "And then they came to Shunnar to reclaim you with a false document? What kind of a magistrate would give them such a parchment?"

"One whom they paid well," Lara replied. "Commerce is the way of Hetar. If a man does not line his pockets when he can, he will die poor."

Vartan shook his head. "Wealth is better, I will agree, but a man's wealth should be gained honestly, not through schemes and trickery."

"A man thought too honest will be considered a fool," she replied. And yet his words were giving her pause for thought. Were there other ways than those she had been taught? She suspected she would learn them in her journeying.

Lara finally found her bed, curling up next to Noss, who was sleeping soundly. But her sleep was a restless one, and the dawn came swiftly. She found herself dozing in her saddle as they rode along the next day. When they stopped to water the horses, Dasras scolded her softly in his deep voice.

"What is the matter with you, mistress?"

"I did not sleep well last night," she told him.

"And you were late to bed as well," Dasras murmured. "Is it the Fiacre lord who disturbs your rest?"

"Why would Vartan disturb my rest?" Lara muttered. "You had better drink while you can. We'll be going again very quickly." She didn't want to discuss Vartan.

Dasras lowered his head, and drank.

It was almost sunset when they reached the village of Camdene.

"Is there an inn or resting place for travelers?" Lara asked Vartan.

He looked slightly scandalized by her words. "You are my guest, Lara, daughter of Swiftsword," he said. "My mother keeps my house. She would be very angry with me if I allowed you and Noss to rest your heads elsewhere."

"You have no wife, no mate?" Lara inquired bluntly.

"I am responsible for my people, and the Fiacre are a large clan. Seven villages belong to us, as well as much land. I have no time for a wife. My younger brother, Adon, took a wife several months ago. Her name is Elin. My mother is Bera."

To Lara's surprise the village looked very prosperous. It very much resembled the villages in the Midlands, but it was better kept, to Lara's eye. Each cottage sat upon a neat square of land with a garden both before it, and behind. The street of shops they traversed showed windows filled with goods. These people did not appear to be savages at all. The men with them dropped away, each going to his own home. At the far end of the village on a gentle green rise sat a large stone house toward which they rode. The house was long, and built to fit into the surrounding landscape. It would have been difficult to distinguish from a distance, it nestled so closely into the land.

They had but reached the house when the front door opened, and a woman stepped forth. "Vartan! What did you find?"

He slid from his horse, and embraced the woman. "Two little girls all alone on the plain, Mother. I brought them home."

Bera looked Lara and Noss over with a sharp and critical eye. "They do not appear particularly helpless to me, my son," she said. "Who are they, and from where do they come?" She was a big woman like her son with the same light blue eyes.

"That is not the welcome I would expect for Lara, daughter of Swiftsword, and her companion, Noss, Mother," Vartan gently chided his parent.

"She is faerie," Bera said suspiciously.

"Aye, mistress, my mother was indeed faerie," Lara quickly spoke. "But she did not raise me. I was raised by my father, who was a mercenary, and my grandmother, Ina. While I have some small magic about me, I mean no harm to any. If you would not shelter Noss and me, I will understand, and seek your inn."

Bera laughed at Lara's words. "And she is proud. She looks delicate, but she is made of iron I can now see. Welcome, Lara, daughter of Swiftsword, and her companion, Noss. Come in! Come in!" She ushered them into the house, leading them into the Great Hall.

"You handled her well," Vartan murmured low.

"I can see now why you are not yet wed," Lara said dryly in low tones.

"I am not wed because until now I had not yet met the woman I wanted for my mate," he responded, well pleased to see her blush.

"You have arrived just in time for the evening meal," Bera said. "We eat simply, but there is always plenty." Immediately servants began entering the hall, bearing steaming bowls and platters. "Sit! Sit!" Bera invited them, noticing that her son put Lara at his right hand. At last, she thought! Was it possible? Dared she to hope? Then she restrained herself. Only time would tell.

Lara's eyes widened at Bera's idea of a simple meal. There was fresh broiled salmon with herbs, a roasted goose, a large joint of beef, and a rabbit pie with the flakiest crust she had ever tasted. There were bowls of peas, onions in cream, butter and pepper, tiny carrots in butter and honey dusted with nutmeg. There was bread, a large crock of sweet newly churned butter and a wheel of hard yellow cheese. And when she thought the meal was over, bowls of peaches and sweet cherries were brought to the table along with crisp little sugar wafers. They drank goblets of ale, and it was the best Lara had ever tasted. Again she wondered why Outlanders were called savages.

"You have another son, I am told," Lara said to Bera when the food had finally been cleared away.

"Aye, but he's wed now and has his own home," Bera said. "'Tis just Vartan and his old mother in this great house that cries out for grandchildren."

Vartan laughed. "Be patient, Mother," he said. "I have only just found the one."

Noss's eyes widened, and she looked to Lara, whose cheeks were again pink.

A minstrel entered the hall, and seating himself by the great fireplace, began to sing songs Lara had never before heard. They were songs of bravery and daring, of battles she had never known and warriors whose names were most unfamiliar. Then he sang of love unrequited, but true, and a hero who died of a broken heart. Bera smiled and nodded with the pleasure the music gave her. A large greyhound sat with his head in her lap, eyes closed, and she stroked him gently as the minstrel played, his music wrapping them all in a blanket of sweetness.

When the musician finally ceased his efforts Bera arose. "Come," she beckoned Lara and Noss. "I will show you to your sleeping spaces." She led them upstairs to a smaller hall with another fireplace, assigning them beds that were tucked into the stone walls on either side of the fire. These were the preferred sleeping spaces for honored guests. "There is water for washing." She pointed. "Good night." But she did not go to her own chamber. She returned downstairs to find her son still by the fire. "Tell me everything," she demanded, sitting next to him.

"She is the one," he said. And then he shared with his mother everything Lara had told him the previous evening.

Bera nodded when he had finished. "But if the Shadow Princes say she has a destiny they do not mean only as the wife of an Outlander leader. There is more, but what more? And she must be willing for she has told you herself that faerie women do not give children to those they do not love. Pleasures she will share with you. But you must have her heart, Vartan. If she favors her faerie blood it is unlikely she has a heart to give you. But if she favors her human side, her heart is there for you to win."

"Have I your blessing, Mother?" Vartan asked Bera.

"You do. My instincts have never failed me yet, my son. Lara is a good woman, and could make you a good wife if she chooses to be, but you cannot force her decision. Woo her, and we shall see," Bera advised.

"Liam was taken with her little companion, Noss, but Lara says the girl is too young yet," Vartan told his mother.

"She seems shy and retiring, the other," Bera noted. "But she could prove formidable if she fell in love, as all women can be. I am pleased that Liam shows signs of wanting to settle down. I have feared for your cousin almost as much as I have feared for you. I will tell my sister, Asta, in the morning. She will be pleased." She arose from her place. "Go to bed, my son. You have traveled long and hard the last few days. I am yet concerned you found naught but Lara and her friend. But perhaps that was the plan of the Celestial Actuary. The plain is vast, and yet you found her. Yes, I see the fine hand of the Celestial Actuary in this." She bent and kissed his cheek. "Good night, Vartan."

Raising his dark head he kissed her back. "Good night, Mother." Then turning back to the hearth he stared into the fire's dancing flames. *Lara.* How could this have all happened in such a short time? he questioned himself. But he knew he was in love. Never before had he felt this way, and his emotions lacked common sense and reason, which was what many said love was like. She said she had a destiny. But was he part of that destiny? Only time would give him the answer to that query. Vartan rose and sought out his own bed, but his sleep was a restless and troubled one.

Chapter 13

LARA SLEPT surprisingly well in Vartan's house. She awoke at first light and washed her face and hands. She very much wanted a bath, and wondered if such a thing could be obtained. She would ask Bera. Perhaps there was a bathhouse in the village as the Forest folk had had. From her pack she drew a simple gown of pale green with short sleeves, a draped neckline and a twisted rope belt of gold silk. She brushed her gilt hair out, braiding it into a single thick plait, and slipped her feet into her sandals. Then she poked Noss. "Wake up, sleepyhead," she said. "I'm going down to the hall. Hurry and join me." Noss grumbled something unintelligible.

The hall was already busy with servants cleaning and sweeping. Seeing Lara, Bera came forward smiling. "I thought surely a girl from the City, and especially one who had spent her time in the palace of a Shadow Prince, would sleep late. Come and eat with me. Vartan will join us shortly. He is in the stables speaking with the grooms. The two horses you and your companion rode have frightened them, and they refuse to care for them now."

"Dasras, my stallion, can be very outspoken on occasion," Lara explained. "Noss's mare, Sakari, is usually quieter. They are a gift from Prince Kaliq, who was my lover."

"Did he want you to leave him?" Bera asked softly.

"No, but he understood I have a destiny," Lara replied. "I feel so foolish saying that, but it is what everyone has told me. I honestly have no idea of what they mean at all. But my mother and grandmother said it, and so does Ethne, my crystal guardian."

"Who is your mother?" Bera questioned the beautiful girl. Yes, beautiful, and yet Lara had not seemed so when she arrived with Vartan yesterday. Now, however, in that feminine gown with her hair revealed, she was a different girl.

"My mother is Ilona, who with my grandmother Maeve's death became the new queen of the Forest Faeries. My father is human. He was a simple mercenary, but now rides as a Crusader Knight. I am sure Vartan has told you the rest of my tale."

"He has," Bera answered. "I stand in awe of you, my child. You have suffered much, survived it all, and seem strong in spite of it. I suspect you do have a destiny to fulfill. But what has it to do with the Outlands?"

Lara shook her head. "As I have said, I do not know. Given a choice between the Outlands and the Coastal Province, I chose to come here. Every instinct I possess insisted. But had not Vartan and his men found us, we would still be wandering out on the plain."

"The Celestial Actuary always leads us to where we should be," Bera said.

"Good morning!" Vartan strode into his hall and going to his mother kissed her cheek. He then turned to Lara, his blue eyes widening in surprise. "You're beautiful," he exclaimed. "Very beautiful," he added.

"A blessing and a curse both," Lara responded with a small smile. "Did I not seem beautiful to you out on the plain?" she teased him.

"You seemed a pretty girl," he replied slowly, "and perhaps a bit formidable with that sword on your back you claim to know how to use, but nothing more. Yet this morning in my hall, you are so beautiful it hurts my eyes just to look at you, Lara, daughter of Swiftsword."

To her surprise Lara felt her cheeks grow warm with his admiration. "Perhaps," she said, "I should wear my leather garments all the time then, lest I be held responsible for blinding you, my lord Vartan." And then she smiled at him. "I understand my horses have frightened your servants. I must apologize to you as you have been so kind to us."

"A bad-tempered stable boy was rough with Sakari, and Dasras objected in the most strenuous terms," Vartan replied with an answering smile. "He was quite right, too, and the lad has been admonished. I explained to my servants that your horses were magical, and they were to be treated with the utmost care. I then asked Dasras not to frighten those caring for him again. All is well now. Would you like to ride out with me after the morning meal? I am going to spend the next few days visiting my other villages. Your company would be most welcome."

Lara considered refusing him, but then she nodded her agreement. "I should like that, my lord." Nothing was beckoning her onward today, and she was interested to learn if all of his villages were as prosperous and well-maintained. Why did the High Council of Hetar insist on saying that Outlanders were uncivilized barbarians? Was Vartan the exception to the rule? She needed to know the answers to her many questions, and she wasn't going to learn them sitting in Vartan's hall with his mother.

Noss came sleepily into the hall just as the servants were bringing in the meal. As they ate Bera engaged her in conversation. Noss became more lively as the hot food and cold cider helped her to awaken fully. And when Bera invited her to spend the day with her Noss looked eagerly to Lara. "May I?" she said.

"Of course. I am riding out with Lord Vartan, but there is no necessity for you to come, Noss. Remain with Bera. You do not enjoy being a-horse as much as I do, and we will be traveling on soon enough."

"Do you know how to weave?" Bera asked Noss.

"Yes, my mother taught me," Noss replied, and then she and Vartan's mother entered into a discussion of threads, and designs.

"My mother has her eye on Noss for my cousin, Liam," Vartan said softly.

"The red-haired man who was so taken with her?"

"Aye, the very same," Vartan said.

"Noss is still a girl, and I have said it before. You must dissuade your mother, and your cousin," Lara told him. "I will not have Noss forced to the marriage bed when she is so very young."

"No one in my care is ever forced to anything," Vartan replied. "I am not a savage like those among whom you were raised, Lara, daughter of Swiftsword. Liam simply wants his honorable intentions known so that when the time comes Noss will consider him for a husband."

"We will not be with you for more than a day or two," Lara said.

"Where do you go?" he asked her.

"I don't know," she said irritably.

"Have you a desire to leave us so quickly?" he demanded of her.

"No," she admitted, "but that is not the point, my lord Vartan."

"You have a destiny," he said taking her small hand in his large one. "I know that, Lara, daughter of Swiftsword, and I will not stand in the way of that destiny. But until destiny calls to you again why not remain here where you are safe?"

"You are confusing me," Lara cried low.

"Then go and change from this clinging gown that reveals the sweet swell of your breasts and hips. Put on your leather garments and strap Andraste to your back, so we may ride out together. I have told Noss we will be gone two nights, and she is not to fear. She is safe with my mother."

"Why will we be gone two nights?" Lara asked him a bit breathlessly. His eyes had all but devoured her when he had spoken to her of her gown.

"I have six villages to visit. I ride out once each moon cycle to make certain all is well, to hold court if necessary, to mediate any disputes," Vartan explained. "I am lord of the Fiacre, and it is my duty to care for and watch over my people."

"I will change," Lara told him, and rising from the table she left the hall.

"I will await you in the stable yard," he called after her.

Lara returned to the small hall where she and Noss had slept the night before. The house, seen from afar, had not appeared to be more than a single story, but on closer inspection Lara realized part of its main level was underground, and the roof over the Great Hall peaked. One side of the building had a second story. Entering her chamber she stripped the gown off, dressing herself again in her riding garments and pulling on her boots. She bound her head in the green cloth, and returned downstairs, hurrying out into the stable yard where Vartan awaited her with Dasras.

"Good morning," Lara said, rubbing his velvety muzzle.

Dasras snorted, and his dark eyes twinkled at her.

"I have explained to Sakari that we will be away for a few days, but that Noss is here," Vartan said. "I didn't want her frightened again." He boosted Lara into the saddle.

Dasras turned his head slightly. "Most thoughtful, my lord," he said.

Vartan nodded his acknowledgement to the great stallion, and mounted his own horse. They rode from the stable yard together, and out into the morning sunlight. Villagers greeted them as they passed by, and again Lara noted Camdene's neat prosperity. "We go first to Orlege," he said. "If there are no difficulties there, we can move on to Leax and Scur today."

"Are all your villages so comfortable?" Lara asked him. "How do you live?"

"The Fiacre's prosperity comes from the land," Vartan explained. "We have vast herds of cattle. Each of our clan families has its own way of earning a livelihood."

"How many clan families are there?" Lara asked him.

"Eight, including the Fiacre. The Tormod and the Piaras live in the north. They mine deep within the earth for gems, and precious metals, but they also husband their lands carefully so it is not destroyed. The Aghy possess great herds of horses. The Felan's wealth comes from sheep. The Gitta are known for their especial strength, but they also farm. The Blathma are growers of grains and flowers. The Devyn are the smallest of our clan families. They are the poets, the bards, the musicians of the Outlands. The minstrel in the hall last night was a Devyn."

"Where is your governing body located?" she asked him.

"Each clan governs itself," he told her.

"What if there is a dispute between clan families?" she persisted. "That is what our High Council is for, my lord. Have you no High Council?"

"Disputes between the clans are rare, Lara. Why would there be? The boundaries separating our lands have been set for eons. The clans intermarry if they wish. We are all prosperous. The Tormod and Piaras supply us with the metals and gems from which we fashion our ornaments. We supply them with what they need in return. Ours is an uncomplicated way of life, and we are happy."

"But there must be a system of governance, my lord," Lara insisted. "How are your clan families ruled? Who decides upon the rulers?"

"Each clan has a chieftain," he began. "Each village has a headman who is responsible to the chieftain. When a chieftain dies, or chooses no longer to rule, his successor is chosen by the elders of the clan family, both men and women. Generally they pick a chieftain from the same family grouping, but their choice is based upon the man who is best suited to take the responsibility of the clan upon his shoulders. My uncle was the previous chieftain, Liam's father."

"Why did they not choose Liam?" she asked.

"He was younger in years than I was, and he did not want to be chieftain. My grandfather was the chieftain before Liam's sire. The elders, knowing this, then chose me. I have ruled the Fiacre for five years now."

They had left the village of Camdene well behind, and now rode at a leisurely pace over the rolling green plain. In the sky above them a hawk soared and, seeing it, Lara could not help but wonder if it was Kaliq. But then she put the thought from her head. She was a very long way from the Desert of the Shadow Princes. Kaliq was her past. She cast a surreptitious look at Vartan from beneath her lashes as they rode. He was a handsome man in a rough-hewn sort of way. She considered what it might be like to share her body with him, and her cheeks grew hot.

Finally, ahead of them they saw another grouping of cottages. It was not as big a village as Camdene, but it appeared every bit as prosperous.

"This is Orlege," he told her. "I have a dispute to settle here today. One of the village men lost his wife, and wishes to have another, but his neighbors will not match any of their daughters with him. I must learn why, and then settle the problem."

Vartan was greeted warmly by the villagers of Orlege. He was led into the headman's house, and seated at the small high board in the little hall. Lara stood quietly at the side of the room, observing all. The headman, Scully, brought forth the complainant to state his case. Pol was a man in his sixth decade. He had been widowed for a year and wished to take a new wife, but, he complained to his lord, the villagers of Orlege would not offer him their marriageable daughters that he might choose. He begged his lord to help him find a wife to take care of him in his old age.

Next, the headman spoke for the villagers. Pol was an old man. No young girl wanted to be shackled to an old man. She wanted a vigorous husband who would give her children, that she not be ashamed at the well when she went to draw water. And no father in Orlege would force his daughter to be Pol's wife. He was an ordinary man with only a small holding he could barely work any longer.

"I must think on this," Vartan said. "Bring me something to drink." He looked to Lara, and beckoned her to him. When she stood by his side he said, "What would you do in a case like this, Lara, daughter of Swiftsword?"

"Ask the headman if there is a widow who would be willing to have Pol for a husband," she replied. "If he has no children to care for him it is unlikely he will have them at his age. He does not need a young wife. He needs a housekeeper, a cook and a companion. What could he possibly give a young wife but unhappiness?"

"A clever solution, Lara, daughter of Swiftsword," Vartan said. He drank from the cup placed by his left hand, and then shared the draught with Lara.

How easy she felt with this man, Lara thought to herself. Their acquaintance was hardly a lengthy one, and yet she felt completely comfortable with Vartan of the Fiacre.

When he had finished his drink, Lara moved discreetly away again to the side of the hall and watched while Vartan settled the issue between Pol and his fellow villagers. First he drew Scully, the headman aside, and spoke with him for several minutes in low tones. Scully listened, nodded and finally smiled. The headman signaled another man, murmured to him. The second man went off into the crowd of villagers, speaking with several women. Finally he led three of them forward. Both Scully and Vartan spoke with them, and then Vartan called for silence.

"Pol of Orlege, you seek a wife to care for you in your old age. Is this correct?"

"Yes, my lord."

"Then choose from among these three fine widows. Women of good reputation with experience in keeping a husband happy," Vartan said. "No father will give you his young daughter. No young girl wants a graybeard for a mate. In this I concur. You seek a companion who will keep you comfortable and well-fed. Here stand three, all eminently suited to your needs, and all willing to have you. You must choose from among them if you would remarry."

Pol looked the three women over, and finally said, "I choose Corliss."

"Corliss, you are willing?" Vartan asked.

"I am, my lord," the plump widow said.

"Then come forward, and be joined," Vartan said, and when the two stood before him he said, "Marriage between a man and a woman is sacred in the eyes of the Celestial Actuary. It is the husband's duty to provide for his mate. It is the wife's duty to care for her mate. Are you, Pol, willing to provide for Corliss, and treat her with dignity and kindness?"

"I am, my lord," Pol said.

"And you, Corliss, will you care for Pol, treating him with respect and kindness?"

"I will, my lord," the widow replied.

"Then it is done, and you are considered husband and wife in the eyes of the Celestial Actuary," Vartan concluded. He drew a coin from his vest pocket, and gave it to the bride. "For luck," he told her, and kissed her cheek. Then he shook Pol's hand.

"Thank you, my lord," the newly wed man said. Then he and his new bride left the hall chattering busily about where they would now live.

"A grand solution, my lord, to a difficult problem," Scully said grinning broadly.

"Do not thank me, but rather my companion, Lara, daughter of Swiftsword," Vartan said graciously. "She is my guest at Camdene."

The headman looked at Lara admiringly. "Thank you, my lady," he said.

"It was common sense," Lara told him, "but sometimes it takes an outsider to see the path through the woods." She smiled at him.

They left Orlege, and traveled on to Leax, Vartan's next village. Again Lara found it a pretty and thriving place. Along the path they traveled, fat cattle grazed on the grass of the plain. There were no problems in Leax that required Vartan's attention, and so they moved quickly on to the next village, Scur, which sat by a swiftly flowing brook. The headman there, Evin, was concerned because in the last few days the fish that populated the brook were turning up dead. He had forbidden anyone to eat the fish, but was worried that if the fish were dying, the water could be tainted.

"Where does the brook flow from?" Vartan asked.

"The north, my lord. In the mountains of the Piaras and Tormod clans," Evin answered.

"I shall send someone north to investigate," Vartan promised. "The village has another well?"

"Yes, my lord. It comes from an underground spring not connected with the brook," Evin said.

"Continue to keep people from the brook and the fish until we learn what is happening," Vartan said.

"You will remain the night, my lord?" Evin bowed when he offered the invitation.

"We will," Vartan said jovially. "This is Lara, daughter of Swiftsword, who is my guest at Camdene."

"You are from Hetar," Evin said.

"We are all from Hetar," Lara told him.

"They do not think it," he replied.

"Then they are fools," Lara remarked, "and I have little tolerance for fools."

The sun set quickly, as was its habit here in the Outlands. Evin's wife invited them to her table, clucking and fussing as the meal was brought forth. Vartan praised her menu, and she beamed, well pleased. Shortly after their meal in the headman's little hall the lord of the Fiacre and his companion were shown to a bedchamber, and bid goodnight.

Lara looked about her. There was one bed. "Where will you sleep?" she asked Vartan. "The bed or the floor?"

"We will share the bed," he said in matter-of-fact tones.

"I have not offered my body to you, my lord Vartan," Lara said tartly.

"I have not asked for it," he replied, his tone amused.

"Then one of us must sleep upon the floor," she told him.

"Why? The bed is large enough for two," he replied. "Evin and his wife have honored us by giving us their chamber to sleep in, Lara, daughter of Swiftsword."

"I will take the floor, then," Lara said, and pulled a coverlet from the bed.

He snatched the coverlet back with one hand, reaching for her with the other. Then tossing the coverlet onto the bed he took her chin between his thumb and his forefinger even as he pressed her slender form against his hard one and looked down into her lovely face. "Do you think I lured you out to one of my distant villages to seduce you, Lara, daughter of Swiftsword? Do you believe I am the kind of man who would share my body with you for the first time in a borrowed bed, in an underling's house?" His blue eyes stared fiercely into her green ones. "If I had desired nothing more than to bed you I could have done it that first day we met out on the plain. When we finally decide to share pleasure with each other, Lara, daughter of Swiftsword, it will be because we both want it. Despite what your Hetarian teachers have taught you, I am not a savage bent on rapine and pillage. Now get into that bed, which I fully intend sharing with you. The nights grow cold in late summer on the plain." Then tipping her face up, he kissed her a slow, hard kiss and, releasing her from his grasp, shoved her toward the bed.

Meekly, Lara complied with his request, but she couldn't resist saying, "I just wanted you to understand that I am not some common Pleasure Woman, my lord Vartan."

"No," he replied wryly. "You could not be called common, and you have a destiny to fulfill." Then climbing into the bed, he turned his back to her.

Arrogant! He was the most arrogant man she had ever met, Lara fumed to herself. Then she reached down to finger the crystal star that hung between her breasts in hopes of calming her righteous indignation.

He is very masterful, Ethne said. *I like him.*

I have a destiny, whatever it is, and I shall fulfill it, Lara returned irritably.

Perhaps he is part of that destiny, Ethne replied, *for why else have you been brought to the Outlands? And why have you been set so neatly into his world? Do not allow your pride to deter you. Remember that the Shadow Prince taught you to be patient, and to consider each situation carefully before acting. You seem to lose all reason with this man, my child. Is it possible you are falling in love?*

Faerie women do not really love, Lara replied. *You know that.*

You are but half faerie, Ethne reminded her. *There is much that is human about you, Lara. Do not deny either part of your heritage. And faerie women do fall in love. Your own mother fell so in love with your father that until she had to, she would not take another mate, or have another child.*

Will she birth a child for Thanos, Ethne? And if she does, will you leave me? Lara asked the guardian of the crystal.

You will have a brother in the next spring, Lara, but I will never leave you. I am the guardian your mother gave you, and I will always be with you, my child. Now go to sleep. The man by your side is already in deep slumber. The flame within the crystal flickered, and dimmed to the tiniest golden dot.

Lara lay silent but wakeful. Vartan was sleeping soundly. She considered her earlier words, and now felt like a fool. Why had she been so sure he wanted to share pleasure with her? He had made no suggestive overtures. She realized, to her dismay, that she did not trust most men. Her own father had sold her into slavery to advance himself, and she had been willing because she saw no other way and she loved him. Now she wondered if he had ever really loved her, or if her striking resemblance to her mother had but added soreness to his broken heart. But he had been a good father when he was there. She had no complaints. He had never beaten her.

But her experience with the Forest Lords had been distasteful at best. She had become hard, Lara realized, in order to survive their brutality and stupidity. Yet Og had been kind to her, and without him she would have never escaped the Forest. And Kaliq had been gentle, patient and generous to her. He had taught her the meaning of passion. But there had to be more to the relationship between a man and a woman than just pleasure for the body. Was that what this love people talked about was?

In the morning, Evin's wife fed them a hearty breakfast of porridge, eggs and ham with fresh bread. She wrapped slices of bread and meat in a cloth, giving it to Lara for it would be afternoon before they reached Doane, the next village. They rode the long morning, stopping briefly to eat again. Evin's wife had not only packed meat and bread, but there was cheese and two pears as well. They sat in the grass while the horses grazed placidly within their sight. Vartan asked Lara to tell him about her life in the City. She was surprised by his curiosity, but complied nonetheless. He listened with open interest, and as she came to the end of her recitation he handed her a piece of pear. The juice drizzled down her chin as she bit into it, and she was startled when he leaned forward to lick the nectar from her skin.

"You are bold, my lord," she said quietly.

"I will always think of you as tasting of pears," he said as quietly.

"What is it you want of me, Vartan of the Fiacre?"

"Everything!" he answered her.

"I cannot give it to you."

"You can, and you will one day," he replied with an assurance that amazed her.

"We should go," she said, rising to her feet and whistling for Dasras.

"Shall I save the other pear for tonight?"

"If it pleases you to do so," she replied, feeling her cheeks grow warm as she pulled herself back into her saddle.

Vartan smiled up into her eyes, but said nothing more.

In midafternoon they reached Doane, another flourishing village. They remained but a brief while, as all was in order. Next they came to Calum village, where again the lord of the Fiacre was greeted warmly and there was no difficulty to be had. The last village was Rivalen, and they reached it just before dark to be greeted by Sholeh, the headwoman.

"My lord!" She came forward smiling, a big-boned woman with dark red hair that hung to her broad hips. "Welcome! I did not know if you would come today. We had heard that you were villaging."

Vartan slid from his stallion, and wrapped an arm about Sholeh. "Each time I see you, my girl, you are more of an armful." He kissed her cheek noisily.

Sholeh laughed heartily. "Away with you! I already have enough children to raise and care for, my lord." Her glance swung to Lara. "And who is this dainty beauty you travel with, Vartan, lord of the Fiacre? She is faerie or I miss my guess."

"She is Lara, daughter of Swiftsword, and only half faerie." Vartan lifted Lara from her saddle. "Eventually I will make her my wife."

"Eventually I will slice you in two," Lara snapped.

Sholeh laughed again, and flung an arm about Lara's shoulders. "I am going to like you, Lara, daughter of Swiftsword," she said. "The key to a successful mating is to never let the man have the advantage. Come in to my hall. You are most welcome!" And she led the way, her arm still about Lara.

The hall into which she led them was large with a great peaked roof. There was a large stone fireplace burning with fragrant woods. They had no sooner been seated at the high board than the servants began to hurry forth with the meal. Lara was surprised, for it was a generous offering. There was salmon and trout from the river that flowed through the village of Rivalen. There was beef, ham, duck, capon and a rabbit stew. There were braised lettuces, asparagus, fresh breads, butter and cheeses of several kinds. And there was Frine and ale both.

"Sholeh is a member of my family," Vartan explained, seeing Lara's surprise. "We are cousins. She is the widow of the former headman here. When he died, the villagers asked that she be put in charge over them."

"She is a woman," Lara said, puzzled.

"She is a competent woman," Vartan replied. "Do not women hold positions of responsibility in Hetar?"

"Not really," Lara said. "They are always responsible to men for their actions. The Pleasure Mistresses, for instance, do not own the houses over which they preside. Those are always owned by a magnate, and magnates are always men."

"Who manages the Pleasure Houses then?" Sholeh asked having overheard their conversation.

"The Pleasure Mistresses do. That is their duty," Lara replied.

"So these women handle all the daily business of the Pleasure Houses? They make certain the girls are happy and healthy? They order the proper foods, wines and other supplies, and yet they are subordinate to those who own the houses, and collect the profits, eh?" Sholeh concluded. "I don't think I like that."

"It is our way," Lara explained. "Are you not responsible for Rivalen and its people to Lord Vartan?"

"It is different," Sholeh said. "Rivalen is mine. It is part of the Fiacre clan family holdings, and Vartan, its overlord, is responsible for our protection in the event of war. I give him my allegiance, but I am a free woman with my own lands."

"I have never heard of such a thing before," Lara said. "I like it much better than the way it is done in the City." Again she thought that these Outlanders were not barbarians in any sense. But perhaps the Fiacre was different from the other clan families. Perhaps they were the exception.

Sholeh's hall was filled to capacity. She was the mother of seven sons and two daughters, all of whom lived with her, and she had twenty-two grandchildren as well. The dogs snuffled beneath the tables hoping for scraps. Two cats, one a large marmalade, and the other an equally large black, lay head-to-head before the fire. There was much good-natured bickering back and forth, but no one fought. And again she was aware of how very respected Vartan was.

Several of Sholeh's grandsons wrestled bare-chested for their
lord's amusement. There was an old Devyn in the hall who entertained them in a reedy voice, but his fingers on his instrument were
yet sure, and the music was sweeter than any Lara had heard before. She did not notice until afterward that Vartan had taken her
hand beneath the table. And when she did realize it, Lara had no
inclination to pull away. Finally the hall began to empty. Vartan
leaned over and murmured a few words to his cousin.

Sholeh arose. "I will show you to your chamber," she said. "You
must share, for my house is full to bursting at the seams. Come!"
And she led them up a narrow flight of stone stairs to a small bedchamber with a large bed. "Good night," she told them.

They slept again, back-to-back, hip-to-hip, in their travel garments without their boots. Lara did not protest this night for to
do so would have been ridiculous. She slept quickly and easily, not
knowing that he at first did not. Instead he lay simply looking at
her. He had waited his entire lifetime for this girl. Until Lara had
come into his view he had never been in love. Had never desired
a woman for his wife. He knew his mother worried that something
might happen to him, and he would die without heirs. Liam did
not want the lordship of the Fiacre. He had made that very plain
to the elders when his father had died. And Vartan knew his younger
brother, Adon, while ambitious for power, was not suited to the
responsibility of the lordship. And then he had seen Lara. He
wanted her for his wife. He wanted children of her body. He
wanted to be her destiny. But she was so intense about it, he did
not think she would see it his way. Lara clearly believed, although
she had never said it in so many words, that she had something great
to accomplish. He sighed. Well, maybe she did. But it did not stop
him from wanting her.

When she awoke Lara found Vartan gone from her side. She was
surprised but, remembering they had reached Rivalen just before
dark, she realized that he was probably conducting the business of
his lordship. She could see it was late by the angle of the sun com-

ing through the small window. She lay quietly, her body sore from all the riding she had done since leaving the Desert. It felt good just to be still. Suddenly the door to the chamber opened to admit a serving girl carrying a tray.

"My mistress thought you might be awake, and the meal is long over in the hall," the girl said, putting the tray down on the empty side of the bed.

"Where is the lord?" Lara asked.

"In the hall holding court, lady. There is a shameful case to be heard. The daughter of the blacksmith had her virginity taken from her by force. The villain is a man she refused when she chose another. Now she is ruined, and it is unlikely her chosen will have her, but she will not have the villain, and has wept for days over it," the servant girl gossiped.

"Has the lord ruled yet?" Lara asked the girl.

"Nay, the case has not even begun, for the girl will not stop weeping, and the lord will not begin the case until she does," the servant said. "She is a foolish creature."

"Tell the lord I will be down to join him quickly," Lara said, snatching up a small loaf from the tray, and tearing it into pieces as the serving girl hurried out. There was butter in a small crock, and Lara scooped some out with her thumb, and spread it on the bread. There was a hard-boiled egg, and a mug of cider. She ate it all, then washed herself in the basin of water that had been left on the wide stone sill of the chamber's narrow window. She rebraided her hair, pulled on her boots and went downstairs.

The hall was crowded with probably every inhabitant of Rivalen. Lara worked her way to the side of the hall up near the high board where Vartan and Sholeh were seated. Her gaze took in the people just below the board. An older man and woman. A sobbing girl. Two younger men, one in chains.

"This hearing must begin, for my journey home is a long one," Vartan finally said impatiently. "Can you not stop your daughter's weeping?"

"My lord, I apologize, but she is devastated by what has happened. Look at her eyes. Swollen with her grief!" the victim's father said.

"We must begin!" Sholeh snapped. "Be silent, Kele!"

The girl howled louder, to everyone's irritation.

Lara moved from her place, going to Kele, and put an arm about her. "I know your grief, for I was used once as you were," she said. "Crying will solve nothing. Now is the time for vengeance, and only the lord can give it to you, Kele, but he will go if you cannot regain control of yourself. Will you allow your attacker to remain unpunished?"

The girl's tears began to abate. "Who are you?" she asked.

"I am Lara, daughter of Swiftsword the Crusader Knight and Ilona, queen of the Forest Faeries. The men who robbed me of my virginity were Forest Lords, cruel and brutal men who held me captive for months. But I escaped them and the taint of their actions to pursue my greater destiny. Now you have the opportunity to change your destiny. You can pine away over something that was not your fault, or you can take your revenge on the man who stole what was not his to take. The lord is here to help you, but you must stop weeping. The shame is not yours, Kele. Choose what you will do, but choose now!"

"Will you stay with me until it is over?" Kele asked.

"I will," Lara answered her, and wiped the tears from the girl's face with the heel of her palm. "Tell the lord what you want."

Kele stood straight, looking up at Vartan, and said, "I ask for your justice, my lord Vartan. I have been terribly wronged."

"Tell me," Vartan said in a kindly voice.

Kele drew a long, deep breath to calm her beating heart, and then she began. "I had two suitors, my lord. My father asked which I preferred, and I chose Key. We have known each other our whole lives, and spoken often in secret of marriage. So my father agreed, and the betrothal was celebrated. But Lonn, my other suitor, would not accept it. He followed me wherever I would go, harassing me to change my mind. Finally I told him by the village well that I would not have him ever. Even if I had to die an old maid. Then Key will not have you either, he told me. There were witnesses to it, my lord."

A murmur arose from the spectators, and Vartan said, "You will have your chance to tell me," he promised them. "Go on now, Kele. What happened next?"

"The next day my cousin and I went to pick berries on the hillside. Lonn came upon us, and told my cousin to leave. He threatened her with his dagger, and she fled back to the village to raise the alarm. By the time my father came, it was too late," the girl said.

"It is not enough, Kele. I need to know exactly what Lonn did," Vartan said. "I am sorry, but the accusation must come directly from you, his victim."

The young girl shuddered.

"Be brave," Lara said, her arm tightening about Kele.

"He ripped my gown half off," Kele began, and tears began slipping down her face again, but she continued bravely on. "He threw me to the ground. He fell upon me, forcing my legs apart with his knee. He pushed his manroot into me, and though I screamed and begged him not to do it he raped me, my lord. And when he did he ruined my chances for marriage with Key."

"If she wants a husband I'll have her," Lonn said boldly, a grin upon his face.

Kele turned, and looked directly at him. "I would die first," she said. "You have ruined my life, but I would die before I took you as my husband!"

"Thank you," Vartan said. "You have been a brave lass. Sit now and I will hear from the others involved in this matter."

Kele's parents spoke. Yes, Key and Lonn had sought Kele for a wife. They did not like Lonn, but they left the decision to their daughter, who chose wisely. Since the horrific incident they had kept their daughter confined, seeing no one. The next witnesses were those women who had been at the village well when Lonn had been told in no uncertain terms by Kele that she would not have him.

"You are certain she was firm in her intent?" Sholeh asked. "She was not flirting with him as young girls will do?"

"No, lady," the witness, an older woman, said. "She could not have made it any plainer, but he kept harassing her. Finally a group of us chased him away, for poor Kele was frightened and trembling. Who knew that he would violate the poor lass?" She shook a fist at Lonn. "Curse you! No decent woman will have you now. May your line die out forever! You are a monster!"

"When did the violation occur?" Vartan asked.

"Almost a month ago, my lord," Kele's mother said.

"Has the lass had her flow since?" he continued.

The mother nodded, blushing.

"It is possible then that Lonn has done no permanent damage," Vartan said. "Where is the betrothed?"

"Here, my lord." A pleasant-faced young man stepped forward.

"Do you wish to sever the betrothal, Key of Rivalen?" Vartan asked.

"No! But they have not let me see her since it happened, my lord. I have not been able to comfort her, or tell her that I love her no matter," he said in anguished tones. "We are to be wed at the harvest. Our cottage stands ready and waiting for us." He turned to the girl. "I love you, Kele! Tell me you yet love me!"

"Oh, Key! I love you, too, but my parents said you would not have me now, and that I had brought this shame upon myself by going berrying with my cousin instead of within a group of girls where I would have been safe. They said I was foolish, and had doomed myself to a lifetime of misery," Kele sobbed.

Key went to the girl's side, and raising her up enfolded her in his arms. He glared at her parents. "You told her these things? Without consulting with me? I love Kele and I intend wedding her at the harvest as we have been planning for months. All I want is justice from the lord. You will not keep my betrothed wife from me again!"

"Then it is settled, but for the matter of punishment for Lonn," Vartan said. He looked at the accused. "We have heard from everyone in this matter but you. What have you to say for yourself, Lonn of Rivalen?"

"I wanted her," he replied. "And when she shamed me before the village I had my revenge on her." He leered at the lovers. "Do you want to know how she screamed when I thrust into her, Key? And struggled? It was glorious!"

"You do not deny your guilt, then," Vartan said, a look of revulsion on his face.

"No!"

"Will you repent of your crime, and make amends to Kele?" Vartan asked.

"No! Why should I? The little bitch got what she deserved."

Lara felt Andraste quivering within its scabbard as it lay across her back.

"Then I condemn you to death for your crime," Vartan said. "The sentence will be carried out immediately."

"Let me!" Lara cried out, stepping forward.

A gasp arose from those in the hall, but a small smile flitted across Vartan's face. He had meant to carry out the sentence himself, but she had said she was capable of killing. Now he would see if she merely boasted, or spoke truth. "Very well, Lara, daughter of Swiftsword. He is yours, and you will execute the sentence. Take him outside, and make him dig his grave in the hillside first." He stood.

"Do you think she can do it?" Sholeh asked, rising from her seat.

"She says she has killed before, and if she fails, I am here. Come, cousin, and let us see this matter through." He stepped down from the dais saying to Kele and Key, "You must witness the execution, my young lovers, for only then will you be free of this tragedy, and able to move on with your lives."

Sholeh's hall emptied as the villagers, Lonn tightly in their grasp, moved toward the hillside just beyond the village. Once there the condemned man had his hands unshackled but not his ankles. He was given a spade, and began to dig. He did so, singing bawdy songs, and laughing almost maniacally as he dug. Finally the grave was done. He looked at Lara, and licked his lips leeringly.

"I should like to have you beneath me just once, faerie girl," he said, and he rubbed his crotch with a dirty hand. "I'll bet you'd scream and struggle nicely for me."

Lara eyes grew cold. She slipped Andraste from its scabbard, and the blade hummed quite audibly. She looked at the condemned man, and a small smile touched her lips. "Nay, 'tis you who will scream and struggle for me," she told him. Then she looked to Vartan. "My lord?"

"Put him on his knees," the lord said dispassionately.

And at that moment Lonn felt icy fear pour over him, certain the faerie girl had bewitched him else he would never be afraid. But he was. He shrieked like a maiden, and struggled against his captors as they forced him to his knees, but he would not bow his head. Lara raised her sword, and he watched in disbelief as the blade swung toward him. He heard the sword singing even as it began to slice his head from his shoulders.

"I am Andraste, and I drink the blood of evil men!"

Lonn's severed head fell into the newly dug grave. There was a long deep silence, and then the villagers cheered loudly as Lara wiped his blood from her sword on the slain man's tunic, and sheathed it neatly in its scabbard. She looked to Vartan questioningly.

He nodded his approval. Then with the tip of his boot he kicked Lonn's body into the grave to join his head. "Whatever worldly goods he had will be given to Kele in reparation," the lord said. "Now I must leave you, for the ride back to Camdene is a long one." He turned to Sholeh. "Give the betrothed pair this from me on their wedding day," he told her, slipping a gold coin into her hand. "Did the monster have kin?"

"None," Sholeh said.

"Good. None to seek vengeance, or cause difficulty over this unfortunate incident," Vartan said.

"You were serious last night when you said you meant to marry her?" Sholeh asked him.

"Very serious," Vartan answered.

"Listen to me, cousin," the headwoman said. "She does have a destiny, and not an ordinary one. I saw it today in my hall when she calmed Kele. I saw it when she offered to be Lonn's executioner, and then slew him without fear or remorse. I do not know why she has come to the Outlands, but if she will wed you, remember that even her marriage, a love for you, or the children she gives you will not prevent her from following her destiny when she knows the time is right. You must understand that, or she will break your heart, Vartan," Sholeh warned him. "You are the first man I loved, and it would pain me to see you harmed in any way, cousin."

He nodded. "I know what you say to me is truth, Sholeh, but I, too, have a destiny, and she is already mounted upon her stallion. The horse talks, by the way, as does the staff she carried," he chuckled at his cousin's surprised look.

"A horse and a staff that talk and a sword that sings." Sholeh shook her head. "There is much magic about Lara. Has she bewitched you, then?"

"There is no faerie magic in my feelings, cousin. I saw her and my heart was gone from me," he explained. "She was raised in the City by her all too human father. She did not know her mother until recently. She has little practical magic about her, but I believe she is blest by the faerie kingdom, and protected by the magic of the Shadow Prince who sheltered her, educated her, and saw she had these weapons."

Sholeh shook her head. "All these years you have been sought after by our most eligible women, but none caught your heartstrings until this faerie girl came into your view. I have to believe it is your fate, Vartan, may the Celestial Actuary help you." She kissed his rough cheek. "Thank you for your judgment in this dreadful matter. I will speak with Kele's parents, who are to my mind a pair of fools, but the lovers are at last reunited and the villain dispatched. Ride safely, cousin."

He kissed her back, and then turning mounted his own horse. "We have a long ride ahead of us, Lara, daughter of Swiftsword," he said. "We will probably not reach Camdene until after dark, but there will be at least one moon to guide us."

"I overstepped my bounds," Lara said as they rode off, "when I came forward so boldly to offer you my services, but the man was despicable, my lord. I ask your pardon."

"How many have you killed before Lonn?" he asked her.

"Just one. Durga, the Head Forester, who was foolish enough to follow me to Shunnar, the palace of Prince Kaliq, my protector and friend. I slew him without mercy for he had shown me none," Lara said.

Vartan nodded.

"It is Andraste," Lara said. "The sword makes me brave, and it will not kill the just, I believe, but only the evil-doers. Lothair, the Shadow Prince, made it and gave it to me. Verica, my staff, is my mother's gift. And Dasras is Kaliq's gift to me. They are all I need to meet my destiny, my lord Vartan. When I return with you to Camdene I must make my plans to leave you."

"I do not believe it is time for you to leave me yet, Lara, daughter of Swiftsword," he told her, "but we will speak on it tomorrow if you like." He must not make her feel that he was constraining her, but he knew in his heart that he could not let her go.

"Yes," she agreed. "I would value your advice for I think you wise, my lord, and I am just beginning to learn this business of living," Lara told him.

And together they returned to Camdene.

Chapter 14

"IF YOU HAVE no destination in mind," Bera said, "then why leave us now? Since the day your father proposed selling you to finance his ambitions you have always known when to go, and where. But now you admit you do not know. The Outlands, Lara, daughter of Swiftsword, can be a dangerous place for those unfamiliar with it. Good fortune has put you in our keeping. Remain with us until you know where it is you must go, and why."

"It is so tempting," Lara conceded slowly with a sigh. She had to admit she felt very comfortable here in Vartan's hall, and she liked the people of the Fiacre who were industrious and filled with humor and the joy of living. Where was she going, and why? The urge to travel, to seek, had suddenly left her. She fingered her crystal, but Ethne was silent. It is my decision to make, Lara reflected. Mine alone.

"The summer is at an end. Autumn will soon come, and then winter. Winter is a bad time not to have a safe place, especially here on the plains," Bera continued. "Say you will stay, and then come the spring you will see how you feel. Noss would like to remain, wouldn't you, my child?"

Noss nodded with a small smile. In the few days Lara had been away with Vartan, something had changed Noss. "I love it here," Noss said. "I have never felt more at home anywhere in my life, Lara."

"Then I suppose it is settled," Lara answered her young companion with a smile. "We will remain until I am called to take the road to my destiny once again."

Bera chuckled. "This is good," she said. "I have always wanted daughters."

The autumn was a busy time for the Fiacre. The last of the grain was harvested, gleaned and stored in stone granaries. Food animals were slaughtered, butchered and hung in a stone building where once weekly a butcher would carve portions for each family in Camdene. The men hunted deer for venison, and geese and ducks, which were hung in each house's larder. The last of the vegetables were taken from the gardens, and stored in a cold cellar. Repairs were made to homes, barns and other buildings. The plains turned shades of gold and brown. The leaves on the trees turned red, purple, orange and gold.

They had been with the Fiacre all summer. The days were growing shorter with each passing sunrise. Twilight seemed to come sooner, and then the cool nights. Vartan's hall was a place of warmth and friendliness, and Lara continued to see how respected and genuinely loved the leader of the Fiacre was. She was beginning to look at him with new eyes. He was not a sophisticated man, but neither was he a simple one. Unlike the Forest Lords, he accepted his responsibilities as an honorable duty and not a privilege. She quickly learned he enjoyed teasing those of whom he was particularly fond. And he was working very hard at drawing her into the society of the Fiacre, especially his own family. Each evening they would play a game called Herder, using a wooden board and beautifully carved figures, two herders and a group of cattle. The object of the game was to gather as many cattle as one could. When all the cattle on the board were herded into a player's designated corner, the herder with the most beasts was declared the winner.

At first Lara did not understand the strategy of the game and Vartan, while explaining how to play, also taunted her unmercifully. But she swiftly realized his purpose was to discommode her. Comprehending his design, she began to tease him back, even as she became quite skilled at the game itself. One evening Vartan realized his pupil had become a very good player indeed. She said, "I shall trounce you quite severely tonight, my cocky lord." And she captured the bull in his herd.

"You cheated!" he exclaimed, surprised.

"I don't have to cheat with you," Lara mocked him. "Now that I have deciphered your game plan you are easy to beat. You always play the same way, Vartan. You have no skill at intrigue, I fear." And she laughed as she took one of his cows. "There are half a dozen ways to play this game, but you practice only one."

"But one way is enough if you can win," he said as he took the last cow on the board. And then he grinned at her.

"You each have the same number of beasts," Bera declared as she counted, "but I think Lara must be proclaimed the winner, for she possesses the bulls from both herds. What will you have for your forfeit, my clever girl?"

"I had not thought of it," Lara said slowly.

"I should have had a kiss," Vartan chuckled.

"Then so shall I!" Lara decided boldly and, standing, she leaned across the game board to give him a brief kiss. But Vartan quickly captured the back of her head with his hand, holding the girl firmly in his embrace until Lara was able to pull free, sputtering with outrage.

"It will soon be time for The Gathering," Bera announced, attempting to defuse the situation.

"What is that?" Lara responded, still glaring at her antagonist. She wanted to strike out at him for publicly discommoding her in such a fashion, but she knew that Bera was trying to keep the peace.

"There is a holy place out on the plain, two days' journey from Camdene. Each year after the harvest, as many as can come from each of the clan families gather together to celebrate the year's end, and welcome in the new year. Each clan is always represented by someone. It is the only time we come together as a single entity," Bera explained. "The rest of the year we keep to our own boundaries, and to our own families. There is a meeting held between clan leaders then as well, and a fair where we barter goods and livestock.

"The Blathma bring apples and pears. The Felan, sheep. The Aghy, horses, and of course we bring cattle to trade or sell. The Gitta grow vegetables we do not, but that we enjoy. And of course the Piaras and the Tormod come with their beautiful jewelry. The Devyn will be there to entertain us all, and some bargain for homes for the winter. It's a lovely time, and then we all return home to await the winter months," Bera concluded.

"And matches are arranged at that time," Noss interjected excitedly.

"You are too young to be married," Lara said.

"I am not!" Noss cried. "I am almost fourteen, and Liam wants me for his wife."

Lara was silent for a long moment, and then sighing she said, "This is what you really want? You realize if you wed him you will have his mother in the house."

"Aye, it is!" Noss replied. "I am grateful to you that your sacrifice saved me from the Forest Lords. And I was content to leave Shunnar with you, and travel into the Outlands. But my destiny is here, and with Liam. I will be fourteen in spring, and I want to marry then. I am a simple girl. There is no greatness in me as there is in you, Lara."

"Then you shall marry, Noss," Lara replied to her friend. "It is a very good match for a poor mercenary's daughter from the City."

"I love him!" Noss declared passionately.

Lara shrugged. She still believed there was no such thing as love but let Noss have her sweet dreams. "I am glad," she said with a smile. "He will get a good wife in you, Noss."

Bera reached out to take Lara's hand in hers. Their eyes met, and the older woman nodded. "You are doing the right thing," she said softly.

"I hope so," Lara replied. "She seems so young to me."

"That is because your life since leaving the City has been the more difficult one. You had little choice but to leave your girlhood behind. The Forest Lords' refusal to have Noss saved her. The Shadow Princes freed her, and protected her. Your kindness and friendship have been her salvation. Now she is where she belongs at last. My nephew is besotted with her, and will be a good husband."

"It seems so simple for her," Lara said, almost sadly.

"There is love for you if you would but have it," Bera said pointedly.

Lara smiled a small rueful smile. "What of my destiny?" she replied.

"None of us can escape our destiny," Bera said wisely. "It will find you when the time is right, Lara. Would you not be happy until then?" She arose from her place. "I am going to bed now. My bones long for the comfort of my featherbed. Good night."

"I'll come with you," Noss spoke up. She stood and, bending, kissed Lara's cheek. "I know you love me, and want me safe," the girl said. "I am safe with Liam. Thank you for your permission to wed him. You are the sister I never had, and I am glad for it."

"Go along," Lara said almost impatiently. "And yes, we are now sisters, aren't we? I am glad for it, too." Thinking herself alone now, Lara stared into the flames. She had lost Og, who preferred to remain in the Desert tending to the horses belonging to the Shadow Princes. She would soon lose Noss, who was in love and wanted to be a wife. Was she meant to continue her journey alone? It was a frightening thought. But for now, at least, she would remain at Camdene. When the spring came the urge to move on would certainly rise in her again, but now the days grew shorter. The nights longer. The air colder. It was only natural that she wanted to bide awhile with the Fiacre. She smiled to herself. She was like a beast seeking a warm nest, and going to ground for the winter.

"I have never before seen that particular smile," Vartan said as he came to sit by her side. "What are you thinking?" He put an arm about her waist, drawing her closer.

"I was thinking how like a rabbit or a fox I am, looking for a winter refuge," she told him, and he laughed.

"So you consider my hall a winter refuge, do you?" he teased her.

"Well, it is," Lara replied. "I can think of none better."

"I can," he said quietly.

"Where?" she asked him.

"My bed," he responded.

She stiffened briefly, but then she relaxed against him. "You want to take pleasure with me," she said.

"I want you for my wife," he answered her.

"And when my destiny calls to me again, Vartan, then what? Will you let me go? Or will you exercise your rights as my lord and master, keeping me forcibly by your side?" She turned to look up into his attractive face. Her hand caressed his cheek. "If you desire my body, my lord, then have it. I am ready to share it with you. But ask no more of me for I cannot give it to you. I must follow my destiny wherever it may lead me. Please try to understand that."

"I do," he replied. "I understand far better than you think, Lara, for you are *my* destiny. You are she for whom I have waited my entire life, the woman I would have ride by my side in the hard days that are coming."

"Hard days?" Lara asked. "What do you mean?"

"The Devyn are more than poets and minstrels. They carry news and messages between the clan territories. While the Fiacre have been involved in the harvest and planning for the Gathering, there have been Devyn in our hall. They tell me that Hetar has begun to encroach upon the lands belonging to the Piaras and the Tormod. Those lands are rich in precious metals and gems, and the Hetarians have grown greedy. They have enslaved many to toil in the mines, and open new ones. They have sent their Crusader Knights to steal these lands, and to keep order over the oppressed. When my fellow chieftains meet at the Gathering we must decide how to respond to this subtle act of war. Hetar cannot be allowed to steal what is not theirs."

"There has been no war between Hetar and the Outlanders for centuries," Lara said slowly. "What can have made them do this?"

He shrugged. "Hetar has always considered itself a perfect world, far superior to those of us in the Outlands. Their society is carefully set, and while advancement is possible, it is only so by following certain rules, as your own father did. Hetar has laws that are legal, but not necessarily just. Hetar is ruled by pride, and by the desire for profit and more profit. For the first time in the history of the Outlands we will have to band together to stop this invasion, or none of us will be safe, and our clans, our ways, will not survive. And the magical beings who share our world will have to become involved. They will not be able to help themselves, for there is power involved here as well as wealth."

Lara felt a shiver run down her spine. Then she said, "Come, my lord, and let me soothe you, for I can see that your concerns are very great. Let me come into your bed, and give you pleasure that you may forget these difficulties, if for only a short while."

"You will share your body with me because I have told you of the threat to our very way of being?" He laughed. "There is still much sweetness in you, Lara, for all you have endured." He bent and kissed her mouth slowly, feeling her lips soften beneath his.

"Before we taste pleasure together I must tell you that I have entrapped you, my beautiful Lara. You say you will not be my wife for you fear I will not allow you to follow your destiny. But when your destiny calls I will not prevent you from heeding that call, and I will probably ride by your side if I can, for I love you. But you are already my wife under the few laws that the Fiacre have, for you have lain with me two nights. And there are witnesses to it. My cousin Sholeh, and the headman Evin and his wife."

"That is not fair!" she cried. "I will not be bound to any man but one of my own choosing! I refuse to accept such a thing, my lord.

It is not worthy of you. Besides, all we did was sleep next to one another. There was no pleasure taken nor given."

"My mother said you would be angry, but what else was I to do? You are the most difficult woman I have ever encountered, Lara. Men have used you cruelly, used you as they would have used a breeding animal, and you have accepted it. Yet I would honor you as my mate, and you scorn me." His blue eyes were troubled.

Lara stood abruptly. "When I escaped the Forest Lords I swore I would never again be used by any man. At Shunnar, Prince Kaliq educated me to make my own decisions. One night in his hall I willingly shared myself with all of his fellow princes, and it was glorious, for I wanted it. I belong to no one but to me, Vartan. If you would be my husband, my mate, then you must acknowledge that not just with words but by your deeds. I do not know if you can do that. For all your scorn of Hetarians, you are much like them in your need for order and discipline."

"I am in love with you, Lara. Whatever I must do I will do, but say you will accept your place by my side as my wife," he said.

She shrugged. "I wish I could feel love for you, my lord," she told him sadly.

"You will one day," he told her. "I promise you that."

"You cannot know that," Lara replied. "You wish it, but you cannot be certain that what you say will come into being, Vartan. I do not want to hurt you."

"Would you shame me before my people?" he asked quietly. "I have only resorted to trickery out of my desperation."

"You could have had my body if you had but asked," Lara responded. "I am not averse to sharing pleasure with you, but I must be free. A wife cannot be free, Vartan." She put her hand on his arm in a gesture of comfort.

"Your body tempts me, Lara—I would be a liar if I denied it. But it is your heart I want. You say faerie women have no hearts, yet you are but half faerie. And as you have told me yourself, your mother cared so much for your human father that she would not wed again until your grandmother faded away, and as queen she needed to sire a faerie heir. I think you do have a heart, but you are fearful of giving it because you do not want to be hurt. I will never hurt you, my love. Never! And if the time comes that you feel compelled to leave me, I will release you, though it breaks my own very human heart to do so. Accept me as your mate, Lara, and know that I truly love you."

Something within her softened. It was a feeling such as she had never before experienced. Was it possible she could actually care for this man? And could she trust him to keep his word? She realized her hand still rested on his arm. She could feel the muscle beneath his shirt. They were strong arms. In a moment of very human weakness, she realized they were arms in which she could hide. And sometimes even she needed a safe place. With a sigh she looked up into his anxious blue eyes.

"Very well, then. I will accept my place by your side as long as you understand that if I say I must go, then I must," Lara replied.

He picked her up and swung her about, his big hands meeting as they spanned her tiny waist. "I adore you!" he told her, grinning happily.

"Put me down, you great fool. It has been months since I have known the pleasure of a manroot inside me, and I long for it, Vartan, my lord!"

He set her upon her feet again, and taking her face between his hands, began to kiss her. His mouth was hot and eager. His kisses touched her mouth, her eyelids, her face. And Lara stood quietly enjoying them. He sat down in his big chair by the fire, loosening his garments to reveal his manroot. She looked at it admiringly, easing her gown off to stand naked before him. His eyes devoured her, and she smiled at him. Her hand reached out to touch him. He was hard, and his skin warm.

"I have never seen a manroot so large," Lara said, stroking the pillar of flesh. "The Forest Lords were big men, but not like this."

"And your Shadow Princes?" He was reaching out for her.

"Skilled, and well-made, but not like you," Lara admitted. She bent and kissed the ruby head of it, then climbed onto his lap.

Reaching out, he began to fondle her breasts while she caressed his manhood. He groaned as her delicate hands reached beneath him to fondle his seed sac. She gasped when he pinched her nipples, leaning forward to lick at the soft twin mounds. He unplaited her thick gilt hair and spread it about them like a curtain. Then lifting her he slowly, slowly impaled her upon his manroot until he was fully sheathed. Lara sighed deeply as their two bodies were joined so neatly and easily.

She wrapped her slender arms about his neck whispering to him, "You fit me perfectly, my lord. More perfectly than any other."

"Because our bodies were created for each other," he told her. Then he said, "You must ride me now, Lara, like the great horsewoman I know you to be. Ride me, and give us both the joy we know awaits us."

She began slowly, rising and falling until he was moaning with delight. Then she moved faster and faster until finally he cried out, and she felt his love juices flooding her. To her surprise, however, he remained hard and when he had recovered slightly he stood, still buried deep inside her. Lara clung to him as he walked across the hall to the high board. Laying her upon the great rectangle of the table, he took the dominant position, and she trembled with excitement. He moved as she had, slowly and deliberately at first, and then more quickly until they were both lost in a white-hot passion that when it peaked left them both weak and exhausted as his juices flooded her a second time.

There were no words to be said. He gathered her up in his arms, and carried her to his chamber behind the hall. It was there Lara awoke several hours later to find herself in his embrace. When she attempted to slip from his arms he growled a sleepy "No!" and his arms tightened about her.

"I must go," she whispered.

"Nay, we will share the lord's chamber from now on. Noss will bring your possessions in the morning."

"I must clean the high board before anyone finds our juices all over it," she said.

"The servants will clean it," he said. "Go back to sleep, Lara, my love."

Obediently she closed her eyes, her fingers going to her crystal as she began to grow sleepy again. She was Vartan's mate, his wife. Yet he had promised he would not stop her from following her destiny. She knew he meant what he said when he said it, but the proof would come when that moment arrived. In the meantime, he was a good man and a passionate lover—the coming winter would not prove dull. But first there was the Gathering to attend. She was concerned by the news he had shared with her this evening. She suspected that Bera did not know it yet. And was Bera aware of the union between her son and Lara? Still more questions.

She awoke with his lips on hers, his big body covering her as he entered her slowly. "Vartan!" she chided him, amused by his great lust for her.

"I cannot resist you," he admitted. "I could spend the next six months in this bed with you, my Lara."

She squeezed his manroot as it filled her, and he cried out. She licked his ear, her tongue tracing the whorl of flesh, pushing into the cavity to tickle him, murmuring to him what she thought of his masculine attributes and what she wanted him to do to her.

"You are a wicked faerie wench," he told her as she wrapped her legs about him. "I will pleasure you more than you have ever been pleasured before, Lara, my love."

"Actions," she said softly, "speak louder than words, my lord Vartan."

In reply he pulled her two arms above her head, holding her wrists firmly in one hand. Then he began a slow, deep, deliberate thrusting. Again, and again, and yet again he pushed into her body with a leisurely measured cadence. Shortly, Lara's green eyes widened with surprise as she found herself responding to him strongly. She had known great pleasure with her Shadow Prince, but it had been an elegant pleasure. The feelings she now felt were wild and uncontrollable. She gasped in shock, for she had never imagined passion could go so deep or be so fierce. She struggled against him, but he gently mastered her, forcing her to his will, yet loving her so sweetly that she found herself weeping.

He kissed and licked the salty tears from her face. "Let go, Lara, my love. Trust me enough to let go." And when she did, his great desire for her burst forth, leaving them both breathless and weak. Satisfied, he drew her into his arms, kissing her face, his big hand smoothing her hair. "We are fated to love each other, Lara, daughter of Swiftsword," he told her quietly. "I am yours, and you are mine."

She burrowed deeper into his arms. What had just happened to her? She could not believe that she had released herself to him so freely. It was all very confusing, and as her tears subsided she found herself falling asleep once again.

He smiled to himself, his hand still stroking her soft gilt hair. In all his life he had never felt so happy. He would need her in the days ahead. This difficulty with the Piaras and the Tormod clans would not be easily solved, and he worried about the other clan families as well. Throughout the centuries past, they had found that keeping to themselves for most of the year was what kept them from fighting among one another. But if Hetar had been bold enough to invade the Piaras and Tormod territories, what was to prevent them from moving deeper into the Outlands? It was very troubling.

When Lara awoke again Vartan had left her side, and Noss was bustling about the chamber putting her few possessions away in a small painted trunk. "Good morning," Lara said, smiling at her young friend.

"'Tis more like afternoon." Noss grinned back. "I had heard he was a mighty lover. He has obviously exhausted you."

"You know not of what you speak," Lara replied, irritated.

"They say you are his wife," Noss answered, not in the least intimidated. "Are you? And how did that happen?"

"They have some law or other that says if you spend two nights with a man you are his wife," Lara said. "While we were visiting his villages we had no choice but to share a bed, but that is all we did. And we never even got out of our clothing."

"Until last night," Noss giggled, holding up Lara's gown which she had retrieved from the floor of the hall.

"There are hard times coming to the Outlands," Lara responded. "I shared pleasures with him to soothe him. Then he told me of this law of theirs. But I shall go when my destiny calls me again, Noss, and Vartan knows it."

"But you are his wife," Noss repeated.

"I suppose I am, even if I was ignorant of these laws of the Fiacre," Lara agreed. "I don't know why our people call them lawless barbarians."

"Perhaps because Outlanders are not like Hetarians," Noss suggested.

Lara nodded. Then she said, "I need a bath. I stink of horse, of man, and of woman's lustful nature. Have you discovered if they have a bathhouse?"

"No," Noss said.

"Then how do they keep clean?" Lara demanded.

"They bathe in their houses in small round tubs," Noss replied.

"Then have a tub brought, and hot water, too," Lara commanded. "It has been too many days since I bathed. My skin is beginning to itch." She climbed from her bed, heedless of her nudity, and stretched. "Where is Vartan?"

"He has been out since just after sunrise overseeing the last of the winter preparations. We leave for the Gathering in the morning, Bera says. I'll go get your tub, but cover yourself, for I doubt your husband wants his serving men seeing you in all your halfling glory," Noss told Lara.

"Halfling? What is a halfling?" Lara asked.

"Half one thing, half another. Bera says you are a halfling. Half faerie, half Hetarian. She is very happy you are Vartan's wife. She says you are strong where he is weak. She says you will be the making of him for she has always thought he could be a great leader of the Fiacre. They are the largest of the clan families, you know." Then turning Noss hurried from the bedchamber to fetch a tub for Lara.

Lara looked about for something to cover her nakedness. Opening the little painted trunk where she had seen Noss store her things, she drew out a chemise and slipped it on. Noss was just full of information, Lara mused. Comfortable in safety, she had become friendly and full of gossip. Bera—or was it Liam?—had worked a magic of her own on the girl. Love, it was said, changed people. If she believed in love she might believe that was true.

The tub was brought, and Lara was amused by its small size. Well, it was all they had, and she was grateful to be able to bathe herself. When the tub was filled Lara disrobed again, washing first her body, and then her long hair. Noss had brought her a small hard cake of soap with a faint fragrance of wildflowers. It lathered well, and Lara was grateful for it. Wrapping herself in the drying cloth, she began to towel her golden hair. She sought for her hairbrush, smiling as she pulled Kaliq's gift from the trunk. It was beautiful. The prince had obviously kept her simple pearwood brush, and replaced it with this gold one with fine boar's bristles. The top of the brush bore a single heart, and twining around it and down its handle was a vine of delicate flowers.

There were several leaded windows set together in the chamber wall with a window seat built in beneath them. Lara sat before one of the open windows and began to brush out her long hair. As it dried in the gentle breeze of the sunny autumn afternoon, the silken stuff flew like a banner from the window. Riding in from the fields Vartan could see it, and felt a surge of contentment well up within him. His wife, he thought happily. His wife was awaiting him.

Her hair dry, Lara dressed herself in one of her two simple gowns, pale green to match her eyes. Then she went out into the hall as Vartan entered it. He immediately enfolded her in his embrace and kissed her mouth tenderly. Lara smiled up at him. She could not help it, and she realized that she was happy for the first time in a very long while. Not relieved at escaping the Forest Lords, or protected by Kaliq, but deeply happy. Was this what love was? she wondered.

"You are beautiful, and you smell delicious," he said, still holding her.

"Of course I am beautiful," she agreed, looking up into his face, "and I have finally had a bath. But your tub is so tiny. It is no bigger than the one I shared with my stepmother back in the Quarter."

"I shall have a larger one made for you," he promised.

"Make it big enough for two," she suggested softly.

His slow smile reached all the way to his eyes. A hand caressed her buttocks suggestively. "We leave tomorrow for the Gathering," he told her.

"So Noss has told me," Lara returned. "I fear I shall shame you, Vartan, for I have but two gowns, and they are more suited to the palace of the Shadow Princes than to the Outlands on an autumn day. I am sorry. Would you prefer I remain behind?"

"Wife, have you not looked in your trunk?" he asked her.

"The little painted one? Aye, I saw Noss storing my things there," Lara said.

"The large one, Lara," he replied.

"That is not yours?" She was surprised.

"Nay, it is yours, and it is filled with the garments of a chieftain's wife," he said. "My mother and her women sewed quite diligently while we were away in the villages. And I have this for you." He pulled a wide heavy gold ring from his tunic and pushed it onto the third finger of her left hand, the finger that connected directly to her heart. "I want everyone at the Gathering to know you are my mate, Lara, daughter of Swiftsword."

Lara looked at the ring in surprise. It was red gold, a very rare ore, and it was simplicity itself. A plain band that when she looked at it brought tears to her eyes.

"The meal is served," Bera's voice broke into the moment.

Vartan took her hand in his and, raising it to his lips, kissed it tenderly. Then he led her to the high board where Bera was already seated and awaiting them. She smiled at them both, her own eyes misty.

"Are you content with this then, Lara, daughter of Swiftsword?" she asked.

"It would appear I have no choice, for the deed is done, is it not?" Lara asked Vartan's mother.

"It is," Bera agreed amiably, and poured Frine into their goblets. "If he is the man his father was you will not be unhappy."

Lara actually blushed. She suspected that the son surpassed the father, for she had never known the kind of ecstasy that she had shared with Vartan. "What happened to your husband?" she asked the older woman.

"He was trampled when a bolt of lightning stampeded a small herd of cattle he was overseeing," Bera replied. "Vartan was ten when it happened, and Adon two. My younger son does not remember his father, more's the pity."

"When shall I meet your brother, my lord?" Lara asked her husband.

"He and his wife live down in the village," Vartan said. "Tomorrow before we begin the trek to the Gathering they will come, for we travel as a family."

The hall was full that night with Vartan's men, and as the meal concluded he arose from his place, drawing Lara up with him. Expectant faces turned to look toward the high board, and the room grew very quiet.

"This is my bride," Vartan told them, "This Lady Lara. Some of you were with me when we found her wandering lost upon the plain. She has accompanied me to the villages, and shown me her wisdom in resolving an unhappy situation at Rivalen. If you honor me, you will pledge your loyalty to her now."

Immediately the men in the hall arose and cried, "All Hail Lara, daughter of Swiftsword, wife to Vartan, lord of the Fiacre!" And then they came forward one by one to kneel before her as she stood before the high board where Vartan had led her. Each man put his hands into her small ones and pledged his loyalty. Lara thanked each man by the name her husband whispered into her ear.

She was surprised by his actions. In the back of her mind had lingered the thought that perhaps he was saying she was his wife so he might cajole her into sharing her body with him. But now, with each loyalty pledged to her, she saw that he had not been playing a game with her. Lara, daughter of Swiftsword, was truly wife to Vartan of the Fiacre. But what of her destiny? She sensed that there was something yet unfinished. Yet it would seem her destiny was here with the Fiacre for now. Had not Ethne approved of her actions so far? Never had her guardian argued against what had happened. For now all was as it should be. But what of the future?

When the last of the men had pledged to her, Vartan led her back to the high board. "You have done well," he praised her softly. "Despite your youth you are a woman of stature."

"In the City I would have had a great bridal celebration," she teased him. "You have shared a bed with me, and called it a wedding party."

"It is our way," he told her.

"Even Pol and Corliss were joined formally in the presence of their fellow villagers," Lara said.

"But under our laws a man and woman who share a bed for two nights are husband and wife," he reminded her.

"Did you plan to wed me?" she asked him.

"Aye, I did. But I did not choose to spend months bringing you around, my love, so I took advantage of Fiacre law. You do not seem too angry with me over it." He gave her a winning grin.

Lara was forced to laugh. Vartan was a very charming man. "I have not decided yet if I am angry at you or not," she told him.

"I hunger for you again, my love," he murmured. "I want you naked and crying out with your pleasure beneath me. I want to fill you full with my passion." He dropped a kiss on her shoulder. "Tell me you want that, too?" Vartan pleaded with her.

"Yes!" Lara heard herself say without hesitation. She arose, and giving both Noss and Bera a kiss upon their cheek she left the high board without another word.

Vartan remained for several more minutes speaking with his captains about the trek that would begin tomorrow. Then he too retreated to the chamber behind the hall. Bera arose, and beckoned Noss to come along to bed. The girl obeyed, smiling shyly at Liam as they passed, which caused the big man to develop a foolish look upon his face as he stared after Noss.

In the morning they departed for the Gathering, and as they traveled along the way they were joined by members of each village. Not all the Fiacre came to the Gathering. It was necessary to leave men behind to defend the villages, and new mothers and the elderly frequently remained behind as well. Vartan's younger brother, Adon, and his wife, Elin, had come to the hall that morning and pledged their loyalty to Lara, although she sensed it was done out of duty and nothing else.

Adon was a handsome young man with auburn hair, and deeper blue eyes than his sibling. His wife, Elin, was a tall thin girl with a look of discontent about her. She stared at Lara boldly, finally asking, "They say you are faerie. Did you bewitch him?"

Adon had the grace to look embarrassed by his wife's query, but he did not scold her over it.

"I am half faerie," Lara replied. "And it was Vartan who bewitched me."

"Oh." Elin's hair was a dirty blond, and she looked enviously at Lara's beautiful tresses. "How do you get your hair that color?"

"I was born with it. My faerie mother has hair this color," Lara told her.

"Oh." Elin said no more.

Taking his brother aside, Adon said, "Is it possible you are enchanted, Vartan? Perhaps the faerie should be killed to protect you, to protect the Fiacre."

"I am not ensorcelled, brother, and it was I who pursued Lara. Let there be no talk of murder, faerie or otherwise. I should not like to have to kill you. It would distress our good mother." He clapped the younger man on the back. "Be glad for me, Adon! I am happy. Really, truly happy."

As Lara stood by her stallion she murmured in Dasras's ear, "No talking. You will frighten many if you do. We will speak together when I think it prudent. I have warned Noss to caution Sakari as well."

The stallion nodded his head.

"Did they tell you I am now wed to the lord? He tricked me, but I am content for now, and you will have a warm barn for the winter." Lara rubbed the animal's muzzle.

"Good!" Dasras said softly that no one else hear him.

Lara chuckled, and mounted the horse.

They rode a full two days, and in late afternoon of the second day arrived at the Gathering place, which sat on the open plain. Tall columns stood in a circle, within which all discussions concerning the clan families would be held. Each clan family had a separate section in which to set up their camp. The fairgrounds and the place for animals and trading was in the very center of the locus. The Devyn were already there, for it was their task to direct the other clan families. The Fiacre, being the largest of them, was given the choicest site. The men set up their tents and the chieftain's pavilion. A pen was erected for the cattle to be sold.

Before dark, the Felan arrived driving their sheep. They were followed by the Blathma, who brought milled grain, flowers, tubers and bulbs; and the Gitta, who came with finely milled flour, baskets of beautiful vegetables, pots of jams, conserves and savory relishes. Their encampments were set up, and the clan families began visiting back and forth. Still to come were the Aghy, the horse lords. There was concern among the chieftains as to whether the Tormod and the Piaras would come under the circumstances.

Vartan proudly introduced Lara to his contemporaries and their wives.

"She's Hetarian," said Rendor of the Felan.

"She is faerie," said Floren of the Blathma.

"I am both," Lara answered them. "I have a destiny that has taken me to the Forest Lords, the Shadow Princes and now to the Outlands."

"Do you not think it odd she came to you now?" Torin of the Gitta demanded. He glared at Lara suspiciously. "What if she is a spy sent among us?"

"I am no spy," Lara told him. "I was sold into slavery by my own father almost two years ago. I escaped, and have been wandering ever since. If you doubt my honesty then speak with Kaliq of the Shadow Princes. He knows my tale. You have but to call to him, and he will come."

"You have gained yourself a most beautiful wife," Rendor of the Felan said, clapping Vartan on the back heartily. "Welcome, Lara, daughter of Swiftsword, wife of Vartan of the Fiacre."

"I thank you, my lord," Lara responded prettily, and the suspicions of both Floren of the Blathma, and Torin of the Gitta were allayed. They grinned and kissed the bride vigorously, leaving Lara laughing and covered with blushes at their enthusiasm.

Afterward in the privacy of their pavilion Vartan told his family how his new wife had stood boldly forth before his fellow chieftains, and won them over.

"I hope they do not think your wife *too* bold, Brother Vartan," Elin murmured, eyes lowered as she embroidered a piece of cloth in an oval frame.

"Our chieftains admire strong women, and a chieftain needs a strong wife," Bera spoke up. She did not particularly like her younger son's wife. Elin was a sly girl, and was always encouraging Adon to some new foolishness. Perhaps she would change with the advent of a child, Bera considered hopefully. In the meantime she had a fine daughter-in-law in Lara, and she would not allow anyone to offend her.

"I hardly consider speaking out to defend myself being bold, Elin. You were not there so you are not fit to judge," Lara said. She already recognized an enemy in Elin.

Elin's lips pressed together in an expression of disapproval, and she gave her husband an arch look, but she said nothing further.

In midmorning of the following day, the Aghy, led by their chieftain, Roan, arrived with a fine herd of horses. The Aghy were the second largest of the clan families. As soon as their encampment was set up and their animals corralled, Vartan took Lara to meet the Aghy. Roan was as tall as Vartan, with a head of flaming red hair and eyes so deep blue they appeared almost black. His gaze swept over Lara admiringly.

"My bride, Lara," Vartan said with a grin. "Keep your hands to yourself, Roan of the Aghy. I would hate to cut them off, for how then would you ride your fine horses?"

"I would trap my mare between my thighs, and guide her thusly," Roan replied wickedly, and he burst into laughter, flinging his arms about Vartan to embrace him.

Vartan was laughing, too. "Welcome to the Gathering, old friend!"

"Any sign of the Tormod or Piaras yet?" Roan asked.

Vartan shook his head. "Nay, not yet, but they do have the farthest distance to come," and his eyes strayed to the purple mountains beyond the plain.

"We can wait another day or two for them," Roan said. "The weather is perfect as it always is for the Gathering, and the longer we linger, the more horses I'll sell," he chuckled. He swung his gaze to Lara. "Do you ride, Lady?"

"I do," she said.

"I have a sweet young mare who would suit you admirably," Roan told her.

Vartan began to chortle, and when Roan looked questioningly at him he said to Lara, "Go and fetch Dasras so that the chieftain of the Aghy may see your mount."

"At once, my lord," Lara told him with a grin, and she hurried off. When she returned she was mounted upon the great golden stallion with the creamy mane and tail.

Roan's mouth dropped open with his surprise. He looked Dasras over with a keen eye. "There is only one place where horses like this are raised. Only the Shadow Princes breed animals so fine. He is magnificent, Vartan."

"Your praise should go to my wife, for he is hers, Roan," Vartan replied.

The horse lord looked up at Lara again. "Lady, whatever you desire I will give you if you will sell me this animal."

"He is not for sale, and never will be," Lara told him. "He was a gift to me from Prince Kaliq. He has magic, and is part of my destiny."

"I can well believe he has magic," Roan said. "But imagine the colts he could sire, and think of the price they would bring! I cannot be content unless you sell him to me. I would even share the profits with you." He ran an admiring hand over the horse.

Dasras drew away from the horse lord. "My mistress has already told you that I am not for sale, my lord," he growled in his deep voice.

Roan's eyes widened. "He talks!"

"But he is not supposed to frighten people," Lara scolded Dasras.

The stallion turned his head to meet her look. "This man has a determined will, my lady. He must understand that I am indeed magic, and your words are not those of some dewy-eyed maiden." Dasras now turned to the horse lord. "My mistress has a destiny, Lord Roan, and I am part of it. We cannot be separated."

The horse lord nodded. "Yes," he said, "I understand, but should you ever long for some pretty little mares…"

Dasras chuckled richly, bowing his head to touch his foreleg. "I shall certainly remember your most kind offer, my Lord Roan."

"Does everyone know he talks?" Roan asked Lara.

"We have tried to keep his talents discreet," she answered with a small smile, and then turning Dasras, rode back to the enclosure where the Fiacre horses were stabled.

"She is not one of us," Roan said.

"Nay, she is a halfling. Hetarian and faerie," Vartan said.

"How in the name of the Celestial Actuary did you ever find such a woman to wed?" Roan wanted to know.

"I found her wandering lost on the plain, although she insisted she was not lost," Vartan said. "She and her companion, Noss, had been with the Shadow Princes. She comes from the City, where her father sold her into slavery to advance his position."

"How typically Hetarian," Roan replied scornfully. "They will sell anything they have of value to gain more. What are we going to do about this incursion they have made into the Outlands, Vartan?"

"I do not think we can make any decisions until we have heard from the Tormod and the Piaras. It is their territory that has been compromised, according to the Devyn, but whatever they may say to us, we cannot allow the Hetarians to eat away at our territory. This is but the first incursion, a test of our wills. They think because we have no centralized government that we can eventually be subjugated. If we do not stop them at the beginning it will be harder to stop them later on, I fear."

Roan nodded in agreement. "Perhaps," he said, "it is time for us to form a stronger union than we have had. We meet but once yearly here at the Gathering. Given what is happening, we may have to form a council of some sort to handle problems like this immediately, instead of waiting for the Gathering. The Devyn who visited me said that the Hetarians came into the Outlands in late winter. It is now midautumn."

"The one in my hall did not know how long they had been in the Outlands. Why did not Petruso of the Piaras, or Imre of the Tormod send to us for help?" Vartan wondered.

"You know how proud the mountain clans are," Roan replied. "We shall have to wait and see if they come to the Gathering."

Three days later the chieftains they had been awaiting rode into the Gathering. There were no women or children with them, and but few riders traveled by their side. The yearly council was called for immediately, and the clan families gathered together within the ring of stone columns. Vartan, as head of the largest clan family, called for order, and when all was finally quiet he said, "We call upon Imre of the Tormod or Petruso of the Piaras to speak to us now. Which of you will tell us what is happening in the mountains? The tales brought to us by the Devyn are disconcerting, and never before has a clan family come to the Gathering without its women and children."

"I will speak for the Tormod and the Piaras," Imre said stepping forward. He was a tall, sinewy man whose ash-brown hair was streaked with silver. His gray eyes swept the gathering. "Just before spring Hetar invaded us, coming into our villages with their Crusader Knights. We were shocked, especially as they treated us as if we were savages. They slew our elders. They penned our women and children into enclosures like animals. They separated our young women, putting them into my house, where they use them for their pleasure. Our young boys are being forced into the mines at too young an age. New mines are being opened every month. They do not restore the land as we always have. Our mountain valleys are becoming a wasteland. They poison the waters with their refuse."

"Why did you not send to us for help?" Vartan asked Imre. "This action was a clear violation of the ancient treaties that separate Hetar and the Outlands."

"We were so shocked at first by what had happened," Imre said, "that we lost the advantage. Petruso and I did manage to meet. We agreed that we had to escape, and reach the Gathering if we could not reach you before. It took weeks of planning, Vartan. The Crusader Knights are a cruel foe, and they were always on the watch, for several of our young men attempted to flee. They were caught and brutally tortured in our public squares before being killed. Our people were forced to watch, and they grew afraid. These few men who accompanied us did so at great risk. And we had to steal the horses we rode. We were pursued in the mountains, but as soon as we managed to reach the plain our captors fell back, and let us go. They could not afford to be caught so deep in the Outlands. When our identities are learned it is certain our families will suffer. We did discuss it with them, and our women agreed we must make the effort, and find help."

Many of the women listening had begun to weep as Imre spoke.

Vartan turned to Petruso. "What have you to say, old friend?" he asked.

"He can no longer speak," Imre said. "When he protested that Hetar was violating a centuries-old treaty, the Crusader Knights cut out his tongue."

Petruso opened his mouth to show his fellow chieftains the stump of what had once been a most active appendage.

The chieftains all paled with this knowledge.

"Hetar wants the ores and the gems, is that correct?" Vartan said.

"Aye," Imre said, and Petruso nodded vigorously.

"Then we will have to drive the Hetarians from the mountains, and kill as many as we can to make our point most clear," Vartan said. "Hetar must not be allowed to violate our borders, or be encouraged by our lack of action to push further into the Outlands."

"Aye!" those gathered in the stone ring cried with one voice.

"Winter is upon us," Floren of the Blathma said. "We cannot fight a mountain war in the winter. And when the spring comes, who will tend to the fields if we are fighting? Can we not send a delegation to the Hetarians and negotiate this misunderstanding? They have always been a most civilized people. Surely they are open to reason." He was a plump man with a perpetually worried expression on his face, but he grew the most beautiful flowers in the Outlands.

"If Hetar comes into your lands, Floren, they will lay waste to your fields and send the daughters of whom you are so proud into the Pleasure Houses of the City," Imre said bitterly. "Hetar did not negotiate with us. They violated our boundaries and murdered our people. This is no small misunderstanding. This is an act of war. We have risked much to come to the Gathering and ask for your help." He stood proudly looking around at his fellow clan family chieftains.

"If we do not put a stop to this aggression," Roan of the Aghy said, "Hetar will push further into the Outlands."

"Perhaps it is just the ores and gemstones that they want," Torin of the Gitta said hopefully. "It is the only real thing of value in the Outlands."

Lara stood up. She didn't know if she should, but she did. "Your lands are the most valuable possession you have, my lords," she told them. "The farmers in the Midlands have no acreage left into which they may expand their farms. They cannot grow enough crops to feed the people. The City is overcrowded, and people need a place to go. They have begun to encroach on the Forest. I know my people. First Hetar will steal the wealth in your mountains, and then they will come to steal your beautiful lands."

"My wife knows well of what she speaks," Vartan said.

"Because she is a Hetarian!" a voice among the crowd cried out.

"Yes, I was born Hetarian," Lara said, "which is why I know the minds of those who rule that land. You must listen to me. Never have I known such beauty as is here in the Outlands. Never have I been treated better than here among the Fiacre. The people of Hetar are taught to believe you are savages, but you are not! I have come to love your ways. If Hetar invades the Outlands you will all lose your way of life. Many of you will be enslaved as the Tormod and the Piaras have already been enslaved. You must listen to me, for I have known both ways, and yours are better."

"I believe her," Rendor of the Felan said.

"So do I," Accius of the Devyn agreed. "We must put a stop to Hetar now. We cannot wait until the spring. How many more people among the two clan families will die if we wait even a few months? We must strike now!"

"There will be snows in the mountains before we can assemble an army and march there," Blathma protested. "It is the end of October."

"And your fields lie fallow and will lie fallow for the next several months," Rendor of the Felan said with a wolfish smile. "I know you, Blathma, and you wish to spend the winter as you always do, safe and snug in your warm house, planning new gardens and dreaming of the spring to come. But there will be no spring for many of the Piaras and the Tormod unless we come to their aid now. We have no other choice."

"There are always choices!" Blathma cried.

"The only other choice is to wait for Hetar to come to you," Lara told him, "and they will. But when the Crusader Knights come, Lord Blathma, your choices will be gone forever. Hetar will drive the Outlanders from their lands, and repopulate them with their own kind. You will be strangers in your own land. Where will you go? What will you do, my lords, when Hetar has taken away your home?"

"Perhaps," Gitta of the Torin said, "they will share the land with us."

"Mayhap," Lara agreed, "in the beginning. But as their population grows again, and Hetarian law takes over here, the people of the Outlands will be squeezed out. You must remain separate from them as you have always done or you will be destroyed."

"Let us take the night, my lords, to think on this," Accius of the Devyn said reasonably. "In the morning we will meet again, and decide what course of action we must take to protect ourselves, and to free the Piaras and the Tormod from the harsh captivity they now bear."

"Aye!" the other clan chieftains said with one voice.

The council adjourned. Usually the evenings of the Gathering were meant for feasting and merriment, but tonight no one felt content to eat and dance. Everyone began to return to their own encampments. Lara walked hand in hand with Vartan.

"I could not help but speak up," she said. "I hope I did not embarrass you, my lord. But suddenly I know what my destiny is, Vartan, and you must not laugh."

He stopped and, smiling down at her, took her face between his two hands. "And what is your destiny, my beautiful halfling wife?"

"My destiny is to save the Outlands," Lara said seriously. "Kaliq knew it, which was why he said I had chosen well when I decided to come to the Outlands. He could not tell me, of course."

"You are certain your destiny is to help us?" Vartan said slowly. Of course! It was all beginning to make sense now. She was a halfling, a woman with certain powers. She had important friends, and a mother who was a queen.

"You must listen to me when I advise you, my lord," Lara told him. "And you must not prevent me from doing certain things, Vartan."

"What things?" He kissed the tip of her nose, releasing her face from his gentle grip. "What do you plan?"

"You must know your enemy, and quickly. Imre speaks from his anguish, but he tells us nothing of the Crusader Knights. How many of them are there? How and where are they transporting the riches they are stealing from the mountains? Who made the decision to invade the Tormod and the Piaras? But most important, just how far is the High Council of Hetar willing to go in this endeavor, or can they be forced out of the mountains if we resist them? These are the things you must know, my lord," Lara told him, seriously.

"But how can we learn all these things?" Vartan asked her.

"I must think on it," Lara said quietly, "but I will find the answers for you, I vow it. This is my destiny! This is what brought me to the Outlands."

"It is, I suspect, but the beginning," Vartan replied. "Your destiny, Lara, I think is much bigger than just this difficulty with Hetar."

And the crystal hanging between her breasts began to glow brightly in response.

Chapter 15

SHE LAY ON THE BED they had made from furs in a corner of their pavilion. Beside her, Vartan slept content with the passion they had shared earlier. But Lara could not sleep. Finally she arose and slipped from the tent. The night was dark, and above her three of Hetar's four moons glowed silver in the sky. She had not shape-shifted in many weeks. Could she even still do it? Lara thought of a young eagle, and silently said the words "Aral go!" She felt herself soar upwards, wings flapping softly. Catching a whorl of current in the air she rose higher and higher above the encampment. It was wonderful. It was amazing! She knew she dared not remain aloft for too long. Already the horizon was beginning to grow light at its edges. But she could do it! She could really do it! But she would need more than the ability to shape-shift to help the Outlanders. She needed magic, and she knew exactly where that magic was to be found. With Kaliq of the Shadow Princes. But not now. She guided herself back down to the ground near their pavilion again. "Lara return!" she murmured, and regained her own shape. Smiling she walked back into the tent, and lay down by her husband's side.

"Where were you?" Vartan asked her softly.

"Seeing if I could still shape-shift," she whispered back. "Go back to sleep, Vartan. I will tell you on the morrow."

"I am hungry now," he told her.

"Hungry? You ate like a pig at the evening meal," Lara exclaimed.

"Hungry for my faerie wife's delicious body," he said with a wicked grin.

"We have no privacy, Vartan," she fretted. "Your mother, your brother, his wife and Noss sleep just beyond our curtain."

"We will be as quiet as mice."

"You are never quiet!" she teased him. But she wanted him now every bit as much as she knew he wanted her.

"If you do not remove your night robe, I will tear it from you," he threatened.

Lara quickly pulled the gown from her slender form. "I will find a way to repay you for this," she threatened, half laughing.

"Oh, wife, I hope so." And he pulled her into his arms, his hands caressing her eagerly. "Punish me with your kisses, Lara!" His mouth took hers in a searing embrace.

She lost herself in his arms. When he had satisfied himself with her mouth he laid her back upon their camp bed and began to kiss every inch of her flesh, not only with his lips, but with his tongue as well. He suckled for a time on each of her breasts, covering her mouth with his big hand to still her cries of delight, his blue eyes blazing down into her green ones. He brushed over her belly, licking and breathing on the quivering flesh as he went. His fingers played between her nether lips, teasing her until she was drenched with her excitement. When he slowly and deliberately put those fingers in his mouth, sucking on them, she almost swooned. Kaliq and his brothers had loved her with exquisite delicacy, but Vartan loved her with a fierce passion that set her afire with longing such as she had never known.

Suddenly eager to return some of the pleasure he was giving her, she pushed him onto his back and straddled him. Her fingertips brushed over his hard flesh, and putting one hand over his mouth, she pinched one of his nipples teasingly with the other. His big body jerked in surprise, but he did not unseat her. "Two can play at the same game, husband," she whispered in his ear, licking it slowly and nipping at the lobe. Lara slithered down his long torso, kissing and licking as she went. Her sweetly rounded buttocks filled his sight. Now and again she would nip at him, but he restrained his cries. His excitement, however, was an entirely different thing, and when her hand reached out to enclose his burgeoning manroot, he stuffed his fist in his mouth to silence himself.

Lara squeezed hard on the pillar of flesh in her hand. Then she bent to let her tongue encircle its blazing tip from which the tiniest milky bead slipped forth. She lapped at it then, releasing the manroot, took him into her mouth even as she felt him move beneath her, raising himself that he might taste her secret flesh with his own tongue. She suckled on him, but as she did her attentions were diverted by the sweet heat that his mouth on her was engendering. Lara bit her lip until it bled to keep from screaming.

"Let me go," she heard Vartan growl low, and when she did he pulled himself from beneath her, still keeping her on her knees and bent before him in a gesture of utter submission. His hands clamped themselves about her hips, and Lara felt him enter her in a single smooth motion. He remained still within her, swelling more until he filled her tightly.

She had never felt a manroot with such incredible intensity. He was hot and hard within her pleasure sheath. She shuddered with pure delight. Then gaining a small mastery of herself, she squeezed him several times until he began to move slowly within her body. Lara thought she would die with the sweetness she was experiencing. He moved in a leisurely fashion, drawing himself out almost to the tip of his manroot, and then plunging back with great deliberation until he was fully encased by her hot flesh.

"I love you," he murmured low against her ear. "I will never love another woman except you, Lara, my beautiful faerie wife."

"Then why do you kill me?" she sobbed back. She felt aflame with her desire, a desire he seemed in no great hurry to satisfy.

In response he began to move faster, and faster and faster, until sensing her impending crisis, he forced her into their pillows that her cries of pleasure be silenced as her ripe body shuddered with release. When she was finally still, he released his grip on her. Lara turned over and looked up at him in wonder.

"I have never before been loved quite like that," she whispered to him.

Vartan smiled a small smile at her, pleased by her words. Then he wrapped her in his embrace, and they were both shortly asleep again.

In the morning she told him of the flight she had taken in the night. "Kaliq can help us," Lara said. "Each province has two members on the High Council. He can find out who ordered the incursion into the Outlands, and if the council is involved."

"It would be a form of betrayal for him, wouldn't it?" Vartan asked.

"No. The Shadow Princes are very isolated from the rest of Hetar. They are feared for their magic, but as no one wants their Desert, they are left to themselves. Kaliq and his brothers have little tolerance for those in the City who make the laws. They are more allied with the Faerie world than with Hetar. He will help us."

"You must take the shape of a bird, then, to reach him," Vartan said.

"I took the shape of an eagle last night. I felt strong and secure as I flew," Lara told him.

"The eagle is the talisman of the Fiacre, as I told you on the day we first met. I can take its shape as well," Vartan said. "I fear to allow you to fly alone. Let me come with you, Lara, my wife, my life and my love."

"If you come you will see that Kaliq loves me, and you will be jealous," she replied. "I do not want you ever imagining what was between this prince and me."

"I do not need to see him to know that," Vartan answered her. "You are an incredibly beautiful woman, wife. I cannot be jealous of your prince, for he was forced to give you up. You are mine for an eternity, Lara, daughter of Swiftsword." He put his arms about her. "I must attend the council today, but we will depart tomorrow. If I leave my brother in charge it will please him, and perhaps his wife will stop her harping."

"What of Liam?" she asked.

"Liam never wanted the position, and will understand why I do what I do. He shall be the only one who knows where we go. Liam knows how to keep secrets," Vartan said quietly.

"I would go with you to the council today," Lara told him. "Let me sit at your right hand to listen and advise."

"Yes," he agreed. "Your position as the wife of the Fiacre chieftain must be enforced and acknowledged here at the Gathering."

"Have Sholeh join us as well," Lara suggested. "That way my presence does not seem so obvious. She is a headwoman, and she is your kin."

"How does one so young have such wisdom?" he asked her.

Lara shrugged. "I suppose it is instinct, and I have always had it."

He chuckled. "We must eat, for the council will last all day, with Floren dithering and attempting to avoid the inevitable while Gitta vacillates between Floren's logic and ours. These growers of crops are reluctant to go to war."

"I have never faced a war, but I learned from my father's tales that war is a futile pursuit, which no one really wins. Yet there are times when it seems the only way to settle a dispute is to go to war. Sometimes men cannot be reasoned with, and only a good bloodletting will bring them to their senses. The day we met you said Hetar would eventually invade these lands, but I do not think you believed it would be in your lifetime, Vartan. I am sorry that it is."

"So am I," he answered her, and then he began to dress.

Lara followed suit. Then they left their small curtained shelter, and came into the larger portion of the pavilion where Bera and Noss had a morning meal ready for them. Adon and Elin were already at table. Adon did not bother looking up, but Elin's gaze was sharp. Lara stared directly at her until Elin turned away, a flush upon her cheeks, and her mouth in a thin tight line.

"Feed us well, my mother, for we will be the day long in the council, I suspect," Vartan said jovially. "Noss, have you eaten?" At her nod, he continued, "Go and tell my cousin Sholeh that I will expect her at the council to advise me."

"Brother," Elin burst out, "should women be at council? Is that not a man's province? Women are not meant to govern. We are too frail, I fear."

"Perhaps you are, dear Elin," Vartan responded, "but there are some women as strong as their men, and in some cases stronger," he chuckled at her shocked look. "My wife shall sit at my right hand today. A woman's opinion is necessary to any and all decisions that the council makes. We are not Hetar, scorning women's wisdom. If we go to war many women and children will be left behind to care for the land, for the elders, to cope with the daily business of living. But some of our women will fight by our side."

"*I* should be at your right hand," Adon said angrily. "Why do you always choose others over me?" he demanded.

"Do you want to sit around all day in debate, little brother?" Vartan asked.

"Of course not," Adon said, "but you might at least have asked me. By your actions you say to the Fiacre that you do not trust me."

"I don't," Vartan remarked bluntly. "You are too greedy for power that you cannot possibly handle. You are short-tempered, and shorter-sighted, Adon, but you are my brother and I do love you. Now cease your carping so I may eat in peace."

The younger man opened his mouth to protest, but Bera said sharply, "Adon!"

"You have always loved him more than you love me," Adon muttered, glaring at her. "Only my sweet Elin understands." He took his wife's hand.

Bera snorted but held her peace, and served the meal.

Sholeh arrived just as they were finishing. She hugged Bera and Lara, nodding to Adon and Elin with a small smile. Their meal concluded, the two went off into a corner of the great tent where they sat down whispering and nodding. She looked to Vartan, who shrugged with a small smile and drank down the contents of his goblet.

The trio departed for the council, to be joined by Liam. They took their seats immediately. The wisdom of the Celestial Actuary was invoked and almost at once Floren presented his argument for arbitration again. Sholeh stood up when he had finished, before anyone else could speak.

"And will you, Floren of the Blathma, lead the delegation to the invaders of the Piaras and the Tormod?" she asked sharply. "Or will you expect someone else to go and plead your case for you?"

"I am not a diplomat," Floren blustered.

"Neither are any of us," Sholeh said. "We are a simple people who prefer a simple life. We have managed to live in peace for centuries, respecting each other and our individual borders. We have no standing armies, no Crusader Knights to protect us from invaders. We are considerate of the land that nurtures us, and we esteem it. We are nothing at all like Hetarians, whose passion is for status, wealth and power. They have always scorned the Outlands, but now they suddenly desire its riches? First it will be the ores and gems of the Piaras and the Tormod. Next it will be for your land, and mine. They will bring their laws and their ethics, or lack thereof, into our Outlands, and we will lose our identities. What makes you think that men who would invade another's lands and cruelly enslave the population can be reasoned with, Floren?"

"We must try," he replied, "if only to save ourselves from a war."

"You are already at war," Lara told the chieftain of the Blathma.

"She is right," Roan of the Aghy said. "And only the Devyn stand between you, Floren, and the invaders. The Devyn will sing of this time in our history, and they will fight. Will you let the smallest of our clan families do what you will not?" He stood tall, his red hair like a beacon, staring out at his fellow chieftains. "Are the Blathma as weak and frail as the flowers they grow?"

"We are not cowards!" Floren cried, his hand going to his dagger.

"Then fight!" Roan roared. "There is no bargaining with murderous thieves!"

"We have not yet decided upon a course of action," Rendor of the Felan said quietly. "Sit down now, Roan. And take your hand from your belt, Floren. Let us discuss this reasonably as we have always discussed matters of importance between us."

Vartan now stood up. "The times are changing, my brothers, my friends. And we must change with the times, else we be left behind. But if we are to control our own destiny we cannot wait for Hetar to come further into the Outlands. We must form a central government, something we have never before done. And we need to speak with one voice. In the past we didn't care that the Hetarians considered our Outlands a barbaric place. We had little if any contact with them. But as the years have passed they have grown to believe what were once merely words. They truly believe that we are savages, and therefore of little account. They will wrest this land from us if we do not stop them." He turned to Floren. "I wish negotiation were possible, but it is not. We must strike these invaders hard. We must strike them now! Much blood will be spilled. The lives of those we know and love will be lost. But many more lives will be sacrificed unless we stop Hetar now. Look on the bright side, Floren. If we can crush the invaders before spring comes you'll be home in time to plow your fertile fields."

A ripple of laughter echoed around the stone edifice at Vartan's words, and a small smile even crossed Floren's plump face.

"We must put it to a vote," Gitta of the Torin said, and the other chieftains nodded.

"May I consider it unanimous?" Vartan asked gazing about the council.

They all looked to Floren, who nodded slowly, saying, "I will hold you to your timeline, Vartan. I have seeds from two plants I crossed, and I want them planted next year so I may see if the flower is as beautiful as I suspect it will be."

There was more laughter.

"What of a permanent council?" Rendor of the Felan asked.

Lara stood now. "With your permission, my lords, I will tell you of the High Council of Hetar," she began. "The High Council consists of eight members, two from each province. They are rotated regularly that no member from any province can be bribed for his vote. The man from each province considered the most important takes his turn as head of the council. Again that honor is rotated, but in this case, every third moon cycle. The council head votes only when a tie must be broken. That is how Hetar is governed, my lords."

"It is a simple form of government," Rendor of the Felan noted.

"And still open to corruption, as all governments are," Roan of the Aghy said.

"All of us are open to corruption, Roan. We need to speak with one voice to Hetar," Vartan replied. "If we do not, they could divide and conquer us."

"Perhaps," Accius of the Devyn suggested, "we would do better to drive the Hetarians from the Piaras and the Tormod regions first, and then revisit this matter of a more formal government for our peoples. I would put Vartan of the Fiacre forth as our warlord, and Roan of the Aghy as his second in command."

"I will agree," Rendor of the Felan said.

"And I," Imre, Torin and Accius said.

"Petruso?" they asked the now mute leader of the Piaras, and he nodded in agreement, drawing his sword and waving it in the air.

"Petruso says that while he can no longer speak, he can still fight," Imre told them.

Petruso nodded enthusiastically, and made several stabbing motions with his weapon to the cheers of his companions.

"Such a shame," Sholeh murmured to Lara. "He had the most beautiful singing voice. As good as a Devyn, and he always entertained us at the Gathering."

"I never knew Hetarians could be so cruel," Lara replied. "I was sold into slavery so that my father could have his chance to become a Crusader Knight. He was a renowned warrior, but had not the means to join the tournament until I was sold."

"Were not his skills enough?" Sholeh asked surprised.

"Nay," Lara said, "they were not. A man who becomes a Crusader Knight must look as if he belongs among them. I hope my father is not among those who have invaded the Outlands. I do not know what I would do if I found myself face-to-face with him in a battle."

"Then you mean to go with Vartan?" Sholeh asked.

"Aye, I do," Lara told her. "I could not sit home at Camdene waiting for word. I am skilled with sword and staff. I must go with him. I am meant to fight this battle."

"Do you love my cousin?" Sholeh said.

"I do not believe in love," Lara told her. "I respect Vartan, and I admire him. I gladly share my body with him. Is that not enough for a man?"

"I do not think it is," Sholeh answered Lara.

"It is the best I have to give," Lara replied.

"You will love him one day," Sholeh told her with a smile. "Come, let us leave the council now. They will discuss how many warriors each of them should give, some saying because they have less land, they should send fewer men. It is the kind of argument that would drive a sensible woman mad."

"They must send a large army," Lara said. "The larger the force, the more impressed Hetar will be. And we must win the first battle, Sholeh. That means we must have the advantage over them to begin with, and I know just how to gain it."

"How?" Sholeh asked her.

Lara shook her head. "I will tell you after it is done, but not before. Vartan and I have already talked about it. Tomorrow you must see that Adon and his wife are kept busy, so busy that they do not wonder where my husband and I have gotten to. Can you do that? Include Noss and Bera as well."

"You will need an excuse for your absence," Sholeh said.

"We will be planning for the war with the other chieftains, and my husband wishes my advice as I have been raised in Hetar, and know them best."

"You do not call yourself Hetarian," Sholeh noted.

"Hetar is all of our world, but if it must remain divided," Lara replied, "then I am of the Outlands, for that is where my heart is. I realized it the moment Noss and I exited the cave in the cliff into the plain. It stretched before me, and I knew immediately that I had come home."

Sholeh smiled at the answer, well pleased. Vartan had taken a good wife. That night she came with several of her children, and grandchildren. She invited Bera, Noss, Adon and Elin to join her the following day in preparing a special feast for the next night. "No one can ready a hot pit like you, Adon," she praised her younger cousin. "And Elin's sauces for the roasted meats and poultry are without equal." She turned to Noss. "You could learn from Elin, my child," she said.

"You have not asked Lara," Elin noted.

"My wife will be with me in the war council," Vartan replied smoothly. "As she has lived much of her life in Hetar her advice is invaluable. Sholeh knew that beforehand, Elin."

"Mayhap she has been sent by Hetar to mislead us," Adon said softly.

"You are a fool, Adon," Lara said, and then she turned to Bera. "They had the same father?"

"Sometimes I wonder," Bera replied dryly.

"Why is it that my words are never considered seriously?" Adon demanded.

"Because," his mother said, "you do not consider your words first, my son."

Later as they lay amid the furs that made up their bed Vartan made plans with his wife, "We must leave just before the dawn, when we are least likely to be seen. How long do you think we will be gone? A day? Two days?"

Lara shook her head. "The magic of the Shadow Princes brought Noss and me through the cliff tunnel to the Outlands. When we looked back those same cliffs were gone, or at least so distant that we could not possibly have traveled that far from them in a single day. Tonight I will put my mind to reaching out to Kaliq. We will leave before dawn as you suggest, and see what happens, my husband." Then her hand went to the crystal.

"Does Ethne agree?" he teased her.

"Ethne has been silent of late," Lara admitted.

He reached out for her, but she pushed him away, and he looked at her surprised.

"We must conserve our strength for the journey ahead, Vartan," she counseled him wisely, and with a sigh he nodded, giving her a chaste kiss. Then turning away from her he fell quickly asleep. *Say something,* she whispered to Ethne.

Rely on your instincts. The flame flickered and banked low. Lara then called out to Kaliq and hoped that he heard her. *I need your counsel, Kaliq. Come to me.* Finally, she slept.

In the dim light before the dawn two eagles rose up from the encampment of the Gathering, and flew toward the Desert. The birds soared in silence throughout the morning, but as the sun reached the midway point in the heavens Lara saw a great tree ahead of them. It stood alone amid the plain, and was covered with golden leaves.

"Vartan," she called to her husband as he flew by her side. "We must descend to the ground beneath that tree."

The two eagles dropped down until their clawed feet touched the ground below, and they uttered the words that restored them to human shape. Under the tree a table had been set for three. There was a joint of meat, bread, cheese, fruit and a jug of wine.

Lara laughed, delighted. "Kaliq! Where are you, dear friend?"

And immediately the Shadow Prince stepped seemingly from inside the great tree. "Lara," he said, taking her in his arms and kissing her forehead, "it is good to see you again." Releasing her he turned immediately to her companion, "And you will be Vartan of the Fiacre. I am Kaliq of the Shadow Princes. Why have you sought me?"

"May we sit down, and refresh ourselves?" Lara said gently.

"I am sorry," the prince apologized. "You have traveled a long way this morning, and you must return to your Gathering by nightfall. Eat, drink and we will talk."

The two men stared at one another. Kaliq, tall, dark-haired and bronzed from the sun of his Desert, his light-colored eyes in vivid contrast. Vartan, tall, dark-haired and bronzed from the winds of the plains, his blue eyes suspicious as he frankly examined the man who had been his wife's lover, and was yet her friend.

"Thank you for coming to meet us," Lara told Kaliq. "And in such elegant fashion! Does the tree belong here, or is it one of your delicious illusions?"

"You see how well she knows me, Vartan," the prince said with a smile. "You were right to make her your wife, but be warned, this small difficulty you now face is but the beginning of her destiny."

Vartan's jaw tightened, but before he might respond the prince spoke again.

"Do not be angry with me for knowing what you cannot. Even Lara does not know. She must follow her instincts," Kaliq said. "And do not be jealous of me, Vartan. I had to let her go. Now, how may I help you?"

They sat down at the table beneath the tree, and while Vartan spoke, Lara served them food, and poured Frine from the jug.

"The Devyn brought word to me that our mountain clan families had been invaded, but only at our Gathering did we learn the seriousness of what is happening, my lord prince," Vartan began. "The leaders of both families managed to escape that they might reach us, but it took them months to effect this escape. The Crusader Knights have killed innocents and are pillaging the land. Hetar has violated a centuries-old treaty between us. We must drive them out of the Purple Mountains before winter, and we have little time to do so. Each day we wait, they entrench themselves deeper into the Piaras and Tormod territories, and their people suffer greatly."

"What do you want of me?" Kaliq asked.

"We need to learn," Lara broke into the conversation, "if the High Council has approved this incursion, my lord prince, and if so, why? Two of your like sit on that council. They would know, and we must know. Even now my lord Vartan is assembling a mighty army to go to our clan families' aid, but the Crusader Knights are a fierce foe, and many will be killed before this is settled."

"I do not know if the High Council approved this incursion into the Outlands, Lara," the prince told her. "I will seek the answer to that question. But I do know the men who invaded the territories of the Piaras and the Tormod are not Crusader Knights. The Crusader Knights are noble in their thoughts, hearts and deeds. They fight only to keep Hetar safe from harm. There is no danger from your clan families to Hetar, and they know this. And Crusader Knights would not enslave a people, and carry on a commercial enterprise. This smells to me of the Merchants Guild, and your old friend, Gaius Prospero," Kaliq said. "It could very well be that the council is in ignorance of what is happening in the Purple Mountains. Or it might be that some of them have been bribed to look the other way. But our representatives would know that."

"I would learn who the head of the High Council was late last autumn, or in early winter," Lara told him.

Kaliq chortled. "It is not a wager I should put money on, Lara, for again I will bet that it was Gaius Prospero. He would have been able to bribe everyone but our princes, and perhaps the Coastal Kings depending on who sat on the council then."

"The Felan have land along the sea," Vartan said. "The gentle hills along the coast are perfect for their sheep. They have always lived in harmony with the Coastal Kings. They allow them to put in for water, and fish in the seas off their shoreline. I believe that Rendor has friends among the Coastal Kings."

"Even one's allies are open to the right bribe," Kaliq said.

"Then why should we trust you?" Vartan demanded. "We do not know you."

Kaliq laughed. "You do not, Vartan of the Fiacre, but Lara does, and she trusts my brothers and me. Do you not, Lara?"

Suddenly she was swept back to that night when Kaliq had shared his passion for her with the other Shadow Princes. She almost blushed with the memory of the delights they had all enjoyed, for she had eventually remembered. Then in a burst of clarity she realized the lesson they had taught her that night. Trust! She had trusted them not to harm her, and they had not. They had instead offered her pleasures such as she had never before imagined. "Yes," she answered him in a strong voice, and their eyes met briefly. Then she turned to her husband. "I do trust the princes, Vartan, and so should you."

He had not missed the silent byplay between his wife and Prince Kaliq, and he swallowed down his jealousy. Had she not warned him he would be jealous, and had he not strongly insisted that he would not? He could not fail her, and shame her before this prince. "If you trust the Shadow Princes, Lara, my love and my life, then I shall trust them, too."

The faintest of smiles brushed Kaliq's lips, and he nodded with respect to the clan chieftain of the Fiacre. He was worthy of Lara, the prince thought. Then he said, "I will learn immediately what it is you need to know. If you will wait for me here I will return before sunset." He waved his hand, and the table with its chairs and dishes disappeared. In its place was a reclining couch large enough for two, a small table by its side bearing a decanter and two small goblets.

"That is not subtle at all, Kaliq," Lara scolded him with a giggle.

"We cannot wait, my lord," Vartan said. "If we do not begin our return journey now we will not be back in time for the evening feasting. It is when we all come together, and speak."

"Take your pleasure while I seek out the answers you need," the prince said. "I will see you are returned to the Gathering place in time." Then, stepping back, he seemed to disappear into the bark of the huge tree.

"We cannot wait," Vartan repeated.

"His magic will put us back where we should be at the proper time," Lara said. "Please trust him, Vartan. I know you said you do, but I also know you said it for my sake, and Kaliq knows it as well. Both of us realize your hesitation stems from your jealousy." She took his hand, and led him to the reclining couch. "Will you deny us the pleasure of this moment when we are alone, and have a bit of privacy?" She undid her gown, and let it fall to the grass beneath her sandals. Her beautiful naked body glowed in the sunlight of the midautumn afternoon. "After last night, I long to be between your strong thighs, my husband. I ache to be filled again with your manroot. Come into my arms, my lord." She began to undress him, and a slow smile lit up his face.

Damn the handsome Shadow Prince who had once known the pleasure of his wife's passion! Lara was his alone. Her soft words, and gentle hands were arousing him. He gladly gave in to her blandishments and helped her so that shortly they stood nude, arms about each other. Her hands slipped down his long back, to cup and caress his tight buttocks. Her fingers brushed over his hot length, running beneath it to fondle the sac holding his seed. He growled deep in his throat, and his mouth found hers in a searing kiss.

Lara sighed at the touch of his lips on hers. Sighed again as those lips traveled first over her face, then blazed a fiery trail down the slender column of her neck. His big hands enclosed her waist, lifting her up to kiss the shadowed valley between her breasts. He licked at her nipples, and her eyes closed in anticipation. His mouth closed over first one breast and then the other, suckling at them hungrily. She clung to him, eager for what was to come as he lay her upon the large reclining couch, but today he surprised her.

She lay spread open to him, but he did not immediately fit himself between her legs. Instead he sat upon the couch next to her, and drizzled a bit of Frine onto her torso. Then lowering his head he began to lick it up, his tongue moving frantically to keep up with the individual droplets running across her body. Soon the liquid was all gone and Vartan moved to kneel between her limbs. His busy tongue moved lower until it was pushing between her nether lips, until he found that delicate nub of flesh that gave such delight when properly encouraged. He touched it lightly with just the tip of his tongue. Then he began flicking at that fleshy kernel until Lara was whimpering, and her slender body trembled with excitement and she cried out. It was a sound of satisfaction that caused him to smile. He was as hard as rock, and without further ado he covered her body with his and entered her.

"Ahhh!" Lara half sobbed as his manroot filled her. "Oh, my lord, yes! And yes again, and yet again!" She wrapped her legs about his hips. Her arms clung tightly to him. Her entire body was atingle with their joining. Her fingers kneaded his broad shoulders. She tried not to scratch him, but he laughed softly in her ear.

"Mark me with your claws, my love!" he encouraged her. He could feel himself swelling inside of her, feel the muscles of her love sheath embracing him. He groaned as her nails raked down his back enjoying the slight stinging pain which but added to his excitement. He began to move on her.

Lara sobbed with the pleasure they were sharing. Her head began to spin, and starbursts in a thousand rainbow hues burst behind her closed eyes. Every part of her felt alive with his love. She could feel her nipples pressing against him as he crushed her breasts against his chest. She savored the great length of him as he thrust again and again into her molten core. And then she sensed the coming storm of passion that would leave them both weak and satisfied. It exploded within them simultaneously and they cried out together with one voice.

Afterward they lay quietly in each other's arms, the soft late afternoon breeze brushing over their damp bodies. Finally Vartan spoke.

"You know that I love you, Lara."

"Yes," she answered. Nothing more.

"Can you not say it, my wife?"

"I do not believe in love," she replied. "I have said it before. Why does it now come as a surprise to you? I have a faerie woman's cold heart, Vartan. But I will tell you that I have never before experienced the kind of pleasure that we share. Never! Not with any man. And I respect you as lord of the Fiacre, and as my husband. It must be enough, for it is all that I can give." Lara slipped from his arms and, standing up, began to dress. "You had best put your clothing back on, my husband. Kaliq said he would be back in late afternoon."

"Is it that you don't want to embarrass him with my magnificence?" he teased her.

"Precisely," she agreed with a little smile.

He chuckled, and then rising proceeded to dress.

They sat back down on the reclining couch, and sipped Frine from the goblets Kaliq had left. The sun was beginning to slip down the smooth silken sheet of the blue sky when the Shadow Prince stepped from the great tree to rejoin them.

"I have word for you," he told them, seating himself between Lara and Vartan.

"Tell us," Lara said.

"I was correct when I said that it was not Crusader Knights. The invaders are mercenaries in the pay of Gaius Prospero, who convinced a majority of the High Council to pursue this small encroachment into the Outlands. The Mercenary Guild needed work. They were becoming restless being so idle, and beginning to cause trouble in the City. Nor did they enjoy paying bribes to their leaders for the small assignments that were coming their way. The Midlands and the Forest Lords voted for the breach in the treaty. My fellow princes and the Coastal Kings voted against it, but as we suspected, the greedy Master of Merchants was council head at that time, and he voted for the incursion. They have taken much ore from the Piaras and the Tormod so far. There is talk in the council of annexing these territories because of the lack of resistance from the Outlanders. Hetar does not understand your ways, and so it believes that you are weak. You will have to strike these invaders hard, and cause them much harm in order to discourage them from moving further into the Outlands."

"A winter war will be cruel for all involved," Vartan noted, "but it must be done. We have no other choice."

"We can help you," Kaliq said quietly, "if you will allow it."

"How?" Lara asked.

"We have the ability to control the weather if necessary. Usually we allow nature to have its way for that is best. But it will be more difficult for your army to fight in the snows and bitter cold. Such winter weather will not touch the Tormod and the Piaras this year. We will keep the worst of winter from the territories involved in this dispute. And the Coastal Kings have agreed to close their lands to the rest of Hetar that you may not be attacked from another direction, and can be certain your women and children are safe in your villages," Kaliq told them.

"And in return?" Vartan asked the prince.

"Nothing," Kaliq replied. "One day we may need a favor from you, and when that day comes I am certain that you will render it to us in kind, Lord Vartan." He held out his hand to Vartan, who gripped it in return. Lara placed her own dainty hand upon the locked hands of the two men. "We are agreed then," the Shadow Prince said, "and now I must return you to the Gathering before you are missed. Lara knows how to contact me. Fight well, my friend, and drive Hetar back within its own borders." Then he made a fluid motion with his free hand, and seemed to dissolve before their very eyes. Blinking in surprise, they found themselves back in Vartan's pavilion.

"There you are," Bera said. "I wondered where you had gotten to! It is almost time for the feasting. I have never known a longer day than this one, with Elin droning on about how important the freshness of ingredients for her sauces is. If they did not taste so good I vow I would strangle the wench, no matter she is Adon's wife. And he was no better as he explained the intricacies of choosing just the right wood for his fire pit. Where were you?"

"We met with Kaliq of the Shadow Princes, and learned much of what is behind this invasion,"Vartan replied. "I will tell you after I have met with the other leaders, and set a time to speak on it," he said to his mother. Then turning he left the pavilion.

"How is this possible?" Bera gasped.

"There has been much magic this day and there is more of it to come," Lara told her softly. "But it has been good magic, Bera. The Outland is not alone in this fight."

"What would we have done without you, my child?" Bera said. "You are truly a blessing to us, Lara, daughter of Swiftsword, wife of Vartan."

"It is my destiny," Lara returned with a small smile, and Bera chuckled.

"Come, help me bring food to the feasting table," she said.

And together the two women carried the bowls, the platters and the assorted dishes adding them to what was already there from the other clan families. The great array of food and drink was quickly consumed as early evening turned into night, and the stars twinkled above them. And then the four moons of Hetar rose, each in its quarter phase. This night the copper Desert moon shone full and bright. A good omen, Lara thought.

It was the last night of the Gathering. The bonfires that had sprung up at sunset to usher out the old year and welcome in the new blazed high. As it grew later and later, more of the clan families departed for their own tents, but Vartan kept his wife by his side until they and the other clan leaders were alone.

"It is time to speak,"Vartan said.

"Why is your wife here in a war council?" Torin of the Gitta demanded.

"Because without her we would have no hope,"Vartan said. "She will be the savior of the Outlands, and her voice is my voice. You will obey it always, Torin. Now hear me. Today Lara and I met with

Kaliq of the Shadow Princes. We have learned that the incursion into the Piaras and Tormod territories is an expedition to test our strength and determination. The Midland Merchants, led by the master of their guild, are behind it along with the Mercenary Guild. Those who invaded you are not Crusader Knights but mercenaries. This scheme was concocted by Gaius Prospero, the Master of the Merchants. The ores and gems stolen from the Piaras and the Tormod have been added to his own treasury. His wealth makes him a powerful man and he heads the Hetarian High Council. The Merchants and the Forest Lords voted to test our determination, while the Shadow Princes and the Coastal Kings voted to maintain our ancient treaty. The tie was broken by Gaius Prospero himself, as he, of course, meant it to be. If only Imre and Petruso had reached us sooner—but they did not. Now we must drive the mercenaries from their lands."

"With the winter coming," Floren of the Blathma reminded them dourly.

"We have allies among Hetar," Vartan said. "The Shadow Princes will hold back the winter from the mountain territories. This will allow us to invade without fear of cold and snow. The Coastal Kings will not allow any from the other provinces into their bailiwick until this matter has been settled. Rendor has made good friends, which will work to our advantage now. We will not have to worry about being attacked from another direction. But most important we shall have the element of surprise, for over half a year has passed since Hetar pushed into Tormod and Piaras. At this point I am sure Hetar believes we will do nothing. But if we do not take back these territories then Gaius Prospero is planning to annex them. Who will they come after next?" He looked about. "The Devyn are the easiest target, and then Blathma will fall, and so on."

"How can we be certain that the Shadow Princes and the Coastal Kings will aid us?" Roan of the Aghy wanted to know. "Can we trust this Kaliq? Why does he offer to help us, Vartan? What does he want?"

"Nothing for now, but he has said that one day they will come to us for a favor, and it is then we must repay them for their aid," Vartan said.

"He has also said we must raise a mighty army in order to impress Hetar," Lara told the chieftains.

"What does it matter the size of the army if we can beat them?" Roan wanted to know. He ran an impatient hand through his bright red hair.

"You must understand that Hetarians are impressed by wealth, strength, status and its like," Lara explained. "If you beat them with a small army they will say it was a fluke, and they will attempt to come at you again. Piaras and Tormod will forever be open to invasions. More people will be killed. If you beat them with a great army then they will feel they have been fairly bested, and in all likelihood the ancient treaty will be once again honored." She shrugged. "I can explain it no better. In order to win against Hetar you must impress them first. And to do that you will have to kill many of the mercenaries, and send their bodies back to the City as a warning."

For a long moment there was a deep silence among the chieftains. Then Rendor of the Felan spoke.

"I understand what you say, but it amazes me that so delicate a female can speak so dispassionately about taking life, for females are life-givers." He looked at Vartan. "Your wife is the most beautiful woman I have ever seen, and yet she has, it seems, the heart of a warrior."

"It is not my heart that should concern you, Rendor of the Felan, but rather your own. How many men will you pledge to this battle?" Lara asked him bluntly.

He laughed. "Every whole man among my clan from fourteen to sixty will fight for the Outlands," he promised. "We are shepherds at heart, but we know well how to defend our flocks be they sheep or people, Lara of the Fiacre, wife to Vartan, daughter of Swiftsword," Rendor answered her.

"We would expect no less,"Vartan said. "What of the rest of you?"

"Every horseman in my clan will fight," Roan of the Aghy said.

"We are few in number," Accius of the Devyn said, "but we will contribute in our own way. Some of our bards will go into the villages of the Piaras and the Tormod, ostensibly to entertain the invaders, but they will pass the word to the people that their leaders have reached their brethren and that a mighty army comes. We will ready them to rise up against their captors. And we will fight. Those who cannot fight will sing you into battle, and if necessary into the realm of the Celestial Actuary."

"Thank you, my old friend," Vartan said. "The nobility of the Devyn is well known among the Outlands."

"Our fields are put to bed for the winter now,"Torin of the Gitta spoke up. "If the Shadow Princes say our villages will be safe, then only women, children and the elderly will be left behind to care for our lands. All who can fight among us will come." He turned to look to his fellow agrarian, Floren of the Blathma.

The plump farmer sighed. "I can do no less than Torin," he said reluctantly. "You are certain our villages will be safe from harm?" he asked of Lara.

"Kaliq of the Shadow Princes has said it, and I have never known him to lie," Lara replied. "They are honorable men, and the oldest among the inhabitants of this world we all share," she explained.

"Then it is settled," Vartan said. "Take your people home, my brothers, and then return here to the Gathering place in ten days' time. By that time we will have a plan readied to punish these Hetarians who have invaded our lands."

"I know I speak for Petruso as well as myself when I thank you," Imre of the Tormod said. "For the sake of our peoples I only wish we had gotten to you sooner."

"Do not thank us until you are back safe in your own house with your wife by your side, Imre. Many will die in this undertaking, but there will be more grief in Hetar than in the Outlands when this is finished,"Vartan said fiercely.

Early the next morning, before the sun was even up, the clan families dispersed from the Gathering place. Imre, Petruso and their men went with Vartan's clan for they dared not return to their own homes yet. On the day following their arrival in Camdene, Vartan dispatched riders to each of his villages issuing a call to arms. Every Fiacre clansman between the ages of fourteen and sixty was expected to answer that call if he was physically able. The villages and the herds would be looked after by the elderly, the women and the children. Any woman able to fight was invited to come as well, although it was not mandated that women answer the chieftain's call. Still, several came from each village, and were put into Sholeh's care. Lara, it was agreed, would fight by her husband's side.

"I will come, too," Noss said bravely.

"You do not like discord," Lara reminded her friend and companion. "This will be terrible, dearest. Remain behind with Bera, Elin and Liam's mother."

"No," Noss replied. "While you will fight with Andraste, I am a better archer than you. Why did I carry the long bow the prince gave me on my back from the Desert kingdom if I was not to use it? And what better use than in the defense of our homeland? And Sakari tells me she, like Dasras, was trained for battle. She is eager, and I feel safe with her. I but ask one thing of you, Lara. Let me wed with Liam now."

Lara sighed. In her eyes Noss was yet a child, but in truth she was not. Lara still saw Noss as the frightened girl who the Foresters had refused to accept as a breeding slave because she was too young, but two years had passed, and Noss was no longer that youngster. She had small, firm breasts, and a way of tossing her head that bespoke someone on the verge of womanhood. Liam loved her. What if he was among those killed in the coming Winter War? Could she forgive herself if she forbade Noss even a brief happiness? "I will have Vartan speak to Liam," she said, and her heart swelled at the look of happiness that engulfed Noss's pretty face.

Tears spilled down that face. "Thank you!" Noss said softly, and she hugged Lara hard. "I was so afraid you would make us wait, and what if he doesn't come back?" She sniffled. "Or I don't?"

"Have you spoken to him about coming with us yet?" Lara asked.

"Yes, and while he is not pleased, he has consented, for he knows that I must go with you. How could I not?"

"You must not think you owe me because the Forest Lords did not want you and took me instead. That was part of my destiny, Noss, as unpleasant as it was," Lara said. "If you would prefer to remain behind I will not think you craven."

"Nay, it is not that. I feel I must do this, just as you feel your destiny so strongly," Noss responded. "I sense no impending doom about me. I shall come home to Camdene again with my Liam when this is all over, Lara."

"Very well then. I shall be glad for your company, as always," Lara told her.

No time was wasted in the matter of Liam of the Fiacre and Noss of Hetar—the marriage was performed that same night in Vartan's hall. Liam's mother, Asta, was pleased with her new daughter-in-law's sweet nature, and equally pleased that Noss would go with her husband to fight by his side.

"Mayhap," she said, "the ordinary Hetarian is not as bad as we have always supposed they were. Noss might have been born here in the Outlands did I not know otherwise. But when this Winter War is over and done with I shall have grandchildren at last!" She laughed heartily. "I am pleased with this marriage."

Vartan gave the bride and groom two days to hide away by themselves. "Be back in my hall on the third morning," he said.

After the brief respite the wedding offered them, Lara and Vartan became engrossed in planning how they would attack and triumph over Hetar's invasion of the Tormod and Piaras lands. All the Outlanders were trained in the arts of war, though they had not been forced to use that tuition in centuries. Their greatest advantage was that neither had the Hetarians, for there had been peace between the two cultures for years. The great Crusader Knights were an army never used. It was the mercenaries who fought in the small squabbles between the law-abiding citizens, and the bandits who roamed all the provinces. But no one in the Outlands could remember a great battle being fought.

They learned from Imre that the householders in each village had been forced to take in their oppressors. Those forced to toil in the mines now were kept in barracks they had been forced to build themselves, and the barracks were enclosed by high wooden fences. The old women were sent into these enclosures to cook for the miners and wash their clothing. The women left behind in the cottages caring for their young children were more often than not forced to offer pleasures to the men now living in their homes. The young girls, as Imre had told them, were confined in his house and forced to act as Pleasure Women for those men in charge and for important visitors from the City. Old men who could work at tilling the fields that fed these clan families were left in peace. Any who were unfit and showed no signs of recovering were slain without mercy.

"They are clever," Vartan said to the circle of men around him in his hall. "They inhabit every house, which makes it difficult to mount an attack."

"Why must a battle be noisy and heroic?" Lara said. "Is not the victory the same even if the battle is a quiet one?"

"What do you mean?" Vartan asked her.

"Death is inevitable in war, but if we can keep all knowledge of our coming from the Hetarians, if we can get word to all in each village before we attack, do you not think they will rise up to aid us? We will move stealthily from village to village until the Tormod and Piaras regions are free of the invaders. In each village we will spare one among the enemy, and they will drive the wagons of Hetarian dead back to the City, to the very door of Gaius Prospero's beautiful house in the Golden District."

The men gathered around her nodded, and smiles wreathed their faces.

"Some Outlanders, for whatever reasons, will have cooperated with the enemy," Vartan said wisely. "They must be rooted out and slain as a warning to any who would betray their own kind. This will be difficult, but we must be hard."

Again there was agreement.

"I would send a traitor from each village with the wagons. They will hardly be welcome, and they will not be able to come back. Execution is a quick death. Exile is a long one. There is no place in the City for strangers," she told them. "They will suffer bitterly before they finally die."

"Is it your destiny to destroy the world that spawned you, my Lady Lara?" Imre asked her politely. "Is Hetar doomed?"

"My destiny for now is to be Vartan's wife, and to ride with you in what is a just and righteous cause. What is to come I do not know, my lord Imre. I am but half faerie." She smiled at him, her green eyes twinkling.

"Will your faerie kin come to our aid if you ask?" he wondered.

"We do not need them in this endeavor, my lord Imre. The clan families of the Outlands are strong because they are pure of heart," Lara told them.

Vartan put an arm about Lara. "You have all heard my wife," he said. "Now we must decide how to execute our plans that all be in place when we meet with the others at the Gathering place in a few days. Speak now, and let me hear your voices."

Chapter
16

THE ARMIES of the clan families convened in late autumn. Lara was very pleased to see how large a force had been gathered, and how impressively they were caparisoned. When word got back to the City, the High Council would be very impressed. The flags flown by each clan family were different. The eagle was embroidered upon the purple and gold banner of the Fiacre. A white horse galloped across the blue and gold banner of the Aghy. The Felan flew a banner of sky blue with a black and gray wolf upon it. The Devyns' red flag was decorated with a golden harp. The Gitta's flag was green with sheaves of grain, the Blathma's green with multicolored flowers. The Tormod flew a banner of silver that twinkled with gemstones. The Piaras's flag was coal black with gold and silver lines running through it.

It had been decided that each clan family would free a single village, but for the last two. Each individual army would move off to secure its designated village, before joining together for the assault on the two villages of the Tormod and Piaras left to be freed. The Devyn would send their bards into the villages beforehand, singing in the ancient language of the Outlands before both they and the Hetarians spoke a single tongue. All Outlanders were taught the old speech in their schooling, and many of their songs were sung in it.

"We are less apt to be seen if we travel singly,"Vartan told them. "Beware of mercenary scouts. Send your own ahead of you. We will lose fewer of our own men if we maintain the element of surprise. Kill all the enemy but the one chosen to drive the cart. We will all meet in the mountains at the Crystalline Falls, and move out from there."

Even with less than half a day's light left, the clan families departed the Gathering Place, their trumpeters and banners hidden until the moment of triumph to come. The Desert moon was waning, but the butter-yellow moon of the Coastal Region lit the way for Vartan's army until they finally stopped to rest themselves and the horses. None of the other clan families was visible to them.

"What if the mercenaries have posted a watchtower on the mountains?" Lara asked her husband. "That could ruin all of our carefully laid plans."

"I will take the eagle's form, and fly ahead in the morning,"Vartan said.

"Nay, you must lead your army, husband," Lara told him. "Nor do you want it known that you shape-shift. It must remain your secret, and it cannot if you disappear from the head of your troop. Yet nothing will be thought if I disappear, and then return suddenly. I am the Fiacre chieftain's halfling wife," Lara said with a chuckle. "I possess faerie magic."

"But what if you are seen?" he worried.

"By whom? An eagle seen flying in the mountains will not be thought unusual, my lord," she reassured him.

He nodded. "Then go with the dawn, my love and my life, but return to me safely." He kissed her brow, his blue eyes filled with his love for her.

"I will, husband," Lara told him, and when the dark began to retreat from the autumn skies over the plains the next day a small golden eagle soared above the sleeping encampment of the Fiacre. The bird's speed was swift, and by late morning it cruised among the peaks of the Purple Mountains, eyes sharply viewing the landscape below. She was pleased to find that there were no sentries' outposts posted on the heights. Obviously the mercenaries felt safe, which seemed rather careless to Lara. Did the men who had escaped them not concern them? Or were they so arrogant as to believe that any Outlanders who came upon them could be easily beaten? Satisfied that their plan would hold, Lara turned and flew back, spying Vartan and his troop as they traveled across the grasslands.

She circled above them calling, and her husband looked up. Lara realized that perhaps now was the time to display some of her small magic to her husband's people. It would put them in fear or awe of her, and one day she might need that advantage. She flew down to the riders, alighting upon her own saddle as Dasras cantered along. "Lara return!" she said, and was immediately restored to her human form. She reached out for her reins, knees gripping her stallion's heaving sides, laughing at Vartan as she did.

Around her she heard the gasps of surprise, and low murmurs. Her husband chuckled. "That was well done, and you are now completely established as a magical creature," Vartan told her.

"It may be of help to us one day that they are convinced of my powers, and perhaps even a little afraid, husband," Lara told him.

Liam rode up, coming between them. "Noss did not tell me you can shape-shift," he said admiringly. "You have frightened many of those who ride with us, especially Adon." He chortled wickedly.

"I suspect that is a good thing," Lara told Liam. "If I should ever have to act for Vartan I do not want to waste my time arguing with him. He is, I fear, a man who has but to open his mouth, and I find I am annoyed."

Liam laughed. "I know," he agreed. "We are blood kin, and I do not know another of our family like him."

"He is greedy for his brother's place," Lara said astutely.

"He shall never have it," Liam said. "The elders would not approve it."

"What did you learn?" Vartan asked his wife, not enjoying the conversation between Lara and Liam.

"There are no sentry posts in the mountains, or even around the villages," Lara said. "It seems rather feckless to me, but they are obviously convinced they are secure in their conquest. Considering that Imre and Petruso escaped with several of their men I would think they would be watching, but they are not." She turned to Imre who had now ridden up to listen, and said, "Was your land always so bleak, lord Imre? There are great open gashes in the landscape, and filth pouring into your streams and lakes. Many trees have been felled and left lying."

"No," Imre of the Tormod answered Lara. "We have always cherished the land, and each time we close a mine we restore the land by planting trees and seeding new growth. Floren can tell you for we have purchased many trees and flowering plants from him. We love our land, and are grateful for the bounty it provides us, but these Hetarians only desire its wealth. They do not care that they are poisoning our water—water which flows into the hills and plains of our land."

"The stream in one of my villages had contaminated water," Vartan said. "The headman brought it to my attention when we visited recently."

"There! You see?" Imre replied. "They will destroy us all if we do not stop them now. And before we managed to flee they had begun cutting the trees on the mountain for its lumber. There is a great need for lumber to build in the City, I have heard it said. But they do not replace the trees, and the mountains need trees to keep them from collapsing. If a mountain fell it could tumble into our streams, or destroy our villages. It has been our custom that whenever we cut a tree we replant a tree."

"Hetar has done much damage. Perhaps you might take your complaint to the High Court of Hetar, and demand reparations for the damage," Lara suggested.

"It would be a waste of time," Vartan told his wife. "Hetarians consider us savages. We would be at a great disadvantage in your court. Better we simply drive them from the Tormod and Piaras so we may begin the business of repairing the land before the damage spreads any further into the Outlands."

They stopped to rest until moonrise. Then they continued on their way. The mountains were drawing closer with every step their mounts traveled. The following midday they were close enough so that they stopped in a small grove of trees, hiding themselves cautiously. Lara shape-shifted once again, flying ahead to see if anything had changed, but it had not. There was no one to see their approach. At moonrise they moved forward once more, finally entering the mountains. They rode single-file along narrow trails amid thick Forest heading toward the Crystalline Falls, which they hoped to reach by midmorning.

As they rode along Lara felt a prickle slide down her back. They were being watched, but not by human eyes. There were faeries in these woods. She felt something light upon her shoulder, and turned her head to see a tiny girl smiling at her, iridescent wings fluttering.

"Hail, Lara, daughter of Queen Ilona!" the faerie said. "I have been sent by my queen to ask if we may help you. Speak to me as you would to Ethne, within your mind. Those riding with you can neither see or hear me. My words and presence are for you."

You are a different tribe from that of my mother, Lara noted.

"Forest Faeries come in all sizes," the tiny creature chuckled. "My name is Esme."

I have taken a bird's form to fly above these mountains and learn of any threats, Lara said. *Have my eyes missed any danger, Esme?* Lara asked.

"They are very arrogant people," Esme replied. "They expect no resistance from the Outlands."

But several escaped, Lara said. *Were they not concerned by that?*

"Those sent to capture them could not, and lied to their masters that they had killed Imre and his band, and thrown their bodies into the river at the Crystalline Falls. They were believed."

How might you best help us? Lara asked.

"We have been friends with the Tormod and the Piaras forever," Esme replied. "We know the Devyn will enter the villages first. We shall be there to aid them. These poor people are frightened, especially having been told that their leaders deserted them and were then killed. The truth will revive their courage. They will be ready when your armies come. We will also warn the Devyn of the traitors among the Tormod and the Piaras, for we know who they are." Her smile twinkled at Lara. "If you need me, just ask Ethne, and she will call me," Esme said.

"Thank you so much!" Lara replied, and the tiny faerie was as quickly gone as she had come.

"Did you see that tiny bird with the iridescent wings at your shoulder?" Vartan asked Lara. "You must have, for you turned and stared at it for the longest time."

"What you saw as a bird was actually one of the Forest Faeries who live here. My mother sent her. She has confirmed what I believed true—the Hetarians are secure in their conquest of these lands," Lara explained.

"Will the faeries help us?" he inquired.

"Esme, for that is her name, says her kind have been friends with the Tormod and the Piaras forever. They will go into the villages with the Devyn bards and spread word that we are coming to release them from their bondage. She says those pursuing Imre, Petruso and their men returned to their masters and claimed they had killed them. The people were beaten down by such terrible news. The knowledge that their leaders are alive will hearten them greatly."

"When we reach the Falls I will tell Imre and Petruso," Vartan said. Then he reached out to caress her cheek. "You are a blessing to the Outlands, Lara, daughter of Swiftsword," he told her.

She smiled. "So you have previously said, husband. But I am not necessarily a blessing, Vartan. It is just that I hate injustice, and what has happened here is unjust."

They arrived at the Crystalline Falls in late afternoon. Lara had never seen their like. It was beautiful. The waters fell in a silvery sheet from the heights above. The torrent dropped into a round rock pool, made its way over a much lower bed of rocks into a river that flowed down and through the mountains. The clear liquid in the pool had so far remained untouched by the impurities the Hetarians were creating. The banks about the pool were soft with moss. The trees soared, most now bare of their leaves. They were the first to arrive, and made their camp without a fire. Lara went to greet the spirit of the falls, requesting sanctuary for the Outlander armies. By moonrise, however, all the other clan armies had reached the Crystalline Falls.

In a tent lit by a single lamp, the clan chieftains and their lieutenants gathered to discuss their next move. Their relief when Vartan told them of the faeries who would aid them was almost palpable. These were not men and women for whom fighting came easily. Vartan also told them that the Devyn bards had already been dispatched into the villages, and that tomorrow the quest to free their fellow Outlanders would begin.

Imre explained that they were less than a day's march from most of the villages. He laid out a parchment map on the tent's single table, showing them where they now were, and how each clan family could reach their assigned villages. "After you have liberated your village," Imre said, "you will go here." He pointed. "These are the Singing Caves. We will all meet there, and continue on to the final two villages we must take. Each of you will be given a copy of this map to guide you. Your individual paths are marked in your clan color."

"Remember," Vartan said to them. "All the mercenaries but one are to be killed. You can show no mercy, for Hetar has showed no mercy. If we are to make them honor the treaties signed between us centuries ago, we must impress them with our determination so that this never happens again. Are we agreed?" He looked about the tent at the nodding heads. "Our cause is just," Vartan said. "The Celestial Actuary will be with us."

"May the Celestial Actuary have mercy on the souls of our victims," Lara told them. "Wars are always said to be just for one reason or another, and the Celestial Actuary's name is always invoked with righteous piety by warriors about to go into battle." She sighed sadly. "Pity those we must kill to make our point, my lords."

"Remember, lady," Lord Roan said, "that it was Hetar and not the Outlands who began this trouble."

"Aye, and I am shamed by it as well as saddened," Lara replied. "My innocence when I left the City was as much of mind as body. My loyalties, however, are with the Outlands, Roan of the Aghy. Not Hetar."

"I did not doubt it, lady," the horse lord replied. "I merely meant to point out that if pity is to be extended it should first be offered to the Tormod and the Piaras."

Lara bowed politely. "I stand corrected, my lord," she said graciously.

He smiled wryly at her and returned the bow, not having expected such a courteous reply. He could see Vartan was irritated with him. But then, Vartan was hopelessly in love with his beautiful halfling wife, and apt to be a bit of a fool over her.

Lara moved into the shadows of the tent briefly, returning with a tray of goblets. "Let us drink to our success, my friends," she said, offering the goblets about.

Each man and woman in the tent took up a goblet and raised it as they looked to Vartan and Lara, who murmured softly in her husband's ear.

"To justice," Vartan toasted. "And to the men and women of the Outlands who believe so strongly in it!"

"To justice, and to the Outlands!" came the enthusiastic reply.

"We will all depart at the same hour," Vartan told them, "that the element of surprise work against all our enemies. Make certain none escape you to warn the last two villages."

In the hour before the dawn the clan families were assembled and slowly moved out, the Fiacre in one direction, the Aghy in another, and so forth. Within a very short time Lara could see no one but those with whom she rode. She reached down and caught her crystal star between her thumb and first finger. Her heart beat very rapidly, and her belly was filled with cramps that rolled rhythmically through it like a melody.

I am here, she heard Ethne's voice say. *Do not be afraid. Fight well, if need be, and you will live to see another day, my child.*

What do you mean if need be? she asked her guardian.

You will see soon enough, Ethne replied. *Now strengthen yourself body and soul, Lara, daughter of Swiftsword, and look ahead to what is to come.* Ethne's flame flickered, and then died to a miniscule point of light within the crystal.

They rode through the autumn Forest. The sky above them was beginning to lighten, but they could see that the day would be a grey one without the warmth of the sun on their backs. Petruso rode with them, for their objective was one of the three Piaras villages. Suddenly the now-silent chieftain raised his hand, calling for a stop. He turned to Vartan and pointed through the bare trees. Vartan moved his horse slowly through the thinning woodlands, and saw they were atop a small hill. Below them lay the village.

It was silent, which the Fiacre chieftain thought odd. Though early, it still should have been bustling with the activity of a new day. His blue eyes carefully scanned the settlement, and then he saw it. In the center of the village square. A large farm cart piled high with bodies. A shudder shook his large frame. Had they been betrayed? Were the bodies those of the villagers? He backed his horse up to where Petruso, Lara and Liam awaited him.

"There is a wagon in the square filled with dead," he told them.

Petruso grew pale. He pointed to himself several times vigorously.

Vartan understood, and shook his head. "I don't know. Have we been betrayed? And if so, by whom?"

"Nay!" Lara said suddenly. "Ethne told me to fight well this day, but then she qualified it by saying, if need be. When I asked her what she meant she said I should see. We must go into the village at once!

I think Petruso's people, made brave by the songs of the Devyn last night, have slain their captors. They hide now, awaiting the arrival of their saviors, but still in fear of the mercenaries."

Vartan nodded. "She is right," he agreed. He raised his hand to signal his troops. "Forward!" he called to them, and, his wife at his side, led the forces of the Fiacre down the hill into the village.

Petruso was off his mount almost immediately. He ran to the cart, examined its contents, and then began to laugh, waving his sword into the air with glee.

"People of the village," Vartan called out, "your lord Petruso has come home to free you. This day you shall rejoice! Come forth, and welcome your lord home!"

For the longest moment all was quiet, and then a door opened, and another, and another as the people of the village poured forth to greet their saviors. Petruso began to weep both with happiness and with sadness as they came forth. The villagers were as gaunt as wraiths, their cheeks hollow, their eyes sorrowful, but they stumbled from their dwellings crying joyfully, surrounding Petruso, touching him, kissing his hands.

"Where is the Devyn bard?" Vartan called over the noisy greetings.

"Here, my lord." A tall, slender man, a harp upon his back, came forward. "I am Adrik of the Devyn," he said, bowing politely to the lord of the Fiacre.

"What happened here?" Vartan asked.

"I came as I was instructed. The Hetarians were surprised to see me until I explained I was a bard, a singer of songs, a teller of tales who traveled the Outlands. As they seem to have a similar tradition, they were not suspicious of me. I suggested they allow me to perform for their workers, pretending I thought all here was as it should be. They agreed, and a great fire was made, and set ablaze in the village square. The workers crowded about the fences penning them in. The mercenaries came with the women of the village, making a great show of fondling and kissing them before their husbands and sons, who were helpless to do anything other than look away. And so I first explained to the Hetarians each song I would sing before I sang it. Then I would sing in our ancient language not the song, but the message we had agreed upon. I warned the listeners not to reveal their joy before their captors, lest the mercenaries realize I was not telling them ancient tales of the Outlands. And while I sang the faeries whispered in the ears of the leaders the names of the traitors so that they might kill them.

"In the night the village men broke out of their enclosure quietly, killing any mercenary in their path. They entered their houses one by one and killed the intruders there. When they reached the cottage where I was housed, I explained to them that one must be left alive to drive the cart of dead bodies from each village back to the City as a warning. And so one mercenary in that last cottage was spared. They have imprisoned him in the cellar." Adrik the Devyn bard bowed with the conclusion of his tale.

Petruso's eyes shone with pride at the story. He tried to speak, but only grunts and garbled sounds emerged. He wept with his frustration.

Lara laid a comforting hand upon his shoulder. "I believe I know what you would say, my lord. Will you permit me to speak for you?"

Petruso nodded eagerly and, taking Lara's hands in his, kissed them in thanks.

"Be silent," Vartan's voice boomed. "Lara, daughter of Swiftsword, wife to Vartan, chief of the Fiacre, will speak to you in the lord Petruso's name. Heed her voice!" His fierce glance swept the square, and all its inhabitants.

Seated upon her stallion, Dasras, Lara look out over the crowd, and began to speak. "Lord Petruso would have you know how glad he is to be among you again. He regrets the sorrow you were caused by being told of his death. This lie was perpetrated by his pursuers who, when they could not capture him, deceived their masters rather than admit the truth. It has been to our advantage that they did, however, for in their arrogance the enemy posted no sentries.

"He escaped with Lord Imre of the Tormod and several others, in order to reach the Gathering that they might gain the aid of their fellow clan families. And so we have come. The Fiacre, the Aghy, the Blathma, the Felan, the Gitta and the Devyn are all here to free the Piaras and the Tormod. To force Hetar to honor the treaty signed so long ago between us. We will not relent until the mercenaries are sent from our lands, never to return." Lara looked to Petruso as Dasras moved restlessly beneath her.

The lord of the Piaras nodded, and then he kissed Lara's hands again.

She smiled a radiant smile at him, and then turned to her husband. "Will you tell them of our plans, my lord?"

"As we stand here in your village square," Vartan's voice boomed, "the other villages in the Tormod and Piaras are now being retaken, but for two. That is why no mercenary can be allowed to escape. Tomorrow we will strike at Fulksburg, the lord Imre's own village, to take it back. Restore your lives as best you can. Where is your headman? He must regain his position as we need to move on to Fulksburg."

"The headman was killed by the mercenaries," a voice in the crowd said.

"Then it is your duty to choose another before the sun sets," Vartan counseled them. "Your village cannot remain without a governor. We leave you now, for we take Fulksburg tomorrow." He turned to Petruso. "Will you remain?"

The chief of the Piaras shook his head vigorously in the negative.

Vartan smiled. "I thought not. You would be with us to the end, eh, Petruso?" And Vartan laughed heartily. "If I were you I would want to be here, too."

They rode on now, following the trail on the map marked with their clan color, arriving at the Singing Caves by early afternoon. The caves were so named for when the winds swept through them it sounded as if a choir was singing, the winds from different directions each sounding quite different. The other clan families were already awaiting them, and all had the same tale to tell. The villages they had been assigned to storm had either already been retaken by their inhabitants, made brave by the knowledge the Devyn imparted, or the villages had risen up in revolt when their saviors had entered them ready for battle. There had been no deaths among any of the clan families, but there were minor injuries.

Imre's own village, Fulksburg, would not be so easy, for it was larger, as was Quartum, Petruso's home village.

"Which is the softer target?" Vartan asked Imre and Petruso as they sat in council after the evening meal. "We have been fortunate so far, but such luck cannot last. I do not believe we can take two more days in this endeavor. We cannot be sure that none escaped the villages retaken today to warn these last two targets. They must both be dealt with on the morrow, my lords."

"I agree!" Roan of the Aghy said. "Let us split our forces. Half will attack Fulksburg, and half Quartum."

"Quartum is more a market town," said Accius of the Devyn. "Both Piaras and Tormod trade there. Its only mine is one that has always yielded us exquisite gems." He turned to Imre. "What think you? Is it an easier target than Fulksburg?"

"Perhaps, and perhaps not," Imre said slowly. He looked to Vartan. "It has more streets than Fulksburg, and those streets wind."

Vartan's next question was for Accius. "We will march early, but what we do must be based upon more knowledge than we have. Can your people scout the two villages, and meet us along our route?"

"I shall dispatch them immediately," Accius replied. "Some of us have an ability that others do not. We can see in the dark. It is an inheritance from a faerie ancestor long ago. I shall gather my night seekers, and send them out."

Vartan said, "If we must split our forces, Roan of the Aghy will lead the Blathma and the Gitta. I will ride with the Felan and the Devyn. Will that suit you all?" He gazed about the circle where they all sat, and his companions nodded again. "Then it is settled. Accius, at first light your scouts must meet us at the crossroads where the road divides the paths for Fulksburg and Quartum. It is then we will decide if we fight as one force, or as two."

The council dispersed, each chieftain returning to his own clan family. Lara watched as several Devyn warriors slipped from the caves. She sat quietly as the fires burned down to small flames and hot coals. The caves sang the softest lullaby as the winds from the west were light. Tomorrow there would be a battle, and she would be in the thick of it. Her belly roiled with the certainty. Should she be afraid, she wondered? Aye! Only a fool would not be afraid. But that fear would not keep her from doing what must be done.

She had always loved her homeland. She had always been proud of Hetar, its laws, its civility, its order. To be Hetarian was to be the best. Now she realized it was but a counterfeit hiding the deceit and rot that was growing within Hetar's heart and soul. A sanctimonious hypocrisy that would spread like a virulent contagion into the Outlands if they did not stop it now. But could they? It would be but a temporary accomplishment. If Hetar wanted the Outlands, if they *needed* them, they would come again—and next time they would send the Crusader Knights, for they would consider the safety of Hetar now at stake. If Hetar wanted these lands they would tell whatever lies they needed to in order to rouse the people, and bring them beneath the banner of war. It had been a very long time since Hetar had fought a real war. But the carts of bodies would be held up to prove the savagery and lawlessness of the Outlanders. The mercenary ranks would once again be filled with innocents eager to share in the glory this war would bring to Hetar. Lara shivered.

"What is it?" Vartan said, coming to sit by her side.

"I am seeing the future," she told him. "It is terrifying. This little war we fight is but a temporary solution. Hetar will come again, I fear."

"Then what can we do?" he asked her. Sometimes Vartan's innocence was endearing, but at other times she worried over it.

"Just what we are doing," Lara answered him. "There is no other way."

"What will happen in the end?" he said.

"I don't know," Lara replied. "Perhaps a new world will come of this all. I just don't know, my husband."

"Come to bed," he said. "You must rest, if only a little." He stood up, drawing her with him, and when they lay together beneath the fur coverlet he put his arms about her.

"That is nice," Lara said, and suddenly weary beyond all she slept in his embrace.

In the misty predawn hour they rode forth from the Singing Caves. The air was now completely still, and oddly warm for late autumn. They came out of the Forest, and traveled along a hard-packed wide dirt road. At the crossroads they were met by the Devyn scouts who had gone out the night before. The news was both good and bad.

Accius listened to his men, and then he said, "The Hetarians have deserted Quartum, and joined with their fellows at Fulksburg. Obviously one or more escaped from the other villages and hurried to warn the mercenaries in those two villages. It was decided that Quartum with its narrow streets was too dangerous a place to be caught, and so they have decided to make a stand at Fulksburg."

"They may have sent someone to the City as well," Lara said. "Our victory today must be a decisive one, my lords. They may even come out to meet us."

"So much the better," Vartan declared. He turned to face the assembled clansmen. "We fight as one, brothers and sisters! Quartum has been deserted, and the Hetarians await us at Fulksburg!"

A great cheer arose as weapons were raised, and the horses danced and snorted nervously at the noise.

Dasras turned his head and spoke to Lara. "I will protect you as best I can, mistress. Concentrate on using Andraste, and leave me to guide myself. I will keep us from danger best that way."

"You may have your head," Lara answered him, "and I thank you." She reached down to touch her crystal.

Fight well, Lara. You will be protected, she heard Ethne say.

They moved out along the road to Fulksburg, and the skies turned bright blue above them. As the sun crept over the horizon, Lara wondered how many of them would live to see the sunset. And then on the flat mountain plain ahead of them they saw the Hetarian mercenaries awaiting them. The Outlanders stopped. Their ranks opened, and the carts from the five retaken villages, piled high with the dead and driven by a single survivor from each particular village, rumbled forth to be displayed to the enemy in hopes of disheartening them. A groan arose from the mercenary ranks.

Then a single man rode forth from the Hetarian forces. He drew his horse to a halt halfway between the warring parties and waited.

Without hesitation Vartan rode out to meet him. When he had reached the mercenary he said, "I am Vartan, lord of the Fiacre."

"I am Odar of the Mercenary Guild. I have come to offer a truce."

Vartan laughed. "You offer us a truce? There can be no truce. You invaded the Outlands in defiance of an ancient treaty that has kept the peace between our peoples for centuries. You enslaved the Tormod and the Piaras. You have committed murder and rapine. Now we have come to take back what is ours. We have already regained all the villages but this one. Now we will regain Fulksburg, and because we are not the savages you seem to believe, we will return your bodies to your masters in the City as a warning to keep to the treaty in future."

"I propose a solution to a battle," Odar said. "We will each send a champion out, and whichever wins shall gain these territories. Your people shall not be slain nor shall ours. Just one man from each side, and the matter will be settled."

Again Vartan laughed. "You obviously do not understand, Odar of the Mercenary Guild. We will not cede one inch of our lands to Hetar. Not now. Not ever! Return to your troops, and say a prayer to the Celestial Actuary that you will die well this day." Then the lord of the Fiacre turned his horse about, and rejoined his fellow clansmen.

"What did they want?" Lara asked anxiously when her husband rode up next to her. She had to let Vartan rule, but he did not know Hetar as she did.

"First they offered a truce, and when I refused they suggested one man from each side fight it out, and winner take all," Vartan said.

"No!" Roan half shouted.

"I told them no. That we would not give up any of our lands," Vartan explained. "Prepare the troops. We are ready for battle. Lara, you and Noss must remain behind here on this little rise. I know your willingness to fight, but I want you safe."

"No," she said quietly, and Andraste began to vibrate against her back. "I am protected, and not afraid now. If you force me to stay, Vartan, I will leave you. What transpires today is part of my destiny. A most important part. You must trust to that."

He closed his eyes for a long moment. Then opening them he nodded. "Very well, Lara. I swore to you that I should never stand in the way of your destiny, and I will keep my promise even though I am afraid for you."

"Do not be, Vartan! I swear to you that I am better protected than any here today. I will see today's sunset, and tomorrow's sunrise as well." *Ethne, help me,* she called out in her mind. *Help me to take his fear away else he be killed in his concern for me.*

Put your hand on his forehead just for a moment, Ethne replied. *You alone are capable of removing his fears. The magic in you grows stronger with each passing day.*

Lara reached out, and placed a hand against her husband's forehead. "You will not fear for me, Vartan. You will know I am protected and worry only about yourself," she told him quietly.

To his complete surprise Vartan suddenly felt the weight that had sat upon him rise up and disappear. His mouth dropped open with amazement.

Lara laughed softly. "It is time, my lord," she said.

"What did you do?" he demanded of her.

"I banished your fears, my lord, did I not?" she replied.

"Aye, most thoroughly," he admitted.

"Can you do the same for me, lady?" Roan of the Aghy asked her with a grin.

"I do not have to for you are fearless, my lord," Lara returned with a small smile. "Like me, you love no one—except perhaps yourself," she amended.

He laughed aloud, and then the battle horns began to sound from the enemy side.

"Lead the second charge," Vartan ordered Roan, who nodded.

And then the battle for the Outlands began in earnest as the armies from both sides charged each other. The thunder of horses' hooves arose into the morning air. The clash of weapons quickly mingled with the cries of the wounded and dying. The Outlanders were ruthless in their pursuit of the Hetarians. Soon the battlefield ran red with blood, and it was difficult not to slip or fall. Steam from both animal and human ascended from sweating bodies. Noss and several of the other archers remained on the rise, their deadly arrows singing in the morning air as they sought and found the invaders, easily slaying them.

As the Hetarians began to fall in greater numbers it became easier to fight on foot. Lara slipped from Dasras, and with him at her back she fought off the mercenaries who, seeing she was a female, thought her easy prey. And with each soldier who engaged Lara, Andraste began to sing louder and louder, sending terror into the hearts of those who would die that day.

"I am Andraste," the sword sang in its rich voice, "and I drink the blood of the unjust, the blood of the invader, the blood of the wicked!"

Lara felt strangely exhilarated as she fought. How odd, the thought twisted through her consciousness, that a girl meant for passion and pleasure should become a warrior. But then suddenly a man engaged her in battle, and to her shock she recognized him, although he did not at first recognize her. With deliberate fierceness she forced him to his knees. He struggled to arise, but could not, and she saw the terror in his eyes as he realized he was but a hair's breadth away from death.

"Yield to me, Wilmot, son of Mistress Mildred," Lara cried. "Yield to me, and live! Continue to fight, and despite my love for your mother I will slay you."

The man's sword blade fell away from Andraste. "Who are you that you know my name?" he asked her, confused.

"I am Lara, daughter of John Swiftsword," she answered him.

Surprise lit his face. His sword dropped from his hand. He didn't know if he believed her, but he could fight no more. "I yield," he said wearily as around him the last of the Hetarians met their just fate, and the battlefield grew silent.

She took a strip of leather from her saddle, and bound his hands before him. Then mounting Dasras, she led him through the battlefield and up the small rise that the Outlanders had held at the beginning of the engagement. The survivors were even now gathering there.

"Well at least one of us thought to save a Hetarian to drive the last wagon," Roan chortled. He was covered with dirt, and sweat and blood, and had a rather nasty gash on his thigh that had cut through his leather trousers.

"Who is he?" Vartan said.

"No one of importance, I'll wager," Rendor of the Felan remarked scornfully.

"His name is Wilmot, and he is the son of the woman whose hovel was next to my father's. Mistress Mildred was my grandmother's friend, and she was always good to me. When I recognized him I spared his life for her sake, for she has no one else. They would give his hovel to another leaving her homeless," Lara explained. "In Hetar if you have no family and no means, there is no provision made for you. The elderly are considered to have outlived their usefulness which is why they must rely upon their family to survive," Lara replied. "If you cannot contribute to society you are deemed worthless. It is their way, Vartan."

"It is a poor reward for those who have given what they could," her husband said, looking to Wilmot. "When you return to the City, mercenary, tell your mother of my wife's kindness. And tell her should you die and leave her destitute, Mistress Mildred will be welcomed by the Fiacre clan, and in Vartan's house. There is always a place by the fire for the old ones among us." He turned away from the prisoner. "How many of our own have we lost?" he asked his fellow chieftains.

"Surprisingly few," Roan answered. "Seven from among my people, five each from the Felan and the Gitta. The Blathma are either incredibly fortunate, or better fighters than I had thought, for they have lost only two, and Floren has not a mark on him although I am told he broke two swords in his enthusiasm."

"Blood is an excellent fertilizer," Floren said calmly.

"Four of the Fiacre are lost, and Noss sustained a small wound when her bow string broke," Vartan said. "Accius?"

"Only one of our people," Accius replied. "We may be poets, but our swordsmen are the finest in the Outlands. Blades and verse are our twin passions," he chuckled.

"Imre and Petruso? They have survived?" Vartan asked, looking about.

"We have," Imre replied. "We are anxious to go into Fulksburg, and tell the people that we have prevailed. And Quartum must be notified as well."

"You two go ahead," Vartan suggested. "We must load at least two more wagons, and they must begin their journey today back to the City. The sooner the High Council receives our message, the better it will be for us all."

Imre and Petruso rode toward the village, and the clansmen began to fill first one cart, and then another with the dead bodies. All weapons, leather breastplates and helmets, however, were removed from the bodies. They would be divided among the victors. Wilmot sat stunned as he watched the activity going on around him. He was still very frightened, and couldn't believe he would really escape these Outlanders unharmed. He began to weep softly in his fear and relief.

Seeing it, Lara dismounted Dasras, and came to sit next to him. "You need have no fear, Wilmot. You are safe now. Are you thirsty or hungry?"

"Nay." Wilmot was silent for a short moment, and then he burst out, "How came you to be among these barbarians, Lara, daughter of Sir John Swiftsword? Were you not meant for a great Pleasure House in the City? That was the rumor."

"Rumors are not always truth," Lara said to him. "The Head Mistress of the Guild of Pleasure Women told Gaius Prospero that I was too beautiful, and she would not permit me to be sold into any of the City's Pleasure Houses. That I was already causing much dissension by the very possibility I might soon be a Pleasure Woman. So I was sent from the City with the Taubyl Trader, Rolf Fairplay," Lara began. And then she continued on, explaining her stay with the Forest Lords, how she had escaped them, her sojourn with the Shadow Princes and her arrival in the Outlands. She did not, however, mention her faerie mother or the relationship they now had. "And I discovered that these people are nothing like it is said in the City," Lara told Wilmot. "They simply prefer a less complicated way of life. They are orderly, and live by their own laws."

"But how do they live?" he asked. "We were always told they were bandits and thieves who preyed on travelers."

Lara laughed. "The Fiacre, the largest of the clan families, raise cattle. The Aghy, horses. The Felan, sheep. The Blathma and the Gitta are farmers. The Devyn are poets and bards. The two clan families whose lands you invaded are miners of ore and gems. They trade back and forth amongst each other, taking only what they need from the land, and restoring the land where it is necessary. Did you not see the beauty of the countryside before your greedy masters began destroying it? Do you not know why the Piaras and the Tormod were invaded? Gaius Prospero, the Master of the Merchants was behind it."

"We were told these people violated Hetar's borders, raping and killing innocents," Wilmot said. "Confiscating their lands was to be their punishment, and by expanding our own borders we would protect Hetar."

Lara shook her head. "Wilmot, these clan families live in peace, each within its own borders, meeting only once yearly at a time called the Gathering. The only roads in the Outlands are here in the mountains. They have been made so the carts from the mines might traverse the land easily. Are you aware that when the clan chieftain of the Piaras protested Hetar's invasion they cut his tongue out? That the women of the villages have been used as Pleasure Women? Their young daughters saved for those among you who lead? Is this our vaunted Hetarian civilization and justice, Wilmot?"

He looked at her, both sadness and confusion in his gaze. "I have known you all your life until you left us, Lara, daughter of Sir John Swiftsword," he finally said. "I did not know you for a liar, but what you say is so hard for me to comprehend."

"When you came into these mountains, Wilmot, were you attacked? No. Your mercenary force swept down on the surprised villages, capturing them and forcing the people into bondage. Did you find the village in which you stayed barbaric or rough? Were those people savage to your eye? Or were they civilized, their homes far better than the hovels in the Quarter you and I have known?"

"I will admit to being surprised," Wilmot said, "but when I remarked on it my captain said it was because they had stolen the furnishings from Hetarian homes. Yet I had never seen their like before, neither in the Quarter nor the marketplaces."

"Because your captain lied, Wilmot. Perhaps he did not know, and said what he believed to be true," Lara said. "But all you have been told of the Outlands is untrue."

"And you came here of your own free will?" he asked her.

"I did, along with the young daughter of another mercenary who was sold into slavery. Her name is Noss, and she was the archer who remained here on the rise shooting with such great skill at your mercenaries. Her husband would not permit her to enter the heart of the fray," Lara said.

"The Outlanders accepted you readily?" he asked her.

"They did. And the clan lord of the Fiacre made me his wife," she told Wilmot.

"Where did you learn to fight as you did today?" he inquired.

"I was taught by the Shadow Princes. They say I have a destiny," Lara answered.

He nodded. "I think they must be right." Then pausing a brief moment he said to her, "What will happen to me now, Lara, daughter of Sir John Swiftsword?"

"We have allowed a survivor from each village we took," Lara explained. "You are to drive the carts of bodies back to the City. This is our message to the High Council. They must abide by the ancient treaties. We will not allow our lands to be invaded by Hetar. If they understand this, the peace between us will be restored. You must tell the High Council that the Outlanders are not barbarians. They simply wish to be left alone in peace as it has always been."

"The High Council? How could I gain their ear? I am a mercenary, and not even one of rank," he said.

"Two of the provinces voted against breaking the peace," Lara told him. "Seek out the Coastal Kings or the Shadow Princes," she advised.

He looked surprised. "How can you know this?"

Lara smiled wickedly. "We have friends," she replied. "Tell whoever you speak with that Lara, daughter of Sir John Swiftsword and wife of Vartan, Lord of the Fiacre, sent you. They will hear you out. Gaius Prospero cannot be allowed to use the council to his own advantage ever again."

"Shall I attempt to speak with your father?" Wilmot asked her.

"Tell him I am well, and happy," Lara responded. Would he care, she wondered? "And tell your mother I send her my regards. I hope she is well."

"She misses your family," he admitted. "You and your brother in particular. She will be happy to learn that all has turned out well for you."

Vartan joined them. "It is time," he said to Wilmot. "Some of us will escort you to the border separating the Outlands and Hetar. You must reach the City, and there may be those who for their own purposes seek to stop you, or even take your life, Wilmot. For the sake of your people the truth must be known, and spread throughout Hetar."

"My lord, I am frankly fearful for my life now," Wilmot said. "Gaius Prospero is a powerful man. If he would engineer a war with the Outlands, then it is likely there will be war. There was a rumor in the City before we left, softly spoken, but heard by many ears, that Gaius Prospero would be called upon by the High Council to become emperor of Hetar. For the first time in memory life has grown difficult for Hetar. When times are difficult, the people clamor for change in hopes that change will bring prosperity once again."

"If what you say is so," Lara noted, "then you will be safe, for Gaius Prospero will use the seven wagons of dead to his own advantage."

"Yet we have no choice but to send them," Vartan replied.

"I know," Lara responded.

The five survivors from the other villages were now led forth, and boosted up on their wagon seats, Wilmot climbing into the first wagon. They moved off, horsemen of the Aghy riding on either side of the wagons. The Winter War was over. Once Imre and Petruso were settled in their fiefdoms again; once the other clan families had donated supplies to get them on through the winter, life could again return to what it had been before Hetar had been foolish enough to invade the Piaras and the Tormod. Yet why, Lara thought silently to herself, did she sense that this was but the beginning?

Chapter 17

GAIUS PROSPERO, a perfumed handkerchief pressed to his nose, stared unbelieving at the seven reeking carts piled high with their dead. The stench was unbelievable, and he wondered that the drivers of these horrific wagons could stand it. But they sat stoic and unmoving upon the benches of their transports, hollow-eyed and gaunt and staring at him as if he were responsible.

"Why have you brought your burdens to me?" he demanded aloud.

"Because we were told to bring them to you, my lord," the man on the first wagon spoke up. "Actually, we thought to drive them up to the door of your fine home, but the guards would not allow us inside. They sent for you instead."

"How could this have happened?" Gaius Prospero said as if to himself. "They are uncivilized barbarians. They are not even united under one government, but live a tribal life. They are savages! Bandits!"

Wilmot held his tongue as he listened to the Master of the Merchants' ruminations. He was good at holding his tongue. It aided in his survival all these years. But he had been in the Outlands long enough to learn that while the society there was different from that of Hetar, it was not the uncivilized place the government wanted them to believe it was. He wondered if the Outlands were not perhaps more civilized than Hetar in a way.

"How did this happen?" Gaius Prospero demanded to know.

"The armies of the Outlands overcame us, and obviously knowing they were coming the villagers rose up against us,"Wilmot said succinctly. The other men nodded in their agreement. What else was there to say?

"And why did you six survive?" was Gaius Prospero's next query.

"It was decided beforehand to spare one man from each village to drive the wagons,"Wilmot answered.

"There were seven villages, and there are seven carts," the Master of the Merchants noted sharply. "Why are there but six of you?"

"The mercenaries from Quartum joined those at Fulksburg to make a stand. One man from the other villages had escaped the Outlanders, and had come to warn us,"Wilmot reported. "They were too many for us. They fight well. All were slain but me."

"Because you were the best of the mercenary fighters?" Gaius Prospero said sarcastically, rolling his eyes in disbelief.

"I have fought in the ranks of the mercenaries for over thirty years, my lord, but I was spared because the last warrior I fought in combat that day was someone known to me. That is why I survived at Fulksburg,"Wilmot said in hard tones.

"Who could you possibly have known among the Outlander warriors?" Gaius Prospero demanded in a suspicious voice. "How could an ordinary mercenary know someone with that kind of authority? Give me his name!"

"It was the wife of the army's general who spared me, my lord," Wilmot replied. He was frankly enjoying having this man who would be emperor squeeze the information from him bit by bit. His conversation with Lara had opened his eyes to things he had been avoiding for several years now.

"You fought with a woman? And lost?" Gaius Prospero's tone was derisive.

"The wife of Lord Vartan is a great warrior, my lord. There were enough woman warriors among the Outlanders to be noticed.

They are fiercer than their men, who are the best fighters I have ever encountered," Wilmot said.

"And how came you to know the wife of this lord?" the Master of the Merchants asked. "Was she one of those used as a Pleasure Woman by our forces?"

"Nay, my lord." Wilmot forced his face to remain impassive.

"Then who was she?" Gaius Prospero almost shouted.

"She is Lara, daughter of Sir John Swiftsword, my lord," Wilmot said. "Her family lived next to mine when she was growing up. Recognizing me, she spared me for my mother's sake. My mother and her grandmother were good friends, and my mother was always kind to the family." He was curious to see what Gaius Prospero would say now. He waited.

"What?" The look on Gaius Prospero's face was a study in amazement. "You are mistaken. You must be! My cousin the Taubyl Trader sold her to the Head Forester for a Pleasure Woman. Though they do not as a rule cohabit with those not of their blood, he was so taken with her beauty he could not resist, my cousin said. The Forester paid a fortune for her."

"She escaped the Forest Lords," Wilmot said, "with the aid of a Forest giant. They fled to the Desert, and from there Lara went to the Outlands where Lord Vartan saw her, and wed her. She is greatly respected among the Outlanders."

"And she is a great warrior? How did such an exquisite creature meant only for pleasure and passion become a warrior?" Gaius Prospero wondered aloud.

"The Shadow Princes gave her the skills, along with a sword that sings as she fights," Wilmot told him. "She is a power now to be reckoned with, my lord."

The Master of the Merchants considered a moment, and then he said, "The High Council must be convened at once to decide upon the disposal of these bodies. Take your carts to the edge of the City, and wait for our instructions." Then turning away from Wilmot and his companions, Gaius Prospero hurried back into the safety of the Golden District. A waiting cart took him back to his home. Entering it, he called for his secretary, Jonah, and told him of the conversation he had just had.

"You must not allow this fellow to speak with the High Council, my lord," Jonah said. "There are those among them who did not approve this little expedition into the Outlands. These carts of dead will become a platform for them to use against you. You must take the advantage while you can."

"But how?" Gaius Prospero said.

"By publicly disseminating the fact that our good men are dead. Slaughtered by a barbarian force who grow stronger each day, and may soon be bold enough to attack Hetar itself, threatening the very foundations of our world. We will shout down anyone who attempts to declare it is our fault for invading the Outlands in the first place. Soon the real truth will be forgotten, and with time and repetition the tale we choose will become the real truth. We will rouse the people against the Outlands, and those who have stood against us in the High Council will be silenced. They will have to join us in our fight, or be declared traitors to Hetar." Jonah smiled a cold smile.

"There is much acreage in the Outlands for the taking," Gaius Prospero considered slowly. "And their mines have brought us incredible wealth in these last few months. I am sorry to lose them, even temporarily."

"And the Outlanders are strong, my lord. You can build your own private army with some by allowing them to retain their own properties within their villages. The rest of them will fill the slave markets of Hetar, making labor cheaper, and our profits greater." Jonah chuckled. The more powerful Gaius Prospero became, the more powerful he became. The richer his master became, the richer he was. He had already purchased his own freedom from the Master of the Merchants while agreeing to remain with him. If the impossible dream could be gained, and Gaius Prospero became Hetar's emperor, Jonah knew he could convince his master to make him his prime minister. And he would gain a lordship. He had already chosen a motto for himself: Make Haste Slowly. He forced the smile back from his lips. "What of Lara?" he asked. "Would she not make you a magnificent empress, my lord?" Jonah did not like the lady Vilia, whose eye was too sharp. The lady Vilia was far more intelligent than her husband, and could not be manipulated as could Gaius Prospero. She would have to be put aside when their plans came to fruition.

The Master of the Merchants' eyes glowed. "You know how difficult it was for me to let her go, don't you, Jonah? You are the only one who knows that. How very much I wanted her. I watched her in the bath through my peephole as Tania bathed her. Had her virginity combined with her beauty not made her such a valuable commodity, I should have taken her before I sold her. If her exquisite faerie beauty has not been destroyed she will make me a perfect empress when the time comes."

"Women like that but grow better with each passing day, my lord," Jonah soothed his master, encouraging the fantasy. But he wondered about the truth of her warrior's skills. If it were true, would she not prove a dangerous opponent? Lara, in their brief acquaintance, had showed him an intelligence rarely found in women. If it were now combined with faerie magic, she could prove deadly. But let Gaius Prospero have his dream. There were other beautiful women with whom to tempt the Master of the Merchants when the right moment came. First things first, and the first thing was to deflect the blame for the loss of the mercenary force sent into the Outlands.

But Jonah was not quite as quick as he should have been with his scheming. Wilmot had driven his cart through the City, his companions behind him, until they had passed back through the main gates, and parked their vehicles. Wilmot jumped down from the bench on his wagon. His posterior was numb with soreness. He did not know the men who had traveled with him. They were new to the mercenaries, but he suspected if he gave an order they would obey it. They looked tired and dispirited, easily manipulated.

"Remain here," he said. "I must go quickly to the Quarter and reassure my old mother that I am safe," he told them. They nodded. Two of them were already falling asleep upon their wagons, their heads nodding in weariness.

Hurrying back through the main City gates Wilmot made his way to the small Council Quarter. Like all the other exclusive quarters it was gated and guarded. Wilmot sighed. He knew his appearance would count against him with the guards, but then he recognized one of the men at the entry, an elderly mercenary no longer fit for serious fighting who had managed to obtain duty as a guardsmen. Walking up to him, he greeted the old man.

"Sim! It is Wilmot. I have just returned from the Outlands."

"I recognize you," Sim responded, and the two men shook hands. "I heard it ended badly. Well, it would have, wouldn't it?"

"Aye, it ended worse than badly," Wilmot said. "Listen, I must see one of the council. A Shadow Prince, or a Coastal King. It makes no difference, but I have a message for them from the Outlands and there are some who would stop me."

"Is this treason?" Sim said low. "I'll have no part of treason, Wilmot."

"It isn't treason, I swear it!" Wilmot said. "The Shadow Princes and the Coastal Kings voted against the incursion last year. Gaius Prospero was council head then, and his vote tipped the balance that led to the troubles. Every man but the six of us saved to drive the death carts died because of the greed some of our leaders encouraged, Sim. My message comes to those who advised peace from those who would have the ancient treaties restored. If that is treason I will fall on my own sword for wanting it."

"Prince Lothair is in right now," Sim said softly. "His apartment is in the rear of the building on the top floor overlooking the gardens. Go!" And the old guardsman deliberately turned his head away so that he did not see Wilmot enter the residence where the council members lived.

The mercenary was very nervous, more so even than prior to battle. He had never seen a Shadow Prince before, let alone met one. He climbed the stairs to the top of the building, and knocked upon the door. It opened immediately, and he was ushered into Prince Lothair's presence by a rather ordinary-looking manservant. Wilmot bowed most politely to the prince, who was garbed in shimmering dark silk robes.

"What message does Lara send me?" he asked Wilmot.

The mercenary's mouth fell open with his surprise, but then he closed it. These men from the Desert were magic. Everyone knew that. "My lord, you know that Hetar entered the Outlands late last year. Our mercenary forces were told to put the native population beneath their heel for they had raided Hetar beyond their borders, killing, looting and raping. We were to make all able-bodied males toil in the mines for us. The ores and the gems were to be sent back to the City. The elderly among the barbarians were to be slain. The woman and children, ours to do with as we chose. Those who sent us lied, my lord prince."

"Yes, I know," Lothair said quietly.

"When the other lords of the Outlands learned of this incursion into their lands they came, and they slew all but six of us. We were sent back to the City driving carts filled with our dead. We were to take them to Gaius Prospero, and we did. He ordered us back outside the gates while a council is called to decide what to do.

"My life was spared by Lara, daughter of Sir John Swiftsword and now wife to Vartan, lord of the Fiacre," Wilmot continued. "I knew her as a child, and she spared me, she said, for the sake of my elderly mother. The lords in the Outlands send this message to the High Council. Restore the ancient treaty between our two lands and there will be peace between us as there was before this incursion. They have repaid in kind the suffering that the Piaras and Tormod clan families endured during this illegal and unjust occupation. You and your allies on the High Council are warned to beware Gaius Prospero, and his ambitions." Wilmot bowed again. "That is all, my lord prince." He started to back out of the room, but Lothair raised a hand.

"Nay, remain, Wilmot. You must come with me to the High Council, and repeat to my fellow councilors what you have told me," the Shadow Prince said.

"Gaius Prospero will have me slain for it, my lord," Wilmot said. "I will be called traitor, and my mother will be sent from our hovel to wander homeless and helpless."

"Did not Lara offer your mother sanctuary, Wilmot?"

"How...how did you know that, my lord prince?" The mercenary was astounded.

Lothair smiled, but did not answer. "I can see your mother is taken to safety, Wilmot. Today. Within the hour. Then you will be free to speak the truth before the council. Will you trust me?"

"How do you know Lara?" Wilmot asked.

"I am he who taught her to fight," Lothair said with a small smile.

"I trust you then, my lord prince," the mercenary replied. "She fought with skill, and with great honor." He shook his head wonderingly. "I would never have thought a girl so fair would become so fierce. Yet she is more beautiful than when I last saw her before she left the City over two years ago."

"Ferocity is a quality that can apply to both pleasure and battle," Prince Lothair replied. "Now sit down, and I will bring your mother to you." He waved his hand while murmuring several unintelligible words, and there was a flash of light. When it had faded Mistress Mildred stood in the center of the room looking quite confused.

"Mother!" Wilmot was on his feet to reassure her. Then he quickly explained the situation that had saved his life and returned him to the City. "You must go to the Outlands, to Lara, Mother, for your life, both of our lives, will be in danger when I have spoken the truth before the High Council. The Guild of Mercenaries was lied to, not that that would have disturbed our captains, some of whom may have known. We invaded and abused a peaceful people, and we have paid for it with our lives. I must speak the truth, but I cannot until I know you are safe."

"Will they kill you?" Mistress Mildred wanted to know.

"Perhaps," Wilmot said. "Their sole rationale has become profit as the merchants themselves. I know for a fact that a portion of the ores and gems mined in the Outlands was given to our guild in exchange for our service. Once each month we were permitted to take a single small gem for our pay, but the captains took more. They will be loath to have their greed and corruption uncovered, and may well try to have me killed."

"Then I would just as soon die, too, my son. You are all I have," the old lady said. "I do not know these Outlands which are said to be barbaric. Why would Lara welcome me? If she is all you have said, then she is a great lady now. She does not want to be bothered with a homeless old woman, my son. No. I will remain here."

The mercenary looked distraught.

"Perhaps another solution," the prince said. "Would you be content to live in the house of Sir John Swiftsword, Mistress Mildred? You should be in the City, and privy to all the gossip that this national problem will engender. And Wilmot could visit you."

"Well," Mistress Mildred said slowly, "aye, I could be content in the Garden District if they would have me. But perhaps Susanna has become too grand for her old neighbor from the Quarter, my lord."

"I will inquire, mistress, but for now you will remain in the sanctuary of my home with your son," the prince said. He had offered this remedy to calm the old woman, but he had no intention of following through. It was too dangerous for Lara's family.

The door to the chamber where they spoke now opened, and a man, similar in appearance to Prince Lothair, entered. "I heard we had visitors," he said with a smile.

"This is my brother Eskil," Lothair told his guests, and then he introduced Wilmot and Mistress Mildred to his companion prince. "He serves with me on the High Council now." Lothair clapped his hands, and the manservant was immediately there. "Take our guests to their rooms," he instructed the man. "I will see you both for the evening meal. You will be safe here with me." When they had gone, he explained the situation to Eskil.

"Once he has spoken before the High Council they will no longer be safe in the City," Eskil said. "I worry less about Gaius Prospero than I do his secretary, the ubiquitous Jonah. He walks within a cloud of ambition. Gaius Prospero is merely greedy for anything his pudgy beringed fingers can grasp. Gold. Power. Beautiful women. Gemstones. Food. Good wine. Nay, Gaius Prospero doesn't frighten me, but Jonah is a dangerous man."

"But he must move carefully or lose everything," Lothair responded. "We yet have time to put a stop to this expansion, especially now that the Outlanders have given Hetar's forces such a thorough beating. Gaius Prospero will be eager to place blame on anyone but himself for this debacle. It is up to us to see he accepts the responsibility of defeat as well as the profits of success."

"He will go to the people," Eskil said, "and fill their minds with confusion."

"We must reach them with the truth first, and have them place the blame where it belongs—on the thick shoulders of the Master of the Merchants," Lothair suggested with a wry smile.

"We will need help," Eskil said.

"I will call upon Lara's kin, the Forest Faeries," Lothair answered.

"Do not interfere with her destiny, brother," Eskil said.

"I will not," Lothair promised, "but do you want to see an emperor ruling Hetar? An emperor named Gaius Prospero? The faeries will unravel the confusion in the minds of the people that the others will attempt to sow. You know that if the people are vocal enough the High Council will heed them, if only to save themselves. It is only when the people become so tired with the games played by their politicians that men like Gaius Prospero can prevail. We both know that change is coming to Hetar, but the time is not quite right. But if we allow Gaius Prospero to interfere in what must be, who knows what damage he might cause? We must consider all aspects of this situation."

Eskil nodded. "Nonetheless, we must get Wilmot and his mother to safety after he has spoken. I would not put it past our adversary to attempt an assassination in the Garden District. John Swiftsword or a member of his family could be harmed. We cannot have that, Lothair. Either they go to the Outlands, or they come to us in the Desert. There is no other way, and they must understand that."

"Wilmot will, and he will make the decision," Lothair said.

A knock at the door, and a messenger entered bowing. "A meeting of the High Council has been called for this evening, my lords. At the sunset hour."

"We will be there, and our thanks," Lothair replied.

"That was quick," Eskil said when the messenger had departed.

"Go and listen to see if Gaius Prospero knows if Wilmot is missing," Lothair said. "I will call Ilona to gain her help."

Eskil nodded and disappeared into a shadowy form that was quickly gone.

Lothair went to a cabinet and took out a round green crystal. Sitting down, he held the crystal between his hands and said, "Ilona, queen of the Forest, I call on you for your aid. Come to me now."

The room was silent, and then there was a puff of purple smoke, and Ilona was there. "What is it you want, Prince Lothair?"

"Sit, oh queen, and I will tell you," he said.

"Do not dawdle, old friend. Thanos, my mate, frets if I am gone too long, and my son still sucks at my breast."

Lothair quickly sketched out the situation for Ilona, finishing with his request for aid.

"How can I help?"

"You must set the tiniest of your faeries on the shoulders of the people so that when they are told the lies that Gaius Prospero would have them believe, they will not believe. We must keep him from gaining too much power."

"I will honor your request, Lothair. How fares my daughter?" Ilona asked.

"Well, I am told. She is wife to Vartan of the Fiacre. She has become a great warrior, and is respected by his people," Lothair said.

"Has she given him a child?" Ilona asked.

"Not yet, to my knowledge," the prince answered.

"Then she does not love him," the queen of the Forest Faeries said sadly.

"Or she does not believe the time is right for a child," Lothair replied.

"Perhaps," Ilona considered thoughtfully. "She is human as well as faerie. The times are unstable, and Lara has always had excellent instincts. I will go now, Lothair. My faeries will aid you." Then Ilona was gone in another puff of purple smoke.

An amazing creature, the prince thought. And while she had never known her mother until recently, Lara was very much like her. He called his manservant, and gave orders that Wilmot and his mother be fed a good supper. "Tender our regrets, and tell Wilmot I will come for him when it is time."

"Yes, my lord prince," the servant responded.

"And bring me something to eat, and some wine. It will be a long night."

Just before the time came for the meeting of the High Council, Eskil returned.

"Gaius Prospero does not know Wilmot is gone from his cart. He thinks the mercenary a stupid man who will blindly obey. He has spent the last hour arguing with his wife, who does not trust Jonah—knowledge we might use to our advantage," Eskil said with a wicked smile. "The lady Vilia is a power to be reckoned with, I think."

"I think her love for her husband could be her downfall," Lothair noted. "One must be totally ruthless when dealing with a man like Jonah. Ah, Wilmot," he said to the mercenary who had entered the room. "You are well fed, I hope, and your mother settled for the night?"

"Yes, my lord, thank you. I did not tell her that the council meeting was tonight, for she would fret," Wilmot said.

"You must make a choice, and make it now," Lothair said. "After the meeting of the High Council I will transport you both from the City. Your mother's presence in the home of Sir John Swiftsword could endanger him and his family. I will send you to either Vartan's hall in the Outlands, or to my palace in the Desert. You will both be completely safe in either place."

"We will go to your palace, my lord prince. The warm dry air will be good for my mother's old bones, and winter is setting into the Outlands now," Wilmot responded.

Lothair nodded. "Your mother will awaken there, then, and you will go to sleep there this very night," he promised. "It is little enough I can do to repay you for your bravery tonight. Gaius Prospero will, once he is over his shock, attack you, and the story you tell, but we will defend you, Wilmot. He is not head of the High Council right now, only the representative from the Midlands. It is our good fortune that one of the Coastal Kings now sits at the council's head, and two of his brothers are on the council. With luck we may be able to put an end to Gaius Prospero's ambitions, at least for the interim. Come now, we must go. Stand between my brother and me, and we will be transported."

Wilmot put himself between Lothair and Eskil. He wasn't as frightened now as he had been earlier. These were good men, though they might have great magic. But he closed his eyes.

"We are here," Lothair said softly.

Wilmot opened his eyes and gazed with amazement about the council chamber. Never had he thought to see it. The room was round. There were eight carved wooden chairs with high backs set upon a marble dais encircling the room. They were arranged in twos. In the center of the chamber was a round piece of marble upon which a ninth chair had been placed. It swiveled about so that its occupant could face whoever was speaking.

"Feel free to look about you," Lothair murmured. "You are not yet visible to the members of the council, nor will you be until it is time for you to speak. The fellow next to Gaius Prospero is

Squire Dareh, the lord of the Midlands. Next to them are the two Forest Lords now serving in the council. They are Lord Albern and Lord Everard. On the other side of the Foresters are the Coastal Kings, Delphinus and Pelias. The council head is Archeron. Ah, he is here. We will begin."

Wilmot looked down at his hands. He could see them. He pinched his arm, and jumped with the sensation. Unable to help himself, he looked directly at Gaius Prospero and made a face, but while the Master of the Merchants appeared to be looking directly at him, he gave no indication that he had seen Wilmot. He was indeed invisible!

At once Gaius Prospero was on his feet. "I beg to be recognized," he said.

"Sit down, Gaius Prospero," King Archeron said rising. "I have something to say before you begin what will undoubtedly be a lengthy diatribe filled with impassioned rhetoric that in the end will amount to nothing. But as your fellow council members we will be obliged to listen to you. First, however, I will speak in my capacity as current head of this council." He stood waiting as the Master of the Merchants took his seat again. Then he began. "Almost a year ago to this very day, my lords, my fellow kings and the Shadow Princes advised you against a most dangerous course of action. At the urging of the Midlands and the Forest provinces, you chose to break the ancient treaty between Hetar and the Outlands. And you, Gaius Prospero, as then head of this high council, tipped the balance. So Hetar invaded a portion of the Outlands, murdered, raped and enslaved the people you found there. Then you stole from their mines, transporting much wealth back here to the City.

"Today we see the results of our foolishness. Seven carts containing the bodies of every mercenary we sent into the Outlands have been returned to the City. Over five hundred men whose women and children will now be driven from their homes, for the Guild of Mercenaries cares only for the families of those who give it service. What is to happen to these women and children? They must be housed and fed. It is only right as their men gave their lives for Hetar. Did you, Gaius Prospero, consider this when you sent those men into danger for the sake of profit? And where is that profit? It has not filled the public coffers, to my knowledge, or am I mistaken? We will need funds to care for the dispossessed, Gaius Prospero."

The Master of the Merchants jumped to his feet. He was surprisingly agile for a man of his girth and years. "You cannot blame me for this tragedy, King Archeron," he declared. "Put the blame where it belongs. With the barbarians of the Outlands! If they had not begun raiding into Hetar it would not have been necessary to annex some of their territory. Are you suggesting that we should have stood idly by while this happened?"

"The Outlanders never raided into Hetar. You fabricated that tale as an excuse to steal their riches," King Archeron said.

"Do you call me liar then?" Gaius Prospero blustered.

"Yes." The word hung heavy within the council chamber. "Unlike you, Gaius Prospero, who bleat and blow about a people you know not, the Coastal Kings do know the Outlanders. Our land borders that of the Felan clan. They are shepherds, Gaius Prospero, not raiders. They gladly share their beaches and water supply with us, and they trade with us. The other clans raise horses, cattle, grain, vegetables, fruit and flowers. One of the clans is made up of poets and bards. The territories you attempted to annex not so much for Hetar, but for yourself, were that of the mining clans. They took from the earth only what they needed, and they always restored the land in which they worked. You came in and scarred their land while you stole its riches. It will take the mountain clans years to repair the damage you have done."

He turned now to address the rest of the council. "Do you know what was done to the clan families in the Purple Mountains? Their elderly were all slain because it was decided they were not useful, and could not be fed. The men and boys were all put to work in

the mines, and those who could not or would not work were slain
as well. The women and girls were used and abused by the invaders. This kind of behavior is not our way, my lords. Hetar has always been proud of its civility. Now history will remember this
time as a time of dishonor, and all because of one man's greed!"

"My lord king." Prince Lothair had stood up that he might be
granted the right to address the high council.

"Speak, Prince," King Archeron said.

"It is no secret that my brothers and I opposed the invasion of
the Outlands. Today there came to me one of the survivors among
the mercenaries to tell me his story, and bring me a message from
the lords of the Outlands. May he speak?"

"A liar! A coward!" Gaius Prospero cried. "Why else would he
have survived the dreadful massacre that took our brave citizens
from us! Do not listen to his words, my lords! They are false, and
filled with guile."

"Thus spoke the snake," Lothair murmured.

"I would hear what this man has to say," King Archeron said, and
the other council members nodded although some less vigorously
than others.

"Step forward, Wilmot," the prince invited, and the mercenary
was suddenly visible to them all.

"What magic is this?" demanded Squire Dareh of the Midlands.

"The kind, sir, that has kept Wilmot safe from murder," the
prince answered.

"You may speak to us, Wilmot," King Archeron said in a quiet
voice.

"My lords," Wilmot began, "I thank you for hearing me. The reason my few comrades and I survived was that we fought to the
end. We were then chosen to be spared in order to drive these
carts to the City. I bring you a message from the lords of the Outlands. They did not begin this war, but it is their hope that it is
now ended. That the ancient treaty between Hetar and the Outlands can be restored."

"And what of reparations?" Gaius Prospero said angrily.

"They are willing to accept the lives of those they slew as rec-ompense,"Wilmot replied. He struggled to maintain a passive face, for he knew that was not at all what the Master of the Merchants had meant by his question.

Gaius Prospero grew purple in the face. He sputtered, but no words came out.

"This is most generous of the Outlanders in light of the damage done to them," King Archeron said, his blue eyes twinkling. Then he grew serious. "Tell me of the occupation that we understand bet-ter, Wilmot."

"It was hard. All you have spoken is true, my lord. Some of the people went mad with the slaughter of their elders, and so they also were slain. The loveliest of the young girls were imprisoned in the largest house in each village. There our captains lived, and these girls were made their Pleasure Women. Many were virgins. Oth-ers, young wives. The ordinary men were billeted in the village houses. They used the wives and daughters for their pleasure."

"Did you?" King Archeron asked.

Wilmot shook his head. "I could not, my lord. What pleasure is there to be gained from a woman who is not willing? I am too old a soldier to change my ways though I be mocked for it. From the moment we invaded these villages I was wary, my lords. The peo-ple are not savages, but people of dignity. They live simply but well. They are governed by a clan chieftain, and each village has a head-man or headwoman. It is not Hetar, but neither is it uncivilized."

"How is it," King Archeron asked "that you were chosen to be saved?"

"I fought a warrior who spared me, my lord,"Wilmot said.

"A woman! He was beaten by a woman!" Gaius Prospero shrieked.

"A woman?"The Coastal King was intrigued.

"Yes, my lord. Lara, daughter of Sir John Swiftsword, has be-come a great warrior,"Wilmot answered.

"She is a slave, my lord," Albern, the Forest Lord said. "She belonged to Enda, our Head Forester. She murdered his brother, and escaped."

"That is not so," Lothair said. "You have been misinformed. Lara did indeed escape the Forest Lords, and lived among the Shadow Princes for over a year. It was then that Enda and his brother, Durga, came with a false document to attempt to reclaim her in clear violation of Hetarian law. We exposed their deception, and when they attempted to force her to come with them Lara defended herself, resulting in Durga's death. Although we did not have to do so, we repaid Enda the monies he had used to purchase Lara, and we paid a bounty for Durga's death. The Forest Lords have no claim on her."

"This warrior woman spared you, Wilmot. Why?" Archeron asked.

"Her father was once a mercenary. His hovel was next to that of my mother and me. I knew her all her life until she was sold into slavery so that her father might have his chance at becoming a Crusader Knight. Her sacrifice was not in vain. She spared me for the kindnesses my mother had done her."

Archeron nodded with his understanding. "And she has become a person of importance among the Outlanders?" he asked.

"She is the wife of their most important clan chieftain, my lord. He is Vartan of the Fiacre. Lara is half faerie, my lords, and she has, it appeared to me, gained faerie magic in her time away from Hetar."

"Lothair, what do you know of this?" King Archeron asked.

"She is the daughter of Ilona, queen of the Forest Faeries, and John Swiftsword. She never knew her mother until she was with us. We reunited them, and Ilona has indeed taught her child of magic. It is as much a part of her heritage as her humanity."

"Who taught her to fight?" Archeron probed further.

"I did," Lothair answered him proudly. "I had a sword forged for her and imbued with my own magic. Her mother gave her a staff that possesses a soul. Kaliq, the prince with whom she stayed, gave her a fine horse trained for battle, and a serving girl with a horse. Her destiny and that of Hetar's is entwined, my lords."

"You speak mumbo jumbo," Gaius Prospero sneered. "Lara is beautiful, but not important. What do you mean to do about the Outlands? They have stained their hands with our blood. Our dead cry out for vengeance!"

"The dead cry out for peace," Delphinus of the Coastal Kings said.

"Aye!" Eskil the Shadow Prince agreed. "If the Outlanders are willing to accept a restoration of the treaty then we are wise to accept it."

"You men of the Desert are always eager to avoid danger," the Forest Lord Everard scoffed.

"And you men of the Forest blow hot though you be cold," Lothair said. "You have no secrets that can be hid from the Shadow Princes, my lord. Beware lest I reveal them to Hetar. Do you understand me, my lords Albern and Everard?"

The two Forest Lords grew pale, and were suddenly silent.

Gaius Prospero's ears almost visibly perked. A secret? A secret of such power that it could quiet the most contentious among them? He must remember to tell Jonah. Jonah could learn what was hidden that could frighten the Foresters. Then he would have power over them.

"I think," King Archeron said, "that we have heard all we need to hear. It is my opinion that we accept the most generous terms offered us by the Outlanders. How do each of you vote? Dareh, Squire of the Midlands?"

"Aye—and do not frown at me, Gaius Prospero. This was an ill-advised venture. We cannot afford a full-scale war, at least at this time," the Squire said.

"Gaius Prospero?"

"Nay!" the Master of the Merchants said with ill-disguised anger.

"Albern and Everard of the Forest Lords?"

"We will abstain from the vote, my lord," Albern said, and Everard nodded in agreement.

"Abstain?" Gaius Prospero almost shrieked. "You were eager enough last year."

The two Forest Lords ignored him.

"King Delphinus?"

"Aye!"

"King Pelias?"

"Aye!"

"Prince Eskil?"

"Aye!"

"Prince Lothair?"

"Aye!"

"The vote is five ayes. One nay. And two abstentions. A majority votes that we accept the Outlanders' offer. Now, will you agree to burying our dead with discretion?"

The High Council members all agreed, though Gaius Prospero was reluctant.

"And will you agree that the Guild of Mercenaries must be made to care for the women and children left behind? They cannot force them from the hovels, or deny them a daily ration."

"The guild must rebuild its ranks," Gaius Prospero protested. "Where are these new men and their families to live? You will cause riots if you do not give them what they have always had."

"Many new to the ranks will be men alone. Have the guild assign them to hovels. The women in residence can care for them. If a man comes with a family then place two widows with their children in one hovel, and give the other hovel to the newcomer," King Archeron said. "It is not that difficult a situation to manage, Gaius Prospero. And you will go to the guild to explain it all. After all, you are partly responsible for what has happened even if you won't admit to it. Now, if no one has anything else to say in the matter I will call for the vote."

The vote was taken and it was unanimous, for while he feared the Mercenary Guild's outrage, Gaius Prospero feared more being called unsympathetic by the people. Things had not gone at all as he and Jonah had planned tonight. He needed time to think. Time to consider his other options. Time to speak with his clever Jonah.

He would go to his favorite Pleasure House, to his favorite Pleasure Woman. The fair Anora would know just how to soothe him. She would calm his fears with her sweetness and her sexual skills. He had been bad, and he needed Anora's whip on his bottom. He needed her initial disapproval, and then finally her approval when she permitted him to have her body. He would not go home to the carping Vilia, who claimed she loved him. He did not want her love. He wanted Anora's sweet abuse. He always felt so much better after she had punished him. Her whip was good for his manroot.

"The High Council is dismissed," King Archeron said. "I will give the order for the mercenaries to be buried."

"Come, Wilmot," Lothair said, and he wrapped his dark cloak about the man. "I will take you to a place of safety now. Your mother is already there."

He was not really afraid, but once again Wilmot closed his eyes, and when a moment later the prince said they had arrived, he opened them. He was standing in a small comfortable room, his mother was sleeping peacefully in the bed.

"You are in my palace," Lothair said, "and you will be well taken care of here. Your chamber is next to your mother's. My servants will see you have everything you need. You are free to wander in our valley of horses. You will meet Og, the Forest giant who aided Lara in her escape from the Forest Lords—your news of her will be of interest to him. When my time in the City is done I will return here, and we will talk further. You are a man used to work, and so we must decide what you will do."

"Thank you, my lord Lothair," Wilmot said gratefully.

"Nay, thank you," the Shadow Prince replied. "I had expected a worse fight tonight, but Archeron was more than well-informed. The Squire is a decent fellow at heart. I could see he thought of his own folk when you spoke. As for the Forest Lords, we know their secret, and that is how we will keep them in line from now on. But without your testimony we might not have had so easy a time."

"Did Lara really kill the Head Forester's brother?" Wilmot asked curiously.

"Yes, she did. It was her first kill, and we were proud she found the courage. Durga was the Head Forester then, not his brother Enda. But when this younger brother was reminded that Durga's death meant his own elevation he began to feel less aggravated about the head at his feet," Lothair chuckled. Then with a wave of his hand he transported himself back to his apartment in the City, where Eskil was waiting for him.

The other Shadow Prince was lounging with a rather large goblet of wine in his elegant hand. "They are safe?" and he smiled when Lothair nodded, helping himself to wine and sprawling upon another couch. "I followed Gaius Prospero to a Pleasure House," Eskil said. "The people in the streets have been roused against him it seems," he chuckled. "They cried out insults at him, and shook their fists. I think he will be busy restoring his reputation for some time, and we need not worry."

"We must always worry," Lothair said. "Gaius Prospero will be concerned with his good name, but Jonah will be considering ways to advance his master's career and so advance his own. He is more the enemy than the fat merchant lordling, my brother."

"Who will send word to the Outlands?" Eskil asked.

"I will speak with King Archeron tomorrow. They must send a delegation to the Outlands, but to whom? They have no central government, and we do not want to insult any of these clan family chieftains. Archeron is the current head of the council. It must be his decision. But I suppose if they want we can go to discover the best way of handling this matter for them tomorrow. But now, I need sleep. I have done much magic today."

"Then rest, my brother, for we will probably be in the thick of it tomorrow. I suspect we must work swiftly lest Gaius Prospero try to subvert our will."

"The people will keep the Master of the Merchants busy for the interim," Lothair said with a smile. "It will be a difficult winter here in the City, and they will blame him for it, too." Then drinking his wine down, he sought his bed.

Gaius Prospero was so distraught by what had happened, and by the people's disfavor as he had ridden through the streets after the council meeting, that he remained two days at his favorite Pleasure House. When he finally arrived home he learned that his wife had taken their children and gone to their country house.

"It is better, my lord," Jonah said. "We have work to do."

"Have you any idea of what has happened? I lost complete control of the High Council. The Squire voted against me! Why he has suddenly gained a conscience I do not know," Gaius Prospero said irritably. "And the Coastal Kings were more than well-informed, Jonah. They knew everything, and so did those damned Shadow Princes! And the people cry out against me as if I was responsible for the deaths of our mercenaries, but I did not kill them. The Outlanders killed them. If anything good at all came out of this, it is that I have learned the Forest Lords have a great secret, and the Shadow Princes know it. *I* want to know it, Jonah! If the Outlands are out of my reach for now, perhaps the Forest realm is not. There has always been too much of it in my opinion. If I can learn this secret then perhaps I can control the Forest Lords."

"Indeed, my lord, you could," Jonah murmured, his facile brain contemplating the possibilities. There were trees to be cut and turned into lumber for the booming building trade. They would harvest the trees on the edge of the Forest first which would open up more land for the Midland farmers. The Squire would stop complaining about the incursion the City was beginning to make into his Midlands, and they could regain his trust—and more importantly, one hundred percent of the Midlands vote in the High Council. So much to do, Jonah thought. And then he recalled the motto he would take one day. *Make haste slowly.* He smiled and then, remembering where he was, he said, "Perhaps, my lord, we acted too hastily in beginning our annexation of the Outlands. Let us consider our other alternatives."

"What of the people?" Gaius Prospero wanted to know.

"We will soothe them, but not quite yet. Allow them the opportunity to express their anger. Then at the midwinter festival you will release some foodstuffs from your warehouses. You will recall the festival was established long ago to help take people's minds off the gloom and scarcity of the season. This generous gesture on your part will go a long way to easing the tensions now between you and our citizens."

"You must go to the Guild of Mercenaries for me," Gaius Prospero said.

"Of course, my lord," Jonah responded smoothly. "Tell me what the council desires done, and I will speak with them."

"I could not do without you, Jonah," Gaius Prospero said.

"Of course you could, my lord," the secretary flattered. "All I have learned I have learned from you. And you are the most respected man in Hetar."

Gaius Prospero smiled, well pleased. "I am, aren't I?" he agreed. "If Vilia is not here then perhaps I shall return to Anora's arms for another day or two. You have enough to keep you busy, do you not?"

"Indeed, my lord, I do," Jonah agreed. His clever mind already pondered the opportunities presenting themselves with this new turn of events.

Chapter 18

"I WILL GO TO THE OUTLANDS," Archeron, the current head of the High Council, told his brothers, Delphinus and Pelias. "My term of office ends with the next moon cycle."

"Let Lothair transport you," Pelias said. "I do not trust Gaius Prospero in general, but right now he suffers from the people's displeasure, and may try to seek revenge on those he feels have wronged him. I understand a mob attempted to storm the Golden District yesterday. They were shouting his name combined with some most unfavorable epithets. They seem to be holding him entirely responsible for what happened to the mercenaries. The Crusader Knights were called out to keep order, for the Guild of Mercenaries would not. Their ranks are weakened, and they must house and feed the widows and orphans of those killed in the Outlands. They are not happy about it."

"They can afford it," Delphinus responded. "They received a fair portion of Gaius Prospero's thievery. But I agree with Pelias. Let Lothair use his magic to send you home."

"Very well," Archeron replied. He was a tall handsome man with wavy silver hair, and eyes the color of aquamarines.

He disliked the City, and would not mind avoiding a long trek through the winter landscape back to his own province where winter came only gently. Winter in the province of the Coastal Kings was a short season when the rains arrived. On fair days the sun sparkled on the sea making it almost seem like a basket of the finest sapphires, aquamarines and emeralds had been tipped among the waves.

"With whom will you speak in the Outlands?" Pelias asked.

"It would seem that the one they call Lord Vartan is their leader. This lack of a centralized government in the Outlands makes it difficult to know how to deal with them, but I shall ask Lord Rendor of the Felan for his counsel."

"Will you go to this Lord Vartan?" Pelias wondered.

"I do not know," Archeron replied. "It is Rendor who must guide us in this matter so we do not offend the Outlanders in our attempts to make peace again. It would be so much easier to deal with them if we were cognizant of their customs."

"But Hetar has never before wanted to deal with them," Pelias said. "It has always been considered they were barbarians, and best left alone."

"Yet we knew differently, didn't we?" Delphinus said.

Archeron grimaced. "Aye, we did, and so, I suspect, did the Shadow Princes. Yet there was never any need for us to share our knowledge, was there? How could we have imagined that any among us would attempt to invade the Outlands? We underestimated Gaius Prospero and his colossal greed. Something is changing in our world, my brothers. We have been too prosperous, I fear, and now the balance is tilting the other way. There are more beggars in the streets now than ever before in my memory. There are too many mercenaries, and not enough work for them. The farmers of the Midlands seem unable to feed us as generously as they once did. Their land is worn out, and the cost of our foodstuffs is rising, yet the farmers see no new profits.

"When the people grow unhappy and hungry they also become restless. They begin to huddle with one another and talk on matters they do not fully understand. Eventually some among them will decide that our way of governing is responsible for their misery. They will revolt against that government, and whether they triumph or do not triumph matters not at all. Many will be killed, which will relieve some of the problem for there will be fewer mouths to feed. The damage, wherever it is, will have to be repaired so there will be work to be had. A new government for good or evil will arise. And prosperity will eventually return to put our world once again in balance." He signed. "May the Celestial Actuary have mercy upon us, my brothers."

"You will be home shortly, Archeron," Pelias attempted to soothe him. "This has been a difficult time for us all. Once you walk along the golden sands by the sea, and feel the clean wind on your face it will seem less distressing."

"Aye, but the problem will still be there," Archeron said. "It will not go away. Hetar's way of life, the Outlands' way of life—it is all changing."

"I will speak with Prince Lothair," Delphinus said, and hurried off.

The Shadow Prince was more than happy to take Archeron home, especially when he heard of the dark mood that had descended upon the Coastal King.

"His words frighten me," Delphinus admitted to the prince. "He has lived longer than any of us, and we revere his wisdom. Sometimes he sees things, as I believe he does now. Is this a vision of what the future of Hetar is to be?"

"He is correct that things are changing," Lothair said, "but do not be afraid, King Delphinus. Everything changes eventually. Sometimes the change is so swift we do not really notice it, and at other times the change is so slow that we can see it coming, and we are afraid. Change, whether for good or evil, cannot be stopped, I fear."

"You feel it, too!" Delphinus cried.

Lothair smiled, and nodded. "When Archeron is ready to travel, come to me," he told the Coastal King. "I will transport him."

A few days later Delphinus bid Archeron farewell. The High Council was now in recess for the winter, but it was necessary for the general council members to remain until their replacements came in the spring. Only the head of the council might leave.

Back home in his spacious palace by the sea King Archeron rested, but the necessity of contacting the Outland chieftains weighed upon him. He sent a messenger to Rendor of the Felan asking that they meet in two days' time on the seaside border between their two kingdoms. There would not be time for the messenger to return, and so Archeron, in the company of his son and heir, Arcas, set off in hopes of meeting Rendor at the designated spot. To their relief he was there. The two men, both of whom knew Rendor well, embraced the Outlander warmly, inviting him to join them beneath a blue-and-gold striped awning that had been set up upon the beach. There were chairs, and servants who brought wine to the three men.

"I have always enjoyed this air of elegance you bring with you," Rendor chuckled as he took a sip of the excellent wine. "We Outlanders are a simple folk."

"Not so simple," Archeron replied, "that you did not destroy your enemy successfully, and with flair. The High Council, while shocked, was most impressed by those seven carts of dead driven into the City by their gaunt and hollow-eyed drivers."

Rendor chuckled wolfishly, but then he grew serious. "It was unwise of Hetar to invade our lands," he said. "I hope they understood the message we sent to them."

"They did, and would return to the boundaries of the ancient treaties, Rendor," Archeron said quietly. "I have come to ask how we should approach the various clans, and their chieftains. We would not offend your lords and add to the problem."

"The offense was in your attempt to annex a portion of our lands," Rendor answered. "But we have had our revenge, and now wish to return to the way it was between us. We have formed our own governing council because of this incident. It is obvious to us that we can no longer live quite as separately from Hetar as we have in the past. The lady Lara has convinced us of that, though some would resist. Your High Council needs to be able to speak to us as one when problems like this arise."

"When was this council formed?" Archeron asked Rendor.

"After the battle. The clan chieftains met at Fulksburg before we departed for our own lands. The council is made up of our eight chieftains. Vartan of the Fiacre was elected its head. He remains in office until he chooses to step down or we vote to replace him, which is unlikely. His clan is the largest, and Vartan is both fair and wise."

"With a beautiful faerie wife, I am told," Arcas murmured.

"The Lady Lara is a halfling," Rendor said quietly. "Her wisdom is as much admired as her beauty."

"And she is a competent warrior, I have heard," Archeron said.

Rendor grinned. "That sword of hers would frighten a demon," he told the two kings. "It sings in a voice that goes from low to high as she battles. And when it is time for the kill Andraste sings of drinking the blood of the unjust and the evil. A man could die of fright facing that ferocious sword. And looking at that delicate beauty wielding it, you would not expect her skill with a weapon."

"She has a killer's instinct?" Arcas asked.

"Nay, my lord, not at all. But her heart cries out for justice," Rendor said.

"Can you take a message to Vartan from our High Council?" Archeron asked the Felan chieftain. "If it is possible I should like to meet with him, and apologize for the actions of our people against yours. Might he come to your hall? Or should I go to his?"

"I think, my lord, that he might enjoy seeing the Coastal Province. I will ask, but I will also offer him the option of having you come to him," Rendor said.

"Thank you, old friend," Archeron said. "Now, please tell me you did not lose many men in that battle at Fulksburg."

"But five," Rendor said. "Our losses were all minimal, unlike those of Hetar."

Arcas and Archeron laughed. The Outlander was enjoying his victory, and they did not blame him. If it had been theirs they would have done the same.

The three men finally parted, and Rendor rode back to his own home. The next morning he dispatched a messenger to Camdene, relaying all that had been said at that meeting. Rendor hoped Vartan would come to his coastal lands that he might meet with the Hetarians. He knew that Vartan had never met any Hetarians but for his beautiful wife, and young Noss. If he was to lead the Outlanders, it was time that he did. To his pleasure, Vartan agreed and he and Lara returned with the Felan messenger. The two men greeted each other warmly, and then Rendor bowed with respect to Lara whose beautiful golden gilt head bowed in return.

"So the Hetarians wish to return to life as it was," Vartan said with a grin.

"Aye, although until you meet with King Archeron you will not have the full tale, which I suspect is an interesting one," Rendor replied. "He was, as I wrote you, willing to come to you at Camdene. Do you wish him to come here to my village, or will you go to him at his seaside palace? I have been once, and it is both amazing and glorious."

"I think it is time I began to familiarize myself with Hetar," Vartan said slowly. He turned to Lara. "What think you, my life?"

"I have never been to the Coastal Province. It is said the Coastal Kings are the true aristocrats of Hetar," Lara said slowly. "I am curious to meet them, but this decision should be yours, my husband." She looked to Rendor. "You have become friends with these men, I am told. What think you of them?"

"I like them," Rendor answered. "They are a people filled with wisdom and honor. We were cautious with each other at first, but our friendship has bloomed into a true one. I believe they are trustworthy, and they did vote not to invade us last year."

"That in itself speaks well of them,"Vartan replied. "How do they live? Have they villages as we have? And how many kings are there? Must I treat with each? Or have they a high king?"

"They are all, it would seem, of one family. Long ago it was decided that the head of each family branch would be called king, that there be no quarrelling over the title. Each king leads a clan family much like ours. The oldest of them, in this case King Archeron, is recognized as the ultimate authority should disputes arise. Each family has a palace built into the cliffs by the sea. These palaces are spread out to house all members of each family, but I would not call them villages in our sense."

"Where does their wealth come from?"Vartan wanted to know.

"No one knows," Rendor replied. "They are as mysterious a people as are the Shadow Princes. Some say they may even be related by an ancient bloodline. They have some magic, but not as much as the Shadow Princes."

Vartan considered, and then he said, "I should like to see these palaces, and I think my going to King Archeron shows a respect for his position."

"Good manners is highly appreciated by these people," Rendor responded.

"I will go with you, husband," Lara told him.

"Of course," he agreed. "Though you have never been in the Coastal Province, you are Hetarian-born, and will advise me to the best of your ability, I know."

Lara smiled and nodded to her husband. He could not guess how much her knowledge of her own people would help him. "I would bathe," she told Rendor. "Have you the means for it? I have brought a special garment given to me by my Shadow Prince that I will wear. I have told you how much the Hetarians value appearance. These Coastal Kings know of my background. They know I was a humble mercenary's daughter, and later a slave. But they also know that my mother is a queen among her own people, and that my skills were honed in the company of the Shadow

Princes. I cannot go with you looking like a warrior, or a simple woman."

"You would display your beauty before these kings?"Vartan said, an edge to his voice. His look was hard.

Lara shook her head. "Have I not told you before that you must not be jealous, husband?"

He flushed. "I cannot help it," he admitted low.

"But you must," she said. "You swore to me that you would not impede my destiny, Vartan. And I warned you that my destiny would sometimes take me from you. I must treat with these people in my own way if you are to succeed, husband. Do not love me so much else I break your heart," Lara warned him softly.

"My wife will see you have your bath," Rendor said jovially. "I have sent a message to King Archeron that you are coming to meet with him, Vartan. We will depart on the morrow for his palace. It is but a day's travel."

"Should we not wait for his permission?"Vartan asked.

"Nay, I told him I would send word when it was decided how you two would meet. By tomorrow evening you will be welcomed into King Archeron's palace. I will come with you. I always enjoy the company of these Hetarians."

Lara enjoyed the bath which Rendor's wife, Rahil, provided for her guest. She poured a small bit of scented oil into the hot water, pinning up her hair so it would not get wet. Rahil sniffed appreciatively as the perfumed steam arose from the water. Seeing her Lara said, "Do you like it? Here." She handed the small vial to the woman. "I think a woman should always have something lovely to enjoy."

"My thanks," Rahil said smiling. Then she added, "I have never seen anyone as beautiful as you, lady. You are careful to hide it in your warrior woman's garments, but here in your bath, as the Celestial Actuary created you, I see how dangerous a burden that beauty is for you to bear. Will you display it before the Coastal Kings?"

"I must, for my legend precedes me," Lara told her as she washed herself. "Like all Hetarians, they will be impressed with Vartan for having such a wife. Because of your good husband they have already begun to make friends among the Outlands. Now we must obtain them as allies, for if I remember Gaius Prospero's passion for profit, his incursion into the Tormod and the Piaras is but the beginning of our troubles." She stood and wrapped herself in the drying sheet Rahil handed her.

"You think Hetar will attack us again?" Rahil said, wide-eyed.

"Yes, I do," Lara replied. "I will know more after we have spoken with the Coastal Kings and I have heard the story of the carts entering the City. That was a very powerful lesson. People in the street, ordinary citizens in the City saw those carts with their dead. More families than not have blood kin among the Guild of Mercenaries. And those among the dead with others dependent upon them for their daily bread would have those family members, wives, children, parents, left now without a home, or a means of support."

"They would lose their homes?" Rahil was aghast.

"There are only so many hovels, and they must be kept for those who give service to the Guild," Lara said.

"And they call us barbaric!" Rendor's wife said angrily.

Lara slipped into a simple gown, and braided up her hair again. "I have found the Outlands more civilized than the City," she said quietly. "Now, how may I help you with the supper?"

"My servants are well-trained and have it all in hand," Rahil said, "but you could pour the Frine." She was impressed by the fact that Lara had offered to help. She might be a great lady, but her human side was mannerly.

After the meal Vartan and Lara were taken to their host and hostess's own chamber. When Vartan protested, Rahil told him it was an honor for the Felan that the new Head Councillor and his wife would sleep there. Then bowing, she left them. Vartan, cautious by nature, threw the bolt on the door, and turning about found that his wife had shed her garment. He smiled a slow smile. "You mean to palliate me, wife."

She smiled back holding out her hand to him. "Yes," she said.

He pulled his own garments off, dropping them upon the floor. "When the Coastal Kings smile at you I will want to kill them."

"I know," she replied.

"When they gaze upon your beauty and desire it for themselves, I will hate them for it," he told her.

"You will," she agreed amiably.

"When I see in their eyes the image of the dreams they will have of coupling with you I..."

She put her hand over his mouth. "But you are the only man I desire, Vartan," she told him. "They cannot have me if I do not wish it, and I do not." She stood before him, and pressed herself against him even as she took his sinewy arms, and wrapped them about her. "I desire you, and you alone, my husband."

"But you do not love me," he said looking down into her small upturned face.

"You know I do not believe in love," she replied.

"Then how will you give me the son I desire of you?" he asked seriously. He could feel every inch of her delicious flesh as it pressed against him seductively. "I know that faerie women do not give children to those they do not love."

"I am only half faerie," she responded softly, her pointed tongue encircling the shape of his ear teasingly. "Do you not want me, husband?"

His length was hard. It throbbed between them. "Witch!" he groaned. Yes, he wanted her! More at this moment than he had ever wanted her, but it was always that way each time they lay together. No matter how much he took of her, no matter how much she gave of herself, it was never enough for Vartan. He wondered if it ever would be. He wanted to hear her tell him that she loved him, but it would seem along with her faerie beauty she had inherited a cold faerie heart. Nonetheless he could not resist her. "I love you, Lara," he told her, and then he picked her up and laid her upon the bed that awaited them. His big hand caressed her small heart-shaped face, his mouth taking hers in a passionate kiss. His long fingers tangled in the soft golden hair with its gilt highlights. *So soft,* he thought as their mouths drank of one another. Everything he touched was soft and smooth, and yet beneath it she was like iron.

He rolled onto his back, drawing her atop him as one kiss blended into another and another. Then she drew away from him, and sitting up, began to caress his broad smooth chest with her hands. Her emerald eyes gazed into his meltingly, and he felt weak but for his manroot which raged, pinned beneath her round buttocks. Reaching up, he began to play with her breasts, and when he teased at her nipples she teased at his in exchange, pinching them lightly, bending to lick at them.

He lifted her up, and impaled her slowly upon his manroot. With a deep sigh she sank down, enveloping him within her body. Taking him deep into her heated flesh, leaning back and sighing again. "Ride me," he growled at her, feeling her thighs close against him as she steadied herself with her hands, tightening her sheath around him as she pressed and released, pressed and released until he began to make whimpering sounds for she was not yet ready to allow him his fulfillment. Raising herself, she leaned forward so he might have the pleasure of her breasts. His mouth closed about a nipple, and he sucked on her hard until Lara began to feel the tension building.

She leaned further forward, burying her head in the space between his shoulder and his neck. She felt his hands closing about her rounded buttocks, kneading them as she thrust, and thrust and thrust against him. Finally unable to endure any more of her sweet torture, Vartan turned them so that Lara now lay beneath him. He thrust and withdrew, thrust and withdrew until it was she who now whimpered. He was so attuned to her that he could sense her impending crisis, and held himself back until they could attain pleasure together. And then the heat enveloped them both. They were filled with their passion, and finally collapsed from their delightful efforts, without another word falling into a peaceful sleep. But Lara, before she closed her eyes, touched the crystal she always wore, as if seeking a reassurance from Ethne that she would not allow herself to find with Vartan.

In the morning she awoke before he did, and she wondered if perhaps these feelings of protectiveness toward her husband, and the yearning she had for his touch, were not perhaps the beginnings of that so human emotion known as love. She was not all faerie, after all, and if she had hardened her heart against love was it possible she had done it in order to survive what she must, in order that she reach her destiny? She was weary, she realized, of the knowledge she carried. She suddenly had a great yearning to be just a simple woman. To carry her husband's child within her body. To birth that child, and care for it.

Stirring, Vartan drew her into his arms, and she laid her head against his heart. "What are you thinking?" he asked her softly.

"Woman's thoughts, husband. Thoughts best kept to myself for now," Lara told him. She wanted to spend the rest of the day in his arms, and not be bothered by anyone, but they had a long ride ahead of them.

"Give me a child, my life," he said softly to her, and he kissed the hand on his chest. "A beautiful little girl like her mother."

"In time I will give you a child, Vartan, I promise you. But now we must meet with the Coastal Kings, and settle this matter between the Outlands and Hetar," Lara said.

He groaned. "Today I am not of a mind to be diplomatic," he said.

"Neither am I," she agreed, "but we must do our duty. And when we have made this fragile peace we will go back to Camdene, and settle in for the long winter. And on the dark mornings we shall not get up at all, but lie in each other's arms and make love the whole day long."

"And you will give me a child," he repeated.

"I will give you a son, husband, who will one day lead the Fiacre as you now lead it," Lara told him.

"And a daughter," he reminded her.

"First a son," she said, and then she climbed from the bed to wash the excess of their night's passion from her skin. She would not meet the Hetarians with the scent of lust on her body. After she had bathed she donned a simple gown. It was white, and the skirt was fashioned in tiny pleats from her waist to her ankle. There was a golden cord twisted about the waist that had tassels at each of the two ends. The bodice was draped from its soft rounded neckline, and the sleeves were full and floated to just below her elbow. About her neck the golden chain with the crystal glittered. She brushed her hair out so that it sat like a mantle about her.

He watched her dress, fascinated. "I have never seen that gown before," he said. "How were you able to carry it with us?"

Lara smiled at him. "Kaliq gave it to me. It is magic, and made to fit within this small coffer," she said holding out her hand to him. In it lay a round wooden peach, perfectly represented, and polished so that the wood glowed with its natural beauty. "The gown can be anything I wish it to be. In this instance the Coastal Kings wish to see the woman who was so beautiful that the Head Mistress of the Guild of Pleasure Women would not allow her to be purchased. The Taubyl Trader who took me from the City meant me for one of the Coastal Kings. I am sure that Rolf Fairplay told them the story."

"Now I am indeed jealous," Vartan said as he arose from the bed, and began to wash himself. "But having a wife whose wardrobe can be carried in a hollow wooden fruit is indeed a great advantage."

Lara laughed. "Our love play has improved your mood," she told him.

He grinned back as he began to pull on his clothing. "It has," he agreed.

The inhabitants of Rendor's hall could not help but gaze in wonder at the halfling wife of Vartan of the Fiacre. But they were also a bit afraid. She had not looked so beautiful the night before, it seemed to them. Her magic was now quite obvious. When they had refreshed themselves at Rendor's board they prepared to depart. The horses were brought from the stables.

As Rendor approached his own mount, Lara's stallion, Dasras, put a leg forward and bowed his head politely. "Your hospitality was exceptional, my lord of the Felan," the stallion said. "I offer you my thanks."

Rendor bowed in return. "I am grateful it met with your approval," he replied. Then he said to Lara as he helped her into her saddle, "I do not think I shall ever get used to hearing that beast of yours speak with a man's tongue, lady."

Lara laughed. "His speech is a comfort to me," she said, adjusting her skirt, which was hiked to her thigh. She patted Dasras lovingly. "We are friends, you know."

Shaking his head, Rendor mounted his own horse. "It is a short ride to the sea, and then we shall ride along the beach until we reach the Coastal Kings. Have you ever seen the sea, lady? I know Vartan has not, for he has never before enjoyed the hospitality of my house. I think it will amaze you with its vastness and its beauty."

Though it was winter the air was very mild, and the sun warmed their shoulders as they rode. They rode first through grassy meadows filled with sheep, shepherds and dogs who loped along with them for short distances, some barking. One irritating animal kept snapping at Dasras's heels until the great beast stopped dead in its tracks.

The stallion turned his head, and looked down at the yapping dog. "Go home!" he said in a firm voice, and stamped a single hoof. The dog stood stock-still for a moment, and then turning, ran yelping back to his master. "Dogs," Dasras said scornfully, "are more trouble than they are worth. Give me an elegant feline to keep me company in my stall. Cats are far better companions, I assure you."

They laughed at the incident and moved on, finally reaching the grassy bluffs overlooking a wide sandy beach that seemed to stretch for miles in both directions. The horses slowly picked their way down the narrow path, Rendor leading, Lara behind him and Vartan bringing up the rear. There was no need for men-at-arms to ride with them here in the Outlands.

Gaining the beach, Lara brought Dasras to a brief halt and stared in amazement. The waters seemed to go on forever. Where did they end, she wondered? Frothy white waves rolled in from the blue sea, racing up the sand and then withdrawing. The sound never ceased, but it was pleasant, and soon she did not notice it at all. Screeching birds hung in the air above both beach and sea. "What are they?" she asked Rendor. "They are beautiful. Look how they soar and dive!"

"They are called Seabirds, nothing more," he told her.

They rode on down the beach which seemed to go on forever, stopping when the sun reached the highest point in the heavens to rest the horses, eat and drink, pouring water from their own water bags into shallow pans they carried for their animals.

"Why can they not drink from the sea?" Lara asked Rendor.

"Taste it," he told her, and she bent down to dip her fingers in the wave that came up to brush her bare feet.

"It's salty!" she exclaimed.

"It is," he agreed. "The sea is where the Outlands obtains its salt. The Coastal Kings supply Hetar with it as well. They collect sea water in great vats, and dry it until only the salt remains."

After their short respite, they rode on, for the winter's day was short. As the sun began to sink toward the horizon Rendor pointed ahead, and said, "Look! We have almost reached the palace of King Archeron, my friends."

"It is that close to your borders?" Vartan asked.

"We came over the border over two hours ago," Rendor said.

"But there was no border station," Lara remarked.

"We do not need it," Rendor responded. "We know where the border is. The Coastal Kings keep to their side of it, and we to ours. It is easier that way. We keep to the same standards as in the Outlands," he explained. "The rest of Hetar may have border stations and guards, but here along the coastland we think it unnecessary."

They heard music, and looking ahead they saw a small procession coming out to meet them. It was made up of young men and women wearing draped fabrics and flowers. They danced, and played upon lyre, flute, cymbals and drums as they came forward to meet their guests and lead them to the king's palace. The travelers rode up from the beach, their escort dancing and making music as they came, and there upon a great marble terrace Archeron waited to greet them. On a lower terrace they dismounted, and their horses were led away. Together Vartan, Rendor and Lara walked to meet the greatest of the Coastal Kings who stood with his son Arcas by his side.

Archeron came forward and took Vartan's hands in his own. "Thank you for coming," he said as their gazes met.

"It would not have been possible to refuse your gracious invitation," Vartan answered. "I have a responsibility to the clan families of the Outlands."

"Then you will accept a restoration of the old treaty?" Archeron said.

"If Hetar accepts a restoration of our original borders," Vartan replied with a small smile.

"It does!" Archeron replied. "I shall notify the High Council immediately." Then he drew his companion forth, "This is my son, Arcas. Our family will be his responsibility one day, and if he lives to be as old as I am he will find himself with the responsibility of all the Coastal Province."

"My lord." Arcas bowed to Vartan, but his eyes were fixed on Lara.

"You admire my wife?" Vartan said in a deceptively bland tone.

"I have never seen anyone so beautiful," Arcas replied candidly.

"My lords, you embarrass me with your words," Lara told them. Then, ignoring them both, she turned to Archeron. "You are a man of peace, King Archeron, and I am glad for it. One day Hetar will realize it as well, and be grateful."

He took her small hand and tucked it into his arm. "Come, Lara, wife of Vartan, and I will show you my palace. We have prepared a banquet in your honor." Together they walked across the terrace toward the white marble building. Its gold-leafed domes, and its slender soaring towers were now both bathed in the blazing colors of the sunset.

"Your palace is every bit as impressive as that of the Shadow Princes," Lara told her escort. "I remember seeing Gaius Prospero's home for the first time and thinking there could be nothing grander. Then I came to the Desert. But this!" She turned, her green gaze sweeping back to the beach, and the great sea beyond it. "What magnificence!" Then she turned again and smiled up at him.

The interior of the palace was light and bright. King Archeron brought them to a banqueting hall where the members of his court awaited them. Their eyes went immediately to Lara, admiring her fair beauty so similar to that of the coastal people, and yet so different. Vartan was taken aback, for never before had he known such luxury, but Lara, standing by Archeron, drew her husband to her side and slipped her hand into his.

"Isn't it beautiful?" she murmured to him.

"I could not have imagined that people live this way," he replied low.

"This is my wife, Alina," Archeron said drawing forward a woman with silver hair like her husband's, but eyes of lavender.

"Lady," Vartan said with a bow, "I must admit to being overwhelmed by such luxury. We Outlanders are simple folk."

The Lady Alina smiled sweetly. "I am frequently overcome by the luxury myself, Lord Vartan," she told him, her eyes twinkling. "I was not born into the noble families of the coast. My father was a fisherman. Our great extended family has those of both high and low station. Yet at the heir's bride-choosing ceremony I was the one to catch my Acheron's eye. Although I have been wed to my husband for over thirty years, I am still amazed by such wealth. Come, sit by me on the dining couch," she invited him.

"Thank you," Vartan replied, hesitant, but then he felt a gentle nudge from Lara, and so he sat. "What is a bride-choosing ceremony?"

Alina smiled as she explained. "When a young man in our society reaches the age of eighteen years each natal day thereafter is marked by a special ceremony in which eligible maidens are displayed before him. He knows instinctively which one is his mate. Sometimes he finds her in that first ceremony. Sometimes he must wait several years. If that is the case the same maidens are never brought before him twice. In this way we keep our bloodlines strong because the same families do not intermarry over and again."

"It seems a wise custom," Vartan said. "May I ask when the king chose you?"

"He was twenty the year I came before him in the bride choosing," she answered, smiling fondly in her husband's direction.

Lara sat with the king, but on a single dining couch at Archeron's right hand sat Arcas, who immediately engaged Lara in conversation while his father was involved with his duties as host.

"Rolf Fairplay was right," he said softly. "You are the most beautiful woman in all of Hetar. I would have paid what the Head Forester paid for you, and more!"

"You would have wasted your monies, my lord," Lara replied. "It is said I have a destiny to fulfill. I would have run away from you as I did the Forest Lords. It is not meant that I be a slave."

"You would not have been!" he declared passionately. "I should have freed you the morning after our first night together. You are not meant to be the wife of a crude Outlander chieftain. You are meant to live in a palace, and be showered with all manner of luxuries."

Lara laughed. "If that were so, my lord Arcas, then I should be exactly where you describe, but I am not, am I? Prince Kaliq gave me the freedom to choose where I would go when I left him. I chose the Outlands because that is where my instincts told me I should go." She reached for her goblet, and sipped delicately at the wine.

"Are your instincts never wrong?" he asked her as he ran a single finger from her elbow to her hand, and his violet eyes met hers.

"No," she told him coldly. "Have you any idea of how insulting you are being, my lord Arcas? For now my destiny is in the Outlands with Vartan of the Fiacre. It will not remain there. I understand that, but I also know that you will not be a part of that destiny other than in a peripheral fashion. I am sorry. It is obvious you have always gotten everything that you desired as a child, but you are a man now." And Lara turned away from the king's son.

He stared at her, surprised. No one had ever spoken to him in so blunt a fashion.

A trumpet sounded, and Archeron leaned over to tell Lara, "I have a surprise for you, my lady. I hope it will please you." He pointed to the doors of the banqueting hall.

Lara's green eyes widened with pleasure, seeing the new arrivals as they came forth from the cloud of purple mist. She arose to greet her mother, Ilona, who came into the hall in the company of her mate, Thanos. Running forward, she embraced Ilona, to the faerie queen's delight. "Come and meet my husband, Mother," she said.

Vartan was already on his feet, wishing desperately that he was clothed in something more elegant, but he owned nothing elegant. The company here was much too rich for him. He was eager to leave and return home to Camdene. Lara brought her mother to him. He took his mother-in-law's hand in his, and kissed it. "I am pleased we have this opportunity to meet, Queen Ilona," he said.

Ilona looked the Outlander over carefully, her green eyes assessing him physically, and peering deep into his heart to see if he truly loved her daughter. What she saw pleased her, but it also worried her. Vartan did indeed love Lara—perhaps too much. Still, it was not yet time. Let the Outlander have his happiness while he could. "I am pleased to meet you, Vartan of the Fiacre," Ilona replied. "This is my mate, Thanos, the father of my son, Cirilo, Lara's baby brother."

Thanos, a courtly faerie man, bowed politely.

"Are you pleased with my surprise?" Archeron asked Lara.

"Very much so," she answered. "It has been some time since I last saw my mother."

"I am happy then to have engineered this reunion," Archeron replied.

Another dining bench was brought, and the faerie queen and her mate reclined upon it as the meal was now served. There were all manner of creatures from the sea, some broiled in delicate wines and served upon beds of greenery with lemon slices; red clawed creatures that had been boiled in their shells, and served with drawn butter; small rounds of succulent flesh set in dainty shells in a delicious cream sauce. Neither Lara nor Vartan had ever seen their like. They carefully watched how their hosts ate these foods, and followed suit. There were silver baskets upon the table piled high with fresh breads kept warm by means of heated stones, and bejeweled silver bowls of newly churned butter.

Vartan particularly enjoyed the red shelled creatures, cracking them open to extract the meat, dipping it into the drawn butter. He ate heartily.

Lara leaned over to speak with her mother. "I do not know what to do," she said softly to Ilona.

The faerie queen did not ask about what, she simply said, "What does your heart tell you, daughter?"

Lara sighed. "I do not think I have ever heard my heart speak. I have been told I have a faerie's cold heart."

"But you are human as well as faerie, daughter," Ilona replied. "And faeries do not always have cold hearts, Lara. That is a choice we make so we may protect ourselves in a world where magic is more often feared than not. My heart was warm for your father. You were born of the love I had, still have, for John Swiftsword."

"I sense I will need a cold heart for what is to come, Mother," Lara said.

"It is not time," Ilona answered. "I tell you this though I probably should not, but I cannot bear to see you so indecisive and unhappy as you wait to meet your destiny, Lara. I honored your father's request, and kept from you as a child although I knew your fate. I have done little for you, but this I can do. You have time, my daughter. These next few years are yours to do with as you please. Have the child you desire to give Vartan. It will comfort him when you must leave him. Let yourself love him."

"But when that moment comes?" Lara said.

"You will do your duty, my daughter, because you were bred to do it whether you knew it or not. As a leader you must know when to show mercy as well as strength. If your heart is always cold, how can you? I have looked into Vartan's soul. From the moment he laid eyes upon you, Lara, daughter of Swiftsword, was his life. He adores you, and to refuse to accept such homage, such passion, would be foolish. Revel in it! Return it! You will not be the weaker for it, but rather stronger, for unconditional love builds strength in those who will accept it. And you will need all of your strength for the road ahead."

Tears slipped down Lara's beautiful face. "I have wanted to love him," she admitted, "but I feared to do so would weaken me."

Ilona reached out, and gently brushed the tears from her daughter's cheeks. "No. Love does not weaken. If my love for your father had weakened me I should not have been able to leave him to return to the duties I owed my mother, and my faerie kin." Her green eyes suddenly twinkled. "I can see that Vartan is much man. No faerie girl would waste him."

"Do you love Thanos?" Lara asked her mother candidly.

"In my own fashion," Ilona said. "But not like I loved John Swiftsword. I took Thanos as a mate because it was necessary to produce an heir or heiress to follow in my footsteps. I left that choice up to fate, and birthed a son. Your brother, Cirilo, will be the first king the Forest Faeries have had in three generations. Thanos understands, for he had courted me for many years before I agreed to have him as my mate."

"I do love Vartan, though I have never admitted it before even to myself. I feared it would weaken me, but as I think on it I realize his love does make me strong," Lara said. "I have felt like I was living on the edge of a sword, Mother. It is a relief to know I may become a simple woman, if only for a short time."

"Do not lose your skills," Ilona warned. "Practice each day with both Andraste and Verica. Until your belly swells ride Dasras regularly so his skills, too, may remain sharp. Remember this is but a respite for you, Lara. When you are finally called you must be ready. I am here for you. Kaliq and the Shadow Princes, also. Do not hesitate to seek our advice when you need it."

Outside the large windows of the Coastal King's banqueting hall, the creamy yellow moon of the province was shining down on the waters of the sea. Inside the feasting continued until very late, and then the guests were shown to their chambers. The bedchamber where Lara and Vartan would sleep was luxurious, and yet deceptively simple in its elegance. A great round window gave them a view of the sea. A bed draped in diaphanous curtains of turquoise silk awaited them. Before the fireplace opposite the window was a large bathing tub filled with hot water, and scented with freesia.

"I'll smell like a girl," Vartan protested as his wife began to slowly remove his clothing.

"You'll smell delicious," she teased him as she unbuttoned the horn buttons on his leather vest, and laid it aside. Her supple fingers undid the laces of his shirt, pushing it off his shoulders, her palms smoothing over his broad smooth chest. "Just like a flower, and I'll be a little bumblebee coming to gather your honey." Lara stood on her toes, and whispered, "Buzz, buzz," in his ear. Then she pulled the shirt completely off.

"Wife!" he said.

"Husband?" she countered as she unfastened his leather trousers, pushing them over his slender hips, her hands now moving to caress his taut buttocks as she pressed herself against him seductively.

Vartan grinned. He could not remember Lara ever seducing him in so bold a manner, and quite frankly he liked it. Reaching out he unfastened her gown, letting it fall to the floor. Then he lifted her from the pile of soft fabric.

Her hands reached out to fondle him. She raised her head up to gaze into his eyes, and he kissed her softly at first, and then as his arms closed about her, and her arms slipped up about his neck, their kisses became fiery, demanding, one blending into another until they were weak with passion. They fell upon the bed, bodies intertwined, and she caught his face between her hands. "Tonight, husband, we make a child," Lara told him, a small smile upon her lips.

"Faerie women only give children to those they love," he groaned, and began the thrusting rhythm that would eventually lead to their mutual satisfaction.

"Yes!" she told him.

"Say it!" he demanded of her, his loins afire with his hunger for her. "Say it!"

She laughed. "Say what?" she teased him as she wrapped her legs about his torso.

He thrust harder and harder, his manroot seeming to swell more as he pushed himself deep into the soft hot morass of her sex. "Say it!" he groaned through gritted teeth. "Say that you love me, you faerie witch."

"I love you," Lara told him, and then the world exploded around them and in them as their pleasure reached its first heights. "I love you!" she told him as it peaked a second and final time. And then as they lay together sated, she said it a third time. "I love you, Vartan of the Fiacre, and I always will, no matter where my destiny takes me. But for now I am yours alone."

"For now?" He was instantly alert.

"Because I love you does not mean I can deny my destiny when it is time," Lara said quietly. "I have never hidden this from you, Vartan. I know you have hoped, but while my time is not yet, the day will come when I must leave you to fulfill that destiny." She kissed his mouth tenderly. "We must take what we can, and while we can, my love."

"How can you be so brave when my heart is breaking at the thought of ever losing you? You are my life," he said to her.

"You will never lose me, Vartan. I may go away, but I will always love you," Lara told him. "Do not think of that distant tomorrow, my lord and my love. Think of the here and now. Think of the life we are meant to share, of the child I will bear you from this love that has grown between us."

He sighed. It was a deep, almost painful sound. "We have time?" he asked her. "You are certain we have time?"

"So my mother says, and I would never dispute the word of a faerie queen," Lara told him.

A small smile crept over his face. "Then, wife," Vartan told her, "we had best make the most of that time." And his arms wrapped about her, and his mouth found hers, and Lara wished that their time together would go on forever even though she knew better. Could happiness slow time? She didn't know. But she could hope.

* * * * *

Look for the next of Lara's adventures in A DISTANT TOMORROW
Book Two of
THE WORLD OF HETAR
coming from HQN Books in 2006